I'm a fair weather friend
I'm a colorless hue but I'm willin' to make a deal
If You think You can make some faith here inside
I'll drive off and marry You

I'm only alive with You
I can't get by and I won't get through
So put me in the river and let me say I do
I'm only alive with You[1]

---

[1] Only Alive, Jars of Clay, Who We Are Instead, 2003

Recipe

For

Disaster

By Susan McGeown

Published by Faith Inspired Books

Magnificent Cover Art courtesy of Laury Vaden
magentaswan@patmedia.net

Published by Faith Inspired Books
3 Kathleen Place, Bridgewater, New Jersey 08807
www.FaithInspiredBooks.com

ISBN: 978-0-6151-4608-9

Footnote credits appear throughout this work.

To My Sister, Amy, and My Brother - In - Law, Michael
And Their International Family: Hannah, Matthew, Jack, and Maggie

Acknowledgements

While this is a work of fiction, some characters in this book are inspired by the wonderful people God has allowed to influence my life. In particular:

❖ To the wonderful birth mothers who made my sister and brother – in - law's international family possible,

❖ To my parents, Herb and Marylynn, who taught me about love and faith and surviving the death of a child,

❖ To Pastor Tammy Abee, good friend, good example, and all around good person to have a cup of tea with,

❖ To the wonderful Navajo people who made me feel so welcome, loved, and appreciated when I served as a summer missionary teacher in Huerfano, New Mexico, during the summer of 1989,

❖ To Robert and Harriet Foster, missionaries at Berean Mission School in Huerfano, New Mexico,

❖ To Theresa Yazzie, (and her daughter Celeste), an amazingly strong and capable woman who taught me about the pride and persistence of the Navajo people, and

❖ To Mrs. Francis Walter, my Sunday School teacher, youth group leader, and one of the finest examples of a Wise and Powerful Christian Woman (second only to My Mom) who went home to be with the Lord during the writing of this book.

Table of Contents

So cut below the surface and try hard not to notice
That I could be so foolish thinkin' I'm alright[2]

July, 2004
Huerfano, New Mexico

Prologue

Nothing was better than a job well done. Dragging tired feet ... no, correction, tired *body* up the long dusty trail to her trailer, Karly Martin rejoiced in her life. It was rewarding spiritually, emotionally, and mentally. Finally, at long last, she felt that she had achieved balance and peace. It was a long time coming. Five years. *Five long, hard years.* Longer than that, should she really be honest with herself. She felt much older than her twenty - seven years, but then, age brought wisdom, right? Karly snorted to herself. She must be *very wise.*

Mentally, she ticked off what needed to be done before tomorrow morning. The summer school classes she'd spontaneously offered for the local Navajo children had turned out to be a rip - roaring success. Such a success that she was on the edge of being pleasantly overwhelmed at the response. She'd need to double her craft supplies for tomorrow and come up with some additional activities for the older boys who had come. She didn't have the heart to turn anyone away even though the classes were filled to capacity. The boys hadn't fooled her, simply arriving to cause harmless mischief and flirt with her. She was old but she still remembered

---

[2] "I'm Alright", Jars of Clay, *If I left The Zoo*, 1999

what it was like to be fourteen. Maybe she'd put them to work helping with the younger ones? Somewhere in the boxes she'd brought with her was a great book that had all kinds of indoor and outdoor games for kids of various ages. Where was that? Maybe the big boys could be in charge of recreational play ...

Lost in thought, at first she didn't notice the silent figure watching her approach from the front steps of her trailer. Spotting him, she slowed, a vague sense of familiarity and unease prickling up her spine. He wasn't a teenager, that was for sure, and even from this distance she could tell he wasn't Navajo. Then he stood, slowly unfolding his massive frame, all 6'5" of it, and she knew exactly who it was. Dear God in heaven. Not now. Not here. Not in this sanctuary of peace that protected her from her bickering family and excruciatingly painful past. Not when her life was finally falling into the nice orderly framework she so craved.

"Hey, Kar," he said to her. He was wearing a Yankees baseball cap, mirrored sunglasses, jeans, and a faded tee shirt. He stood stock still, not approaching her. "You look as beautiful as I remember. I know this is a shock, me being here and all. I would have called but you probably know better than anyone that phone service isn't the most reliable out here." He tried to joke a bit, shrugging and saying, "I was just in the neighborhood and thought I'd stop by and say hello." He gave her a heart-stopping grin that tore her apart with its familiarity - even after all these years.

She continued to stand and stare, incapable of speech. Around her she felt all the carefully stored containers of unwanted memories popping open like sprung jack – in – the - boxes. A wave of anger washed over her. *How dare he come here to this place! He had no right.*

He thrust his hands in his pockets, awkward and unsure. Maybe even a bit frightened of her reception. *Good.* "Look, I can leave if this isn't a good time, and come back later if you'd rather. I've had weeks to get up the courage to come here. I could at least give you the courtesy of a few hours."

"A few hours won't do it, Paul. I think I need about ten more years." She walked towards him. God, he was bigger than she remembered. She strained her neck to look up at him and was rewarded with a double image of her pale, stricken face reflected in his sunglasses. "Excuse me. I need to get into my home."

"We need to talk."

"No, *you* need to talk. I feel no need whatsoever." Karly stepped around him and climbed the three steps to her trailer door. It wasn't locked. That would change *now.* She ripped open the door, stepped in, and slammed it shut. The lock turning could have been heard all the way to Tucson.

Leaning against the trailer door, she listened to the retreating crunch of footsteps walking down the hill.

"Paul," she said in an anguished voice, "don't do this to me again."

THE FALL

Growin' up I overheard
All the grown ups sayin'
You better be prayin'
And sayin'
All the right little things
At the right little time
And I had it down
At least on the outside
I'd put my best side forward
I could smile with the best
And dress like the rest
Of the messed up church folk singin' a song[3]

---

[3] "God Did", by Shane Bernard, Shane & Shane, *Clean*

So we crossed the line and can't turn back
Happy endings never last
Cause there's always more to stories never told[4]

June, 1999
Watchung, New Jersey

One: Good Christians Never Make Mistakes

The morning of her wedding dawned bright, brilliant, and beautiful. At 6:00 a.m. Karly hauled herself out of bed, pulling on shorts, tee shirt, and sneakers. It was no use trying to get more sleep. Was it possible to make yourself tired trying to fall asleep? She needed to get out of the house. She needed to get out of her life. These last two weeks she had suffered such profound insomnia that finally, in desperation, she had bought some over the counter sleep aides.

They hadn't worked.

She now felt like her body was gradually being filled with lead, making every movement slow and more difficult. Peering into the mirror, she felt a wave of hysteria hit her. She looked like absolute hell. Dark circles outlined her eyes, her skin had a dull, gray pallor, and her eyes were red and bloodshot. She had to pull herself together! Today was her wedding day for goodness sake! The single most important day of her life! Her shining opportunity to once and for all escape the clutches of her

---

[4] "Where We Were Before" Blessid Union of Souls, By Eliot Sloan, Jeff Pence, 1997, Capitol Records

parents and join herself forever and always to the man that she had given *everything* to.

She sighed and went to get the dog's leash hanging on the back of the kitchen door. Reality was, thinking of Paul only caused her greater anxiety. No two people had looked more miserable and out of their depth than she and Paul had last night at the rehearsal dinner. Karly had caught a glimpse of the two of them in a mirror at the restaurant and they both looked … haunted. Desperate. Lost. All around them was laughter and gaiety, joy and excitement, and the two of them looked like they were at their best friend's funeral.

But the biggest clue about how bad everything had all become was that even Karly's mother had begun to be nice to her.

What was going on? She refused to believe that this marriage was a mistake. *They loved each other. They had made a commitment,* with their hearts as well as with their bodies. Both of them had finished college, Paul had sent out over twenty resumes to neighboring towns in Kentucky looking for a job as an accountant. Karly had literally done everything within her power to please and accommodate him. And yet Paul looked like the shell of the man he once had been. Where was that smiling, carefree young man with whom she had found safety and connection that first night she had met him at the frat house party? What had happened to the laughing, jovial, teasing young man who could charm her out of her most serious of pouts? Why did it feel that whenever she was with him she was slowly and surely sucking the life right out of him? *What else was she supposed to do?* She'd done everything she could.

She'd given him everything she had to give.

"Calm down, Max," she mumbled as she tried to catch hold of his collar. "You dumb dog, *sit!*" Hooking the leash on Max, she reverted to the same old litany she been singing to herself these past two months. *Once we're married and off on our own, everything will be fine. All of these concerns and stresses and strains will disappear. I'll make him happy. He'll never regret this marriage.* It was just the pressure of the wedding. It was just the uncertainty of their future. It was just the fear of venturing into uncharted territory. It had nothing to do with their relationship. *Their relationship was absolutely fine.*

"Let's run off some of this excess tension, boy," she said as she opened the front door.

Karly tripped on her shoelace as she was fumbling out the front door. "Hold on you dumb dog! Let me tie my sneaker or I'll break my neck. What are you so excited about?" Something made her look up.

Standing on her front lawn was Paul, looking worse than he ever had in the last two months. A full growth of stubble covered his face and he wore the same clothes from last night's rehearsal dinner, now all wrinkled and mussed. He stood standing at the end of the front walkway, hands thrust in his pockets, looking for all the world like he had been standing there the whole night just waiting for her to step out the front door. "Oh. Hi Paul ..."

Karly made herself put on a dazzling, megawatt smile and walked down the pathway, stopping directly in front of him. "What are you doing here, Honey? Don't you know you're not supposed to see the bride before the ceremony?" She touched his shoulder and tried to draw him down for a kiss. It was like bending a hundred year oak tree in half and kissing a marble statue.

Suddenly she desperately needed to get away. She needed to walk the dog. She needed to get some air. *She needed to go ...*

"I can't do it, Karly." The voice that came out of his throat sounded like it hadn't been used in ten years.

Can't do it? Surely he didn't mean what she first thought. *Of course not.* He meant he can't stay away from her before the wedding. He's got cold feet. He needed to see her and get reassurance from her. How sweet. The evil twin in her head said, "*He doesn't look like he's being sweet.*"

"Can't do what, Paul?"

"I can't marry you."

His words were like an unfamiliar foreign language. They just didn't process. Did he really say what she thought he said? *It was his idea of a bizarre joke.* They had both been under such tremendous pressure.

Okay. She'd be funny right back. No, not funny. She'd shift over to sarcasm. That worked better for her right at this moment. "What are you saying, Paul? Are you saying *now, today,* on the *day of our wedding,* after almost four years of dating and the *level of commitment* that we've shared, that you're changing your mind *now?"*

"Yeah. That's what I'm saying." Her head exploded. Like a minefield being triggered in one small corner that then set off a massive chain reaction of explosions, Karly's brain simply overloaded and shut down. *I'll think about all this tomorrow. Good-bye. I really need to go and walk the dog right now. See ya.* As she turned to walk away from him, Paul caught her arm roughly. *"I mean it,* Karly. Do you want me to come inside so we can talk to your parents together?"

Find me a gun. It was the first stunningly clear thought that entered her conscious mind. Then the words began to roll out, boiling out of her mouth like a spewing, angry kettle. She gripped his arm and felt her fingernails sink into his flesh. *"You can't do this,* Paul. Things are set. Done. Finished. Planned. I've given you *everything* I've had to give. You know who I am and what I am and what my hopes and dreams and plans are. We are in this together. *Two have been made one,* Paul. The vows maybe need to be spoken today, but this deal is already signed and sealed."

"I can't marry you, Karly. I don't love you." He had the temerity to look embarrassed.

She felt herself begin to physically shake and tremble. The rumble of a bodily earthquake, of a volcanic emotional eruption. *"You don't love me?"* She heard herself scream hysterically and the dog began to jump up at her and whine. *Hello? Is anyone home?*

"We're sleeping together!" Karly screamed at him. "We're considering a missionary call to Appalachia! We've got two hundred and fifty people getting dressed as we speak to come and see us officially become husband and wife in less than five hours! *AND YOU HAVE THE GALL TO STAND HERE AND TELL ME YOU DON'T LOVE ME??"*

All of a sudden her mother and father were there beside her, looks of concern carved across their faces. She felt her mother's hands on her shoulders trying to calm her. Bile rose up in her stomach and burned in her throat. Karly could not abide her mother's kindness *now.* Too little, way too late. *Get away, Mother.* Furiously she jerked herself away from her mother's grasp and turned to her father. *"DO YOU HEAR WHAT HE'S TELLING ME? DO YOU HEAR?"*

"Come inside, dear, and we'll talk," and she felt her mother grip her arm and forcibly propel her back towards the front door.

They got her as far as the front room before it hit her. She was never going to escape from here. She was going to stay here in this house and *die here.* She would never be a teacher or a missionary or a wife. She was trapped, mired, cemented, imprisoned ... Oh Dear God. Please. No.

"I'm sorry," Paul choked out to her, standing amidst the chaos of her life trying to ignore her mother and father's presence. "I never wanted to hurt you, Karly. You don't see it now, but I'd only make you more miserable if you married me. I'm sorry it took me so long to realize that."

Come on Babe, don't you love me?

Hey, you know we'll be together to the end, Love.

Don't hold back anything from me, Karly.

I'm giving you everything. It's just you and me.

This is what committed couples do, Babe. This isn't wrong. It can't be when we love each other so much.

She wanted to clamp her hands over her ears and never, ever hear another lying sound come out of his mouth. *"GET OUT,"* she choked as the tears began to pour down her face. "I don't want to see your face or hear your voice. You are weak and cowardly, afraid to make a choice and take a stand! You're right, Paul, you would have made me miserable! You would have dragged me down into the depths where you seem so desperate to be! Get out! *GET OUT!"*

The rest of the day was a blur for Karly. She sat in a corner of the living room on the formal couch while hushed voices flitted around her. The phone rang constantly and even, for once, Michael, her little brother, was quiet and subdued. At one point he brought her a glass of water and set it by her on the coffee table. Hesitating for just a moment in contemplation, he finally plopped down on the sofa next to her, curled up against her and played his GameBoy.

She slept. *At last.* Completely and deeply, waking only to drink the glass of water that Michael kept fresh and filled for her on the table, and to stumble to the hallway bathroom when necessary.   Vaguely she remembered someone trying to move her, but she put up such a fuss that they finally just left her alone.   Someone brought her a bed pillow. Someone covered her with an afghan. Yes, she'd feel better after a nice long sleep ...

"Karly?" A warm, tentative hand was put on her bare thigh that hung out from beneath the cover. "Karly? You need to focus and listen to me."

"Go away. Can't you see that I'm trying to sleep?"

"Yeah, Karly. I see that. Everyone's tip toeing around you like you're an atomic bomb ready to detonate, but I don't think they've realized that you've already exploded, haven't you? Open your eyes and look at me, Karly."

For one brief second, Karly looked at the harbinger of sleep interruption. Tammy. *Reverend Tammy,* minister of youth and education at church. Minister second, though, best friend, first. The two of them had bonded over cups of tea and laughter and mutual interests.

"Go away, Tam. I'm tired. I want to sleep."

"I won't go away. I'm your friend and I love you and I'm worried about you. Your parents are on the phone *right now* with a hospital. A *psychiatric* hospital, Karly. Attempting to make suitable accommodations for you," Tammy said in a hushed but persistent voice. The hand on Karly's thigh gripped her leg tightly and shook her. "You've been sleeping on this couch for almost a *full week,* Karly. They don't know what to do with you and have decided maybe you need to be hospitalized for a while. Does that sound like a good plan to you? Or don't you care?"

A full week? She'd been asleep on this couch for a full week? God, her mother would kill her. No one was allowed in the formal living room but special company. But she was still so tired ... Just a few more hours of sleep ...

"*Karly.*" The persistent voice and hand were there again; shaking her and intruding on her much needed nap. "*The reality is not going to go away.*

I'm sorry about that. But I'm here and will be here. *I* won't go away. You've got to face it all sooner or later. Are you going to do it now, with me and those who love you, or in a hospital? Give me an answer one way or another." There was another persistent shake. *"NOW, Karly."*

Karly was too tired even to cry. "I can't …" she moaned.

"Yeah, I know," Tammy's voice said with real compassion. "One step at a time, okay, Sweetie? Let's start with a shower …"

Karly was never aware of her parents, although later, in retrospect, she suspected that they had been there, hovering. Tammy stripped her and shoved her naked and numb into the stall shower and then leaned her back across the door. "You can wash or just stand there until the hot water runs out, Kar. Either way you'll be cleaner than when you started. Remember, making no decision *is a decision.*" In the end Karly made a vague attempt to wash her hair and her body.

Tammy helped her into clean clothes and made her brush her teeth. Combing out her hair for her, Tammy said, "You can either trust me or your mother to pack for you. What do you want to do?"

"Am I going to the hospital?"

Tammy shrugged. "That's still an option. I'd rather you went with me to my family's cabin on the Outer Banks. I was planning on going soon for a few weeks' vacation to refresh and renew. The church has let me rearrange my schedule and take time off now instead. I'd like you to come with me. We'll just sit on the beach and relax."

"It won't be much of a vacation for you."

Tammy made a dismissive sound in the back of her throat. "If all you do is sleep in a semi - catatonic state on the couch down there like you've been doing this past week I don't see what difference it will make having you with me."

Karly met Tammy's gaze in the mirror over her bureau. "Outer Banks or the hospital," Tammy said firmly to Karly's pale face reflected in the mirror. "You decide. And remember: making no decision is a decision." Karly picked the Outer Banks.

Tammy and her mother packed for her and her father walked her to the car. "You know we love you, right, Baby?" he said, and Karly saw tears in his eyes.

Karly's eyes felt dry and tight. The tear bank was empty. "Yeah Dad, I know."

"You tell me what you need. Anything. Just name it. If it's within my power to do it, I'll do it. I'm telling you this now, but you put it in your mental bank for when you feel up to processing it. I may not have always seemed like I was there for you, but I'm telling you now *I am.*" Her father gripped her hand and a tear slid down his cheek. "Do you believe me, Baby?"

Until this very moment, had she been forced to admit it, no, she wouldn't have believed him. The man she knew as her father spent a majority of his home time trying to stay under his wife's radar and out of range of her vicious tongue. But staring into her father's tear filled blue eyes, she felt her heart skip a beat. "Yeah, Dad," she took a deep, shaky breath and reached out to wipe away the tear, "I believe you." He seemed to relax visibly at her assurance.

"Here, Kar. Dad says it's a long drive to the Outer Banks. This will help pass the time." Michael held out to her his brand new, too – precious – for – real - words GameBoy. "Super Mario Brothers," he said by way of explanation as to what game was in it. "I'm on level five but can't get past it. See if you can beat my score."

Karly's heart skipped another beat. Tenderness and love from the little brother who delighted in causing mayhem and catastrophe wherever he went. The child who was a living example that negative attention was preferable over no attention at all. The brother who earned his nickname from putting a live snake in her bed because he wanted to hear her scream. "Thanks, Snake," she managed and curled her fingers around the game. "Are you sure?"

He shrugged, trying desperately to appear nonchalant and detached. "Yeah, I'm sure."

Then her mother was there. For the first time, Karly thought she looked old. *Haggard* came to mind. "It, it was nice of Pastor Tammy to offer this," she began. "I'm not good at kind, soothing words, Karly." Her mother made a face. "You know that." She reached out a tentative hand to touch Karly's cheek and Karly willed herself to not pull away. *"I'm sorry. I should have done a better job."* She took a shaky breath and bit her lip. "Call us if you need us, okay? We'll come and get you if you want to come home sooner than Pastor Tammy does."

Come home sooner. Like that would ever happen. "Thanks, Mom."

Karly and Tammy drove for hours, spent a night in a low budget motel, and then drove for more hours. Late in the afternoon of the second day they stopped at a Foodmart and bought a pile of groceries. Not more than twenty minutes later, Tammy took a right onto a hidden, weed choked dirt and gravel road.

"Are we here?" Karly asked. It was the first thing she'd said that wasn't a necessary answer to a direct question from Tammy.

"Yup. Home sweet home. Rustic, but private. The place has been in the family for close to a hundred and fifty years. Always passes down to the oldest child in the family. One day it will be mine."

The private road went on and on it seemed until it finally stopped at a dead end. "We walk from here," Tammy said throwing the car in park and turning off the key. "Plan on making at least two trips. Just grab your suitcase to start." Hauling her case from the trunk, Tammy walked off onto a vaguely definable path into the woods.

It was a charming, two bedroom, honest to goodness log cabin, carved out of real trees that had been felled from the very forest they were walking in. Bare planked floors and a fieldstone fireplace were the dominating features inside. But it was the outside that drew Karly. The back of the house through which they had entered faced the forest that they had walked through. But the big wide windows at the front of the house faced the ocean. Bright sunlight bounced off the water and white sand, all of which was framed with wild flowers and greenery. "Ohhh ..." was all Karly could manage.

"Yeah," said Tammy behind her, her voice filled with pride and satisfaction. "This first view – no matter if it's night or day – always makes the long drive completely worth it." She walked forward and opened the front door. "Come on! Race you to the water!"

There was no phone. A generator had to be fed with gasoline every three days and the well water that was so cold it made your teeth ache. "We're not totally uncivilized though," Tammy said with a grin as she opened a door. A fancy flush chemical toilet and a stall shower greeted them. "A solar heated water tank on the roof gives us warm water in all but the coldest times of the year so we can stay clean and happy." She winked at Karly.

They spent blessed hours in companionable silence: sitting in the rocking chairs on the porch reading, swimming in the warm ocean water, or walking for miles along the sandy beaches that seemed to go on forever. Tammy seemed content with the silence, and Karly thought it was miraculous that she was managing to eat two meals a day and bathe herself.

"Paul's father and mother, John and Hannah Williamson came and visited me about four weeks ago," Tammy said casually one day towards the end of the first week as they waded in the gentle waves collecting shells. It was a casual statement in and of itself, however the fact that the two of them had barely spoken of *anything* other than 'Are you hungry?' or 'Want to come swimming?' made the choice of topic monstrous. And the implications of what the visit four weeks ago implied made the statement as volatile as an eighteen - wheeler full of nitroglycerin.

At Karly's silence, Tammy continued. "They were worried sick about the two of you. Wanted to know my perception of things. Asked for advice as to what I thought they should do."

It seemed to Tammy that Karly was never going to respond, but finally she said, "What did you tell them?"

Tammy shrugged. "Oh, all the proper stuff I'm supposed to say as a minister, like you were both adults, we need to keep you two in constant prayer, and that they should continue making themselves available to both of you whenever the need arose." Tammy sighed. "I did finally share with them that I was greatly concerned, too." Karly felt Tammy look at her but she stared straight ahead at the curving coastline. "You and Paul were like walking zombies those last weeks. It was horrible to watch. Anyone who was surprised at what happened had to be deaf, dumb, blind, and stupid."

"I guess that sums me up then."

Tammy grabbed Karly's arm and dragged her over to sit in a shady spot on a huge fallen log. "You look me right in the eyes, Karly Martin, and tell me you had no clue anything was wrong," she said rather fiercely.

Karly picked at her fingernail polish, remnants of the wedding manicure. She shook her head. She couldn't do that. In an anguished voice she finally whispered, "*I gave him everything*, Tammy. *And he took it.* Gladly. Willingly."

Tammy made a rude noise in the back of her throat. "Join the club."

Karly looked up at her. "What do you mean?"

Tammy looked out towards the ocean and squinted at the brightness. She shrugged. "We've been really good friends for years but we never talked about sex stuff. Did you ever wonder why? We're way past the whole "pastor" barrier, so why do you think?"

Karly frowned in thought. The two women had known each other for almost four years now. Tammy had just been hired to take the youth pastor position at Karly's church as Karly was leaving to go off to college. It had been an immediate friendship, rooted in similar sense of humor and like - minded Godly goals.

Tammy didn't wait for her answer. "We both avoided it for our own reasons. I avoided it because I knew I couldn't lie to you. If you asked I would have had to say that I was stupid in college, fell in love with a fellow ministerial candidate, got stars in my eyes and mush in my brains, and gave up the farm – lock, stock, and virginity. Only to have him dump me for someone else who, I think his exact words were, 'Stayed closer to his spiritual and moral values'. I may be a minister, but I know what it's like to be young, hot, and in love." She looked at Karly. "Why did you avoid the topic?"

"I liked the image I thought you had of me. I so much wanted to be just like you: honorable, pure, dedicated, solid ... How could I talk to you about what I was struggling with? It never occurred to me that you'd know what I was going through."

Tammy looked at her incredulously. "Why's that?"

Karly looked at her with impatience. "You're a *good Christian!* You're a *minister!*" Karly said impassionedly. *Certainly that explained it all.*

Tammy looked at her like she'd grown two heads. "Karly, being a *good* Christian means you have an extra resource to rely on during the wild and crazy ride we call life: God. It doesn't mean things are easier, or things make better sense, or life takes on a constant rosy glow." Tammy shook her head. "It for *darn* sure doesn't mean that we are summarily good the moment we make a profession of faith, or that we don't sin and make horrendous mistakes even when we should know better." She grinned at Karly. "I'm a minister and a good Christian, but it doesn't mean I'm *dead!* I appreciate a handsome man just like the rest of you and dream of …" she sighed in a dreamy far away fashion, "some handsome 6'2", blonde haired, green eyed," she looked at Karly and winked, "*Christian,* construction worker who has a heart of gold and a personality of the utmost patience, who sweeps me off my feet and drives me off into the sunset." Matter – of – fact she added, "Where we will establish a small country church – which he repairs and brings back to life with his wonderful God - given talents and skills – as I minister to the congregation." She looked out at the ocean again and said in a tone that implied Karly's complete foolishness, "Who says ministers don't have passion, huh?"

"I, I can't be what I thought I was going to be, Tammy. Look what I've done with my life already. I just don't have what it takes to go out and be a good Christian example, let alone a missionary."

Tammy squinted at her. "Describe a good Christian to me, Karly."

"Well, a good Christian knows God's plan for his or her life, a good Christian doesn't make huge mistakes like I do – I mean *big stuff* like sex or drinking or drugs, a good Christian is happy most of the time, good Christians have solid marriages and productive lives, good Chr -"

"I feel like I should be playing some smarmy movie sound track in the background while the camera shows shots of laughing loving couples and cooing babies and puppies romping in fields of flowers," Tammy said with a voice filled with disgust.

"What? You don't agree with me?"

"I don't agree with one single perception you have about good Christians. No," Tammy shook her head in emphasis, "no, I don't believe any of it."

Karly opened her mouth to say more but Tammy interrupted her. "So, let me get this straight then. This is what you're telling me." She stuck out her index finger, keeping tally, "Number one, someone like *me* who made a huge mistake while I was away at seminary by getting sexually involved with another student is not a good Christian." Almost to herself, she added, "I'll add King David, because he had the whole Bathsheba incident and everything. Number two," the second finger came out to keep tally, "people like your parents who struggle regularly within the bounds of their marriage are not good Christians. We'll have to add in the Samaritan woman because she had a number of failed marriages under her belt, and let's not forget Jacob who ended up with four wives, two of them sisters." She rolled her eyes, again seeming to mumble to herself, "What a mess ..." Karly went to open her mouth but Tammy held her hand up so she wouldn't interrupt, her voice getting a bit louder with suppressed emotion. "Number three, people who genuinely love the Lord but struggle with alcohol and drug addictions are not good Christians." Tammy was really working herself up into a real lather. "And I have an entire group of high school seniors in my youth group who have no idea what God wants them to do with their lives so I guess I should just give up on them because they're certainly not good Christians either."

Tammy looked intently at her friend. "Karly, are you listening to yourself? Do you really hear what you're saying?" She gripped Karly's arm. *"Do you really believe that?"*

Karly sat there in stunned silence with her mouth slightly open.

"Did you come up with all this yourself or did someone convince you of this?" Tammy asked quietly.

"How about no one ever proved me wrong?" Karly said as her powerful emotions rolled beneath the surface. "I've spent my whole life being dragged off to church, and everyone I saw there looked perfect to me! Everyone smiled and had hopes and plans and dreams and worked toward goals that with dedication became accomplished. You saw people who were capable and sure, calm and collect, purposeful and determined. Everyone was all cleaned up and spanking clean. No one was fighting or crying or moaning or yelling. There was no tension, no criticism, no anger …"

"Like it was at home …"

"Yeah, like it was at home," Karly said with real fury. "Why wouldn't I be drawn to something like that? Why wouldn't I want to have a life like that, full of smiles and laughter and joy? I've been soaking this stuff in since I was tiny, Tammy, and as soon as I had it all figured out I was determined that this was what I was going to get for myself come heck or high water. I've been holding on, looking toward the eventual goal that I'd get out of the house and lead a good Christian life and *at last* find happiness and contentment."

With her chin stuck out like she was ready to fight the world, Karly said, "And yeah, I don't think my parents are good Christians! My mother hasn't managed to say *one positive thing to me* my entire life. She's probably one of the unhappiest people I know. Same with my father. He's been miserable for as long as I can remember. You're telling me *that's* what being a Christian is all about?"

Tammy shook her head and looked grave. "Don't judge. Unless you've walked in a person's shoes, lived a person's life, and know a person's innermost heart, you *cannot* ever presume to know what they are all about. Only God has the ability to do that." Tammy took Karly's hand and gripped it tightly, "Karly, this life we're living is *hard*. There are sorrows and difficulties and pain and sickness that *destroy* us. *Kill* us. We're a selfish, fickle, unfaithful lot, we human beings. We think we're better than God! We think we have better answers and smarter solutions and despite reams and reams and reams of advice given to us, think we can make better choices on our own than with God's guidance. *We are so unbelievably self -*

important! Yet, God loves us anyway. Talk about unconditional love! He sent His Son to *die* for us, to take *all the blame* for all the *lousy, horrible, wicked* things we manage to do on a daily basis." She leaned in to make sure that Karly was focusing on her and what she was saying. "And do you know the only thing we have to do to be *good Christians*, Karly? The only single, solitary thing we've got to do is *believe* in Him. We've got to believe that we're sinners, believe that Christ is God's son, believe that He died to take the blame for our sins and then was victorious over death, and believe that Jesus is the only way for us to get to heaven.

"That's it. Nothing else. The Bible says we can't be 'good' by doing lots of works, or by giving lots of money, or by speaking fancy, flowery words, or by smiling all the time. We just have to believe. Have you done that? Have you given over the control and destiny of your entire life to Christ? Or have you been trying to steer it? Have you really committed your life to Christ, or are you dealing with some artificial image of what you should and shouldn't be and working toward that goal all on your own? You'll never find contentment and never please God until you turn your life over to Him."

Tammy gave Karly a huge grin. "And you know what? Once we believe, and we turn ourselves over to Him, we still have to deal with this *hard* life. We still get dragged down, we still make mistakes, we still cry, we still hurt, and we still disappoint God. But He never gives up on us. Like the most loving of parents, He is always there, always forgiving, always willing to give advice or support if we only ask for it. We are God's children. He's our loving mother *and* father. It is the only sure thing in this life, the only real example of unconditional love, the only safe haven when things are *really bad*."

Tammy glared at Karly. "But don't you dare judge yourself, *or me*, based on the load of garbage you just spouted about what a good Christian is. *Don't you dare.* You're doomed to failure before you even begin. Talk about a recipe for disaster! Good grief, Karly ...

"I don't have any concrete proof, but I personally think that the bad parts of life sometimes become more alluring once you make that decision to walk in the light and not in the dark. But that just could be my own personal struggle." Tammy gave Karly a wry smile.

Karly put her head on Tammy's shoulder. "Thanks for all this."

She felt Tammy shrug. "That's what friends are for. It's a corny saying but it's very true. I couldn't let you spend these two weeks we've got in silence without facing some important stuff. Let this make you stronger, better, wiser. Don't let it destroy you. Don't lose all the good things that God has given you." She hesitated. *"I won't let you, Karly.* You shine, you know. You've got beauty inside and out. *People are drawn to you.* You may not be aware of it, but when you walk into a room the entire room becomes different because of your presence. God has given you many, many gifts and I believe He has great plans for you." Tammy laughed. "I'm not saying you have to rush right back into the land of the living, but I'm telling you that whatever you do, don't you dare give up on God. You stay focused. You spend time grieving. You work at healing all of these atrocious hurts that you have. You take a good hard look at your life and organize and take stock. But then you make sure that you continue on the path that God has set before you. To be a teacher. To be a missionary. To be a woman after God's own heart. Don't you dare let what happened between you and Paul convince you that you are not a 'good enough Christian' to continue on with your plans. There isn't *one* Biblical man or woman who was perfect and without sin. *Not one.* Jeeze! David was an adulterer! Rahab was a whore! Judah got his own daughter – in - law pregnant! Martha worried all the time!" She all of a sudden looked sheepish. "Sorry, you're getting a sermon here, aren't you?"

Karly gave her a small grin. "And I thought you didn't like to preach."

"One - on - one I'm okay."

"I get what you're saying."

"Do you?" Tammy said earnestly to her. "Really? Because, you see, that's what almost happened to me. I spent about six months just lost. In limbo. I convinced myself I was so obviously *not* minister material after that time that I didn't know what to do with myself. It's the worst feeling in the world to give up on your God - given dreams. Just stand up, brush yourself off, and say, 'Okay. *Well let's not make that mistake again!'* and move on.

"It would be a truly sinful loss if you decided not to be a missionary because of this, Karly. There is *nothing,* and I mean *nothing* that should keep you from that goal. You should be praying about all this stuff 24/7. Are you doing that? Do you spend time in prayer and thought regarding God and His purpose for you daily? *You must if you want to succeed. You must if you want to know what God wants for you and your life."*

Tammy laughed a soft laugh, seeming to remember some private joke. "If you don't spend time in prayer, listening carefully to God's still small voice, He sometimes has other ways of getting your attention. Like letting you steer your life right into a brick wall. Dump all of this into God's lap, your problems, your shortcomings, your hopes, your dreams, your worries, your fears, and say, 'Here, I can't do it by myself. I'm all Yours, Lord. Every good and bad part. Use me, guide me, and change me to be the person You want me to be. I'll follow wherever You lead, just point the way.

"He loves you. He wants a relationship with you. That's all He requires of you. Just drag yourself over to Him and say, 'Help'."

Karly spent the second week at Tammy's cabin on the beautiful Outer Banks of North Carolina almost as silently as the first week, but not as numb. She did a lot of thinking and forced herself to take a good hard look at the reality of her life. And the reality was that she had been in love with Paul but she knew, *had known,* that he didn't return the same level of emotion back. How many times had she visited his family and watched the interplay between Paul's parents and *longed* for that same connection between her and Paul? *You only long for things that you didn't already have.*

The frantic desire she continually felt to make him happy, make him love her, *make him see* the way things were between them loomed up before her just like a glaring recipe for imminent *disaster.* Just why had she had to work so hard? For almost four years Karly had done everything in her power to be good enough, happy enough, loving enough for both herself and Paul. Good grief. Between trying to keep the perfect girlfriend plate spinning and the perfect good Christian plate spinning it's a wonder she was still functioning at all! Why had it been necessary to turn herself inside out, compromise her values, justify her beliefs, battle to find the ever-illusive acceptable middle ground that could keep everyone satisfied? The truth of the matter was just what Paul had said to her years ago. *You're good enough for both of us, Babe. Keep up the great work.* And Karly had tried to love enough for both of them, too. And look where that had gotten her.

As their final week ended, Karly was able to have brief flashes of an emotion that had long escaped her: peace. Suddenly, the future that stretched out before her no longer seemed so frenetic. She fell asleep at night pondering the course of her next step rather than organizing battle strategies for upcoming skirmishes. Sitting in the rocking chair on the porch watching the sky dim into night, she found herself, for the first time in her life, seriously praying: asking forgiveness, appreciating all she had been blessed with and requesting continual guidance. Maybe, just maybe, she really was going to survive this …

Karly's prayers were not big fancy impressive minister prayers, but quiet, hesitant, sometimes fumbling-for-words prayers. Sometimes her prayers almost had a conversational dialogue about them rather than the formality of the by rote, 'let me dazzle you with my eloquence' prayers she had grown up on. She found that her relationship with God took on a different perspective: it became more personal, more tangible, and more accessible. God no longer seemed to be the imposing and authoritative presence she always imagined Him to be when she attended church. He became a friend and confidante, someone who had created the beautiful flowers and the particularly odd sand crabs that she saw on the beach. Heck, if God loved her as much as Tammy said, *and He knew more about her shortcomings and abject failures than even her mother knew,* then He had to be unbelievably tolerant and forgiving. Didn't He?

The cabin had lots of traditions, Karly learned. (Tammy said 'traditions' sounded better than 'rules'.) As they began to prepare to leave, the traditions came out in force. It had to be left spotlessly clean, fully stocked (gas for the generator, water in the solar tank, chemicals in the toilet), beds stripped, and sheets and towels ready for the next person.

Other less obvious traditions included the purchasing of new books for the next visitor, making sure non - perishable items such as coffee and tea and canned goods were readily available and the dusting of every corner and floorboard with baby powder (kept the mice away and the smell of mold down). "Hey, wouldn't you figure?' Tammy burst out onto the porch as Karly shook out the numerous throw rugs that were scattered throughout the cabin. "I just got my period three days early. Thought I'd have time to go get supplies before it hit. Do you have anything with you? I'm desperate -" Tammy stopped and looked intently at Karly. "Hey, what's wrong? Are you okay?" Tammy came to stand next to Karly and reached out to touch her bare arm. "What? *Talk to me ...*"

"I, I ... I haven't had my period in a while."

"No biggie. I'll just run into town then."

"I thought it was because of all the stress and strain surrounding the wedding ..."

"Yeah, that's probably it. You've been through major stuff these last few months."

"Tammy, we never used protection."

"WHAT?!"

"I was a good Christian girl, Tam. I didn't need to think about birth control because I wasn't going to need it."

"And Paul ...?"

Karly shrugged. "We never discussed it. I know it's stupid. I can't tell you why."

Tammy swallowed. "Got any symptoms?"

"My breasts are tender, but that often happens before I get my period. I've had cramps the last few days thinking my period was going to start any day now ..."

"Maybe I'll pick up a home pregnancy test while I'm at the pharmacy, huh?" Tammy said quietly.

"Oh, God, Tammy ..."

"Don't go catatonic on me yet. Let's get the facts straight first. How late are you?"

Karly had to think and then was aghast at what she realized. "I'm at least five weeks late!" Her voice raised in panic.

Tammy grabbed her arm and dragged her back in and through the cabin. "Come for the ride with me. It's better than sitting here by yourself slowly going nuts."

They got home and sat on the front porch in the big rockers reading the detailed instructions on how to do a home pregnancy test. "It says first morning urine is optimal, but not required. What do you think?" Tammy asked.

"Let's do it now. I don't think I can wait until morning. There are two tests in the package anyway. If this one's … negative, well then I can always do the second one first thing in the morning."

Fifteen minutes later the two of them stood side - by - side at the kitchen sink staring at the indicator strip on the test stick in absolute silence. Tammy reached over and took Karly's hand and sighed. "Dear Lord," she said out loud in a voice filled with firm resolve, "please be with Karly and this baby she's carrying. Keep them both healthy and strong throughout this pregnancy and continue to guide Karly through this next difficult phase of her life. Help Karly to remain firmly within your protective embrace and trusting in You completely."

A baby. *A baby.* Wasn't her life in enough turmoil without this? Driving home, Karly stared at the window and felt bitterness rise up in her throat. What a joke. Wasn't it just yesterday that she was thinking that she was finally beginning to feel at peace? Did she actually entertain the thought that her life was calm enough – at last – so she could begin to plan what she was going to do next?

Oh God. *Oh, God …*

Karly must have moaned out loud, for Tammy said suddenly, "Don't fall apart on me. My mother used to say, 'The Lord never gives you more than you can handle.'" Karly looked at Tammy like she was absolutely insane. "Are you going to tell Paul?"

"No."

"Why? It's his responsibility, too. I'm not disagreeing with your answer, mind you. You've got some time to think, but eventually, like it or not, everyone will know about this. I know your head is all in a whirl right now – I can't imagine it being anything else – but if you want to keep control of this whole situation, you better make sure your decisions are all based on sound, rational reasons." Tammy glanced at her for a moment and then looked back at the traffic in front of them. "I'm thinking of your parents mostly, your mother in particular."

"Oh, God, my mother …" she put her face in her hands. "Just drop me off on the side of the road here. I can't face her. *I can't.*"

"Maybe they'll surprise you."

"Have you learned *anything* about me and my family over the course of our friendship?"

Tammy sighed. "Yeah. I have. I know for a fact that you being good and perfect hasn't made your mother happy. Maybe being *human* and all the disasters and mistakes that comes along with that quality is something your mother can more easily deal with now."

Karly shook her head. "You're crazy. You have absolutely no clue."

Tammy shrugged. "You're probably right. What was I just saying a few days ago? Unless you walk in a person's shoes and live her life you can't presume to judge? No one knows better than you about your situation right now."

"Now you're being sarcastic."

Tammy laughed. "No, no, really I'm not! I didn't mean it to sound that way if it did. Honest." After long moments of silence, she said, "I think you should tell your family sooner rather than later. No sense sitting on this time bomb and going insane over the stress of it."

"What, I just show up and say, 'Hi Mom, Hi Dad, I'm no longer catatonic, now I'm pregnant?'"

Karly's good friend shrugged. "Works for me. They're going to be on pins and needles waiting for us to show up tomorrow anyway, wondering what state you're in. Got a better idea?"

"No. No, I don't."

For the rest of the ride Karly tried not to think. There was no topic she could safely venture towards that the baby and her current situation didn't color with an unwelcome shade of imminent catastrophe.

Once again, the circumstances of her life overwhelmed her.

It was time to put a stop to that.

A garment of praise for my heaviness
Beauty for ashes
Take this heart of stone and make it yours[5]

June, 1999
Watchung, New Jersey

Two: Good Christians Are Always Wonderful Examples to Others

Michael was waiting on the front lawn when Karly and Tammy pulled up in front of the house. "What level did you get up to?" he asked without preamble.

Karly grinned. "I made it to level nine before I decided that my life was fading away before my very eyes while I was trying to help Mario rescue the princess. That thing's addictive."

Snake studied her intently. "You're better."

Karly shrugged. "Only marginally." She and her brother had a unique relationship. On one level, it was as everyone would expect; a bickering, no holds barred, I hate you, you pain – in – my - neck existence. They fought endlessly: he snooped, she teased, he tattled, she outwitted him. But on another level, although they never spoke aloud and acknowledged it, they were each other's support network, each other's champion amidst the chaos and confusion of this place they called home.

---

[5] Beauty For Ashes, By Shane Barnard and Kendall Combes, Shane & Shane, *Upstairs*, 2004

She looked up at the house. "How's it been here?"

Snake looked over his shoulder at the house and then back at his sister. "Quiet. Really quiet. Creepy quiet. They've been polite with each other and twice I saw Dad putting his arm around Mom." He shuddered at the bizarreness of it all. "It's wiggin' me out big time."

"Well, buckle your seatbelts, because it's going to blast off again I suspect," Karly said with a sigh. The enormity of the situation, that she was not leaving this place that she called home, but was quite possibly here for a lengthy time, crashed down on her like a piano falling from the sky.

"You want me to stay?" Tammy murmured from behind her, as Karly stood frozen in place.

With a shake of her head, Karly picked up her suitcase. "Nah, I might as well jump into this with both feet." She turned, put her suitcase down, and threw her arms around Tammy. "I heard everything you told me, my friend. *Everything.* I'm still processing it all, but I heard and understood. Thank you for these two weeks. I'll go to the Outer Banks with you anytime instead of a hospital psychiatric ward." Karly grinned at Tammy and picked up her suitcase again.

"Well that says a lot for my hospitality." They both laughed.

By the time Tammy's car had pulled out of the driveway, both of Karly's parents were standing on the porch looking concerned and uncertain. With her suitcase in hand, Karly made her way towards them. "Hey, Mom. Hey, Dad."

"Hi, Sweetie," Tom Martin said, looking at his daughter intently as she walked towards them. "It's good to have you home."

Hold all judgments, Karly's Evil Twin said smugly. *You have no idea what you're saying.*

Standing at the bottom of the steps of the porch with her suitcase in hand and Snake behind her, she looked up at her parents. "We've got to talk, and Tammy says that it's best to do it right off the bat. I think I'll follow her advice. Can we go sit somewhere?"

"I know, I know, 'go find something to keep yourself amused, Michael'," Snake said behind her in a poor imitation of his mother's voice.

Karly turned around to look at him. "No, I'd like you to stay. It's going to affect you too." She walked up the front stairs, and her parents parted like the Red Sea. Leaving her suitcase in the front hallway, she avoided the formal living room and went back toward the deck. Her father's newspaper and iced tea glass were on the patio table.

Once all four of them were seated, Madeline Martin looked at her daughter and said, "Why all the high drama, Karly?"

Karly and Michael had talked about this theory of her responsibility for the tension between her parents. The first time Michael had told her that her parents fought more when she was around Karly had thought he was trying to be cruel. But Michael's sincerity and obvious puzzlement over the reality of it all had soon convinced her. How could that be? She was always cooperative, never controversial ... *until now.* While over the day – to - day business of life Michael made every effort to be disruptive, Karly had always made every effort to be good. And it hadn't helped, ever. The reality was like a knife in her heart.

"I wanted to tell you all, first, that I'm sorry. Sorry for what I've put you through and sorry for ..." she shrugged, "I don't know, not making better choices I guess."

"You have nothing to apologize for!" her mother exploded, "It's Paul that has all the answering to do! He bears the full responsibility -,"

"No, Mom, your wrong," Karly interrupted. "Yes, he showed up and called the wedding off and yes, if he hadn't done that we would be married right now, but I can't let you put the full blame on him. We were both in it together and I carry as much," Karly stopped and looked at the three serious faces staring at her. *Aw heck,* Evil Twin said, *why not wipe the slate clean once and for all?* "or probably more responsibility for all this than Paul does. I knew he was unhappy, I knew the proposal was a ... spur of the moment thing, I knew he really didn't want to get married." She looked down at her tightly clasped hands, "I just thought that if I worked hard enough and loved him enough he'd eventually see the light and be happy in the end." Karly sighed all the way from her toes. *"I was a fool."*

"Nobody's perfect, Karly," her father said quietly. "As far as I'm concerned a person is only a fool who doesn't learn from his or her mistakes and instead keeps repeating them."

Her mother spoke passionately. "You've got your entire life stretching out in front of you, Karly. You can pick and choose what you want to do and where you want to go. You've graduated from college with high honors and have a stellar record of volunteering. Once you get your resume together, I'm fairly certain you can write your own ticket as to where you end up."

Karly looked up at her mother. It was the most positive collection of comments she could remember ever coming out of her mother's mouth. How ironic was it that at this monumental moment in time, when Karly had the chance to be in her mother's greatest favor, she was going to completely destroy whatever good feelings there were between them? Karly sighed. "I don't think that's true, Mom. I'm pregnant."

"Oh dear God," her mother said.

Snake's mouth dropped open. For once in his life he was speechless.

Her father closed his eyes in obvious agony.

"Well!" her mother exploded, recovering first, "I knew that young man was a liar and a coward, but it never occurred to me that he would be such a low life individual that he would abandon not only the young woman he had compromised but the baby ..."

Karly held up her hands to stop her mother's tirade. "He doesn't know, Mom. I didn't know until about three days ago myself."

"A phone call can remedy that in a matter of moments." Her mother rose from her lawn chair and headed for the house.

"Where are you going?!" Karly shot from her chair to stand and look at her mother's retreating back.

Her mother stopped and turned. "I'm calling the Williamsons. I'll be interested to see exactly what influence that family can exert on that son of theirs. It's time he accepted his responsibilities."

"If you call the Williamsons – *any of them* – I will get in my car and drive away and you'll never see me again, Mother. I have no intention of telling Paul about this baby. He left me to deal with everything on my own and that's what I plan to do. I refuse to allow him to walk back in my life because of this. *I mean it, Mother."*

Her mother slowly walked back to the porch, her posture and steps a walking illustration of fury. "I have dedicated my *entire life* to my children. I have raised you and your brother at the sacrifice of hopes and dreams that were never allowed to be fulfilled. It was only once you were away at college that you began to make these *glaringly poor choices* that have led to your present circumstances. What should I have expected? Why should I have hoped and aimed so high for you? Why did I waste my *time?"*

"Maddy, enough …" her father said.

"*Shut up*," her mother hissed turning on her husband, "just shut up and keep out of this. Just go back to reading your paper and sipping your iced tea and selling your little pieces of electronic trash that no one needs but everyone wants. *I'll* continue to keep everything on the straight and narrow, everything under control." Madeline Martin turned her furious eyes back on her daughter. "So. You don't want the Williamsons involved, huh? You don't want Paul to assume any responsibility for this baby? What are your grand plans, Karly? Where exactly do you envision yourself in five months or five years? Am I expected to stay home and care for this baby while you go to work to support yourself and this child? Are you planning on living here with us? Have you thought about medical bills? You're no longer covered under our policy because you're *too old* now. Are you thinking that Appalachia will welcome you and your illegitimate child with open arms to go ahead with your missionary work?" Hands on her hips her mother glared at her and spat out, "Come on Karly, let's hear your plans."

"THAT'S ENOUGH," Tom Martin said as he surged to his feet. Gripping Karly's hand he began to forcibly drag her from the deck into the house. "You've said more than enough, Madeline. I will not sit here and watch you eviscerate her any further. You'll have to postpone your fun until another time."

"How dare you!"

"STOP," Karly shouted at the top of her lungs. "*Just stop!*" She pulled her arm away from her father's grasp and glanced at Michael, wishing she'd not allowed him to hear all this after all. He looked pale and lost. "I'm twenty - one. That qualifies as an adult." She looked at her mother. "Maybe not a *wise* adult, but an adult nonetheless. I've got about seven months to think about what I'm going to do with myself. I'm asking you two," she glanced at her mother and father, "to allow me to stay here and live during this time while I make arrangements and try to get my life in order. Will you allow me that?"

"Of course, Karly," her father said instantly.

Her mother remained silent and Karly made eye contact with her and waited. *We might be here all night,* Evil Twin said with genuine concern. "I'll not allow you to remain here even one minute if you are considering an abortion," her mother said through gritted teeth.

"That's not an option for me, Mother. Anymore than marrying Paul is."

Her mother just stood and stared at her. Waiting, it seemed.

Karly sighed and said quietly, "Adoption is an option, though."

"You'd give your own flesh and blood away?" her mother hissed in horror.

Karly was so terribly tired again. "Isn't that exactly what you'd expect from such a disappointment of a daughter?" she said in a dead voice and walked into the house retrieving her suitcase and slowly climbing the stairs to her bedroom.

If Karly had thought that the first twenty - one years of her life at home with her parents had been difficult, she had no words to describe the situation once she'd announced her pregnancy. Like achieving a new level that had previously been unattainable, the interplay between the four members of the Martin family took on an entirely new course. Her mother and father ceased arguing, for to the best of Karly's knowledge, they no longer spoke. Like two enormous tanker ships trying to negotiate safe passage in the smallest of harbors, the two of them avoided each other as much as possible. Her mother's criticism of Karly continued unabated and, if possible, escalated. She went so far as to criticize the glass that Karly brought her a drink of water in and the tone Karly used when she answered the telephone.

Michael reached an all time new level of being unique. He became a vegan.

"A *what*, Snake?"

"A vegan. I've been reading up on it and I've decided that I am no longer going to support – either subtly or blatantly, the misuse and ill treatment of animals."

"Don't you mean 'vegetarian'?"

"No, I mean *vegan*. Veganism is much more than vegetarianism, it is the belief that *all products* derived from animals – meat, dairy, eggs, honey, gelatin -,"

"Gelatin?!"

"Yes," her brother said in a very superior tone. "Vegans hate unnecessary killing, cruelty, and exploitation of animals. And it's more than an eating style," he continued with an absolutely straight face, "it's a *lifestyle*. In embracing the vegan lifestyle I can influence world hunger and the misuse of our natural resources.

"I just asked Mom and she said that you would take me shopping. I need to get new shoes. My sneakers and sandals are leather and I no longer wear leather." Looking down at his feet Karly took note that he was wearing his blue plastic pool flip - flops.

Karly rubbed her forehead and then pinched the bridge of her nose. "Look, Snake, *I'm sorry* about all the stuff that's going on. Really I am. Don't do this, okay? You and I will stick together and weather this storm and everything will be okay."

"I resent that you think I'm doing this for attention," he said in a supercilious tone. "If you can't drive me, I'll ask Dad when he gets home from work. There's a health food store down town that supposedly has a small clothing line that is endorsed by the Vegan Society of America."

"*The Vegan Society of America?!*" When he turned to walk away she said, "Okay, *okay*. I'll take you."

Most disturbing of all though, was her father. He simply stopped interacting with Karly. There was no light conversation, no defense in the face of her mother's criticisms, and no tender smiles across the room. Karly seemed simply to become invisible. *So much for him being there for you,* Evil Twin said with real sarcasm.

By the end of the second month home, Karly found herself sitting in Tammy's office at the church with her head in her hands. "I can't do this, Tammy. I can't live there with them anymore! *Not one more day.* I thought I could stick it out until the baby was born but I don't know if I can. Michael's driving everyone absolutely nuts. He threw out everyone's leather shoes, belts, purses, briefcases, and suitcases last night. You should have seen my mother and father out at the front curb at 5 a.m. going through our trash trying to get everything of value out before the garbage men came. The little nutcase even implied that all silk garments were inappropriate, and so my mother is having my father put a *lock on their bedroom closet!* My mother quite literally cannot stand the sight of me, and my father behaves as if he doesn't even have a daughter anymore.

"I've found a doctor I like downtown at the women's clinic. Of course, my Mother's furious because I've refused to go to her OB/GYN for my prenatal visits. I've got a job working at the mini - mart doing cashier work. I *know* it's not a career for goodness sake but it's putting money in my pocket so I don't have to ask my parents for any. But I'm going to have to find another place to stay. I'm having trouble sleeping and even eating. At my three-month check up today the doctor was concerned with my *weight loss.* He said pregnant women are supposed to be worried about the opposite problem."

Tammy leaned back in her chair. "You want to come live with me? I've only got a one bedroom apartment, but the living room couch folds out."

Karly hesitated, looking desperately at her friend. "Could I? I'd help with the rent and expenses."

"Of course you would."

Karly looked at her. "I thought you'd fight me on that."

Tammy shrugged. "Would it do me any good?"

"Nope."

"So why bother?"

"I have another request."

"Shoot."

"What do you know about adoption?"

Tammy sighed. "Some. I had a girl at my last church where I worked who gave a baby up for adoption. She did something called an 'open adoption'. Do you know what that is?"

Karly shook her head.

"In an open adoption, there is a certain level of communication between the birth parents and the adoptive parents. Depending on the two parties it can be a lot or a little. Or, you can do the old - fashioned closed adoption, where once the baby is handed over the door shuts, never to be opened again."

"I didn't know ..." Karly said with real desperation. "In these past two months I've gotten *no where* with what I think I should do. I'm too busy just trying to cope with getting out of bed. As each day goes by I just feel more and more ... overwhelmed. Now I'm starting to feel *desperate*. I thought maybe if I started asking questions I might be able to come to some conclusions about *something.*"

Tammy smiled and nodded. "Lots of people think closed adoption is the only available option. The girl from my youth group got to choose the adoptive couple that her baby went to and was able to have some input with the amount of visitation she would have with the baby."

"You mean she stays in touch with the adoptive parents?!"

Tammy smiled. "She could have. She was from Taiwan, an exchange student, and so she opted to have only minimal email contact once she gave the baby up. But she could have stipulated that she wanted to see the baby once or twice a year."

"I had no idea ..."

"I can't get you her name, but I remember the name of the agency – Agape Christian Services. Come here. I'll look it up on my computer." Minutes later they were scrolling through pages and pages and pages of letters from prospective adoptive couples looking for babies to adopt. "There's an office not too far from here. Why don't you go visit and talk to someone there? I'll go with you if you want."

"You think this is what I should do, don't you," Karly said watching Tammy intently.

Tammy held up her hands, shaking her head furiously. "Oh no you don't! This is *your* decision. I'll support you in whatever you do. The bottom line is that whatever you decide, you're the one who's going to live with this choice, not me. You asked me what I knew and I told you. I'm just trying to be a supportive friend. Heck, Karly. I can't even imagine what I'd be doing or thinking if I were in your position. It's smart for you to gather as much information as you can so you can make an informed, correct decision. Are you praying 24/7?"

"I'm trying! Being home, the whole peaceful, Godlike, Christian person I want to be just seems to disappear. They all just seem to suck it right out of me. I'm too busy trying not to scream in frustration and pull my hair out."

Tammy looked at her, checked her desk planner, and then picked up the phone. While she dialed she said to Karly, "Jimmy Morriset just got a new truck. He came by to show it off this morning. Parents got it for him for graduation." Tammy rolled her eyes. "Hey Jim, it's Pastor Tammy. You know that new truck you were showing off this morning? Want to put it to good use already?" She paused, listening, "Yeah, I have a friend who needs help moving some of her stuff over to my place. She's going to be staying with me for a while. Great. What day's good for you? Saturday?" She looked at Karly and arched her eyebrow in question. Karly tried to read her expression. She wouldn't extend the offer if she didn't mean it, would she? Slowly she nodded at Tammy. "Saturday would be fine, Jim. Is 10:00 a.m. too early? Super, here's the address ..." When Tammy hung up she looked at Karly. "Well, you've got two days to get packed, and I've got two days to clean my apartment!"

"Are you sure ...?" Karly asked.

"Yes."

Things were immediately better at Tammy's. Karly was still plagued with insomnia, but her appetite improved. She went out of her way not to be intrusive, and by the end of the second week Tammy kissed her and said, "My apartment's never been cleaner, and I've never enjoyed so many delicious home cooked meals! Will you marry me?"

Karly spent every free moment that she wasn't working or sleeping (something she wished she could do more often but it seemed as if her brain would not cooperate with her very exhausted body) reading the letters of the adoptive parents on the Agape Christian Services website. Pages and pages of them. Karly seemed to gravitate toward the website any free moment she had. When not at the computer, invariably her mind was replaying all the pictures and words, over and over. Standing at the checkout counter working at the mini - mart, she realized that certain couples she'd read about stood out in her mind. *Help, Lord. Give me direction on this. I feel so alone. I don't know what to do. Help.* At what point did one make a decision as huge as adoption? Did you just wake up one morning and *know?* Did you all of a sudden have a blinding flash of the obvious and realize with crystal clear clarity what needed to be done? Karly had this reoccurring nightmare that she was on her way to the hospital to give birth, in excruciating pain, and they wouldn't let her in to see anyone until she could tell them what she was planning to do with the baby. More times than she could count she had awakened from the dream, heart pounding, drenched in sweat shouting, "*I still don't know! Help me! I need someone's help!*"

At her five month check up the technician did a sonogram. There on the screen in black and white was the baby. As the technician punched buttons and rolled the sensor across Karly's belly, the woman said, "Do you want to know if it's a girl or a boy?"

Karly swallowed. "You can tell that?"

"Not always, but your baby is being cooperative today. I could make a pretty reliable prediction."

Did she want to know? Would it make any difference? She stared at the screen, watching the wiggly little thing skitter around inside her belly. "Is it sucking its thumb?" she said incredulously.

The technician smiled. "Seems like it. That's pretty common."

"Oh."

"Look, if you're not sure you want to know now, I could make a note in your chart and you could ask another time."

"No, I'd like to know."

"It's a boy." The technician gave Karly a brilliant smile. "Congratulations."

A boy. A baby boy. She was going to have a boy. The technician's smile slowly faded, and Karly realized she needed to make a response. "A boy! Well! Thanks …"

"Here." The technician handed Karly a small square of paper. "I thought you might like to have a picture to take home."

She went right to work from the doctor's appointment and spent the day studying the variety of people that came through her line at the mini - mart. What a mass of humanity. Laborers and business people, teenagers and the elderly. She found she was drawn to the mothers who occasionally showed up with their children in tow. Some looked harried and fit to be tied, but quite a number of them were patient and loving with the kids. Two mothers in particular stood out. One came in with two older children, a boy and a girl who were obviously bickering with each other and from the look on the mother's face, it had been going on for some time. "I said sorry," the boy said in a tone that implied anything but.

"You're *not* forgiven," said the girl who appeared to be a year or two younger.

"What do you want me to say then?" the boy exploded in frustration. "You know we can't have electronic toys until everything's settled between us." The sister remained purposefully mute.

The mother, looking tired but purposefully blank regarding the exchange between her two children, placed two gallons of fat free milk on the counter.

"Can I get a candy?" the girl asked her mother. Karly hesitated, waiting to find out if she had to ring anything else up beside the milk. The mother stared straight ahead at Karly, never answering her daughter's question.

"Will there be anything else, Ma'am?" Karly asked the woman.

"You know you can't get any candy," the boy hissed at his sister, "*nothing* good happens until we settle this. *You know that.*"

"Mom?" the girl looked expectantly at her mother's back.

Karly exchanged looks with the mother who rolled her eyes and then winked. *Just one more second, please,* her look seemed to say.

The girl gave a world-weary sigh. "Okay, I forgive you."

"So I can tell Mom it's settled between us?"

The girl glanced at her mother's back and said in a resigned voice, "Yeah."

"Mom, Gracie and I have things settled. Can we get a candy?"

"Do you have any money in the bank?" the mom said seemingly coming back to life.

"Yeah, we've both got $3 left from our allowance."

The mom turned. "Okay, it's your money. But hurry up, okay? We need to get home and start dinner." As they wandered out of the store Karly heard the mom say, "You two did a good job settling that on your own. I'm proud of you."

The second mother had a toddler with her that was at the age where he wanted to touch everything. Especially stuff that the mom said 'no' to. Standing in line waiting to pay for a pack of disposable diapers, the little boy kept trying to fling himself out of his mother's arms to reach the display of candies in front of the register. "No, Jack, you're too little for those candies. Mommy has pretzels in the car for you. You can have some of them." The little boy screamed in fury and leaned so far out of her mother's arms that the mom finally had to put the diapers down and hold him with both hands. "No, Jack."

"Wanna dat!" Jack screamed and pointed. "Wanna me dat!"

Under her breath the mom said in a low quiet voice, "I ... need ... a ... kiss ... from ... a ... red ... haired ... boy!" The mom pounced on the neck of the little boy who squealed in delight as his mother nuzzled him.

By the time the mom got to the register to pay for the diapers, the little boy was snuggled against his mom's shoulder sucking his thumb contentedly.

In both instances, Karly felt she never would have had the patience to do the right thing with those children. She heard her mother's voice rising in sharp criticism about each child's behavior and the feeling of impatience of being at the mercy of disobedient children. Was it different with your own children? Did you learn how to diffuse volatile situations with experience? She supposed it had to be. But what did that say about her mother? The idea that she might end up just like her mother caused a wave of terror. *Dear God in Heaven!* Was that possible? The awful truth stood up straight and tall so it could be fully noticed. What did she know about the right way to raise and deal with a child? She touched her stomach that extended enough now that she wore stretch leotards and big blousy tee shirts and tops as her standard uniform.

A baby boy. Shouldn't she feel something positive other than tension and indecision and … in the deepest recesses of her heart … indignation? A baby boy.

The reality that in only a few months she could actually be living her nightmare of indecision outside the hospital made her heart pound, her palms sweat and the baby kick. Oh, God. She was going to have a baby boy … She felt absolutely and completely alone with nowhere to go because the reality was that it was only she who could make this decision. And like it or not, no matter what she decided, her life would never, *ever* be the same again. No matter what she decided.

Dear Birth Mother,

We don't know you, but believe it or not we are already praying for you. We have never been in the situation you are currently in and can only begin to imagine what you must be going through. We pray that you have someone to talk to who will listen and console and give you good, solid advice. We pray that God makes His presence known to you at each and every moment of your day and that you feel His gentle guidance. We pray that you are healthy and safe. We pray, that if it is the Lord's Will, this letter will speak to you in some special way.

Our names are Viv and Darin. We live in a home that is filled with love and laughter. I'd like to say it's always clean and tidy, but we're trying to be honest here! Viv is a schoolteacher and Darin is a financial consultant for a local investment firm in our town. We have a great life. The Lord has blessed us continually in more ways than we imagined possible. We have each other, strong family ties, and a wonderful church community that is as close and as important to us as our families.

We would like to share our wonderful life with a child. Perhaps that is the child you are carrying right now. But we don't know for sure, do we? If this letter speaks to you, and you would like to correspond with us, please take that as the Lord's guidance and contact us by our email address here at Agape House. Just as you would like to get to know us better, we would like to get to know you better.

Yours sincerely,

Viv and Darin

It was late and Karly was so tired, but still she could not sleep. Moving into Tammy's apartment had given her a huge semblance of peace and a big boost in the independent ego category but had not truly helped the insomnia. Lying in bed at night she felt like she had a gigantic hairy elephant sitting in the bed with her, waiting and watching for her to make some sort of decision. And that's where the trouble began. Her restless brain kept running over and over in an endless loop. Gotta decide what to do about the baby. Gotta think about the future. Gotta make plans. Gotta make a choice about adoption. Gotta choose a couple. Only four months to go …

She knew that she and she alone had to make these decisions. Tammy had been patient and loving in giving her time and advice but the reality was just as Tammy had said, *This is your decision. The bottom line is that whatever you decide, you're the one who's going to live with the choice.*

She had to decide if she was going to keep her baby or give it up for adoption. *A baby boy.* That was the first and greatest hurdle. Once she chose one of those paths, then there were five billion more decisions she had to make, but she couldn't do anything at all until she made the first decision. And just how could *anyone* make a decision like that?

Are you praying 24/7? Tammy's voice in her head seemed always to zero in on the glaring inconsistencies of her plans.

No, she was not praying 24/7. She had no idea what she wanted to pray about! She felt this overwhelming regret that she hadn't started praying a *long time ago* – like *years* ago – and since she hadn't done it then, what could she do about it now? What was she supposed to do? Pray something like 'Dear Lord, my whole life is screwed up. I've made more mistakes than I can count. Could you please help me untangle this mess?' Karly snorted sitting in front of the brightly lit computer screen. *Yeah, right.* That would work.

No decision is a decision. Who'd said that to her? For the life of her she couldn't remember. It sounded like something snide her mother would say to her.

We don't know you, but believe it or not we are already praying for you. Karly looked at the computer screen at the words this couple had typed to a faceless, desperate, pregnant woman. She clicked back a screen to look at their picture. This Darin was dark haired, fair skinned with glasses. He looked just like the investment type his wife had described him. The woman, Viv, looked … *happy.* Relaxed. Some of the photos of some of the other couples just wreaked of desperation and sorrow. At least in Karly's eyes they did. But this couple looked *content.* Karly clicked ahead again to their letter. *We have a great life.* They didn't talk about the enormous hole their life had as a result of no children. They talked about it being so great they wanted to *share it* with another. *The Lord has blessed us continually in more ways than we imagined possible.* They weren't whining about anything. Their happiness and joy kind of oozed off the computer onto her hand holding the mouse. All of a sudden, Karly really wanted to email them.

Dear Viv and Darin,

First, please don't get your hopes up in receiving this email from me. Yes, I am a single, pregnant young woman (I'm twenty - one and five months along) but at this point in my life I've made no decision one way or another about whether to give this baby up for adoption or keep it. I just liked your email and thought I'd take you up on your invitation to correspond.

If my indecision right now seems to be too insecure and potentially hurtful to both of you I understand if you don't want to answer me back. Honest I do.

Sincerely,

Karly

Karly clicked send before she lost her nerve and then was awash with panic. *What have you done?* Evil Twin said in a furious tone, *Are you out of your mind?*

It's okay. It's just an email. There is no harm done.

Her shift at the mini - mart ended at 7:00 p.m. the next day, and as she walked out to her car she was stunned to see her father leaning against it. He was dressed casually in khaki shorts and a button down short-sleeved shirt, looking tired and old and tremendously uncertain. She stood in the parking lot with the waves of heat rolling up around her from the bubbling asphalt. *Oh great,* Evil Twin said, *Just what you needed today after a long sleepless night and a hard day on your feet.*

The heat made her light headed, having come from the cool of the air conditioning. The promise of car air conditioning is what forced her feet to step forward towards her father. Nothing else.

He thrust his hands in his shorts pockets as she approached him and fished her keys out of her purse. "Hi, Karly. I thought maybe I could buy you dinner if you don't have any other plans."

She felt the perspiration trickle down between her breasts and back as she looked up at her dad. "I'm kind of tired, Dad. I've been working since eleven, and I've not been sleeping too well." She looked down as she sorted through her keys to find the right one. *Let him have it,* Evil Twin said. Looking her father right in the eye Karly said, "I'm better off at Tammy's, Dad, but still on edge. I've lost the ability to be polite or even tactful in certain areas. *I don't think it would be a good idea to try to have a nice father daughter conversational dinner."*

He stepped forward and took her arm, steering her towards his car. "Good, because that wasn't what I had in mind."

Her father took her to a quiet, cool, out of the way bistro style restaurant that offered them privacy and little in the way of distraction. Karly's anxiety level continued to escalate as the silence between them went on unabated. What did he want from her? She felt a wave of tiredness overcome her. Sleep. That's what she wanted. Sleep ...

"Look, I'm gonna just talk, okay? I don't expect you to say anything. I can't promise to make a lot of sense, but I'm going to start from the beginning and try to clear up a few things."

"Dad, I don't know what your agenda is or what you're hoping to accomplish with all this. I'm tired and I'm confused. I don't really need you to try to pressure me into making decisions ..."

"I'm not here so much about *you* right now, Karly. I'm here about me. And your mother. You're entitled to know some things and maybe, in telling you some of this ... *stuff* ... it might help you understand your mother and ... me a little better. If that happens then perhaps it will help you ... directly or indirectly. I don't know." He ran his fingers through his normally impeccably combed hair and it stood up all over his head at odd angles. Toying with the salad fork he said, "I can't sleep, I can't eat. I can't concentrate at work and I can't abide going home. Last night I laid in bed and tried to think of the last wise decision I made." He looked up out the window at the traffic whizzing by. "The only thing I could think of that had any semblance of quality to it revolved around times with you, talking, laughing, loving." He looked at Karly then. "Let's start with a simple question before I begin. Do you believe that I love you?"

Yes. The answer was quick in her head, without hesitation. "Yes, I know that, Dad."

Her father visibly relaxed at her answer. "Oh, thank God. I panicked last night when I thought that perhaps I'd messed up even that." He gave her a tiny smile. "I do you know. Love you. Love you with *all my heart*. I've gotten my greatest joy and my greatest sense of self worth and accomplishment watching you grow into the young woman you have become."

Her gut clenched and rolled as she looked over his left shoulder avoiding his eyes. "Until recently," she said bitterly. Until she showed her true colors.

Karly felt her father's warm hand clasp hers as it rested cold and stiff on the table. "But that's where you're wrong. The way you've behaved these last few weeks and months has made me just as proud, if not more so. That's why I realized I had to defy your mother's wishes and come and speak with you. I really had no choice."

"Mom doesn't want you to see me?"

"No, it's not the seeing that she objects to. Your mother doesn't want me to talk with you and tell you some truths. You see, she's worked her whole life to establish a certain … I'm searching for a word that doesn't have negative connotations, but it's hard … *veneer* I guess. She wants very much to appear to be a person that she feels, deep down she isn't." He released Karly's hand. "Damn, I'm not doing this well at all."

The waiter came and brought their drinks, took their orders, and left. "Karly," her dad said after he took a sip of his soda, "when we were in college I got your mother pregnant."

Criminal espionage, middleman for a major international drug cartel, a bigamist with three other wives … but getting *her mother pregnant in college?* Get out of town! Karly sat there unable to hide her shock or shut her mouth. Good thing he said he didn't expect her to say anything.

"We were both seniors and really hadn't been dating for all that long when it happened. I think maybe five or six months. We were serious though. I'd already told her that I loved her, but she hadn't told me back yet." *Had Karly ever heard her mother say she loved her father? Karly didn't think so …*

"When we met we both had had grand plans. She'd accepted a position with the International Red Cross in Washington, D.C. for an entry-level position that had great promise for advancement. I had already accepted a position, with the company I still work for today." He shrugged.

"We were pretty impressed with ourselves, I guess ... Both of us had friends who were still worrying about getting an interview, and she and I were waltzing around campus with jobs already in our back pockets." He gazed at Karly. "She was pretty. More than pretty actually, she was in that small stratosphere of women on campus that qualified as *gorgeous*. Just like you." He shook his head and popped a cherry tomato in his mouth, lost in memories. "I had heard of her before I met her. When I laid eyes on her that first night I was *just gone*. She was witty and vivacious and in – your - face sure of herself. She exuded a message that said *you can look but don't bother even asking to touch.*

"But I was pretty sure of myself, too, you see. We hit it off that first night like a nuclear explosion." He gave Karly a wry grin and scratched the side of his cheek. "I'll spare you the ... details ... but things moved fast with us. I can't actually tell you for sure if it was love at first sight with me but it was pretty darn close."

They were silent for a while, her father lost in memories and Karly trying to wrap her head around the image of her parents young and carefree, *hot and horny*. Hell, it was impossible to picture her mother simply happy. "What about Mom? Was it love at first sight for her too, Dad?"

He smiled a sad smile. "I think we both know the answer to that question, don't we? I don't think Maddy does too well in the love department."

"What happened when she found out she was pregnant?"

Her father snorted. "She absolutely freaked out. Went ballistic, ranting and raving about her plans and her career and her life. She was furious with me, with her circumstances.

"I insisted that we speak with her parents together. You've got to remember, the times were different, the Midwest, conservative ... I was trying to do the right thing, willing to accept my responsibilities. Heck, I knew I was in love with her, deep down was excited about the possibility of a child. For me, the future as it was suddenly materializing wasn't all that far from what I eventually wanted for myself anyway."

"But not for Mom."

"You know, Karly, we've been married for all these years now and I can honestly tell you that I don't know what you're mother wanted or planned for her future. We never got around to really discussing it prior to her getting pregnant, and after that, well, there didn't seem to be much sense. Somehow, I get the distinct impression, however, that the course of your mother's life was *not* the way she hoped or planned it would be," he finished rather bitterly.

The waiter brought their meals and left their almost untouched salads still at the table. Her father looked out the window again and sighed. "We did the 'right thing': we married, she dropped out of school two months shy of graduation because she had complications with her pregnancy and had to take it real easy. I graduated and we moved up to where my job was, I worked my tail off to do the whole provider thing, she dedicated her life to home and family and we both lived miserably ever after. The End."

Karly frowned in confusion. "What happened to the baby?"

"You're that baby, Karly."

"I can't be! If you *had* to get married then my birth date would only be a couple months after the date of your marriage. You were married well over a year before I was born."

Her father shrugged. "We lied."

"What?"

He shrugged again like it was no big deal. "We lied about the date of our wedding. Remember, we moved right after we were married so we told everyone at the new job and the new neighborhood and the new church that we'd been married a year longer than we really had been. The longer we were together the less it mattered anyway. You're going to be twenty - two on your next birthday and we will be married twenty - *two* years, not twenty - *three,* on our next anniversary."

Again she was speechless. Then it seemed to fall into place. "That's why Mom hates me."

"She doesn't hate you Karly."

"Like hell she doesn't! Even Michael's noticed that you two fight less when I'm not around. That's why I never can seem to do anything right for her. I was a big, gigantic, unwanted, mistake for both of you. At last it all makes sense ..."

Her father leaned across the table and said furiously, "*I didn't tell you all this to make you feel worse.*"

"Then why did you?" She shot back. Karly felt like ice was slowly filling her veins, starting gradually with her face, freezing away her tears, immobilizing her facial expressions, and working down to her heart to numb away the hurt.

Her father spoke urgently now, seeming to realize that if he was going to make a valid point he had better move fast. "Despite the fact that I am your father, I know something of what you are going through right now: the fear and the indecision, the worry and the regret. In some ways you are similar to your mother, but thankfully there are many ways in which you are not. You're beautiful, smart, talented, focused, and committed. Those qualities are from your mom. In addition, you care little for appearances, have a hunger to do what is right and good, and don't have a selfish bone in your body." He hesitated and rubbed his face with both hands, seeming to shore up his courage. Looking at Karly he said, "Those are qualities that make you different from your mother.

"A few people spoke to Maddy about adoption, Karly, when she was in your position. She wouldn't hear of it. But it wasn't because she loved the baby she was carrying too much to give it away, she loved her *image*. It's always been about prestige and what others think for Madeline. Above and beyond anything and any*one* else. These last few months that we've known you were pregnant, I've asked myself over and over the question, *would you have been better off had we put you up for adoption? Would your life have been more full of love and peace and happiness and goodness?*' Her father's eyes filled with tears as he looked out the window again and said in an agonized whisper, "Every time I ask that question of myself I am forced to answer *probably yes.*

"I told you when you went down to the Outer Banks with Pastor Tammy that I would be there for you, and the first thing I did when you got back and needed me was to retreat. I'm telling you that whatever you decide to do about this baby, I will support you one hundred percent with anyone and everyone regarding your decision. No questions asked, no waffling. *I promise you.*

"I have every confidence that whatever choice you make will be, not the best for you or this family, but for this baby. And you will have the courage to do it, too. That is what makes you different from both your mother *and* me."

"You said what qualities I got from Mom and what qualities I had that were different. What qualities do I have that are from you, Dad?"

"Oh, that one's easy," he said with a tremulous smile and a fresh spill of tears down his cheeks. He fished out his handkerchief and wiped his face. "From me you got the quality of unconditional love." He took a deep shaky breath. "It can be a blessing and a curse, Baby. As you are already discovering."

I've recklessly built all my dreams in the sand, just to watch them all wash away ...[6]

August, 1999

New Brunswick, New Jersey

Three: Good Christians Can Withstand Temptation

"Paul! Grab me another beer, I'm a little busy here! Make yourself useful instead of sitting there staring out the window. What's a matter with you, guy?"

Paul hauled himself up, wandered into the kitchen, his feet sticking to the grime on the cheap linoleum floor. He pulled open the fridge, grabbed two beers and wandered back to claim his seat.

Twisting the cap off, Paul took a long pull while he held out the other unopened bottle to his friend, Vince, sitting happily on the couch with a gorgeous redhead curled up in his lap. The girl twisted off the cap for him and Vince held it high in salute to Paul. "Cheers, man. What's up with you? We've been waiting six years for our team to have a chance at making the playoffs! You could show a little enthusiasm!"

Turning to stare out the window, Paul took another swig of his beer and remained silent. If he had no answers for himself about why he

---

[6] "Faithful To Me", by Jennifer Knapp, *Faithful-To-Me*

behaved like he behaved, how could he possibly explain himself to someone else? How could someone appear to have everything he could possibly want on the outside and feel so empty and unhappy inside? That was the question of the moment, the question of the week, the question of *his life*. For Paul Williamson could not remember a time when he felt happy or satisfied with anything that was going on with his life.

On the outside, no one's life appeared more charmed. He had had a free ride through college from his parents. Hell, he only pumped gas over the summer to guarantee pocket money. He had been popular and well liked by just about everyone. Naturally smart, he rarely had had to study. When his parents had pushed him to decide on a career, he'd settled on accounting simply because math was something he could do *in his sleep*. And he had dated for almost his entire college career the most gorgeous woman on campus. Jeeze, guys *talked* about her because of her looks even when she wasn't around to stare at. The reality that some of his reputation on campus was directly related to the fact that he was Karly Martin's boyfriend had caused him a certain level of discomfort.

Paul snorted to himself in disgust and stared down into his half empty beer bottle as the crowd around him roared their approval over something happening on the television screen. Maybe he really deserved to be still called the 'baby of the family'. As a toddler, his earliest memory was sitting on the curb staring at his bloodied knees, howling at the top of his lungs, while his two older brothers laughed and ran away from him. Here he was, twenty - one years old, sitting in his friend's disgusting apartment, mentally crying into his beer over the hopelessness of his life. What a waste. He was such a waste.

It seemed to him that he had spent his entire life trying to catch up, grow up, or keep up. Not once had he ever led or planned or initiated something. It was absolutely miserable being the youngest in a large family. Everyone considered him the spoiled baby, and yet he never, ever seemed to get anything he really wanted.

Hand – me - down clothes and sports equipment had been his lifestyle. His parents only started buying him his own clothes when he got bigger than anyone else in the family and the hand – me - downs no longer fit. He was sure his sister Rachel would accuse him of growing big on purpose to get more attention. Heck, his first brand new piece of sports equipment had been his mountain bike that *he had bought with his own money*. Everyone in his family had told him how foolish and wasteful he had been when he'd done it. "What do you expect?" his oldest sister Connie had said with complete disgust, "He's never had to assume *any* kind of responsibility so why should we expect him to be wise with his money?" He'd wanted a damn mountain bike, for God's sake, not his older brother Elliot's eight year old ten speed. He still had that mountain bike, too. It had been a good investment, even if no one but he appreciated it.

The hardest thing he had to deal with, which had been part of his life *forever*, had been living in his brothers' and sisters' shadows. There was literally no area where Paul could shine or be outstanding because *someone* had always been there before him. Not at home, not at school, not even at church.

Way to go, Paul! You hit it right out of the park! You're a chip off the old block, that's for sure. Just like Elliot and Brian. I could always count on them to bring in the runs.

Paul, it's my pleasure to recognize yet another Williamson into the Honor Roll Hall of Fame here at Brentridge Junior High School. Well done, young man.

Quarterback? Sure, I'd expect that from a Williamson.

And the Bible Verse Memorization Blue Ribbon goes to yet another hard working Williamson child, Elll-, oops! Sorry! PAUL Williamson!

But finally, after much hard work and thought, Paul had found a way to distinguish himself from his brothers and sisters … Unfortunately, it was at the cost of his parent's happiness, peace of mind, and the family's tranquility.

What do you mean you don't want to be in the church play? Your brothers and sisters have always been willing to perform in the church productions when they were asked.

Oh my, this is very unexpected. We've never had to deal with a Williamson child failing an academic subject.

Quit in the middle of the season?   Who the hell are you?   You're no Williamson, that's for sure!

DROP OUT OF HIGH SCHOOL?! 'Maybe' take your GED instead? No son of mine is going to be a high school dropout and spend the rest of his life sitting on his butt doing nothing but causing trouble.

You can do one of two things, Paul. You can go back to high school or take your GED this coming Saturday. Otherwise, we're shipping you out to Aunt Nancy's in Texas and you can have a fresh start there going to high school. Those are your only choices. And your father and I will not even discuss whether you will be attending college or not. YOU WILL. We want the best for all of our children and by God, you're going to get it whether you like it or not!

He was such a coward. He should have stuck to his guns and not taken the GED or, at the very least, refused to go to college. Maybe that would have helped bypass this latest great disastrous turn of his life: dumping his fiancée on the morning of their wedding. After all, if his parents hadn't forced the whole college issue down his throat then he'd never have met Karly and ended up spending the last four years of his life with her.   Four years of following her around like a pet dog, tongue hanging out and tail wagging, dancing to whatever tune she played. He took a swig of beer and grunted. Nah, with his luck, if he'd turned out to be a bum she probably would have been volunteering at the homeless shelter and they still would have run into each other.

Paul couldn't stand being home. Not that he'd ever felt completely part of the whole perfect family scenario, but since the morning of the wedding he'd avoided anyone that qualified as family like the plague. Over the last six weeks, he'd spent a total of sixty minutes in the presence of his family. Today's past thirty being probably as bad as the wedding day's previous thirty. Long enough to make his mother cry (again), his sisters to roll their eyes (as usual), his brothers to call him an idiot (what else was new), and have his father tell him what a great disappointment he once again was (been there, done that). Anyplace was better than being home amongst all his perfect siblings playing his role as the only – family – screw - up. No one said it, but the thinly veiled "typical Paul" looks along with the more obvious disgusted head shakes were par for the course with most of his family these days. Sleeping on friend's couches and floors, even occasionally his car, had been preferable to getting anymore well meaning lectures or thinly veiled pieces of "sound advice".

He took another swig of beer and ground his teeth. Yet here he was, twenty - one years old and *still* letting his family influence him and drag him down further. All he'd tried to do was sneak into his room and grab some clean clothes today. As soon as they'd spotted him, they'd gone after him with both barrels. Again. Still. As usual. Even with the wedding disaster behind him, even with his personal life in complete shambles, *still* his father and mother were pushing him to get his resumes mailed out so he could get an accounting job! *He didn't even want to be a freakin' accountant!* God, the look on their faces when he'd screamed that at them had been priceless. Maybe *now* they'd leave him alone. Finally. At last.

God Almighty. At a time in his life when everything should be coming together he never felt more scattered. Were Paul to be pressed by someone, anyone, he couldn't, for the life of him, tell you one thing he believed in or felt strongly about. *Not one thing.* Worse yet, he had no desire to do anything. No wishes, no hopes, no dreams, no goals … Nothing.

Looking down at his empty beer bottle he allowed himself a small smile. Well. He could do with another beer. That's one thing he'd sure as hell like right now …

If he could just get Karly off his mind. She haunted him. Breaking up with her, *finally*, had not eliminated her from his life as he'd thought it would. He couldn't stop thinking about her when he was awake and she filled his dreams at night. Over and over again, his mind replayed the look on her face when he had told her he didn't love her. The expression on her face as she screamed at him to get out. What would she have done if she knew that the question, Did he really love her?, had been rolling around in his head for almost three years? Jeeze, her head probably would have spun around.

Sure, he *had* told her he loved her. All the time. In all honesty, until lately he hadn't been able to picture his life without her after all of these years. But during their final year at college, in his very deepest hidden parts, there were times when he had actually hated Karly. She was kind and good and loving and … spiritual. Literally every damn thing he was not. Although that's what had originally drawn him to her, once he got past those looks of hers. Karly Martin was everything he knew his parents wanted him to be and a constant reminder of what a complete and abject failure he was in every department. How screwed up was he? Even the most elementary fact of his life, loving his girlfriend of almost four years, hadn't been a certainty for him.

Paul knew what a loving relationship was all about. He'd grown up with one, watching his parents' give and take, support and defend, love and argue. His sister Rachel had a poster in her room at home that said, *Love is patient, kind, does not envy or boast, is not proud, rude or self seeking, does not easily rise to anger nor keep records of wrongs, never delights in evil but rejoices in truth, always protects, trusts, hopes, and perseveres. Love never fails.*[7] Before he became such a cynical bastard he recognized how much his parents lived that style of love. Paul had claimed to love Karly with words, but to the best of his knowledge he hadn't fulfilled even one of the qualities about love that Rachel's poster talked about in his heart or by his actions.

In fact, were it possible to do a before and after analysis of one Karly Martin, pre - and post - her relationship with one Paul Williamson … Well, let's just say that she was close to becoming tarnished beyond repair. Which had led to his decision that was the noblest thing he'd ever planned to do in his entire worthless life. Break up with her. He should have done it long ago. Certainly much sooner than the morning of their wedding. Damn it, he'd tried! Really he had. But for all of his blustering and big tough guy facade, the secret shame that he hid from everyone but himself was that he was the greatest of cowards. No decisions were made, no stands taken, no actions embarked on because he was afraid to fail. It was a hell of a lot easier and more fun just to coast through life with the tide seeing where things took you. Nothing was ever your fault if you never agreed to it in the first place, right? *Right.*

---

[7] I Corinthians 13:4-8

Paul had *tried* to do something about Karly when they were in their senior year of college. Increasingly when they were together that last year, he'd felt like the biggest creep, the greatest disappointment, and the most monstrous of failures. The guilt he felt when he was with her far outweighed any happiness. He had begun to think, as their senior year rolled by, that if he could eliminate her from his life completely, then perhaps he could saunter off into the future foot loose and fancy free. And then maybe, *just maybe*, find a bit of happiness and contentment. (It was about time as far as he was concerned.) Only, just like everything else in his life, nothing had worked out the way he'd planned. *Nothing.* Just like everything else in his life, he managed to make things astronomically worse … It had been this past January. Could it only have been eight months ago? God, it felt like years …

Last January, after a miserable holiday shuttling between families and dealing with all the nightmares *that* entailed, Paul had finally made the decision to break up with Karly. But he had rationalized that he owed her, after almost four years together, the courtesy of a full explanation. He couldn't just walk up to her, or worse yet call her on the phone, and say, "Sweetheart, it's been great, but I really think we should end this before we finish college and move on." Right? A real man would sit down with her, do his best to explain what was in his head and heart, and then let her down as easy as possible. How hard could that be? Paul at least had the fortitude to do that, didn't he? After all this deep analysis of his personal arsenal of faults and destructive behaviors, Paul had honestly thought he had that much in him.

Now the greatest thing lacking in college was privacy. Paul sure as hell had none at the frat house and Karly's current insane roommate never seemed to leave their dorm room. And no one sat down and had a personal discussion in the common room. No, he'd decided to take her up to their friend Donna's parents' cabin in the Pocono Mountains and have it out with her there. She'd cry, he was sure about that, and want to have a heart to heart talk – that was a given, too. But for once, Paul Williamson was determined to do the right thing.

The drive to the cabin had taken longer than they'd anticipated because it had snowed the night before and the roads were still treacherous. Besides dodging the questions about why they were driving up alone rather than with the other couples Karly thought were also going, there had been little conversation. Karly had seemed tense and lost in thought as she stared out the side window and watched the snow - covered landscape slip by. Every time Paul had glanced at her, she had been chewing on her lower lip and twisting a stray lock of her hair, a sure sign that she was stressed out.

Often in his dreams, Paul remembered how Karly had looked that day in the car. Sitting all quiet and withdrawn. God, she was beautiful. She made no effort whatsoever to enhance her looks, and yet whenever Paul looked at her he got lost in her loveliness. The reality was, as corny as it sounded, she was as pretty inside as out. That day that they'd driven up to the Pocono Mountains, he remembered she'd worn a dusty blue turtleneck underneath a huge bulky wool sweater. Karly was always trying to hide her body, and Paul sometimes didn't blame her. He'd watched guys walk up to her, more times than he could count, and literally have a conversation with her breasts. How demeaning must that be?

"The new snow should make it perfect for snow - mobiling," Karly had finally said into the silence that surrounded them.

"Yeah, perfect," Paul said. For a moment he had forgotten he'd said that was why they were going up to the Pocono Mountains.

As they had pulled into the driveway of the cabin it was obvious that no one else was there. "Where is everyone?" Karly had said in confusion. "I thought you said that they left before us?"

"Did I? Nah, I knew we'd get here first."

She'd looked him right in the eye. "Paul, you're a terrible liar."

He had sighed and looked straight ahead out the windshield, hands clutching the steering wheel. He was *not* going to tell her why they had come up here in the front seat of the car. That's exactly what he had been trying to avoid. "Look, I just wanted an opportunity for us to be alone. So we could talk and stuff. Okay? Things haven't been the best between us lately and I thought, well, maybe, we needed to get away."

Karly's face had looked pale and drawn. With a sudden rush of panic, Paul had thought, *she knows*. Karly knew that he'd planned to break up with her. Now, thinking back on it, Paul wasn't quite so sure he had read her right. Suddenly, Paul had wanted to put her fears to rest, at least temporarily. "Look," he remembered himself saying, "everything's going to be okay. *Relax*. Can't we just take this one step at a time?" At her silent response and stiff nod, he'd opened the door and unfolded himself out of the car. *Coward,* the voice had taunted him in his head. *You are such a coward.*

After they'd hauled in all of their bags, Paul gave her a smile. "It's cold as hell in here. That's a contradiction in terms, huh?" While he had fumbled with the thermostat, he'd said to Karly, "Why don't you build a fire?"

Bending down in front of the fireplace all she needed was to strike a match. Someone had lain a fire before they'd left. Without even having to stand up, she'd reached over for the brass container that held the matches and within minutes the fire was blazing brightly.

"Hey, you're speedy," Paul had said coming over to sit next to her on the rug. "Ahhh," he'd stretched his hands out to the growing blaze, "that feels great." He studied Karly for a minute, frowning, and again he had made an excuse to stall. "You hungry? I brought some cheese and crackers."

Food. Yeah sure, like they could eat anything. Karly had shaken her head.

Paul sighed and had taken a deep breath for courage. "You look so sad all the time, Kar. I can't remember the last time you really, truly laughed. Do you laugh when you're away from me?"

Unable to find any words, she had stared numbly at the fire and shook her head again.

"We've not been doing so well these past few months, have we?" he'd said quietly to her. He remembered thinking that maybe, just maybe, she was on the same thought path as he. Maybe it wouldn't be so hard after all to break up ...

Karly had refused to look at him and shrugged her shoulders. Reaching up, Paul tucked a loose strand of her silky, blonde hair behind her ear while his gut clenched and he felt himself start to sweat.

"I -, I'm, I've been unhappy, too, you know that, Babe," he had stammered out.

Karly nodded and the tears started welling up in her eyes. She took a deep breath trying to keep herself together.

"Don't cry," Paul had said and pulled her into his arms. "I hate when I make you cry. I feel so much better when you're laughing and smiling, but I just seem to have lost the capacity to make you do that."

He remembered the feeling of having her in his arms as being so familiar. Almost four years together. *Four years.* Practically their entire college experience had been as a couple. Karly had turned her face to Paul's chest and buried herself there. The two of them had sat in front of the fire for a long, long time lost in their own thoughts. Paul felt his shaky courage begin to disintegrate. Maybe he shouldn't ...

In those minutes before the fire with her in his arms, Paul experienced every one of the emotions he had ever felt for Karly. Sorrow. Regret. Some level of love. Tenderness. Protectiveness. Joy. Fear. Everything about her was so familiar. The smell of her hair, the feel of her in his arms, even the way she snuffled as she tried to keep from crying. It was as natural as breathing to tilt her face up to his and kiss her. With a renewed surge of determination, Paul had thought just before their lips met, *I'm going to let you go. I'm not good enough for you. I'm destroying you and your spirit. You know it and I know it. This is a goodbye kiss, Karly.*

Karly had wrapped her arms around his neck, pressed herself against him and opened her mouth to kiss him back. And then Paul had remembered the emotion that had been stronger than all the other emotions he had ever felt for this beautiful woman lying in his arms *combined.*

Lust.

Between the two of them Paul had *always* been the aggressor and Karly had *always* been their conscience. As much as he fought and grumbled, pouted and cajoled, Paul always counted on Karly to be the one to put the breaks on when things got 'going' between them. For him it was a game that he played, knowing that at the appropriate time, no matter what the action or how close the score, when the end of game buzzer sounded that was it. Karly had principles that were carved in granite. Not once had he been able to reach the summit of sexual gratification with her. Not once. And he'd tried more ways than he could count with words, actions, and promises to try and change her mind. But she had always been unshakable.

But this time there had been no buzzer. Karly gave him no resistance, and seemed at times to even have encouraged him. His brain and his conscience just completely shut down. Nothing became more important than the feel of her in his arms and the opportunity to take what was offered. His body had done the victory dance, taken the ball and ran. Finally, when Paul had least expected it, the summit had been reached. *At long last.*

Afterwards, when his worthless brain finally kicked in and his conscience gasped in stunned, shocked horror, Paul had sat there silently while Karly did everything possible to smile tremulously at him and not cry. She'd failed miserably. Paul's mind had reeled with the magnitude of what they had done, of what she had given, of what he had taken. It had risen up like a gigantic tidal wave and swept everything else away. The words he had said, time and time again, trying to convince her to give him everything she had to give rose up and danced around them both: *Come on Babe, don't you love me? ... Hey, you know we'll be together to the end, Love ... I don't hold back anything from you Karly, don't hold anything back from me ... Come on! This is what committed couples do, Babe. This isn't wrong. It can't be when we love each other so much ...*

At long last, Karly had offered him her virginity, and he, selfish bastard that he was, had happily taken it. *Moments before he had planned to break up with her.* As Karly cried in Paul's arms, he had felt the jail door slam and the key turn in the lock. Struggling to comfort her, rocking her back and forth in his arms and stroking her tangled hair, he had whispered against the top of her head the only thing that came to mind, "Karly, will you marry me?"

Ever the fool.

Ever the coward.

Over the months that had followed Paul had floated along while the wedding plans swung into full gear, letting Karly think he'd set up an accountant's practice wherever she was called to be a missionary, enjoying the sexual relationship that seemed to work overtime to make up for four years of abstinence, and watching both of them become more and more miserable as each day passed. Karly practically turned herself inside out in those months leading up to the wedding trying to make him happy. And it hadn't worked.

For reasons Paul couldn't explain, Karly's constant desire to please made him begin to loathe her. He found himself becoming more sullen and withdrawn, angrier and more impatient. Which only made her try all the harder to please. In the end it had taken him months to get up enough courage to decide to break up with her again. Reality was, he knew he couldn't spend the rest of his life with her. He couldn't stand the way he was with her anymore than he could stand the way she was with him.

In a way, the morning of the wedding had turned into the biggest joke of all. When he had finally found enough courage to break things off, *finally* had really followed through on something that he'd set out to do, *and really accomplished it,* what had she called him? *A coward.*

Karly's words still roared repeatedly through his head now, to this day, louder than the ball game that played on the television in front of him, louder than the guy's shouts, and louder than anything his own miserable voice in his head whispered. *You are weak and cowardly, afraid to make a choice and take a stand!* The one time in his life Paul had decided to do something and followed through on it and she'd called him a coward, afraid to take a stand. What a scream that had been.

Paul tipped his beer up to his lips. Hell. His beer bottle was empty again. Time for another cold one. He hauled himself up and wandered into the kitchen.

"Hey! Paul! Don't forget your best friend!" Vince shouted. "And his best girl!"

Wandering out with three beers, Paul looked down at Vince's smiling face. "Dana's got a friend who's lonely. Want her number?"

"Sure," Paul said as he lowered himself back into his chair. "Got nothing else better to do."

Here in the valley walk close beside me
Don't look back
For Love is growing vineyards up ahead[8]

August, 1999
New Brunswick, New Jersey

Four: Good Christians Have All The Right Answers

Karly played over and over in her head the startling information her father had given her at dinner. She had been conceived out of wedlock. Her parents had lied about the date of their marriage. Her birth had caused all of her mother's professional dreams to fade away into ashes. Equally stunning was her father's willingness to support her in any decision she made about the baby. He believed that she would make a wise choice. He loved her. He thought perhaps Karly herself would have been better off had she been adopted.

What did she think about that, really? Her father had not said it in so many words, but had implied that not only did her mother not love him, she did not love Karly either. *I don't think Maddy does too well in the love department.* What would it have been like to have grown up in a home full of unconditional love? Karly couldn't begin to imagine … Once again unable to sleep, she padded barefoot to the computer, turned it on and checked her email.

---

[8] Acres of Hope, by Shane Barnard, Robbie Seay, *Clean*, 2004 Inpop Records

Dear Karly,

Thank you for your email! Darin sits beside me as I type this and no doubt will be continually kibitzing as I write. (Already he is mumbling under his breath.)

We will address, first and foremost, our concerns for you. Are you safe? Under doctor's care? Do you have other's helping you and watching out for you? Do you have someone you trust to confide in and talk to? For Darin and I, all of these things are of the utmost importance regarding you and your well-being – both emotionally and physically. Whether you plan on keeping your baby or placing your baby up for adoption, all of these things are critical for you to make a wise, educated, peaceful choice. We pray for these things for you, now with your name attached to them! Please let us know what else we can specifically pray about for you.

Darin says we should tell you a little bit about ourselves and that's why we are trying to do this email together.

I'll start with Darin since I'm in control of the keyboard and am nowhere near as keen on talking about myself as I am about him. (He says just wait until it's his turn ...) My perception of him is that he is extremely patient and loving; he rarely looses his temper or becomes frustrated. He is a tease, which gets on my nerves at times but I have come to learn to ignore it in the worst of times. He has the amazing ability to be able to fix just about anything from a broken china figurine I've accidentally dropped to the carburetor in our car. But what attracted me to him first was his strength of character; he has his priorities straight, is not easily swayed by peer pressure or that powerful force of the Macho Persona. Real men in our house are the better cooks, know how to dust and vacuum, iron their own shirts, thank you very much, and think I look beautiful when I first wake up in the morning with bed head. We've been married for just under ten years and marrying him was, by far, the best thing I ever did. (He says I'm getting mushy now and I should stop.)

Regarding myself, I'm organized, but at the same time, flexible. I love children and have enjoyed being a teacher for the past twelve years. I believe my career of teaching is a gift that God bestowed on me early and I treasure it. I tend to be too intense about certain things; worrying about students in my class who have tough times at home etc., and poor

Darin must regularly bear with me as I bring my work home with me. Darin says I must tell you that I am talented. I enjoy doing crafty things like knitting, crocheting, and sewing, etc. I am not one to sit idly watching television and regularly bring "toys" with me in the car when we take long trips. Until I met Darin, I tended to be a bit of a loner, content with myself and whatever amusements I could find at hand.

Uh oh, now Darin insists on typing. Look out ...

Hi Karly, this is Darin typing now. You take it easy with all this stuff, okay? You must feel pressure twenty - four hours a day and seven days a week with the decisions that you are facing. Don't let anyone rush you one way or another. You need to get quiet and pray about this. Listen to God's still small voice. (Although for people like me God at times uses bull horns and sledge hammers.) Viv says I'm being irreverent. Do you think so?

Write and tell us about yourself. What are your interests and hobbies, hopes and dreams? Remember to tell us anything you specifically wish us to pray about for you.

You have been added to our prayer list by name now, Karly. We look forward to hearing from you again.

In God's Love,

Darin and Viv

Twice the email had made her smile. Once when Viv said Darin loved her with bed head and once when Darin encouraged Karly not to let anyone rush her into a decision. She immediately began typing a response. And it was time. She would call Agape Christian services to make an appointment and talk to a counselor. Whatever decision she finally made would be an *informed one.*

In November, by the start of her seventh month of pregnancy, Karly was pleased with her progress. For the past months she had prayed and prayed and prayed and prayed so that it had almost become as common as breathing. Whenever the worry and the panic seemed to begin to drag her under she would begin to pray; whether she was at work, in the car, or lying alone in bed with the baby kicking. Staying attuned to her head and her heart, she listened and watched for God's guidance. Her first meeting with the counselor, Lynn, at Agape Christian Services had gone better than expected. Lynn had been low key, kind, and willing to answer any and every question Karly came up with in addition to giving Karly information and additional things to think about that had never occurred to her. Besides regularly corresponding with Darin and Viv, Lynn had provided Karly with five Family Profile Books. Prepared by the prospective adoptive couples these profiles were personal pictorial introductions to each family Karly might wish to consider. Karly saw houses and backyards, pets and gardens, wedding pictures and family reunion shots. She read personal narrative accounts of each family written with detail, love, and sincerity.

Originally, Karly had only wanted to see Darin and Viv's book, but Lynn had insisted that Karly be introduced to at least four other couples. "You're only going to do this once, Karly, and you must do it right. Each one of these couples match the stipulations you put down that were a must for any adoptive parents you would consider. On the flip side, each one of these prospective adoptive parents has provided Agape with its own list of criteria for birth mothers. This pile," Lynn patted the pile of five books, "represents a perfect match sample for both sides." Lynn looked intently at Karly. "Take these home, *pray about them*, and read each one. I would suggest you do one a day, but some women can't wait. If you do one a day then you can take your time, not get any of the facts mixed up and have at least one night to digest all you've read before you go on to the next one.

"I know you are corresponding with Viv and Darin via email. Each one of the other four couples has email accounts with us, too. Feel free to contact them as well. Just please, do not make any promises that you cannot keep. I know this is a highly stressful time for you, but you must understand that these couples are in their own private states of turmoil and stress."

Karly brought all five books home and she and Tammy poured over them. At first, she had felt deceitful looking at books other than Viv and Darin's, but Tammy had agreed with Lynn. "What was that slogan I used to hear on TV? 'An educated consumer is our best customer.' You want to make the wisest choice possible, Karly. Viv and Darin sound great, but can you imagine finding a couple *that's even better?* Make sure there isn't one out there, okay?"

In the end, examining all the books had been the best possible thing she could have done. For Karly, Viv and Darin outshone all the other couples by far. And finally, Karly was able to make her decision. One morning she simply woke up and wanted Viv and Darin to have her baby. The love she felt for the life inside her was great enough that she wanted only what was the very best for him. Consequently, the reality of her situation was that at this time in her life she was not the very best person to raise her baby. Yes, she wanted children some day! At some point Karly was even able to truly believe that with maturity and stable circumstances, she *would* be a good mother, too. The truth was, she wanted the best of opportunities for both herself and the baby to not just succeed, but to *thrive*. Staying together was not going to provide that - for either of them.

She would put her baby up for adoption. With that decision came a wave of relief and a vivid burst of contentment. *Thank you, God, for helping me make this decision.*

With Lynn's blessing, Karly wrote to Darin and Viv asking them to consider adopting the baby boy she was carrying. Joyous emails flew back and forth full of plans and questions. How was Karly feeling? Was the baby active? What did the doctor say? How did her last checkup go? Was she gaining weight? Karly shared with Viv and Darin the difficulties she had with her parents, although she didn't go into detail about the private information her father had shared with her. Viv and Darin added Karly's parents *and Snake* to their prayer list, asking for peace to settle within the Martin family during this highly emotional time. Karly spoke of Tammy and what a blessing she was, allowing her to live with her during her pregnancy and her continual support and wise counsel. Viv and Darin rejoiced with Karly for this spiritual foundation on which Karly could rest and rely. Lastly, the topic of Paul Williamson could not be avoided. Karly spoke only briefly and tentatively of Paul, not wishing to open old wounds and unwilling to speak with hatred or anger about the baby's birth father.

Karly would have proceeded on without ever informing Paul of the baby, but Lynn, from Agape Christian Services, was adamant. "The adoption cannot go through until the birth father signs all the same papers that you will, Karly. You must contact him."

"But he doesn't even know I'm pregnant, Lynn! I don't even know where he is! The last time I saw him was the day of my never - happened wedding when I told him to get out of my parent's living room. He's made *no* effort to contact me, *no* effort to find out how I'm doing, and I have *no* desire to have him back in my life again – *even for the five minutes it takes for him to sign the papers*." To her mortification, Karly felt her eyes fill with tears. Fishing for a tissue in her purse, she blew her nose and said, "These last few months I've cried more tears than my whole life! Everyone keeps telling me it's hormones."

"Probably that and everything that's going on. Are you still sleeping better?" Although Karly still struggled with falling asleep each night, since she had made the decision about the adoption and Viv and Darin, she had been sleeping better.

"Yeah, I'm getting about five hours of sleep a night now. I wish I'd had this insomnia when I was at school. I could have used the extra hours for studying."

Lynn smiled at her. "Look, let's try the easy way first. We'll send Paul all the paperwork via registered mail. If things go well, he'll sign them, have them notarized, and then mail them back to us. If he needs to speak with us, either we'll get him to come in and sign the final stuff in our office or we'll send a representative out to him to get his signature. Either way, you don't have to have any contact whatsoever."

"What if the easy way doesn't work?"

Lynn smiled at Karly sympathetically. "I'll be honest with you and tell you to pray hard about this! If the birth father can't be located, for example, then for six weeks the adoptive parents will have to advertise in all major newspapers in all major cities around the United States giving specifics regarding the baby's birth asking for him to step forward and claim responsibility. If he doesn't, then we go to court and have his parental rights legally terminated."

"You're kidding …"

Shaking her head, Lynn continued. "Nope, sorry. And you must understand, Karly, that he could not only refuse to relinquish his rights but also state his wish to gain custody of the child himself."

"NO!"

"Yes, Karly," Lynn said sympathetically yet firmly, "he can do that."

"If he says he wants custody, then I won't sign the papers. I'll keep the baby myself."

"Let's cross that bridge only if we come to it, okay? How about you get me Paul's address and we'll try the easy way, first."

Which brought Karly to the position she was in; the need to call or visit Paul's family and try to get his current address. "What do I do," she moaned to Tammy, "call them up and say, 'Hey, remember me? The girl your son almost married? Well, surprise! I'm pregnant with your grandson and I'll need Paul's address to get him to let me give the baby up for adoption."

"You could try that," Tammy said, looking dead pan at her over their dirty dinner dishes. "Doesn't Paul have sisters and brothers? Could you contact one of them?"

Karly shook her head. "We only ever had contact at family get-togethers at Paul's parents' house." The memory box opened and Karly was assailed with the wonderful memories of those times she had been almost part of that family. "They're a great family," she said to Tammy rather wistfully. "That was one of the best parts of marrying Paul, getting to be officially a Williamson …" She had a flash of the dinners and Paul's father bustling around the kitchen ordering everyone around. "Hey, I just remembered something …"

"What?"

"Every Tuesday night is 'Mom's Night Out' at the Williamsons. Mrs. Williamson goes off to a friend's house to play some card game or something and Mr. Williamson cooks elaborate gourmet dinners for himself."

Tammy got a big grin on her face. "You're kidding."

Karly smiled. "No, it's true. They've been doing it since the kids were little. Even though the kids are all grown, they still do it. He often has 'surprise guests' that show up and he always cooks enough food in case he gets company."

"You thinking of being a surprise guest?"

Nodding slowly Karly said, "Maybe …"

The second best thing about marrying Paul (after, of course, getting him) was going to have been getting his family. Paul may have ranted and raved about how his brothers and sisters had made his life miserable and his parents drove him nuts with their constant suggestions and inappropriate concern, but Karly had always thought they were all just about ideal. In the three and a half years that she and Paul had dated, Karly had come to love the Williamson family with all her heart. Over the course of their engagement, the idea that she was going to be a part of that big, loud, boisterous family had made all of the other concerns she may have felt fade in comparison.

It was one thing to say she was going to show up unannounced at the Williamson's house on a Tuesday night but it was another to actually do it. Sitting in her car outside their house, Karly realized that the two - hour drive to get there had not calmed her nerves, but had only made them worse. Alone with her thoughts and the baby rolling around in her belly she realized she had no idea how to approach the situation. Should she just stand there and let them take it all in and then answer whatever questions they asked? Sooner or later they'd probably get around to, "And why exactly are you here?" Maybe she should be cocky and in your face with stuff like, "Let me tell you how it's going to be …"

Perhaps she should start the darn car, do a k-turn and get the heck out of here.

Just as she was reaching for the keys to start the car and run (like the cowardly fool she was) Hannah Williamson stepped out of the front door and headed to the car parked in the driveway. Then John Williamson was at the front door calling out to her. Hannah turned, put her hand on her hip, and responded. He threw his head back and laughed. As he turned to go back into the house he stopped abruptly, turned back and looked right at Karly. *Well, that settles that,* Evil Twin said.

Karly opened her car door, and with all the grace a seven - month pregnant woman could muster hauled herself out of the car. Hannah Williamson stood frozen in the driveway as Karly walked slowly and tentatively toward her. John Williamson, as if in a slow motion dream, came to stand by his wife. Karly stopped a few feet away from them and stood in their driveway, letting them get a good long look. Finally, she said, "As you can see, we've got a few things to discuss." *Looks like you're going with the cocky, in your face technique, huh?* Evil Twin said.

Karly took in the fact that there was already a meal in high production based on the smells that emanated from the kitchen and the mess that could be seen on the counter tops. "I remembered that this was 'Mom's Night Out' so I thought it would be okay if I stopped by unexpectedly."

"You always have been and always will be welcome here, Karly," Hannah Williamson said firmly. "No matter the day, no matter what is going on."

"We've called a number of times to speak with you at your parents home," John said as the three of them sat down in the formal living room, "but were always told you were unavailable or out."

Hmmm. That was interesting. Karly had never gotten any of those messages. "I think they are trying to protect me." She smiled a little. "Too little, too late, mind you, but I guess we can't fault them for their good intentions. I'm sorry, I never got the messages that you'd called."

Hannah and John Williamson looked at each other and then back at her. "We were afraid of that," Hannah said quietly.

Karly took a deep breath. "I'm seven months pregnant and plan to give this baby up for adoption. I'd appreciate it if you'd give me Paul's current address so the legal papers can be sent to him and the agency can contact him."

Hannah Williamson blanched. All color left her face and she made a small mewling noise in the back of her throat. John shifted so he could put his right arm around her shoulders and his left hand reached out to cover both of hers as she clenched them in her lap. Karly suddenly had an overwhelming wave of tenderness for them. They were so very different from her parents in the way they dealt with each other and the people around them. She didn't want to hurt them anymore than she had to. There was no reason for cruelty, no purpose for animosity. They had always been so kind, loving, and welcoming to her. Even from the first.

Karly would give them information. It had helped her in her decision; maybe it would help them in their acceptance? "I've been living with the youth pastor at our church. Her name is Tammy O'Hara. She welcomed me into her home when things got out of hand living with my parents. She's been a good, solid support system while I've worked through the many decisions I've had to face over these past months." Karly looked at Hannah Williamson fighting back tears and John Williamson trying to be strong for both himself and his wife.

"Tammy has encouraged me to pray and I've done that. God has guided me to Agape Christian Services which is a Christian based adoption agency and through them I have been in email contact with a couple that I believe will be able to give the baby everything that I could hope and dream for … him." John Williamson's hand tightened around his wife's hands. "This isn't a decision I've come to without a lot of prayer and thought and research," she said earnestly to them. *Please let them hear what I'm saying and believe,* she prayed all of a sudden. "My Dad is supportive of my decision to pursue adoption. My Mom," she hesitated and then shrugged, "well, my Mom is just my Mom. Being pregnant hasn't really made things any better between us, as you probably could have guessed."

Karly looked at Paul's parents, *the baby's grandparents.* "I have to be honest with you and tell you that had I been able to do this without contacting Paul I would have. I don't want him in my life for any reason. And I'll also tell you that should Paul decide to fight me on this and try to gain custody of the baby, I'll forego the adoption and keep the baby myself." Karly felt tears well up in her eyes and blinked furiously. "I want what's best for this baby. Not what's best for me or my family, but the baby. I want him to have things that I never had, as well as opportunities that I could never offer him with my life the way it is right now.

"The couple that I've been emailing with," Karly hesitated and looked out the curtained window, "they're like the parents I'd always wished I could have had. They're solid with each other and already happy with their life. God plays a huge role in their thoughts and decisions. They don't want to adopt a baby because they feel like they're *missing* something, they want to adopt a baby because they've got so much that they're overflowing and want to share." She looked back at them. "They remind me of you two in a lot of ways. Every time I came here ... with Paul ... the love and acceptance and belonging that radiated out of the two of you was visible, palpable ... contagious. I always loved coming here because this was a place that really felt like a ... home.

"I hope one day I can give that to a child, but I know for certain I can't do it now. I've made some poor choices, but I'm trying really hard to remedy that. I certainly don't want to make any more bad decisions. That's why I've thought and prayed long and hard about this. I pray you'll understand where I'm coming from. I need ... Paul ... to support me in this."

"Paul won't fight you for custody of the child," Mrs. Williamson said in a strained whisper. "He's not in any position to care properly for himself, let alone a baby."

They spoke of their son as if he was some quadriplegic invalid living upstairs in the back bedroom. "Is he hurt?" Karly asked.

"No, nothing like that, Karly," Mr. Williamson said. "He's just working hard to accomplish all the things we've always warned him against. He's working mighty hard at reinventing himself so that he never has to do a decent, respectable, productive thing again in his life."

"I'm so sorry ..."

"Yes, we are too," Mrs. Williamson said taking a deep breath. "We may still love our son with all our hearts, but we also don't like him too much right now."

That makes three of us then, said Evil Twin.

Karly drove directly from Paul's parents' home to her own parents' house. Why postpone it and have to look forward to another painfully difficult day? It was dinnertime, and aside from a major international incident, nothing much changed the Martin family schedule on a day – to - day basis. Not even visiting daughters that were failures and pregnant. Tuesday was almost always meatloaf night, and as she walked into the dining room she saw that the meal her parents and Snake were eating did not prove her wrong. Except that Snake's plate had a pile of pinto beans where the meatloaf should be. Guess the Vegan kick was still on.

"Hey Baby, it's good to see you! Pull up a chair." Her father rose, went to fetch a glass from the sideboard, and poured her a drink of iced water from the pitcher on the table.

"Tom, don't you think "Baby" is a rather bizarre nickname for Karly given the present circumstances?"

"Hello, Mom. Hey, Snake." Karly sat down and sipped her water, shaking her head no when her dad offered her to get her a dinner plate. "Thanks, no. I ate at Taco Bell."

"Do you think that kind of food is healthy for the child, Karly?"

She was *so* not in the mood. "Yeah. Yeah I do. I think it's great." She refused to elaborate that she'd had a rather healthy taco salad. It wouldn't make a bit of difference.

"My, my, pregnancy seems to have made you a bit testy, Karly."

Again she didn't respond. *Stay with the cocky in – your - face technique,* Evil Twin encouraged. Karly took a deep breath and plunged in. "I've just gotten back from driving up to see Paul's parents. I've got Paul's current address and I'm going to provide it to the adoption agency so they can contact him and get him to hopefully sign all the required papers. I wanted to inform you of my plans and ask you to pray that he does this without a fight." Karly looked directly at her father as she spoke but it was her mother who answered.

"So you're really going to do this, Karly. You're just going to *give away* your own flesh and blood. Just return it to a different store because it didn't fit."

Karly continued to look at her father. Their eyes locked across the table. *I will support you one hundred percent with anyone and everyone regarding your decision. No questions asked, no waffling. I promise you*, he'd said.

Her father swallowed what he had in his mouth and then said, "I'll certainly pray for that, Karly." Not exactly jumping to his feet, standing in front of her, drawing his sword, and preparing to defend her to the death, but something nonetheless.

"Be quiet, Tom. We both know whose side you're on - whatever one is against *me*."

Karly looked at her father again. He had a buck in the headlights look about him. "I don't always support whoever is against you, Maddy. But I do support Karly if she's chosen the path of adoption for the baby."

"You can honestly sit there, Tom, and tell me you're comfortable with the idea that *your very own flesh and blood* is going to be given away to be raised by absolute strangers?"

Her father had not broken eye contact with Karly for this entire exchange but now he turned to his wife. "Yes. I can honestly sit here and tell you that."

The force of her mother's disapproval blew across the dining room table like a hot wind. Snake let out a huge belch. "Sorry," he mumbled, "it's the beans. They do it to me every time. Can I ask you a question, Karly?"

Karly glanced at him. He wore his blank I'm-not-up-to-anything expression, which told her he was up to something.

"No, Michael. Be quiet or you'll be asked to leave the table," his mother hissed.

Karly looked at her mother. "I'm sorry this upsets you so, Mom. I've prayed long and hard about this, I've done a lot of research and spoken with ..." She stopped. What could she say? 'Dad'? 'People she trusted'? 'People whose opinions mattered'? 'Those she knew wanted only the best for her and the baby'? Each one was an indirect criticism of her mother.

"Spoken with whom?"

"A lot of people," Karly mumbled vaguely. *Oops, there goes the cocky – in – your - face technique*, Evil Twin said.

Sensing imminent victory, her mother swooped in for the kill. "Oh, I know. You spoke with people whose opinions mirrored your own. Those who have no real experience in this area but who …"

"She spoke with me Madeline," Tom Martin finally said firmly. *"At length."*

"You." Volumes were spoken in the silent looks her parents exchanged across the dining room table.

"Yes. *Me*. At length over dinner a few months ago. I believe I told her that whatever decision she made I would support her one hundred percent. I know it would mean a lot to Karly if you would say the same thing to her, too."

Her mother rose from her seat at the dinner table like a queen standing up from her throne. "And do you know what would mean a lot to hear you say to me, Tom?" In the face of his silence, Madeline Martin continued. "It's something that you have *never, ever* said to me in all of our years together. It's something I've hoped for, hungered for, *dreamed of* hearing you say." She walked the length of the dining room table until she was standing by his side looking down at him. "'You're my top priority, Maddy. Nothing comes before you. Not job opportunities, or church responsibilities, or family obligations, or parental duties.' From the moment we first met in college," she whispered to him but both Karly and Michael could hear her clearly, "I've felt first like a potential acquisition, then like a necessary merger, and lastly like a burdensome liability."

Madeline Martin looked at her daughter. "I support you in all you do, Karly. Perhaps adoption is the best solution. God knows I certainly have no clue how to live happily ever after." As she walked from the room, Tom Martin put his head in his hands.

I built another temple to a stranger
I gave away my heart to the rushing wind
I set my course to run right into danger
Sought the company of fools instead of friends[9]

December, 1999

New Brunswick, New Jersey

Five: Good Christians Are Certain of God's Plan For Their Lives

The pounding sounded as though it was inside his head. "Yo! Paul! You in there?" He heard his bedroom door open. "Wow, man, you still in bed? It's two in the afternoon." There was groaning and grumbling next to him, and Paul felt movement in the bed beside him. Then he heard Vince's sly chuckle. "Oh, sorry. Didn't realize you had company ..." Something hard and sharp hit Paul in the side of the head. "This just got delivered for you. *Registered mail*, man. I had to sign for it. You win the lottery or something? Got a sick relative who died and left you money?" Again Vince's sly laughter. "Good thing I offered to let you move in with me if you're on the road to being wealthy ..." The bedroom door slammed shut.

God Almighty his head hurt. What time had he gotten to bed? He remembered 4:52 a.m. and he was still standing in the kitchen. Jeeze, his mouth felt like a bird had made a damn nest in it or something.

"Paul? What time is it?"

---

[9] "Jealous Kind", Jars of Clay, *Who We Are Instead*, 2003

Turning to the right he squinted out of his right eye to see who was talking to him. Paul took in her mussed blonde hair and smudged eye makeup then let his eyes travel down to her naked breasts. Opening both eyes, he looked back up at her. She had five earrings in her left ear and a tattoo of some Chinese character over her heart. Even if you offered him a million dollars he'd be unable to tell you her name. "Sometime after two according to my roommate."

She sat up and threw her legs out of bed. "Crap. I've got to do the three to eleven shift at the hospital." She rose from his bed in all her naked glory and padded into the bathroom. Immediately the shower began running. *What the hell was her name?* "Do you want to go dancing at Thirsty's again tonight?" she called over the sound of the shower.

Oh yeah. The blonde at Thirsty's. Jilly or Nelly or Kelly or something. She'd played real hard to get for most of the night, but he'd known all along it was just a game with her. She would dance a couple of slow dances with him and be all over him and then waltz away to come on to a few other guys. In actuality, he preferred her type, because aside from the cost of a few drinks they were pretty much no strings attached relationships. Just the kind he wanted. Sure enough, as he'd made his way to his car at closing last night, she'd followed him and offered him her number on a piece of paper. He'd crumpled the paper up, thrown it on the ground, and told her that if she wanted to see him again she'd better get in the car, otherwise all bets were off. As she climbed into his car it was *score another one for the master.*

Paul sat up and scratched his bare chest, let loose with a jaw - popping yawn, and stretched high overhead. The sharp corner of the envelope Vince had thrown at him slid off the pillow and poked him in his bare butt. He reached down, looking at it with a frown. *Agape Christian Services* was the return address. Wish he were as certain as Vince that it was good news. Dropping it on the bedside table he decided he wasn't looking at anything until he had a cup of coffee.

"So?" Whatever – Her - Name stood there dripping water on his bedroom carpet while she toweled her hair dry. "Wanna make me late for work?" She grinned at him and let him look all he wanted. Wasn't this supposed to be everything he'd ever dreamed of? Hung over, tired, and crabby, Paul struggled to remember what her great appeal had been last night. His mind was numbingly blank and all he saw before him was a hard edged, well used, and overly impressed with herself young woman making his carpet slushy.

"You're making the rug wet," he said, and tossed her a towel he'd left by his bedside, still damp from last evening's shower.

"Guess that's a no, huh?" Padding over to Paul's dresser she began a casual process of getting dressed. "Wanna meet at Thirsty's again tonight?"

Last evening had been only moderately enjoyable. He had no desire to do a repeat. "Nah, I've gotta work the eleven to seven shift."

"Oh. Okay. I'll leave you my number."

"Yeah, sure."

"Got anything I could eat before I go?"

"I'll go see." He stood, found a pair of boxers on the floor, and pulled them on.

"I had a good time last night," Whatever – Her - Name gave him a tentative smile as she watched him dress. Out of her purse she whipped out a bag, unzipped it, and began the process of applying makeup. "Of all the guys last night, you were the only one who tried to get to know me and talk a bit. *Except for the name part,* his conscience said with disgust. As he pulled a tee shirt over his head, her reflection in the mirror grinned and winked at him, "And you're sure not bad on the eyes or in the sack."

Padding barefoot into the kitchen he had a wave of ... disgust. He felt ... used. Wasn't that what girls always complained of? Yeah, he'd heard that a few times already. "You can't just use a girl like a paper cup and then toss her away!" He didn't exactly feel like a paper cup. More like a crumpled Doritos bag. "What's her name?" Vince asked, sitting in their messy kitchen eating a PopTart.

"Billy or Kelly or Nelly. How the hell am I supposed to remember?" Paul grumbled.

Vince chuckled. "I hear ya, man. I'll just call her Beautiful. That always works."

"What is there to eat? She's hungry and wants to eat something before she goes off to work."

Vince held up his half eaten PopTart. "We've got cinnamon and strawberry. Coffee's hot. No milk though."

Paul pulled open the refrigerator and gazed into the unappetizing interior. He felt like he was still living in the frat house with a bunch of out of control morons only now he was a working stiff renting his own apartment. Same crap different location.

"Hi Honey. What's for breakfast?" She breezed in like she did this all the time with not an ounce of embarrassment or hesitancy. What did he expect really?

"Coffee's hot, Beautiful," Vince said gesturing to the coffee maker by the sink. "Sorry, you have to drink it black though."

"That's fine. Got any sugar?" she said as she poured herself a cup. Paul threw some sugar packets on the counter by her and set the two boxes of Pop Tarts in front of her. "Oooo, gourmet!" she said and Vince laughed out loud.

"I like a lady with a sense of humor in the morning," Vince said.

"I like a man with a libido," What's – Her - Name said.

"Aww, my roomie let you down?" Vince crooned to her from his seat. "Paul's never the best in the morning.'

"Oh yeah? What about you?" she sashayed over to the table and sat down.

"I'm good *all the time*," Vince said and grinned at her.

"Paul's busy tonight, but I was hoping to go over to Thirsty's after my shift is over. Think you might be there?"

Vince glanced at Paul who shrugged indifferently. *You want her, you can have her.* "Yeah, I just might be there. What time's your shift over?"

"Eleven."

Paul padded into his bedroom sipping his coffee. Christ, when was the last time he'd changed those sheets? They had a grayish pallor to them, and for the life of him he couldn't recall the last time he'd washed them.

He hated doing laundry almost as much as he hated food shopping almost as much as he hated cleaning almost as much as he hated ...

Damn. He'd forgotten about that registered letter. He sat down, picked it up, and then set his coffee cup down. *Agape Christian Services*. Paul had a bad feeling about this. Tearing open the enveloped he scanned the contents. His brain read the words but had trouble comprehending the reality of what was being communicated. *Karly Martin ... parental rights ... legal rights ... adoption process ... birth father ... birth mother ... adoptive parents ... counseling services ...*

For long moments he sat on the end of his unmade bed holding the paperwork in his hands. Oh. My. God. Karly was pregnant with his child. Karly was going to give the baby up for adoption. A wave of rage hit him with sudden, all consuming force. Did she hate him *that much*? Was her fury and desire to hurt him just as he knew he had hurt her really to this level? The papers crumbled in his hands. *No freakin' way*. No way was she going to throw away a child of his just because she hated his guts so much she wanted nothing of him as a remembrance – *not even a child*. He stood up and paced around his room, kicking dirty clothes, shoes, sports equipment, and garbage out of his way. He'd fight this. Fight this with every speck of his being. She didn't want his baby? *Fine*. He'd take the baby. He may be living a screwed up existence right now, but he had a decent paying job, he had ...

What the hell did he have? Paul looked around him in dawning horror. He had exactly what he had set out to get: a life of no real responsibility, no real demands, no real consistency, no stability, no goodness, no faith, no one to answer to, no one to rely on ...

He had nothing.

Not a single damn thing to prove that he was a solid, reliable, positive human being. The anger left him just as quickly as it had come like an overfilled balloon suddenly loosing all its air. Oh sure, they'd give him his baby. *Here Paul, where shall we set up the crib? How about over here near these empty condom wrappers?*

Setting the crumpled papers on his dresser, he began to methodically pick up all the dirty clothes strewn about his floor and stuff them in a grayish colored pillowcase he'd taken off of the bed. Next he picked up all the garbage that was laying around: food wrappers, plastic shopping bags, and store receipts. He shoved all the sports equipment he could under his bed – hockey skates and pads, baseball cleats and two bats. In the corner behind the door he put his hockey and lacrosse sticks. Carrying the garbage out into the kitchen he took note that both Vince and What's – Her - Name were gone. Slowly he began cleaning up the dishes and wiping the kitchen counters. He carried the garbage out and threw it from the back porch balcony down into the dumpster behind their apartment.

A wave of longing to talk with someone hit him so strongly that it brought tears to his eyes. But who? Certainly not Vince or any of the other guys he had gotten friendly with at work. He'd only been working for the power company a couple of months anyway. His thoughts naturally drifted to his parents, The Voices Of Reason, but he still felt their heavy disapproval over his current choice of lifestyle. The stubborn rebellious side of him stiffened his backbone. Hell, he didn't have to talk to his parents, he already knew what they'd say anyway. Forget his brothers and sisters. He didn't ask their advice when things were *good.*

Suddenly he wanted nothing more in the world than to talk with Karly. Hear her voice. He remembered her laughter and her smiles. The way she said, *"Oh Paul,"* when he teased her. Sometimes at a bar, when he danced with women, they had a certain scent – shampoo or perfume – that reminded him of Karly and it was like someone had just turned on a video show in his head. Karly had always had the voice of common sense and goodness until he'd screwed her up. Maybe, if they could just talk, he'd be able to understand where her head was. Maybe she could help him understand how to deal with the huge, gaping, bleeding hole he had in his chest where his heart used to be.

He walked over to the kitchen phone but didn't reach for it. Was she home at her parents? God, how many times had she spoken at length about getting away from them and starting her life? She had had so many plans. If you wanted to see Karly light up like a Christmas tree, all you had to do was ask her about her plans for the future: missionary work, teaching, children, far away countries, meeting the needs of those less fortunate, *changing the whole friggin' world.* He'd left her disgraced, pregnant and alone with no one but her wimp of a father, a witch of a mother, and a brother named Snake. Looking back in the wake of his life, he'd left nothing but destruction and despair. He could only vaguely comprehend the misery she must be going through trapped in her parents' house under their authority *pregnant with his kid.*

No wonder she hated him. No wonder she didn't want the baby.

But something didn't fit. Paul could not conceive the image of her hating him so much that she would ever hate or want to hurt a child. Even his. *I love you, Paul.* He sighed. Especially his.

So why would she do it? Why wasn't she all goo – goo - eyed over the thought of having a baby of her own? Why give it away? Maybe she still wanted to go off and do the whole escape – and – become – a - missionary thing. Maybe the torture of living home, relying on her parents was too much for her. Paul knew what that was all about. The thought of him going back home to live with his parents made his skin crawl – and his parents were *nice.* Maybe Karly just decided to put herself first and say *finally,* 'The hell with all of you, I'm doing this for myself.'

Walking away from the phone, he got himself a can of Coke from the refrigerator, popped it open, and drained it in one gulp. "No way," he said out loud to himself, "she'd never do that." He wasn't certain about much in his life but he was certain of that. Karly would have sacrificed her future and her dreams and even her freedom if she thought it was the right thing to do for the kid.

And suddenly, there it was in a nutshell. Karly must have thought it all out, researched every angle and decided that this whole adoption nightmare was the best way to go. Someone or something would have had to convince her of it. She would have turned herself inside out before she would have done something that she didn't think was best for their baby.

Oh God. *Their baby.* His chest hurt, his throat closed, and his eyes burned as he fought down the well of grief and sorrow that threatened to erupt. Paul had known that he had screwed up, he just had no idea of the sheer magnitude of it all until now.

Going back to his bedroom he retrieved the papers, and smoothed them out. It took a while to find a pen, but finally he did. He flipped through the pages, signing in all the spots with the little yellow arrow that said SIGN HERE in red letters. He didn't even bother reading anything … he just kept signing.

He signed away his baby along with any hope of redemption. He had always been a coward. Now he could add loser to the growing list.

THE ASSENT

There's a time for love and a time for healing
Can't go back and undo what's been done
Word of mouth, time is revealing
Just how far we've let this kingdom come
Hand in hand we're finding our way
And today is just tomorrow's yesterday[10]

---

[10] Susan Ashton, *All Kinds Of People*

Six: Wise Christians Raise Perfect Children

April 3, 2000

Dear Karly,

Our little boy is growing so quickly! Already his eyes have turned a dark brown and at his two month checkup he is up to twelve pounds! Even the doctor chuckled at that.   He is sleeping through the night, eating heartily, and as long as there is always someone around to fuss and coo over him he is quite content.

Thank you for this gift, Karly. Darin and I cannot believe this tremendous blessing God has given us through you. You are in our hearts and prayers always.

Love, Viv

---

[11] International Love Song, By Moore, Goodcame, Osenga, Caedmon's Call, *Share The Well*, 2004

April 20, 2000

Dear Karly,

I had forgotten the information about Benjamin's birth father being 6'5" tall! Darin had a good laugh at that as he is barely 5'8" on a good day. (Don't tell him I told you that!) At least we know who will be in charge of changing all the ceiling light bulbs and dusting the ceiling moldings! And it seems that Ben has brown eyes from his birth father, too. Thank you for sharing with me some information about Paul and his personality. It will be interesting to see if Ben will exhibit the same easygoing character and affinity for sports. Darin has always been a frustrated baseball player. Perhaps he can relive his misspent youth watching Benjamin make the big leagues.

Tell me of your personality traits, Karly. When Ben smiles and coos at me, he reminds me of your sweet smiles at the hospital on his birth day. I think he has your mouth and chin.

How are you doing? Have you gone back to school to get your Masters' degree as you spoke about? Have you looked into taking a missionary assignment? I pray that God will continue to lead and direct you with Big Black Arrows to where He wants you to go.

Write soon.

Love, Viv

May 5, 2000

Dear Karly,

Today Ben rolled over in his crib! I was walking by his bedroom door and heard his sweet baby chatter and peeked in to check on him. He was on his stomach, peeking at me through the bars of his crib, gurgling and drooling. When I crept up and peeked at him through the bars, he laughed at me! It was the sweetest music I have ever heard. I checked one of the many baby books we have, and the fact that he's done this amazing feat at only 2 ½ months convinces Darin and me that he is destined for Great Things. Darin's thinking President of the United States. I'm thinking Doctor who finds the cure for Breast Cancer. What do you think?

It sounds to me as if the Lord is offering you many choices, Karly. What will you do? Go to college, accept the job in town, or travel down to Appalachia and meet with that minister? Do you have someone to talk to that you admire and trust? Take advantage of those people God has placed in your life. God wants you to succeed and be happy even more than Darin and I do.

With love and prayers, Viv

June 2, 2000

Dear Karly,

You sounded so discouraged in your last email. You must remember that God says 'no' just as He says 'yes'. Obviously the Appalachia opportunity was not a fit for you. Better to find out right away than once you get down there, right? So one door has been closed for you, but God will open other ones. I think you are wise to consider pursing the Masters Degree in teaching. The district I taught in previously had instituted a policy to only give tenure to teachers with M.Ed. degrees and I suspect that will be the trend in all towns soon. Will you stay at school? I know you struggle at home with your parents. Why don't you look into a room and board opportunity? Darin and I have a friend who's hired a young woman to care for her two small children while she and her husband work full time. The young woman is taking college courses nights and weekends. I believe my friend called one of the local colleges and was given this young woman's name. Perhaps your college offers the same services? It can't hurt to check it out, can it?

Ben has a trick. He spits. And spits and spits and spits and spits ... By the time he stops, his entire face is covered, and the other day my bed pillow was drenched as well. Darin and I have decided he may possibly be more brilliant than Albert Einstein.

Please call the college.

Love, Viv

June 20, 2000

Dear Karly,

Hah! I knew it! I will pray that The Perfect Family calls the College Opportunity Center in search of The Perfect Nanny to watch their Perfect Children.

I am sorry about your mother's continued lack of faith regarding the decisions you are making in your life. You must pray and trust your head and your heart on these things. I will pray for her as well as for you. When do classes start? What have you registered for?

Today I came in to get Ben up from his nap and he was standing in his crib! Darin and I think that perhaps he might win an Olympic Gold Medal as he seems so progressive in his physical abilities. We've got it bad, don't we?

Keep me posted,

Love, Viv

July 20, 2000

Dear Karly,

The Poys sound like the Perfect Family to me. The twins sound adorable – if a bit of a handful, and the older daughter sounds so sweet. Is she in second or third grade? How perfect is it that they live within biking distance of the college? The living accommodations sound wonderful, too. God is taking wonderful care of you, Karly. He is faithfully guiding you and preparing you for extraordinary things.

Tammy is a great friend. Her advice sounds right on the money regarding how to handle your parents. She sounds like someone who values your opinions and desires and yet is firmly grounded in love and good sense. Another blessing the Lord has put in place for you.

We had quite a scare with Ben yesterday. He somehow managed to find and swallow a penny. You should have seen Darin and I at the hospital emergency room, both absolutely hysterical, while Ben laughed and cooed and drooled at all of the doctors and nurses. X-rays did confirm that he is exactly $0.01 more valuable than he was the day before. We were told to go home, relax, and wait for nature to take its course in reducing his value over the process of the next few messy diapers. Darin thinks he has fifty new gray hairs as a result of all of this. I've decided to enclose Ben in a plastic bubble until he is fifteen. Darin said I couldn't do that, though. I guess I'll have to strip the house down to bare wood. But then he'll get splinters …

We love you, Karly.

Viv

August 15, 2000

Dear Karly,

How is it at the Poys? Are you able to get your school work done and at the same time keep all your plates spinning at the Poys? I am worried that you are taking too much on yourself with your plans to get your degree in one year while at the same time being a full time nanny to three active children. Was it much of an adjustment moving in? Do you have enough privacy? Tell me what I need to pray for you about. I need specifics!

How are your courses? I remember that I enjoyed my master's courses much better than my undergraduate courses. I don't really know why, I just did. Maybe the Masters courses were meatier and seemed more applicable.

I do not think that you should set aside your strong desire to do missionary work. I will keep praying for you to have guidance in that regard. You sound as if that is no longer something you wish to do. While I am glad that teaching is still a passion of yours (something tells me that you are very, very good at it) I wonder exactly what God wants you to do with it. God never wastes anything, Karly. Your passions and desires, hopes and dreams are all part of His Gift and Plan for you. Just because the Appalachia experience left you with a sour taste in your mouth doesn't mean that you should eliminate the entire option of mission work from your plans. Pray about it. You have time. I will ask for the Lord to send you more Big Black Arrows for the direction He wants you to take.

What does Tammy say? Does she know of anyone or of any organization you could contact and speak to? How about the college?

Where did you originally hear of the Appalachia opportunity? It never hurts to ask questions, you know.

Ben says "Da, Da, Da" and Darin says he's won the bet over who's name he would say first. But here's the catch. When Darin is holding Ben, Ben puts his arms out to *me* and says, "Da, Da, Da." I think that means that I won. What do you think?

Love, Viv

December 12, 2000

Dear Karly,

Please don't be mad at me, but when your package arrived for Ben I just couldn't wait until Christmas so I've already opened it. I am having trouble writing this letter for the tears that keep blurring my vision. The book you made him is beautiful, Karly. It is a treasured keepsake that he will value for his entire life. The pictures are magnificent! And your narration about each and every photo, telling stories and funny anecdotes is priceless. I particularly love the picture of you and Michael (Snake!). The look on Michael's face is so hysterical and then to read what you wrote about what was going on just prior to the picture! I laughed and cried at the same time.

Thank you in particular for the pictures of Paul. Having never met him and having no contact with him, the pictures and things you wrote about him are particularly precious. I appreciate the kind and loving things you wrote about him, knowing how terribly he hurt you. You have a loving and forgiving spirit, Karly.

In regard to your present, it is enclosed. Darin and I prayed long and hard about this and both feel strongly that this is the right thing to do. The enclosed open - ended plane ticket can be used anytime in the next six months. It's time for you to come and spend some time with Benjamin and us. Perhaps you'd like to come and help us celebrate his first birthday? I hope that you will take us up on this offer.

We love you and can't wait to see you.

Love and a Blessed Christmas to you, Viv

March 30, 2001

Karly,

Did the Poys survive without you for a long weekend? They are so fortunate to have you with them all the time. Thanks for bringing pictures so I can put faces on the names. That Karen is one cute little girl! And the twins! That picture of them with the peanut butter made Darin and I rearrange our kitchen cabinets after you left. I could see Ben painting the cat with peanut butter just like Steven and Max painted each other!

Ben says "CCC", "CCC" and I think that it is "Karly"! Darin says I'm nuts, but what does he know, anyway? Wasn't it a wonderful visit? I am so glad that you came here for Ben's first birthday. I've been thinking about how unique our relationship is. God has blessed you, Darin, Ben, and me with this wonderful, special bond. I don't know about you, but I feel stronger and more secure with this loving correspondence and contact we have. I am so happy that we were able to go and get the portraits done as well.

Now here is something you need to consider. Our church funds a mission school out in Huerfano, New Mexico. It is a small school (a little bit more than a one room school house, but not by much) that does an educational as well as spiritual outreach to the Navajo Indians. The missionary couple that has been running the school for over thirty years is rapidly reaching retirement age. In their monthly newsletter, Edith and Samuel Jamison have notified the church mission board that they plan to retire in about five years. In addition, this coming September they will be in need of a teacher. (The school has two, one of whom is retiring in June.) Darin sits on our church mission board and came home all excited after reading the Jamison's letter. He insisted that I tell you about this, for he said that as the committee discussed the Jamisons he couldn't get his mind off of you. He felt that it was the Lord speaking to him. I have enclosed the Jamison's address, and thought that perhaps you could correspond with them a bit and maybe feel them out? Perhaps this might be something you would be interested in? As always, I would encourage you to pray about this and trust the Lord's guidance.

I pray that this causes you great excitement and that God continues to use his Big Black Arrows to show you direction.

Ben took three steps last night! Our baby is turning into a toddler before my very eyes! Darin sits and reads Ben the book you sent him for Christmas. It is the cutest thing.

All our love, Viv

April 12, 2001

Dear Karly,

Do you see the wonderful way the Lord is working in your life? The Jamisons seem like delightful people from what you've shared and I think the opportunity to teach down in Huerfano sounds like challenging fun. Are you going to visit and check it all out? How soon do you have to make a decision? Will you have to recruit support? I'm sure our church mission board would be willing to consider taking you on as a new missionary prospect. Please let us know what we can do.

I've been meaning to ask. Who in your or Paul's family has curly hair? Ben's hair has gotten curly at the ends with the warm weather and I was just curious. He climbed out of his crib last night. We heard a thump and when Darin and I went running in he was standing there with the proudest grin on his face. Good grief. Now what do we do?

Keep me posted about the Jamisons.

Love, Viv

May 6, 2001

Dear Karly,

When do you finish with college? Darin said something last night and I thought, "Oh NO! Is she done already?!" I still can't believe you managed to get it all done while seeing to all your nanny duties. When you're old and crotchety like Darin and I you're going to look back on this time and think, "How did I ever manage?!" Ha.

If you decide to fly down to Huerfano and meet with the Jamisons, Darin and I would like to pay for your plane ticket. You can consider it a graduation present if you want, but we will not take 'no' for an answer, okay?

I think Ben must have Paul's sister Connie's hair. It is thick and rich, and when the weather is humid it curls in the most adorable way all over his sweaty, big head. Darin says I must take him soon for his first haircut or we are going to have to change his name to 'Benilita'. He thinks he's so funny. I try not to humor him but sometimes I do just laugh out loud at that man. Today, when Darin called from work, Ben listened carefully to his voice on the phone and then got all excited. I think he understood it was Darin. Isn't our baby brilliant?

Let us know about the ticket.

Love, Viv

May 30, 2001

Dear Karly,

Mercy it's hot and the summer isn't even here yet! Today Ben spent the entire day naked on the deck in his paddling pool. I think I'll just give him a bath in it tonight before I put him down. I sat in a lounge chair on the deck with my feet in the pool reading. It was nice.

Thank you for my life, Karly.

Thank you for this beautiful baby boy we share, Karly.

Darin made the reservations for you last night and arranged for the ticket to be mailed directly to you. Remember, Karly, God says 'no' as well as 'yes'. If you get down to Huerfano and it just doesn't feel right then trust your gut and God. I am praying for Big Black Arrows for you to follow and that might mean that Huerfano is a nightmare that you can't wait to get away from. But maybe not as bad as Appalachia! (I hope that made you smile.)

I can't wait to hear how things go.

Love, Viv

June 2, 2001

Dear Karly,

So Ben's birth mother is going to be a world famous teacher missionary at Huerfano Navajo School in Huerfano, New Mexico! What do you know! Your enthusiasm over the people and the opportunities down there just poured out of your letter. Keep that spark going, Karly, and you'll get your support money from sponsor churches in no time flat. Would you consider flying here to see Ben and speak to our church about your missionary plans? Both our church and Darin's parents' church would love to meet and hear from you. Think about it and let us know. You are going to have to move quickly if you want to have enough sponsorship in time to be there to start teaching in September. I will pray, pray, pray!

Ben has a fat lip. He fell yesterday and his top tooth bit right into his bottom lip. Oh, the crying and sobbing and screeching and wailing! And that was just me! Ha. He was a tough little soldier. Wouldn't let me put ice on it but did enjoy FIVE orange ice pops out on the deck instead. I wish you could have seen the look on Darin's face when he walked in the door from work. He looked at me like I was The Worst Mother In The World. That made me burst into tears all over again. What a day.

Come and visit us.

Love, Viv

July 12, 2001

Dear Karly,

Our church is still talking about your presentation on Sunday. What do you mean you were nervous? You sure couldn't tell by looking at you! You were so enthusiastic telling us about the school and the things you wished to do that I almost wanted to go with you! Darin's mother said her church was equally impressed. Who would have thought that you would be able to raise all the sponsorship money you needed in less than six weeks? Big Black Arrows, Karly. I told you that God's got wonderful plans for you.

After you left, Ben toddled around to every room in the house saying, "Kar?, Kar?" looking for you. He couldn't seem to understand where you'd gone. I told him you would talk to him on the phone. Call us collect when you've got a few free minutes, okay? He loves that stuffed bunny you brought him. Carries it everywhere (even the bathtub once before I could stop him!)

How are the Poys doing in their search to replace you? (As if they could!) I will pray that they find someone soon because I know that you are worrying about this almost as much as they are.

Are you excited? Nervous? Terrified? I think I would be all three ... I'll keep praying!

Love, Viv

August 9, 2001

Dear Karly,

I'm rushing this letter off to you because I know you are leaving for Huerfano this Saturday. I've been meaning to ask you how your family has reacted to all of this? Positively, I hope. Something tells me that your mother will never change though, Karly. You must (unfortunately) accept that and perhaps learn to love her for what she is. Sometimes if you love someone and learn not to have unrealistic expectations regarding him or her then that takes the pressure off the relationship. I'm sure your dad will be supportive and Snake (I love calling him that) will have a few choice words for you. But as for your Mom, why don't you ask her for some advice? If it's good then great and if it's bad just smile and nod. She'll never know if you do or don't use it, right? Just a suggestion.

I have the PO Box you gave me for mailing things to you. Darin pointed out that technically you will be closer to us living in New Mexico than you are now. I hadn't really thought of that. Ben had fun 'talking' to you on the phone. Did you hear him say, "Bye"? He's picking up more and more words every day. I've become official translator because Darin still struggles to understand what Ben's trying to communicate to him.

I'm praying that these last few days with the Poys and your family are smooth and easy. Huerfano, here you come!

Love, Viv

August 27, 2001

Dear Karly,

How many days until the first day of school? How will you manage teaching in a standard classroom with such a broad age range? I taught different age groups when I taught those gifted classes, but I never taught all three different grades at one time. Have you had a chance to meet any of the children yet? Tell me about the people you associate with.

Darin and I got out the atlas last night and found out where Huerfano is. You're right near Four Corners. Darin was there once many years ago, and he said it was the most beautiful countryside he had ever seen. Still until this day! He called it "God's Country" and said that it's natural magnificence made you stand in awe of our great God and Creator.

Our toddler boy told me 'no' today. Put up his tiny little grubby finger, pointed it at me, and in a very firm tone said, "No!" I caught myself biting the insides of my mouth to keep from laughing out loud. I decided to set a good example so I 'obeyed'. I hope I'm not creating a monster!

Darin and I have made a commitment that each morning, lunch, evening and bedtime we will stop and say a specific prayer just for you. We pray for peace, strength, wisdom, and most especially, joy. Let us know how we are doing for you!

Love, Viv

P.S. I came across this Bible verse today during my devotions and wanted to send it to you. Zephaniah 3:17 'Your God is present among you, a strong Warrior there to save you. Happy to have you back, He'll calm you with His love and delight you with His songs.'[12]

---

[12] The Message, Zephaniah 3:17

Did You smile when You made the moon and gave the sky its color?
Did Creation dance in rhythm to Your song of life I wonder?[13]

Second Week of August, 2001
New Mexico

Seven: Dedicated Christians Eventually Understand The Big Picture

After changing planes in Denver, Karly landed in Albuquerque, New Mexico at 10:37 p.m. Bleary eyed from a day of travel and frazzled with nervous exhaustion, she scanned the arrival lounge looking for Edith and Samuel Jamison.

"Karly! Karly! Over here!" Turning she saw Edith waving frantically as Samuel picked up the pace to approach her.

"Here, let me take your bag," Sam said as he took Karly's small carry on out of her hand. She let him, knowing that with his bad back and arthritic hands there was no way he could manage the two huge suitcases waiting for them on the luggage carousel. "How was your flight?" he asked politely as they walked in a pace that was slow enough to accommodate his painful, shuffling gait.

"Long, but fine. A bit of turbulence, but nothing big. How are you feeling, Mr. Jamison? Is your back any better?"

---

[13] Sacred Delight, Sunday Drive, *Sunday Drive*

"Nah, it's about the same. Edith wants me to try some new fangled exercise class over at the civic center on Tuesday nights but there's no way you're going to get me in stretch purple leotards." He grinned at Karly. "Not in public anyway."

Having heard the last bit of conversation, Edith Jamison huffed disapprovingly and tried to frown in an intimidating fashion. She failed miserably. "You *don't* have to wear purple stretch leotards, you stubborn old man, and you know that." She looked at Karly, smiled, and leaned over to give her a quick buss on the cheek. "Hello dear, welcome back. He's still complaining about his bad back, *whining continually* if the truth be told, and I just suggested that he try the yoga class that Valarie Lee started over at the civic center on Tuesday evenings. You'd think I'd asked him to slip into a pink tutu and strut his stuff!" She rolled her eyes and shook her head. Turning to her husband she said, "You know what the doctor said, Samuel. Exercise is the key to making your back better. You've got to strengthen those back muscles!"

Karly laughed with genuine affection for the both of them. "I've got two suitcases I've got to claim. Try lifting those, Mr. Jamison! We'll have to hire a Skycap to lug all of it. I hope you brought an 18 wheeler to haul them home."

"Oh, we'll get there in the Escort, right Sam? I hope you're not too anxious to set up house. Sam and I decided you'd spend the night with us at our place. It'll be way too late to get settled down at your new place tonight."

"Sure, that's fine with me. Will you make me some of your buttermilk biscuits for breakfast?"

Edith gave Karly a delighted smile. "I sure will!"

Sitting next to one of her enormous suitcases in the back seat of their pale blue Ford Escort that was fifteen years old *at least*, Karly had a flashback to the first time she'd visited the Jamisons over two months ago. What a study in comparisons of then versus now: nervousness versus excitement, trepidation versus certainty, and insecurity versus determination. That first night, sitting in the dark with nothing to see but the twin cones of light projected in front of them by the car's headlights,

Karly had had such an all consuming wave of panic that she had been reduced to trembling and tears in the backseat darkness.   Evil Twin screamed, *What have you gone and done NOW?!!* Embarrassed about her fear and weakness, she'd prayed fiercely for the Lord to help her get herself together before she made a fool of herself yet again – this time in front of absolute strangers. *Talk to the Jamisons,* a soothing voice had said. *Ask them some questions.* Voice trembling with emotion, Karly had asked the Jamisons what had originally brought them to Huerfano, New Mexico. For the hour and a half drive, she'd gotten lost in their story and had forgot all about her panic …

"The Navajo Mission School at Huerfano," Edith had explained, "was begun over thirty years ago. Its purpose was to educate, encourage, and empower both spiritually and intellectually the children who passed through its doors. Sam does the preaching and a million other things, I coordinate the school and a million other things. Over the years the school and the church have grown, with the Lord's blessing and guidance, to what we are today: a church with an average Sunday attendance of about fifty and a kindergarten through eighth grade school which provides numerous opportunities for almost thirty - five students. Twenty of the students board with us during the school year and we have two dormitories with live - in adult chaperones." Edith had turned and Karly could just barely make out her smile, "We call those brave souls, 'Dorm Parents', but they really should be called 'Saints'." Sam had chuckled with humor in the dark but said nothing. "The rest of the children are transported by family or friends _"

"Or me," Sam had put in. "I'm a jack of all trades around here, one of which is local bus driver."

"Or Sam," Edith had reiterated patting her husband on the shoulder and then looking forward again. "The children come from far and wide to learn both academic skills as well as spiritual lessons. Each year, depending on the abilities of the staff we have and the availability and enthusiasm of the numerous volunteers we are continually blessed with, we manage to offer a substantially impressive variety of opportunities besides the basics of Biblical studies, reading, writing, math, science, and social studies. We try to include Native American history and culture, and often we have parents who are adept at certain skills who will come in and teach. We have a darling old woman named Verna Werito who comes in once a week and teaches basic Navajo: speaking, reading and writing it. Sometimes we have cooking and craft clubs, sports teams ..."

"Don't forget the photography and computer classes we had last year," Sam had murmured.

"Oh, that's right! I did forget!" Edith had turned to her husband and Karly could see her smile fondly at him as she said, "For a small school, the Lord blesses us and has provided us with an abundance of resources."

"Except for ..." Sam had said and let the open sentence hang in the darkness of the car interior.

Karly hadn't been able to keep herself from asking, "Except for what?"

Edith had sighed and said somewhat impatiently, "What's the purpose of bringing it up before the young woman even sets her eyes on the school, Sam?"

His dark outline had shrugged. "Let her know what we're all praying for. She'll hear about it sooner or later anyway."

Edith's profile had been quiet and serious for long moments as if debating whether she would pick up what Sam had started or let him take it from there. When she finally began to speak, she spoke to Karly, but did not take her eyes off her husband. "Our dream, Sam's and mine, when we came here over thirty years ago, was to start up this school. Like a child that you love and treasure, we wanted to raise it, encourage it, and then send it off on its own. We never planned to stay here our entire lives only to retire and see our 'child' fade away, but that seems to be what ... the Lord ... intends."

Edith had turned then to look at Karly, her serious expression partially lit and partially shadowed by the car's headlight illumination. "We always believed that someone from the school or the community would pick up where we left off. We never, ever wanted this to be The Jamison School in Navajoland. We wanted this to go back to the community, run by community people, supported by community churches and business. Our dream has always been that the school would become an independent and self - sufficient Christian mainstay within this Navajo community."

"And? Why hasn't it?" Karly had asked, puzzled.

Edith had sighed. "Because no one has stepped forward to replace us. Sam and I were so certain that over the course of our ministry the Lord would provide us with someone with a history and a heart for this place – a young Navajo man or woman. There have been times when we thought the Lord had answered our prayers, but … Right now we are just like you are with your ministry, Karly - dependant on the generosity and faithfulness of your supporting churches and individuals. Sam and I felt that when the school reached fruition, it would be self - sustaining both with manpower and with money." It was her turn to shrug. "Wouldn't that be the ultimate accomplishment? To build something from the generosity and good will of others that eventually could stand on its own and, perhaps in years to come, repeat the process?" She had shaken her head. "The Lord has always blessed us with teachers and financial support and supplies. Lately though, we find ourselves struggling to fulfill needs that we fought for *a long time ago*. We feel, to some extent, that we're going *backward* all of a sudden instead of forward. And after all of these years, with Sam and I seriously beginning to think about retirement, we still have nobody that has stepped forward to take over for us when we leave." Edith had sighed. "We're *tired*. We're *old*."

"Speak for yourself, Old Woman," Sam had growled, but it had been said with love and humor.

Edith had ignored her husband and forged on. "Sam has trouble doing what he used to do with no effort. His back is bothering him. He sprained his ankle a few months ago and I don't think it will ever be right. I have high blood pressure and have already had one bout with colon cancer." Sam had reached over and touched her cheek. "We find it hard to understand, but it seems that perhaps the Lord intends this school to exist only as long as we're able to run it. These last few years we've had trouble just finding *teachers* and *dorm parents* willing to come down here and live and work, let alone ministers and educational directors!"

Sighing, Edith had said, "We know God has it all mapped out and knows best, but we battle with discouragement as each year slips by and nothing seems to materialize to answer these needs."

She had smiled reassuringly at Karly. "You're a tremendous blessing. When Janine Swanson unexpectedly decided to make this past year her last, we were thoroughly unprepared. Do you know your letter asking about opportunities here at the school arrived just two weeks after she told us that she was going to retire? I pray that what you see at the school this week will excite you and encourage you. Please, you must promise to ask any and all questions that come to mind. We want you to make the most of this visit."

You can do this, the voice had then said. *Just take it one step at a time. You are the one who is needed here. Relax and be yourself.* And Karly had. She'd literally given up all her worry and self-doubt in the darkness and silence of the backseat. She had ceased trying to be something she was not or something she thought she should be. During her weeklong visit at Huerfano with the Jamisons she developed a 'This is what I am, like it or lump it attitude' and was positively stunned that everyone seemed to like her quite a lot. They laughed at her witty perceptions, listened to her casual observations, and gave thoughtful replies to her sincerely asked questions. The Jamisons had turned out to be a loving, committed couple who had devoted their entire lives to their mission of serving the Navajo Indians in the best way they knew how: teaching. And the Navajos she had met – just those that worked at the school and attended Sunday services at the small chapel – had been welcoming and witty. They'd teased her unmercifully about her "silly white girl ways" and her "eastern Yankee" accent, and she'd loved every minute of it. At the end of the week, she'd cried real tears when she'd said good - bye to them all.

Traveling in the car this second time, she leaned her head against the cool glass of the car window and gazed up at the night sky. A star display that took her breath away was her reward. What had Viv said about Darin's impression of this part of the world? *God's Country.* Never had she felt more in awe of God's power and majesty than here. Standing and looking at the world from the top of Huerfano Mountain had turned out to be The Defining Moment Of Her Life. Just before she'd flown back, at the end of that first visit, Edith had said, "Have you been to the top of Huerfano yet, Karly? No one can come visit without having made the pilgrimage. Go take a walk. If you move quickly you should be there in time to see the sunset. And it was on the top of Huerfano Mountain nine weeks ago that God had said to her loudly and clearly, *This will be your home, Karly. Get back here as soon as possible.* If He'd sent a hand written note or appeared directly in person and shouted it in her face, the message couldn't have been clearer. She had fallen on her knees in the dirt and scrub grass while the sun set with glorious splendor, bowed her head, and recommitted her heart and soul and life to God. *Show me those Big Black Arrows, God. I'll follow every single one of them.*

The powerful feeling of *rightness* that had begun that moment on the top of Huerfano Mountain had been so all consuming that it had overridden every obstacle that should have held her back or slowed her down once she got back home. No one recovers from such a disastrous wake of pitiable life choices, no one has a friendly, loving and open relationship with the couple who has adopted her baby, no one raises support in less than six weeks to become a missionary, and no one could fight the monumental force of her mother's disapproval. But Karly had, with a strength of power and enthusiasm that had stunned even herself. Karly Martin was energized, alive and sure.

Help me or get out of my way.

However, standing next to Sam Jamison the next morning and looking into the trailer that was to be her new home, Karly had to admit she was horrified. Gazing at the revolting interior of the trailer she was expected to live in and call home, Sam Jamison said from behind her, "I, uh, know it needs some work. The last person who lived here wasn't much of a housekeeper. I was afraid to let Edith come down here and see it because she would have killed herself to get it back in shape." Karly turned to look at him pointedly. "Okay, *okay,*" Sam said in the face of her direct stare. "Well, she would have killed *me* making *me* get it back in shape. Look, I'll send over Earl. Did you meet him last time you were here? No? He does odd jobs now and then, and you just tell him what you need ... hauled away and burned." Sam glanced toward the right end of the trailer at the bed. "I'd start with that mattress. I'll call around immediately to find out if anyone's got a spare one to give you."

Karly sighed. So much for starting to set up her classroom and getting her lesson plans written. "What cleaning materials do you have?"

"Oh, there are plenty of things up at the school in the janitor's closet. Help yourself. And Karly?" When she turned to look at him he gave her a sheepish grin. "Could we keep it to ourselves about the, um, er, *poor state* of this place? Edith would have my hide if she knew how bad it was."

Karly narrowed her eyes. "Did you sign up for that yoga class yet, Sam?"

"Why no, I told you that there was no way I was going to be wearing pur -,"

She interrupted him and said firmly, "I *said*, did you sign up for that yoga class yet?"

"Oh, man, Karly. Don't do this to me! You've got to get a *floor mat* and stuff."

Karly turned and crossed her arms. "Did you sign up for that yoga class yet, Sam?"

Sam sighed a world - weary sigh of resigned defeat. "I'll do that on the way to Earl's." He shook his head, mumbling as he turned to walk away, "Man, I'm *doomed* with the two of you after me."

Standing in the doorway on the grimy linoleum floor, Karly looked around her at a loss as to where to begin. *Earl will haul ...* That's what she'd start with. She'd toss out everything she was absolutely certain she couldn't clean or recover. Out went the mattress, followed by every curtain and throw rug she could find. Old newspapers, magazines, and miscellaneous bits and pieces got tossed into the dump pile, too. She suspiciously sniffed pillows and couch cushions. Most of the pillows went, but she was relieved that the couch cushions just seemed musty. Around back in a rickety old enclosed shed with it's door propped up beside it, she found a working washing machine and half a container of clothes soap. Gradually, she began to work her way through anything that could be reclaimed with a thorough washing … or two or three. She propped all the foam couch and chair cushions outside in an attempt to air them.

What to do next? She had a passionate desire to scrub every available surface, even the ceiling. The school was a fifteen - minute hike down the hill. Commandeering buckets, sponges, a mop, rags, and anything that said "chemical cleaner" on its label, she trudged back up the hill.

The inside of the refrigerator was the most frightening mess she had faced in years. If she could have, she would have hauled it out and left it for Earl to take away with the mattress. But she squared her shoulders and attacked the grime and fur bits with stiff lipped resolve. Next came the stove, sink, and counter tops. Karly's shoulders, neck, and back ached fiercely when she was done, but she was beginning to feel as though she was at least making some serious headway. Stretching and bending to get the kinks out, she jumped practically three feet and slammed her head on an open cabinet door when a voice said, "Need all this stuff out here taken to the dump?"

"And hello to you, too," Karly said more sharply than she intended as she rubbed the back of her head. Standing peering in her open door way was a handsome, unsmiling Navajo man with dark hair, dark eyes, and dark skin. He had on an old pair of Levis, a tee shirt, cowboy boots, and a well worn cowboy hat.

"Sorry to startle you," he said quietly. "I called from outside but you must not have heard me."

"I take it you're Earl?"

He nodded and removed his hat. "Earl Nezbegay and his truck at your service. I've got a mattress for you, too. Sam said you needed one."

"Oh, that's great! Yeah, I do need one. Would you let me quick wipe down the bed frame and then I'll help you carry it in?"

"Yeah, sure, take your time. I'm in no rush."

She grabbed a fresh rag, filled the bucket with fresh warm water and cleaning solution and headed over to the bed frame.

"So you're the new teacher, huh?" He'd let himself into the trailer and was leaning against the wall of the 'living room' watching her work.

"That's me," she said over her shoulder as she cleaned the bed frame. "Karly Martin and her teaching skills at your service. Although right now, my cleaning skills are much more valuable."

He didn't laugh or respond to her joke, but simply said with a matter - of - fact voice, "You'll be teaching my niece."

She straightened and looked at him. He was of above average height with a strong, muscular build. When he turned to examine his surroundings she noted that he wore his black hair long and pulled back in a casual ponytail. It reached almost to his waist. "Oh? What's her name?"

Earl didn't look back when he answered but pulled a screwdriver from his back pocket and began to tighten some of the screws on the kitchen cabinets. "Marion Goodluck. She's in fifth grade."

Karly dropped the cleaning rag into the bucket of soap and said, "I'll watch out for her." He turned to look at her and she smiled at him. He walked out of the trailer without further comment.

In silence, the two of them wrestled the 'new' mattress into the trailer and onto the freshly cleaned bed frame. It was of significantly better quality than the original mattress, and suddenly the idea of a good night's sleep seemed very appealing. When they had loaded the back of his truck with everything for the dump he simply climbed in the cab and drove away without a word of exchange or goodbye.

"Charming personality," Karly mumbled to herself as she made her way around the back to hang up the fresh load of washing on the line.

She was exceptionally pleased with herself when she crawled into bed that night. Though sparse, the trailer was clean from top to bottom (even the ceiling!). Now it was ready for Karly to add whatever touches she wanted to finally make it her home. The position of her bed allowed her to see out the window into the night sky and its glorious display. The beauty of it all called to her from the bed, tired bones and all. Pulling the quilt off the bed against the evening chill, she padded outside, barefoot, to stand underneath the exquisite beauty that affirmed loudly and clearly God's power and majesty. Out loud to the darkness Karly prayed, *"Thank you for my life, Lord. Thank you for this place. Thank you for my skills and talents that fit so well here. Thank you for your guidance. Thank you for the peace in my mind and body and soul. Thank you for getting me here. Please be with ... Benjamin, and Darin and Viv, Snake, and Dad and Mom. Help my being away make things smoother at home for everyone. Be with the children I will be teaching that they will have open hearts and ears to everything I try to teach them. Be with me and continue to bless this mission school and all those near and far who honor, pray for, and support it. Help me to stay focused and close to You. Guide my words and my actions, my head and my heart, help me to know good choices from bad, wise directions from foolish ones. Let me make You proud with all I say and I do. Thank you for my life, Lord. Amen"* She stood for long moments in the glorious evening, soaking up the strength and power and peace that seemed to pour into her from the sights and sounds and smells around her. *I am peaceful.*

The excitement to get working and planning got her out of bed earlier than she intended the next morning. One moment she was fast asleep and the next moment she was wide - awake trying to figure out how she was going to manage teaching fifteen children ranging in ages from nine to twelve. Technically, she was responsible for grades four through eight, although Edith Jamison had said that in reality some of the children's skills were probably significantly lower. "The older ones, just like any group of preteens and teens you would encounter anywhere in the world, think they know everything and that school is just a concept invented by the old to suppress the young." She'd grinned at Karly. "Trent Patterson told me that last year when I gave him a hard time about completing his homework requirements in order to pass." She chuckled. "You've got him in your eighth grade. *Good luck."*

Edith showed her where all the teaching materials and supplies were stored. "We tend to lock everything up in the one store room at the end of the school year because the school is often empty for long periods of times and we've had some trouble with vandalism. Come on, I'll show you where the key is.

"Over here are Naomi's things. She's the one I said teaches the kindergarten through third grade." Edith hesitated and then looked at Karly. "She's been with us a good seven years and is close to retiring. I'm not exactly sure what brought her out here to no - man's - land to teach. Her resume' showed an impressive school career in upper New York State, and she had only a few more years until she would have had enough years in to collect a pension. She certainly didn't come here because of the money." Edith sighed. "I'll not say anything else, but let's just say if you have any questions, I'll promise to answer them as honestly as I can, okay?" Karly nodded. "Naomi's currently back east visiting her sister, and should be returning sometime in the next week or two."

Edith placed her hand on Karly's arm. "See the shelves with the blue stickers on them?" Karly looked up at about a dozen shelves with small blue dots stuck on them. "Those are Naomi's shelves. *If at all possible*, don't put things on those shelves or take things from them. You'd be better off asking me first, okay?"

"Sure, that's no problem," Karly said. "But all the rest of the stuff in here is okay to use?"

Edith nodded. "Yes, those are all the textbooks you'll need. You can see they're carefully labeled with the subjects and grade levels. Here are the craft supplies, additional learning materials, consumable supplies. We have a minimal budget from which we can order things that you feel are critical to you this year, but otherwise we hope you'll just be able to make do. When in doubt feel free to ask Sam or me. As we told you, I tend to run the school and business end of things and Sam tends to deal with the preaching and building and people issues, but neither one is ever far removed from the other that we can't usually provide an answer to a question."

As it turned out much of the teaching materials were of miserable quality. Old and outdated, the textbooks appeared to be cast offs from a number of old schools in the area. In general, the math and literature materials were adequate, the science material dull and boring, and the history and geography materials woefully obsolete. Craft supplies were basic: glue, paper, pencils, erasers, markers, and crayons. The 'teaching materials' consisted of numerous hundred – year - old flashcards for math, a game of Scrabble, two boxes of chess and checkers, a globe that was so old that Thailand was still called 'Siam', and a set of fifteen videos entitled *Learning The Bible: Serious Lessons for All Ages.* In addition she found one hundred gross of Popsicle sticks (what does one need with 14,400 Popsicle sticks?), seven very dried up sets of watercolor paints (not all with paint brushes), and a huge gallon vat of Elmer's School Paste.

Fishing through her book bag, she got out a pad of paper and began to make a list. Tapping the pencil in thought she decided to make three columns: Have to Have, Like To Have, Big Wishes and started writing furiously. The rest of the day she kept reaching for the pad, adding to the columns. Tonight, when she got back to the trailer, she'd rewrite the list, write a cover letter, and send it out to all her supporting churches. In the meantime, she would make the best with what she had.

Something was different with the trailer when she got home that evening, but, staring at it, for the life of her she couldn't immediately put her finger on it. What was it? The sun was busy doing its spectacular sunset, and as the beautiful pinks, oranges, reds, and purples reflected off the windows it hit her. *Her trailer was clean on the outside.* Walking up to the front door, she tentatively touched the metal siding and felt a warm, smooth, *clean* surface. The windows shone, the siding was a surprisingly bright white, and even the window awnings showed a hint of their original forest green color. Karly walked around the trailer to the back and stood with her mouth hanging open. The door had been rehung on the washer shed and the single sagging clothesline had multiplied into a sturdy triple line accessible from the 'living room' window. "Well I'll be," she said to herself. Then Karly narrowed her eyes. If Sam Jamison thought he was going to get out of that yoga class he had another thing coming.

Over the next few days Karly got frequent dinner invitations from the Jamisons. As cooking was a skill tremendously low on her list of capabilities, she was more than happy to accept, and, she suspected, the Jamisons enjoyed the company.

"Guess what!" Edith said as Karly chopped tomatoes for the salad and Sam got their drinks ready. "Sam joined that yoga class after all! I had to go to town today and buy him a sweat suit and a yoga mat. He looked so cute going off to class in the morning. I hope he keeps it up."

Karly smiled at Sam who had a blank expression on his face. "Good for you, Sam! How many other men are in the class?"

As Sam went to open his mouth, Edith burst out laughing and said, "The *poor guy*. He's the only one. I told him he's setting a good example and should start trying to get some of the other older men in town to try it out."

Sam had begun to perspire slightly as Karly continued to glance at him while she began slicing the celery. She took a little pity on him. "Thanks for all the hard work you did on the trailer, Sam," she said with a smile. "I really appreciate it."

His eyebrows arched and he gave her a pointed, deer - in - the - headlights look.

"I mean it," Karly said, trying to get him to understand she wasn't giving him a hard time, simply trying to communicate how much she appreciated what he'd done as a surprise the other day. "It was so nice to come home to the trailer all spick and span clean. The new clothesline is great. And the door you repaired on the washer shed, too. *Thanks.*"

Sam Jamison looked at her with a pained blank expression for a moment and then sighed. "You're welcome, Karly. *Anytime.*" Then he looked at his wife. "Do you think maybe Josiah would try out the yoga class?"

Edith beamed. "What a great idea! I'll call his wife right now." Rushing to the phone, Edith began an animated conversation with the person at the other end. Hanging up with a satisfied smile, she said to her husband, "Nancy thinks it's a *great* idea and is going to start working on Josiah *immediately*. I'm so glad you're taking such an interest in your health *finally*, Sam."

"Yeah, well, just call me Sam La Lanne. The next thing you know I'll be opening my own fitness center just like Jack," he mumbled as he turned to the cupboard to get out the dinner plates.

Those first two weeks Karly was settling at the Huerfano Mission School flew by. Twenty - seven letters (which she photocopied at her own expense at the local Foodmart's copy machine) went out to all of her supporting churches asking for help and donations to her "Karly Supply List". Before she dropped them in the mailbox she'd said a quick prayer, "It's all up to you God!" She purchased a second hand car in Farmington (using the money from the sale of her old car at home and some of her small savings she had horded with Scrooge - like miserliness) that gave her some much needed freedom and mobility. After becoming friends with the elderly librarian in Farmington, Karly was able to make an arrangement with her for borrowing books for longer periods of time. Books that complimented the core subjects she was planning to teach – Social Studies, Science, Geography, and Literature - that could be set up in the classroom on a rotating basis. The local school system took pity on her and miraculously had a substantial pile of "old" materials – maps, extra yet outdated workbooks, some moderately used textbooks, and even some old playground equipment that they willingly gave her. Karly elicited a promise from them that before they threw out *anything* they'd call her. Lastly, at the local crafters market she had discovered while searching for a parking space in Huerfano, she managed to convince three of the local craftsmen – a silversmith, a potter, and a Navajo rug weaver – to come into the class on a rotating basis to do some demonstrations and perhaps teach some skills and history. Things were starting to look up.

Then, Naomi returned.

School was due to open in a week when Naomi French appeared at Karly's classroom door. "You must be Karly Martin," she announced in a businesslike tone, strolling confidently into the room and extending her hand. "How do you do?"

"Hi," Karly said, struggling to appear somewhat dignified as she swallowed a mouthful of her tuna sandwich. "Pardon me," she smiled sheepishly.

"When did you arrive?" Naomi asked, taking in the preparations Karly had made in the room.

"A little over three and a half weeks ago. I'm just starting to feel like I *might* be ready on time."

"Organization is the key to success, I always say. I take it Edith has shown you around?"

"Yes, she's been very helpful."

"She's not the best teacher but does do an adequate job keeping all of the plates spinning."

"Excuse me?" Karly wasn't certain she'd heard correctly.

Naomi looked at her. "*Edith.* She's great in a pinch if she needs to cover for you, but don't count on any stellar teaching skills. That's my first tip for you."

"I see," Karly said cautiously. "I've helped her out two Sundays at church school and she seems to have a wonderful flair with the children."

"*Church school* is light years away from actual school, Karly." She sighed and strolled around Karly's room, picking up books and reading posters Karly had decorated the walls with. "This is your first teaching job, isn't it?"

"Yes. I graduated from college this past June."

"Experience will be your greatest teacher. Just wait until you've got a room full of children who encompass five plus years of negligent academic skills, half of which are on the cusp of raging hormones and puberty. I've been doing this for almost thirty years and I'm still learning." She began to impart to Karly a collective mass of teaching wisdom that, from Karly's perspective, was part common sense and part dictatorship. Naomi stopped at the bookshelves in the back of the room and halted her detailed explanation of her disciplinary procedures. Looking pointedly at Karly she said, "Where did you get these books?"

"The librarian at the Farmington public library agreed to let me borrow pertinent books for the subjects I'll be teaching. She said that I could take up to forty books and keep them for two months. I'll return them just before the start of the next marking period and get a new collection. You're welcome to borrow some. I thought I'd assign one of the kids to be the class librarian."

Naomi shook her head emphatically. "That will never work. They'll steal you blind. My experience has been that anything that isn't nailed down is considered free game. I'd keep a close handle on these books and, in fact," she gazed around the room, "I'd store them in the bookshelves behind your desk so you can keep a better eye on them."

"You've had lots of instances of theft here at the school?"

"No, actually it's not been much of a problem because of my vigilance. At the school where I used to teach back east, anything I considered valuable was eventually stolen."

"I'm sorry to hear about your experience, but I'm glad to hear that it's not been so bad here."

Naomi gave her another pointed look. "Did you hear me? *Because of my vigilance.* Kids are kids, no matter the location or the skin color. Remember that."

Somehow, the implication was not a favorable indictment regarding the classification of 'being a child'. Karly sighed. "I appreciate your advice, Naomi. Will you be going to the Tent Meetings this coming weekend?"

Naomi shrugged and nodded. "Sure. The food is great. There isn't a lot to do here in Huerfano, New Mexico. You grab the opportunity when you can. After all the excitement back east with my sister, I'm going to be struggling with withdrawal symptoms over the next few days. It happens to me every summer."

"What brought you here?"

"Life," Naomi said as she breezed out of the door. "Life brings all of us here, Karly."

My happiness is found in less
Of me and more of You[14]

Labor Day Weekend, September, 2001
Huerfano, New Mexico

Eight: Perfect Christians Have An Easy Life

The Tent Meeting was a yearly event that drew people to Huerfano from far and wide. Held over a long weekend – Friday, Saturday, and Sunday – the best way to describe it, according to Edith, was a 'religiously based party weekend'. Sitting at the Jamison's dinner table the night before the first meeting, Edith was as excited as some of the children had been. "Sam preaches each and every night, I do extensive activities with the children, partly because I enjoy it and partly because it's good promotion for the school, and then there are games and contests and craft displays. It's loads of fun and is held over three nights down in Huerfano Canyon.

"It will be a great opportunity for you to meet everyone. Oh, that reminds me. Have you met Theresa Goodluck?" When Karly shook her head, Edith continued. "Sam went to see her the other day and she's been asking to meet you. Normally, she'd be the first one to greet you but she's been bedridden for the past few weeks, and it looks like it's going to continue for a while."

---

14 The Answer, by Shane Barnard, Shane & Shane, *Upstairs*, 2002

"Is she sick?" Karly struggled to remember the name or the facts, but she'd met and heard of so many people over the last few weeks that it was close to impossible.

"Yes and no. A little over ten years ago she was in a car accident and ended up a quadriplegic. Her brother is Earl Nezbegay and her daughter Marion will be one of your fifth graders. Anyway, she spends most of her life zipping around causing trouble in her wheelchair, but she's developed a rather serious bedsore and the doctor's told her she must stay completely off it until it heals. Last time that happened, she was in bed for almost six weeks."

Karly remembered Earl, the silent, rather abrupt 'handyman' who had helped her that first day as she cleaned the trailer. "Oh, how horrible. She must be going stir crazy."

"Oh believe me, *she is*. And she's probably making Earl and Marion miserable."

"They live together?"

"Yes, Earl does primary care of Theresa and the rest of us fill in the holes."

"Wow, that's quite a responsibility he's taken on."

Edith looked pained for a moment. "Yes, he's been caring for his sister since she came home from the rehabilitation facility, and prior to that he cared for Marion who was only a baby when the accident happened. I pray for Earl continually." Edith sighed and walked over to the coffee pot, carrying it over to pour everyone a cup. She glanced across the table at Sam who was surprisingly quiet. "If you're up to it and could spare the time, I think Theresa would really enjoy your company."

"I'll go over tomorrow."

School was set to start the following Wednesday after Labor Day and finally, on the Friday before, Karly felt that she was ready. Driving over to Theresa, Marion, and Earl's house she felt slightly anxious about the visit. *Please guide my words,* she prayed.

"Hello? Anyone home?" Through the screen door a small but neat kitchen was visible.

"Who's there?" came a female voice from deep inside the house.

"Karly. Karly Martin. I'm the new teacher at the mission school. Sam and Edith Jamison gave me directions and said you might like some company."

"Come on in!"

Karly let herself in and wandered slowly into the house. The kitchen led to a roomy living room. Following the hallway at the living room's opposite end she eventually came to the bedrooms. "First one on the left," came the voice.

"Hi."

"Sorry I can't get up and greet you proper," came a voice tinged with sarcasm. "My evil brother sets me up like this to stare at the wall all day."

"Can I help?"

"Sure, come over here and turn me. That way I can at least get a good look at you and we can talk face to face."

"I don't know what to do ..." uncertainty poured out of Karly.

"Don't worry. I won't break. That happened already." Bitter laughter followed. "Come behind me and kneel on the bed. That's right. Grab a firm hold of my right knee and right shoulder ..." Theresa proceeded to talk Karly through the turn and flip and adjust and slide. "There, that wasn't so bad now, was it? Nothing like getting to know someone by climbing into their bed first thing before you are properly introduced, huh?" Theresa gave her a level stare.

You can't do this, Evil Twin said. *Get going. Quick.*

Remember, be yourself. You were called here because YOU were needed, came a calmer voice of reason.

"I'm not too good with quadriplegic humor," Karly finally said slowly. "But if you'll be patient with me, I'll try to learn."

Theresa studied her for a moment with sharp eyes. "Shoshanna said you were too beautiful for words. She was right."

"I've spent my adult life with men having long conversations with just my breasts."

"Hmmm, and what I wouldn't give for a little of *that* action," Theresa said and then winked at Karly. "Quad humor again."

"Oh." Karly pulled up a chair and sat down next to the bed. "Does your brother really make you face the wall like that on purpose?"

"Yeah, I scream and cry every morning and he just flips me over and leaves me there." At Karly's serious expression Theresa looked a little bit impatient. "Look, don't believe everything I tell you. Or, better yet, take everything I say with a grain of salt. Usually it's the truth but it's fun sometimes to twist things up a bit." She sighed. "Yeah, he makes me lie like that, yeah sometimes I scream and cry and even throw out a few good curses. But, if he doesn't shift me every couple of hours then I'll just get another bed sore. This is my favorite side because I can see best from here. But if no one's going to be around, I might as well just lie here and look at the damn wall."

"What do you do when you lie here?"

"Sometimes I listen to the radio or watch television. Reading's a pain because even though I have some movement of my arms and hands," she did a brief demonstration, "turning pages is a bitch. I get visits, too. I've got a lot of loyal friends."

Karly looked around. "How long are you left alone?" The idea would have terrified her.

"Earl ran some errands to help with the big Tent Meeting tonight. Marion went along to escape me and my vicious tongue. They'll be back in time to flip me. You'll see. They're as steady as clockwork." She looked at Karly's breasts. "Guys really talk to them?"

Karly laughed. "Go figure, huh? Yeah, sometimes I put up with it and some times I don't depending on my mood."

"So, what's your impression so far of good old Huerfano? Who have you met?"

They ended up talking for almost an hour and a half. Karly had expected to talk longer, but Earl and Marion came home just as Theresa had predicted. Theresa heard the truck before Karly did. "Here are the troops."

The sound of running feet came to a halt in the doorway. "Hey, Mom! You should see the new tent they've got this year! It's almost twice as big. Uncle Earl says he thinks that almost a hundred and fifty people can sit under it."

"That should keep Pastor Sam happy, huh? Marion, say hello to Ms. Martin. She's going to be your new teacher I hear."

"Hey, Miss Martin."

Karly stood and walked over to Marion with her hand outstretched. "Hey, Marion. It's a pleasure to meet you. I hear from Mrs. Jamison that you're a wiz at memorizing just about anything. You're going to have to teach me any tricks you have, because I can't memorize to save my life."

Marion shrugged, blushing with pleasure at the compliment. "It's no trick, really. It just seems to stick in my head. Uncle Earl says it's because there's so much empty space up there to fill."

"He does, does he?" Karly said.

"Speaking of Earl, where is he?" Theresa piped up.

Marion glanced at Karly and then at her mother. "Said he had stuff to do in the shed."

"Tell him I said to get his tail in here and be polite."

"Aw, Mom."

"Go on now."

Minutes later two sets of steps could be heard making their way down the hallway. Marion preceded her uncle into the bedroom but it was his voice that filled the room with anger. "What are you doing on that side, Tee? You know you're not supposed to be on that side until after 1:00."

"Aww, go to hell Earl. What was I gonna do? Sit here while Karly here visited and have her talk to my ass?"

Karly had stood when Earl and Marion came into the room. Speaking to Earl she said, "I'm sorry if I've done something wrong. Theresa asked me to help turn her, so I did."

"Rule number one about quadriplegics, Karly," Theresa said in a tone tinged with anger and impatience, "They don't like to be talked to like they're deaf and dumb."

Horrified, Karly turned to Theresa, "I didn't mean ..." she began.

"Tee ..." Earl interrupted in a warning tone, and began to advance toward her with purpose. Karly backed up to the wall. He pinned Karly where she stood with his unblinking dark eyes. "What time did you turn her?"

"I didn't note the exact time ..."

With a sigh of impatience, Theresa volunteered, "She got here a little after 11:30. I had her turn me right away. So you can punish me and flip me and keep me talking to the damn wall until 3. Okay?"

Without any further response to Karly or his sister, Earl used quick, economical movements to get his sister repositioned onto her other side. Looking at Karly he seemed to struggle with himself for a moment. Finally he said, "You shouldn't feel like you've got to go, but she's got to stay on this side for a bit now."

Karly looked at him, sucked up her courage, and said, "If rule number one is quadriplegics don't like to be talked to like they're deaf and dumb, why do you do it?"

"You go, Sister," Theresa said in a delighted tone, "let the S.O.B. have it."

For a few moments Karly didn't think he was going to answer her. But then he did. "Because, I'm the one that's got to live with the complaints and deal with the problems when she insists on doing *stupid, stubborn* things." He turned and directed his comments to his sister's back. "Like insisting on being in her wheelchair for *hours* longer than she knows is wise. Like refusing to rest in bed for a *few days* when the pressure point started. Like being unwilling to listen to the *good advice* she gets from doctors and nurses who've dealt with this situation many times before." He turned and looked back at Karly. "That's why."

Karly, wisely, kept her mouth shut.

The Tent Meeting was as much fun as Karly had expected and then some. Delicious food smells wafted in the air and the breathtaking view of the sunset, and then subsequent nighttime sky, were spectacular. Plate piled high, she sat at a picnic table in the food tent and ate corn on the cob and fry bread (which was rapidly becoming a favorite), delicious barbequed meats, and blue corn mush drenched in butter.

"Miss Martin?"

Looking up from her plate she met the smiling eyes of a vaguely familiar young man. "Hello …"

He smiled at her. "You don't remember me, do you? Mind if I sit?" he gestured to the space on the other side of the picnic table.

"No, please, go right ahead."

"I'm David Shafer. We met when you came into Farmington a few weeks ago and spoke with the high school about supplies? I teach high school science …?"

"Oh yes," Karly said with a smile, relieved to finally have her memory kick in, "I remember now. Please forgive me." She gestured to the hundreds of people milling around. "I'm a bit overloaded with new names and faces."

He smiled in return. "No need to apologize. We only met briefly and I was up to my neck unpacking supplies. How has your hunt for better quality materials worked out?"

Over their meal they had an easy conversation about school issues and general topics like the weather. They shared sketchy information about their lives and their families. David was a born and bred New Mexico boy, his great grandparents having traveled out west with the lure of free land and a new start back in the early 1800's. He shook his head. "But I'm not rancher or farmer material. That was obvious early on. I've got three older brothers though, so my father wasn't too disappointed. And I love the area. Teaching seems to fit and when I need a cowboy fix, which does happen now and then, I just drive out to the family ranch and get it out of my system." He smiled as he took a bite of corn. "Do you ride?"

"Ride?"

"Horses."

Karly shook her head and smiled. "Oh, no. I've always been fascinated with them, but you don't have much opportunity to play cowgirl back east."

"I'd love to take you riding. I could teach you the basics quite quickly and we've got some very gentle horses that I'm sure you'd feel comfortable with. Would you be interested sometime?" A lock of brown wispy hair fell across his forehead as Karly looked into his sincere green eyes. He had a tan from a lifetime spent outside chasing around the family ranch with his three older brothers. He smiled at her silence. "No pressure. But I do think I should be honest and tell you that I only came to the Tent Meeting in the hopes of meeting you." His smile turned into a grin and he waggled his eyebrows. "Does that get me points?"

She laughed delightedly. It felt like such a long time since she'd had the opportunity to consider a casual date. "You won't put me on a wild bucking bronco or anything?"

"Nope. Pony level or one step up."

"Sounds like fun."

"Are you available tomorrow? I know it's short notice, but if your life is anything like mine, once school starts things switch into high gear. I always look at this final weekend before school starts as my last chance to relax and enjoy myself."

"You're so right. I've been running myself ragged trying to get everything set up, but just yesterday I finally felt like I was actually going to survive and be ready." She smiled. "Tomorrow would be fine; I've got a free day."

They settled on a time and she agreed to drive out and meet him in Farmington. From there he'd drive them to his family's ranch.

"Miss Karly!" a breathless voice sounded behind them. "Mrs. Jamison says she needs you quick!" It was Roderick Yazzie, a cute seven – year - old who attended both the school and the church.

Glancing at her watch, Karly rolled her eyes at David. "I'm on. I promised I'd help with the puppet show." She stood and began gathering up her empty plate and cup.

"Maybe I'll stay and catch the show," David said.

As Roderick grabbed Karly's hand and began to pull her away, she laughed at him. "Find something better to do with your time!"

Saying her prayers that night under the stars, Karly was overwhelmingly thankful for the feeling of belonging that she experienced in this place. It was new, it was different, it was still unfamiliar, but she never felt out of place, awkward, or lost. In fact, it seemed as the days passed that she felt more and more like ... *herself.* And with that feeling came a confidence and joy that was empowering. *Thank You, thank You, for Your love and faithfulness,* she prayed. *Guide me and help me to please You in all I do.* Her thoughts were suddenly filled with Theresa. Karly tried to wrap her head around the kind of life Theresa led, and felt a measure of her joy slip. *I thought you sent me here for the children, Lord. But maybe there are others here that I can help, too. Please ease my hesitancy and insecurities where Theresa is concerned.*

Be yourself, Karly. Just be you.

David Shafer's family's ranch was nine thousand acres of prime grazing land about forty - five minutes north of Farmington. Driving down the "driveway" that seemed miles long Karly turned a stunned expression to him and asked, "This is all your family's land?"

David laughed at her. "Don't be too impressed. It's really small by ranch standards. Land out here is in no way as expensive as back east. Yes, it's a nice spread, yes, it's profitable, but the family works their tails off just to break even most years. On my miserable teacher's salary I'm often the rich member of the family when it comes to available cash."

"It's so beautiful out here. I hadn't expected to fall in love with the countryside, but I have. I have a friend who calls this "God's Country", and I have to agree with him. You really feel God's power and majesty here."

David seemed to study the scenery as they drove. "Maybe you become jaded when you've lived here as long as I have."

"I hope I don't ever take it for granted. I still can't believe the stars I see at night! I had no idea. Don't laugh, but I say my evening prayers outside under the night sky because it's too beautiful to stay indoors and miss the view."

"I've never been much of a fan of religion," David said hesitantly.

"You really did come to the Tent Meeting just to meet me?"

David glanced at her and said in complete seriousness, "I sure did." He looked back at the road and smiled. "I didn't stay for the puppet show, though. I hope that doesn't make me lose too many points."

"Actually, the way things went, knowing that you didn't see it *gains* you some points." Karly went on to regale him with the disastrous performance that had turned into an unintended comedy show.

David was true to his word, showing her the rudimentary basics of riding and providing her with a horse that was gentle and sweet. Afterwards, they drove back to Farmington and had dinner at a small Mexican restaurant that was one of his favorites. Driving home to Huerfano, Karly marveled at how smoothly their time together had gone and how much she had enjoyed the day. *He's nice, Lord. Make Your direction known to me, please. Guide my head and my heart. No more mistakes for me.*

On Sunday, Karly arrived at Theresa's unannounced with gifts. "Hello? Anyone home?"

"Nobody here but us crabby chickens," came Theresa's reply.

Karly let herself in and walked to Theresa's bedroom. "Hey! How are you today? How's your conversation with the wall?"

"It sucks as usual. But this is a nice surprise. Come and turn me over."

"Oh, no you don't! I'm not getting caught in *that* trap again!" Karly burst out. "But," she came around and squeezed between the narrow space between the bed and the wall so Theresa could see her, "I've been thinking about this room of yours all day. I *think* if we did a little bit of furniture moving we could arrange this place a whole lot better. Is there a reason it's set up like this? Some reason it has to stay this way?"

Theresa looked at her skeptically. "It's set up like this because this is the way it's always been. That's all I know."

"Well, I was thinking, you could move the bed more to the center of the room, put that bookcase over there and that chest of drawers over there. I *think* that chair will fit in the corner. The only problem I can see is whoever goes in and out of your closet won't be able to open the door fully because the nightstand might be in the way. If this works, then visitors could sit comfortably on either side of the bed and talk to you. On your right side you'll have a view out the window – instead of the wall – and on your left side you should be able to see into the hall and a little bit of the living room. What do you think?"

"Where have you been all my life?"

Karly burst out laughing. "Does that mean yes?"

"Sure, as soon as Earl gets home we'll get him to move -,"

"Who needs Earl? I can move this stuff," Karly said putting down her gifts. "Oh, I forgot. I was in Farmington yesterday, and I went to the library and got you some books on tape. I picked two I think I'd like and two I think I'd hate since I don't know your tastes."

"Ooo, let me see. Which ones are which?"

"I'm not telling. You'll have to listen to them and then tell me what ones you think I'd like. Do you want to put one in now and listen to it while I start tearing apart your room or, do you just want to gab?"

"Oh, I want to gab. Tell me about the Tent Meeting."

So Karly did. She regaled her with the hysterics of the puppet show, told her about the sights that impressed her, and even gave her a run down on David Shafer and her date with him yesterday.

"Boy, you move quick," Theresa said when she heard about the Shafer ranch.

"What's that supposed to mean?" Karly shouted. "I didn't do anything but sit there in the food tent eating my meal. *He* sought me out."

"What part of you did he talk to?" and when Karly looked at her with a puzzled frown Theresa gave her a wicked grin and glanced down at her breasts.

"Oh," Karly said laughing and blushing all at once. "He was a perfect gentlemen. If he looked he did it without being obvious."

"You gonna see him again?"

Karly shrugged. "I don't know. We hit it off nicely. I prayed about the whole thing last night. If it's not going to be good for me in the long run I'd rather God just put an end to it right away. I can't deal with getting my head and my heart messed up again."

"What do you mean 'again'?"

"Oh, I've got history. *Lots* of history."

"That sounds juicy. Am I going to get to hear about this history?"

Karly gave her a wink. "Maybe. Maybe not. We'll have to see."

It was like a Marx Brothers movie when Karly started moving Theresa's bed. The two of them were laughing hysterically as they tried to shift the big, hospital style bed around in the small bedroom. In the end, the bookcase and the nightstand had to be dragged out into the hallway just so the bed could be turned. Once it was in place though, Karly put her hands on her hips and said, "Okay, before we go any further tell me if you like this position. No sense going to all the trouble to put everything back in the room if you don't. What do you think?"

"Well, I'm already on my 'hated side' and seeing more than I've ever seen before. Hey, I can even see a bit of the road out the window! This is great. Turn me over so I can see what's on my other side."

"Oh no you don't. What is that, quadriplegic trickery? I'm not flipping you over until your done cooking on that side," Karly said, and Theresa burst out laughing. "Here, I'll tell you what you'll see." Before she could think it through, Karly lay down with her back against Theresa's back, lying on her side. "This is what I see. I can see the hallway and the door to the, what would that be, the car port?"

"Yeah, that's the carport."

"And I can see into the living room and the end of the couch and the easy chair. I can't see the TV though."

"Can you see in the carport? Like if a car pulled in could you see who was driving?"

"Yeah, I think I could. Definitely if they were in a truck, and I'm pretty sure I'd be able to see if they were in a car."

"That's great then, I like this new arrange -,"

"What the hell's going on in here?" a furious male voice sounded from out in the hallway. "I can't even get into my own bathroom with all the stuff that's in the hallway!"

Karly scrambled up out of Theresa's bed and rushed to the door. "Hi Earl. I was just rearranging Theresa's room."

"And you thought you should do this because ...?"

"Mind your own business," Theresa's voice came drifting out from behind Karly. "It's my bedroom and I'm tired of staring at this freakin' wall!"

"Tell me, Tee. How come changing around your room is okay when someone else suggests it but not when I want to do it? Huh?" Earl stared unblinkingly into Karly's eyes while they both waited for Theresa's response.

After long moments of silence, Theresa finally said, "You holding your breath for my answer, Earl? That would make my day."

Karly smothered a laugh behind her hand. "She's real funny," Earl said to her, "as long as you don't have to live with her." He sighed and took stock of the pile of stuff in the hallway. "How long are you going to be? She needs to be turned in about forty - five minutes."

"I'll be done by then. I'm sorry, Earl. It seems that every time I'm here it causes a problem." Karly gave him a tentative smile in the face of his stoic expression.

"I'll be in the shed when you're finished. Have Marion come and fetch me." He turned and stalked away.

"He's off sulking in the shed, huh?" Theresa said when Karly came in dragging the bookcase.

"That's what he said. He said to send Marion when the coast was clear for him to come in and turn you in about forty - five minutes."

"He needs to get a life. Jeeze, he drives me nuts."

"You're so tough on him."

"He carries the weight of the whole damn world on those shoulders of his. Always so busy beating himself up, day in and day out."

Stacking the books back in some semblance of order, Karly said, "Why's he beating himself up? I don't get it."

"Oh," Theresa said, "I thought you knew. He was driving the car the night we had the accident that paralyzed me. He was the one that dragged me out of the wreckage, afraid that the car would burst into flames. The doctor's told me that had I not been moved that *perhaps* – and that's a big perhaps – I might have been able to fully recover from the initial injury.

Earl blames himself for everything, even though I was too drunk to be driving myself anywhere, let alone Marion, too."

Karly sat in the middle of Theresa's floor, stunned. "I had no idea."

"No? I thought the Jamisons would have told you. He had his life all mapped out for himself, I tell you. He had a college degree and a job offer up in Colorado. He was finally to get himself out of this place once and for all and make something of his life. How he used to go on and on about the worthless punks who wasted their time and intellect and energies on the pursuits of wine, women, and song. 'Course, I used to get an earful from him, too, about how many foolish mistakes I continued to make: drinking, having babies out of wedlock, never holding down a job for long. Oh, he was going to show all of us the right way to do things, and instead he ended up as a nanny and then a nurse and finally now an on - call handyman and nursing home assistant."

"What was he going to be? What's his college degree in?"

"Wow," Theresa was genuinely surprised, "the Jamisons really do keep their mouths shut. Earl's an ordained minister, Karly. He's a gen – u - ine Preacher Man."

The look on Karly's face made Theresa laugh out loud. "Man, I wish I had a camera. Man, I wish I could *operate* a camera. You had no clue, huh?" Karly shook her head. "Yeah, he's got a *Master of Divinity degree* in Biblical Studies from Princeton Theological Seminary. Got it on a full ride scholarship because he showed such 'promise and dedication' in high school. Spent a few years after he got that degree doing missionary work in Mexico, Europe and Africa. At the time of the accident, he was one of two candidates for an associate pastor position at some big, high - fallutin' church up in northern Colorado. By the time I became aware of things though, that had fallen through. I suspect he withdrew his candidacy, but I never came right out and asked him.

"So now he's my glorified nurse and butler and Marion's mom and dad all rolled into one. Paying his dues to society by being a martyr that nobody loves or appreciates."

"That's not fair, Theresa."

Theresa rolled her eyes. "*Life's* not fair, Karly."

And I long stopped dreaming those crazy dreams of mine
These days get so long and my heart grows weak
And, honey, we ain't living on no easy street[15]

Second Week of August, 2001
Huerfano, New Mexico

Nine: Pious Christians Never Loose Their Tempers

Karley was the most beautiful woman Earl had ever seen in his life. She stole the breath from his lungs and the thoughts from his head, making him become a rude, bumbling idiot. Driving his truck away from Karly's trailer to the dump that first day, Earl felt blinded by the image of her that was seared into his brain. His world, as orderly and monotonous as it was, felt skewed, as if someone had picked it up, shaken it forcefully, and then sat it back to watch the consequences. *She's just one woman,* Earl told himself. *Nothing special, nothing to get yourself all worked up about. So, she's pretty. No, breathtakingly gorgeous. So what?*

Why did he feel that his life had all of a sudden been disconnected from the normal train and hooked up with a super - sonic engine whose destination was a mysterious unknown?

In those brief minutes they had been together in her dirty, cramped trailer and he had stumbled through a poor imitation of conversation, every single solitary thing about Miss Karly Martin was imprinted on his mind.

---

[15] "Walk On" By Borders & Borders, 1994, *Along The Road*, Ashton, Becker, Dente

She was a study in opposites, a monument of contrasts: fair to his dark, smiling to his sullenness, purposeful to his aimlessness. Who had gold hair that moved like silky ribbons? Who had eyes blue like the mountain sky? Who had a smile that was like a blinding flash of light in the darkest of nights? He *was not* some hillbilly, back woods, uneducated, Hogan - living Indian. He was educated and traveled, had had his fair experiences with Life and The World Beyond The Reservation, but ... Great God Almighty, nothing had prepared him for one Karly Martin.

He should have known the moment Sam had shown up asking for a favor. When Sam had asked him to go help the new teacher haul some trash away from her trailer, he'd gotten a niggling flash of suspicion at the look in the Old Coot's eyes. Earl was never sure of Sam's agenda, and never took anything he said or did at face value. Never trust a Preacher Man. His Mamma had told him that, fed it to him alongside his fry bread and blue corn mush, but he'd ignored her then. No siree, he didn't listen to the wise words of his elders. Worse yet, he had to go off and become a preacher man himself. *Then he learned how true his Mamma's words were.* Only by then it was too late.

The dump wasn't a formal dump. It was just a spot at the end of a long dirt road near a wash that was dry most of the year. People backed up their trucks, dropped the tailgate, and hurled stuff down into the gully. Then all the punks who had nothing better to do than drink, drive their cars around, crash into each other, and kill themselves would come and set fire to the garbage when the mood struck them. He knew about that too, because he'd spent almost as long a period of his life being a no good punk as he had being a worthless preacher man. Fact is should he sit down and consider the reality of his world; he was still a punk. Even at age thirty - two.

Watching the putrid mattress make cartwheels down the gully wall, Earl heard the distinct sounds of an approaching vehicle. Turning, he watched LouRay Betselie back his battered truck up next to him.

LouRay was a hundred and fifty years old if he was a day. Bent over and spare he had been old when Earl was a kid. Now he was positively ancient. Spry as an old coyote, he scrambled up into the back of his truck and squinted at Earl with his one good eye. "Morning to ya, Earlie," he said scratching the stubble on his chin and reaching for a broken rocking chair. "Ain't seen ya in a pile of days."

For as long as Earl could remember, LouRay had had only one eye, a stooped back, and long gray hair that reached past his waist in a ratty pony tail. As kids, they used to make up tall tales about how LouRay had lost his eye and got such a bent back. The truth, though, was still a mystery, and LouRay never seemed too inclined to solve it. "You know where we live. How have you been LouRay?" LouRay had been on his own *forever*.

"Can't complain, Earlie, can't complain. Been thinking about stopping by for a bit of your excellent cornmeal fritters." Being on his own, LouRay was always searching for someone to cook him a meal.

"Stop by anytime, LouRay. You know you're always welcome."

"Ah, you're too good to this old man, Earlie. How's Theresa doing and that little girl of hers, Marion?"

That sister of yours still in that wheelchair you put her in? was the unasked but implied question that Earl heard. "They're both fine, LouRay. Bossing me near to death some days, but fine all the same."

LouRay chuckled and shook his head. "There's something wrong with a picture of a bachelor boy such as yourself tied down with all the responsibilities of supporting your sister and her kid and getting none of the benefits." His rheumy old brown eye looked at Earl. "If you know what I mean."

Still paying your dues for the horrendous mistakes of your misspent youth, was the unspoken implication Earl heard loud and clear. "Ah, well, LouRay, you take what hand you get dealt, I always say."

"I hear ya, Earlie, I hear ya." Earl watched as LouRay unfastened his pants and proceeded to pee a stream of urine down onto the pile of junk at the bottom of the ditch. Rearranging his pants, he winked his one good eye at Earl. "You make sure you're stocked up on cornmeal. I'll be over soon."

"I'll do that LouRay. You watch out for yourself."

Just a half hour later Earl greeted his niece Marion as he walked in the front door of their home. "Hey, Little Prairie Dog."

Hand on her hip, she gave him a sassy look. "You better come up with a new nickname for me, Uncle Earl. I'm the tallest kid in my grade and Mrs. Jamison says she thinks I'm almost as tall as that new teacher. 'Little Prairie-Dog' doesn't seem to fit me anymore." Earl had been calling her that nickname ever since she was a baby. She had a habit of looking at him with the same kind of intent curiosity as a prairie dog does when it peeks out of its burrow to examine the world around it.

Marion was a long, tall 'drink of water' as someone at the Foodmart had called her. She had a classic beauty that was already developing at an alarming rate, with cocoa cream skin, snapping dark eyes, and jet - black hair. Just like her Mama, only she could walk and dance and run and twitch her butt at you when she was stalking away in a huff. The best Theresa could do was roll away and throw a few choice curse words over her shoulder as she left. "How's your Mom?"

Marion flipped her long hair over her shoulder and gestured to the bedroom. "I think the phrase she used just moments ago was 'bored as hell'."

Earl sighed. He wished that Theresa would watch her language around Marion, but he wasn't in much of a position to say much. She was always mighty quick to point out his own glaring faults and that just ended up with the two of them not speaking to each other for days sometimes. Which was pretty difficult considering he was the primary lift and shift and dress and clean person on staff. It sure was awkward helping someone wash and get herself dressed when you were both so mad at each other you couldn't manage a civil word. Nah, it was just plain easier to keep his mouth shut.

"Well, she's got about four more weeks to go as I see it. Doc said that she had to stay out of her chair and off of her back until that bed sore was fully healed and the way it looked last night when I gave her a bath makes me think it's going to take the full time."

"Just like last time," Marion said with resigned defeat. Both she and Earl suffered when Theresa was bedridden.

"I'll go talk to her. Maybe ..."

"Good luck," said Marion as she headed for the kitchen, "I'm going to get her some lunch."

"How ya doing, Tee?" Earl asked his sister as he entered her bedroom.

"Oh, just peachy," came a voice dripping in sarcasm. "I've been lying here, looking at this friggin' wall all morning, and am so mentally stimulated I just can't stand it anymore."

"Want me to turn you?"

Silence for moments was his answer. Even after all these years, she still hated asking for help. From anyone, but most particularly him. Finally she sighed. "Yeah, that would help a little."

He'd performed the movements a hundred times, like an orchestrated dance. Shift, pull, slide, lift, flip, turn, adjust. "Okay?"

"Can you fix the pillowcase by my ear? It feels wrinkled." His sister was a quadriplegic. Although she had gross motor use of her arms to some extent, and of her hands to a lesser extent, she was unable to manage the fine motor coordination required to do something as simple as smooth an irritating wrinkle away.

"Good?"

"Yeah. So, what do you think of her?"

"Who?"

"Don't play stupid with me. The new teacher. I know you met her today. Everyone's buzzing about her. Shoshanna says she's unbelievably beautiful. Marion said Sam asked you to go do some favors for the new teacher – haul away some junk or something? - so I know you've been over to see her. Is it true? Is she as gorgeous as they say?"

Now Earl was really in trouble. There was actually no way he could win. Theresa had the ability to read everyone, particularly him, like a bold-typed, wide - open book. It might almost be easier to tell her the truth about how one Karly Martin had just about turned his own personal world right up on it's side. Then Earl mentally shook his head. Nah. No way. He'd never hear the end of it. So he settled with skirting around the reality of his life with carefully spoken understatements. "Yeah, I met her. She's pretty. Busy sweating and cleaning out the pigsty of a trailer she's stuck with."

"Sam didn't clean it out before she moved in? Edith will kill him."

"Yeah, probably, but I'm not going to tell on him. I'll leave it up to you."

Theresa sniffed. "I love Sammy. He brings me candy every time he comes to visit. There's no way I'm going to rat on him. So why don't you go over and help the pretty new teacher out a bit? I'm sure she'd appreciate it."

"She seemed like she was doing fine all on her own, Theresa. I'm going to do what you should do. Mind my own business."

"You know, whenever you call me Theresa, I know I'm getting close to a hot topic. What does she look like? Is it possible that she's your type?"

Earl shrugged and picked up the basket of clean clothes that Marion had just washed and folded. He started to put them away. "No woman's my type, you know that. You're the only girl for me. You and Marion." Theresa's silence was as effective as her crossing her arms and tapping her foot with impatience. Earl sighed. "She's blonde. Blue eyed. She's gonna stick out like a sore thumb with all of us."

"What did you talk about?"

He began matching socks and putting them in the drawer. Marion hated matching socks and always hid the unmatched pile at the bottom of the basket of neatly folded stuff. "Nothing much. I told her she'd be teaching Marion. I brought her a new mattress Sam got for her." He tried to change the subject. "Marion cooking you something for lunch?"

Theresa studied him for a moment and then squinted her eyes. "Maybe she'd come and visit me seeing as I'm stuck in this damn bed for four more weeks and all. Maybe we'll become the very best of friends and she'll be over here ever day. Maybe I'll get an opportunity or two to watch how you twitch and stutter when she's around and then I'll know what you *really* think of her." She grinned a wicked smile at him. "Why don't you invite her over?"

Time to abandon ship. Fast. Earl hurried his motions so he could get out to the peacefulness of the shed. "I'm not inviting her over here, Tee. As soon as you're mobile, I'll bring you over to visit her at the school or her place, okay? I'll say it again, *mind your own business.* Don't get any ideas. Do you hear me?"

His sister made a face at him. "Ideas are *all I've got,* big brother." Earl sighed. He knew darn well that if Theresa wanted Karly to come over here and visit, Karly would end up over here visiting. Like a spider at the center of a web, if pulling his strings didn't get the reaction she wanted, she had a million other ones to tug on. There was no doubt in his mind that Karly Martin would be invading his home, just like his thoughts, *soon.*

Earl found out from an off - handed comment Sam Jamison made the very next day that Karly had declined to eat dinner with them because she was going to work late at the school getting her classroom and lessons ready. Knowing she was going to be away most of the day from her trailer, Earl decided to do a few things at her place that needed doing: hosing the dirt off the trailer, repairing the washer shed door, hanging a new clothesline. Yeah, that's what he was good at, behind the scenes handyman stuff. It was the least Earl could do and it would save Sam the hassle of having to do it himself. Earl argued with himself the entire time he worked that the good deed had everything to do with the obligation he felt toward the Jamisons and their continual help with Theresa and nothing to do with the most beautiful woman he had ever laid eyes on in his whole, God - forsaken life.

It had nothing to do with Miss Karly Martin. Absolutely nothing at all.

So why was it, just a few weeks later, Earl felt as if the woman had entered his peaceful existence and completely destroyed it? Jeeze, who did she think she was anyway? Wasn't his life stressful enough with a quadriplegic sister who had attitude to spare and a preteen niece who had the makings of a playboy centerfold? If the woman wasn't questioning his technique and style in handling things that he'd been handling *for over ten years,* then she was literally in his house *rearranging it.* By what right? When he tried to talk with Tee about it, she'd just given him a sly smile and a smart comment, because he'd once again called her *Theresa*.

It was his worst nightmare come to life.

Earl couldn't even avoid her. Since he'd gone a little bit ballistic the first time he'd unexpectedly found Karly in his house and she'd moved Tee before the scheduled time, Karly had absolutely refused to ever move Theresa again. While he was able to acknowledge that Karly had the common sense at least not to believe everything his sister tried to tell her or get her to do, it didn't help Earl's situation any. Just as Theresa had predicted, she had become a regular visitor at the house. Earl couldn't even avoid the house if her car was in the driveway because he *still had to meet all of his responsibilities* in the day to day, hour to hour care of Theresa. It would make Theresa's day to know how much Earl would like to avoid Karly. And nothing would delight Theresa more than in being able to let that very person know.

His only escape from life was the shed. Only Marion came in sometimes when he was working. He'd made no effort to make it handicap accessible, so even when Tee was ripping around the planet stirring up trouble in her wheelchair, he was still safe in the shed. Only here could he find peace. Woodworking. Carving. Building. Creating. Designing. He could go in the shed once Tee was down and settled for the night, and get lost in there for hours. He was moderately pleased with some of the pieces he'd done. There was the small footstool he'd intricately carved and then stained a deep dark cherry color. A bookshelf in Marion's room was sturdy and true. Most of the stuff looked worse than most of the things he'd seen guys do in high school woodshop, though. Had he not inherited the various tools and machines from his grandfather, he probably never would have bothered. But sometimes, after a tough day with Tee, or a particularly worrisome day regarding Marion, or more often than anything else, a moment when the reality of his life and his screw ups and his poor choices and his inability to fix *anything* just about choked him, Earl would wander out to the shed and start puttering. Before he knew it, five hours were gone and it was three in the morning. But by then he'd be calmer, vaguely at peace, and possibly able to sleep for a few hours before the nightmare and tension began again.

But with Karly Martin's invasion of his life, the brief peaceful moments that the shed had brought him disappeared and were filled with thoughts of a woman who was too beautiful for words.

"Uncle Earl, Miss Martin says she prays standing outside at night watching the stars. Isn't that cool?"

"Did you tell her to watch out for rattlesnakes when she's outside stomping around in the dark doing such a foolish thing?"

"No, Uncle Earl, I didn't. Want me to tell her that tomorrow at school?"

"No Marion, I don't ... "

"What in God's name is that on your toes, Tee?"

"Toenail polish, you Neanderthal. Tell me you've never seen a woman wear nail polish on her toes."

"Sure I have, but not on you. Who put you up to such foolishness?"

"No one you know."

"What's that supposed to mean? You have a stranger that I don't even know come into the house and paint your toenails? Are you out of your mind? You know I don't think it's safe, you having people come in that I haven't met. What were you thinking?"

"Well, next time she's here, I'll send her out to the shed so you two can talk and get to know each other better. Karly was asking what you do all the time in that stupid shed anyway."

"You know what that fool teacher did the other day when she came into my shop, Earl? She asked me what kind of flowers she could plant 'round her trailer to spruce the place up. I told her you got any trash lying around in that yard? She tells me no. I say you got any old cars that need to be hauled away? She tells me no. I ask her if her outhouse is on the front lawn where everyone can see it? She tells me no sir, it's not. I tell her it sounds like her property's first class to me. Why go to all the trouble of planting a bunch of flowering weeds when things sound in such good shape already?"

"It's a wonder he's learning anything, that son of mine. Last year I had to threaten to whup him good if he didn't stop skipping school. This year he's spending an hour in the morning primping and posing in front of the mirror and goes out of the house smelling so sweet I'm thinking he's drinking aftershave instead of orange juice. What do you think that new teacher's up to that's got all the boys tripping over themselves to catch her attention? Have you noticed how young and pretty she is? What boy with half a brain in his head can learn anything worth while with something like that standing in front of him day in and day out?"

"Hear tell the new teacher is dating David Shafer from Farmington. He's been courting her since the Tent Meeting and they seem to be hitting it off just fine. Think if they hitch up we'll be stuck looking for another teacher for the mission school, or she'll hang around and keep teaching, Earl? Those Shafers own a passel of land up north of Farmington, and I hear tell they have close to eight thousand acres of prime grazing land. Don't you wish someone from the Shafers would come courtin' us, Earl?"

"Hello? Earl? I hope I'm not interrupting. Theresa wanted me to come out to the shed and find out if you were going to take her food shopping this afternoon. I told her I'd be happy to drive the van and take her myself, but she's insisting that I come out here and speak with you about it.

Oh ... my ... is this what you spend so much time doing in here? Theresa said you played with wood but I had no idea you were a craftsman. Oh, Earl, look at what you've done! I've never seen anything so fine-looking. Did you really carve and build this? What a wonderful gift you have to be able to create such beauty ..."

By Christmas, the shed was the only place that offered him even the barest chance of solace. There seemed to be no place else he could escape to, no job he could do, and no person he could talk to that Karly Martin didn't come up. He wasn't sure things could get much worse until he got an invitation to the Jamison's annual New Year's Eve Party and Tee said, "You and me are gonna double date with Karly and her boyfriend, David. If you think I'm sitting home that night you've got another thing coming, and I'll be damned if I'll be a third wheel."

"So you'd rather go on a date with *your brother?*" Earl said in a particularly vicious tone. Rarely did he allow his sister to bate him into cruelty, but he was truly living on the edge these days.

Tee didn't even blink. "You betcha sweet cheeks, because it gets me there. Once I'm at the party I can dump your ass and not feel guilty. Oh yeah, and it's fancy dress up so you've got to take me out to get a new outfit. How's tomorrow afternoon sound? Maybe we can find you something new and half way decent to wear, too."

It was a miserable evening. Tee was her usual irreverent, provocative self, Karly was exceptionally lovely in a deep green velvet dress, and particularly sweet with the hoards of children who continually demanded her attention over the course of the evening. And David Shafer was the perfect gentleman: smiling, polite, attentive, and witty. Feeling like he was about to suffocate, Earl escaped out the back door into the cold evening air. Given the elevation of Huerfano and the time of year, it was highly probable they would experience snow, or at least a hard frost, one of these nights very soon.

"Trying to escape the crush of the party, too?"

Good God. The object of his pain and misery stood quietly under a huge red oak wrapped in the colorful woolen stole she had worn as a coat. "I'm not much good at making pointless conversation," Earl allowed as he yanked at the tie Tee had insisted he dress in, although he'd refused to relinquish his jeans. "Sometimes it starts to wear on me, and it's just best if I get away for a bit." He looked at her. "What's your excuse?"

"I enjoy the company of people, but sometimes its best for me to go off by myself, regroup, and pray. It keeps me focused."

"Oh? What's so desperate that you need to miss the thrill of the party, regroup and pray?"

She looked at him for a moment, seeming to consider whether she would answer him or not. "The direction of my life."

"Get any answers?" he said in a flip tone.

Again the hesitation. "Yes, I've got some answers."

"Aren't you the lucky one."

Karly sighed and turned her back on him, obviously annoyed. She began to walk away, dismissing him.

Earl had to ask. "Have I said something to offend you?" he called to her.

She didn't bother to turn around, saying in a low, firm voice, "Pretty much everything you do offends me, Earl Nezbegay."

He was stunned. *"Excuse me?"*

Shrugging, Karly continued to walk towards the house. "Never mind. My opinion isn't important. Forget I said anything."

Like hell. His boots crunched on the gravel of the Jamison's driveway, his long strides catching up quickly with Karly's shorter ones. "You think you can drop something like that and I'll just ignore it and walk away?"

She nodded, matter of fact, seemingly calm and collected, still with her back to him and still walking away. "Yes. Yes, I do. That's pretty much how you handle most things in your life from what I've seen. You pretend it doesn't exist until you can find the opportunity to run away."

A fury like Earl had not felt in years ignited, and without thinking he reached out and grabbed her arm, forcing her to stop, turn and look at him. "You've got a hell of a nerve," he ground out through gritted teeth.

She gave him an unblinking stare, making no move to pull away from his grasp. She did look down at his hand on her arm and then back up to meet his furious gaze before she spoke. "You have a sarcastic streak whenever something spiritual is mentioned in your presence. I find that particularly offensive about you. In addition, you have a general air of latent anger that I also find rather ... *oppressive* I guess is the best word."

"Care to give me the courtesy of explaining why my sarcasm is *particularly offensive* to you as opposed to just *plain 'ole offensive?"* Earl worked to keep his hand from bruising her arm.

Karly gave him an impatient look. "You're a *trained minister*, Earl. Your rejection of God and His Call, not to mention the advantages you were given to achieve your schooling, is ... offensive." She appeared to loose a bit of steam as the words were spoken aloud.

"As a *trained minister* I know that judging others ranks right up there with some serious sinning, Miss Martin. You'd best watch yourself before you offend the Almighty in your valiant quest to champion Him."

Eyes snapping, she didn't back down an inch. "I'm not judging you, Earl. I'm simply stating facts and my reaction as a result of them. Perhaps it's your own deep - seated issues that make you feel like I'm passing criticism over your life's choices."

"What do you know about my life's choices?" he said in a low voice.

She tossed her hair over her shoulder and lifted her chin a notch. "I know that life's a test, one big giant pass or fail exam that doesn't finish until we die. I know that things happen. *Terrible, terrible, hard things.*" Earl felt her tremble, a tremor that seemed to travel right through her. "I know that some of us bend and some of us break as a result of these things." He watched in stunned silence as her eyes filled with tears and her voice shook as she whispered. "I just would have thought your faith would have kept you from breaking, that's all. I would have hoped that even being stripped bare and ragged, your faith would have held you from going over that edge."

Earl looked at her and her tears and all of a sudden felt that she was talking more about herself than him. Releasing her arm, he mentally shook his head and then took a small step back from her. "Well," he said calmly, for suddenly all the anger had simply disappeared, "about me, you thought wrong."

They stared at each other for a moment and then Karly reached her hand up and palmed his cheek. He felt the heat of it pass through his body and his toes curled in his boots. "In my prayers each night, I'm drawn to you," she whispered. "Your ... sorrow and anger and ... *angst.* I pray for peace and happiness for you, Earl. I pray for you to have joy and laughter once again. For some reason I can't explain even to myself, I want that for you so very much. I know God wants that for you, too. I know He has forgiven all of us from the Grand Mistakes of Our Past." She laughed and smiled bitterly. "We're the only ones that still struggle with the guilt of it all. We're the ones who just can't seem to *let it all go.*"

Earl couldn't resist, and reached up to put his hand over hers as it still rested against his cheek. He would have given just about anything he had if she would stay here, like this, touching him and looking at him like she really cared for him. "It's mighty impossible to let go of the guilt when it stares you in your face each and every day," he said quietly.

"Trust me," she said with a wry look, "something doesn't need to be present staring you right in the face to make it impossible to forget. Out of sight does not mean out of mind, or heart, or soul ... *believe me.* I don't want this part of your life to be your defeat, Earl. I want it to be your victory. That's what I pray for. Triumph. Success. I pray that for you each and every night."

"Under the stars?" he said in a mocking tone. It slipped out before he could help himself.

Karly pulled her hand away from his cheek and his grasp and took a step back. His cheek felt achingly cold where her palm had been. "There you go again, Earl. Are you sarcastic because it's an easier emotion to handle, or because it keeps people at a distance? Do you even know the answer to that?"

He shrugged and stuffed both hands in his pockets, suddenly tired to the bone. "Probably a little bit of both."

"You must be *some guy* to want nobody's company but your own."

He pinned her with his stare. "Uh oh, be careful. Do I detect a little bit of sarcasm from you, Miss Martin?"

She sighed and wrapped herself more tightly with her shawl. "Yes. Yes, you do. And if this is the way you feel on a regular basis then I'll add another emotion to my list of what I feel for you: pity."

Earl cocked his head to the side, and his long dark ponytail swung out behind him. "Hmmm. I've heard "offensive", "oppressive", and now you're adding "pity". Seems like that's the best one of the bunch, really."

"No," Karly said, "believe it or not there are some much, much better ones that I think about in regard to you. But that's just another thing I've got to pray about." And before he could get out another word, she walked back into the party, leaving him alone with the wonderful company of himself.

But you don't have to stand up all alone
Just put your hand in mine
Climb on a back that's strong
Yeah, you can get what you want[16]

December, 2001
Huerfano, New Mexico

Ten: Persistent Christians Save Everyone They Meet

David Shafer was the perfect man. *Almost.* He was kind, hard working, and had a great sense of humor. His family was loving and supportive, happy that he had found a place in his life that suited him, seemingly unconcerned that it wasn't part of the family business, and positively delighted that whatever it was it had kept him relatively close to home. Over the course of the past weeks and months, Karly had gotten to know David's mother and father, Neil and Elaine Shafer. Both were down to earth people who welcomed Karly with a genuine burst of love and affection. Karly never saw Neil Shafer in anything more than a battered old pair of jeans, a rough flannel shirt, mud spattered boots, and a sweat stained cowboy hat, and yet he carried himself with a pride of purpose that would have done a Wall Street banker proud. Elaine Shafer had that take – no - prisoners style of behaving that came from being a life - long rancher's wife and the mother of four strapping sons. "All of them were taller than me before they hit

---

[16] "Climb On", by Shawn Colvin, John Leventhal, Caedmon's Call, *40 Acres*, 1998

their teens," she told Karly during one of their many conversations over a hot cup of tea in the homey Shafer kitchen. "I knew that was coming and established early on that I was a lot tougher than I looked. I remember Andrew giving me sass one day saying, 'Momma, pretty soon I'm going to be bigger than you and you won't be able to make me do nothing.' I looked at him – almost right in the eye at the time - and said, 'Son, pretty soon you're going to be just like your father and covered in hair from head to toe. All I need to do is get one good handful and tug and you'll wear a pink tutu if I insist on it.' That ended that little spate of rebellion."

"But as I recall, Momma," David felt inclined to point out during that same conversation, "Andrew is also the one that you claim caused you the most gray hair."

"Now, David, no sense giving away family secrets. Karly thinks I'm this lovely *natural brunette*, she doesn't need to know I've got more invested in Clairol Nice 'N Easy than I do in my retirement fund," but she laughed out loud and smiled delightedly when David gave her a quick kiss on the cheek.

Karly enjoyed the similarity both she and David shared in their respective careers. They traded ideas and suggestions for problems with difficult students and spent many evenings grading papers, writing plans, and doing a hundred other things that teachers never have time to do during class time. Like Karly, David seemed to view his teaching profession as more of a 'call' than a 'job', and it was novel and nice to have someone who naturally understood that frame of mind.

David was attentive and affectionate without being overbearing. One night, after about two months of dating, Karly told him, in fits and starts, about Benjamin. Had she not thought he was a wonderful man before, afterwards she would have had no doubt. He'd applauded her difficult but noble decision, seemed genuinely delighted that she had regular contact with Darin and Viv, and understood her chosen stand on celibacy outside of marriage. He'd embraced her and given her a firm hug and kiss and said, "Guess that means I'll just have to rush you down the aisle all that much quicker, huh?"

They shared a passion for the outside, in particular the natural flora and fauna of New Mexico, and spent hours of free time hiking and exploring the absolutely spectacular landscape that surrounded them. To the delight of both of them, Karly had a natural affinity for horseback riding, and rarely a week went by that they didn't show up at the ranch for dinner, visiting, and a long trek out on their favorite horses. Most Sundays after church found Karly with the Shafer family, laughing, joking, and relaxing.

And that's where the almost perfect man had just one, tiny crack. David had no interest in God or church or anything spiritual. "Look at me, Kar," he'd said during one of their many conversations on the subject. "I'm healthy, happy, content, well adjusted … I don't need God. Why mess with things? Why make changes when things are so fine already?"

"I think you'd find a wonderful blessing if you opened up your life to God."

"But your life has not been like mine. You've had a difficult family life and have faced some trials and hardships that could have destroyed a weaker person. You made wise choices and found support and reassurance in a commendable place – church."

"What about you? What if you faced trials and hardships at some point in your life?"

"I probably will. But look at my network of support: I've got my family, loads of friends, even a terrific relationship with colleagues at work. I'm not saying I'd never seek out God, that would be foolish, but I have to honestly say that right now I can't imagine a scenario in which God would fit into my life."

David had given her a quick kiss and a gentle caress across her back. "What's the big deal, anyway? I *support* you in your passion and interest in Godly things. I think that's one of the things that initially drew me to you. *Your goodness.* You care about people and the world and have a general commitment to doing the right thing. That's why we are such a good match, I think. Because I have a high standard of defining right and wrong, too. I just do it based on my own definition, not based on an organization like a church or a book like the Bible, setting all the ground rules. I'd never stand in the way of your religious convictions."

"What if we got married and had children?" for David regularly spoke of a life together for the two of them.

He'd given her a sweet smile and drew her into an embrace. "If going to church and doing all that God stuff makes them just like you, I'm all for it." David had touched her face and run his hand through her hair. "Why are you making such a big deal about this, Love? Look how well things are between us, now. Take Sunday, for instance. You go off and do your little God things that you gotta do, I sleep late and read the paper. We meet up for lunch and then have a wonderful time at my family's. I've come to some of the churchy little functions you've asked me to go to." He gave her a teasing smile. "Hey, I even braved that big Tent Meeting and I wasn't even sure what I was hoping to catch. *Now I know.* I'd walk through fire for you, Karly, and you know it."

Yeah, he'd walk through fire, but he wouldn't attend church Sundays with her or even entertain the idea of doing something Godly together like attending a local Bible study that one of the young married couples who attended the chapel had tried to initiate. Again, David had supported her in her attendance but had declined to go along with her. There was something about his attitude toward her spiritual self that bothered her. Almost like it was equivalent to a passion she might have for baseball or knitting or jogging. It was a nice *hobby* in his eyes that he was quite happy to have her pursue. Just don't think he'd ever develop an interest, thank you very much.

As Christmas approached she battled with herself on a continual basis. Did she love him? He'd told her he loved her. Did she want to spend her life with him? He'd told her that he had a major surprise for her for Christmas, and she suspected it was a proposal. Was passive acceptance to her religious stand really any better than Paul's blatant challenging of it? Karly found it was ironic that the relationship she shared with David was light year's better *already* than her parent's marriage, and yet one of the few things her parents *did* have in common was their mutual interest and commitment to God.

Increasingly, she began to feel like she had felt during those dark, terrible days when she had been with Paul. Only this time there was two distinct differences: she prayed continually for God's direction and she talked to people she trusted.

Prayer had become a substantial part of her life. Besides praying at night under the stars, she prayed when she drove and when she walked back and forth to school each morning. Because it was a Christian school, she had the added perk of being able to pray with the children as well. She never asked for specifics. Tammy had told her that wasn't the right way. She simply prayed for the Lord's guidance, for clear direction, and for the Lord's continual peace and wisdom.

She called Tammy and asked for her prayers. She spoke to her at length about David (in the mission school office, calling collect, as her trailer was too remote to have a phone line installed economically). And both of them had made a pact to pray for the other regarding specific life issues. They tried to speak at least once a week to keep each other's needs and concerns up to date. Hanging up with her friend, Karly felt peace and assurance because someone who loved and cared for her, *and who had a similar mindset in regard to spiritual things*, had made a committed stand to pray for her.

Finally, the Lord opened up a rather unexpected source in the form of Edith Jamison. Their frequent meals had continued as the school year progressed, and Karly found the adult camaraderie with Edith and Sam invaluable, even though the Jamisons were old enough to be her grandparents. The three of them, setting their age differences aside, shared a common bond in the Lord, a passion for the missionary call, and a genuine love for the people and place in which they lived. Karly had grown to love and respect them, delighting in their funny quirks and the frequently sassy conversations that two people married for close to forty years naturally develop.

One afternoon, after she had turned out the lights and locked up the school building, rather than making her way home Karly had walked to the Jamison's house. It was a small, ranch style building, built out of stucco and painted white with a slate roof like most of the homes in the area. The front door faced east. *All* front doors faced east in Navajo homes. "Originally, when the first missionaries came, they made a big to do about trying to break the Navajo's superstitious customs," Edith explained. "They argued with the Indians that doors *did not* need to face east, that a home with a door facing west was not going to be filled with bad luck as the Navajos claimed. Those missionaries built houses with doors facing west, *the exact opposite* of the way "good luck" houses should be built to prove their point." Edith gave Karly a grin and waited for the inevitable question.

"And? Did the missionaries have houses that were filled with good luck with doors facing west?" Karly asked with a grin.

Edith laughed. "Oh, I don't know if they ever were able to determine the level of luck they had in their houses. They were too busy sweeping and dusting and cleaning, trying to keep the sand and dust and dirt that continually blew from the west into their front doors. Back in those days, you didn't shut a house up tight with air conditioning, you kept every available door and window open so you could catch a breeze." Edith chuckled. "There were quite a few missionaries who learned the hard way to ask *why* some Indian customs and traditions were put into place before they preached the need for change."

Letting herself into the *east facing* front door, Karly called out, "Anyone home?"

"Hello dear! What a nice surprise. Here to help me fix dinner?"

"No, you weren't going to feed me tonight and you know it. You're just being polite."

"I'm never polite, but I can be diplomatic," Edith chuckled.

"Can I ... pick your brain about something?" Karly sat down in 'her' chair at the table after helping herself to some cookies from the cookie jar.

Edith poured two glasses of iced tea, then sat down facing Karly. "Of course. Shoot."

At first, Karly kind of tripped and fell over her story. But she finally told Edith the unedited version: her family history, her Paul history, everything about Benjamin and brought Edith right up to the current David chapter. She tried to paint an accurate, unbiased profile of her life, and when she finally fell silent, thought she had done a pretty good job.

"I can't tell you to marry David or not marry him, you know."

"Even if I offered you real cash?" Karly teased.

"How much are we talking?" Edith teased back.

"No, seriously, I know you can't," Karly said, "and quite frankly I don't think I want that from you."

"Then what do you want from me, dear?"

"You've been married a million years, Edith ..." Karly said.

"A million and three," Edith laughed.

"I don't want a marriage like my parents, but I would like a marriage like yours and Sam's. So, I guess what I want from you is advice. Any kind of advice you can give me."

Edith sighed. "Oh dear, this gray hair is making people think I'm wise again." She shook her head. "That's *sooo* dangerous." She looked at Karly. "Let me go get something, okay?" She walked back into her bedroom and returned shortly, holding a framed picture. She handed it to Karly. It was an old fashioned black and white portrait of a young boy, freckle faced with slicked down dark hair and dark, smiling eyes. He sat with his hands folded in front of him on top of a picture book. He looked about seven. Edith let Karly study the photo for long moments without speaking. Finally, Karly looked up at her questioningly.

"That's Rudy. My oldest son." Karly knew that the Jamisons had one son named Tim who lived in California with his wife and two children. "Rudy died when he was nine of a genetic disease known as Cystic Fibrosis."

"I'm sorry ..." Karly began.

Edith waved an impatient hand. "I'm not showing you the picture and telling you about Rudy so you'll feel sorry for me. You asked me about my marriage. I'm showing you and telling you this," she pointed to Rudy's picture, "because of that.

"Sam and I met in a church youth group. We were high school sweethearts and married right out of college. We've been together for a lot more years than the forty - plus we've been married. We've always had a lot of common purposes: love of each other, God, missionary work, the Navajos, our children. I put up with his disorganization and laziness and he puts up with my temper and need to control every speck of my existence. Those differences are part of what makes us so good; we compliment each other and make each other better by being together. We've accomplished far greater things for the glory of God together than we ever would have done apart. We knew it when we were seventeen and we know it now when we are sixty - four.

"Rudy was our first child. He was born two years after we were married, when we were in training to be missionaries in Africa. We had learned all of the language and cultural information and were simply trying to drum up enough support to get us to the Congo and keep us there. My getting pregnant with Rudy was a surprise. We'd wanted to wait a bit, worried that we wouldn't be able to give enough attention to our child *and* our work in those first years, so the original plan had been to wait for about five years before we tried to start a family." Edith got quiet and took a sip of her iced tea. "When I got pregnant, it set us back a bit in our plans, for you see we needed to raise even more support because now we were not a couple but a family. We were frustrated already with how slow the support was coming in and were devastated when we realized our timetable was going to have to be pushed back even further." Edith drew a deep sigh, "I've always carried guilt about those initial reactions to Rudy ...

"Sam was working as an assistant pastor at a large church in Michigan and I was teaching at the local public school. Rudy was sickly almost from the moment of his birth with all kinds of problems: lung ailments, digestive problems. He was born at the start of the summer, and his first visit to the hospital was from severe dehydration from the heat. Before he was one we received the diagnosis of Cystic Fibrosis. We were told it was a genetic disease that affected the lungs and the digestive system, and that with treatment we could expect him to live *maybe* to ten or eleven."

Edith looked at Karly. "Sam and I were devastated. It was like *we* had been given a death sentence ourselves. We took our little boy home from the doctor's that day and sat on the back porch of the little bungalow the church had provided us with and Sam and I just sat and cried and cried.

"We withdrew the request to go to Africa. We knew that we could never take Rudy to such a remote location, and decided instead to try to find something here in the United States near hospitals and other medical necessities. Within a year, the opportunity to come here to Huerfano came up. Property had been deeded to the Senior Board of Missions with the stipulation that the facility had to cater to the Navajos and have a Christian base. It was Sam and I who thought of the school and dreamed initially of what we hoped it would become, but it was hundreds of people praying and supporting and encouraging us that got us to where we are today.

"This climate turned out to be good for Rudy. I firmly believe that we had a longer time with him because of the dry air. He died at the Farmington Hospital just a month after he turned nine. He'd wanted to be a missionary you know."

Edith smiled and took a deep breath. "When I got pregnant with Tim, all our family and friends *went nuts*. They couldn't believe we would be so cavalier as to risk another child with a genetic disease. But you know what, Karly? It was something that Sam and I prayed about and came to a decision about *together*. We both felt that the Lord was supporting us in the decision and went ahead with it. We put it with the Lord and went from there. Tim was born healthy and without Cystic Fibrosis. His children are healthy, too."

Edith smiled at Karly. "So, you're probably wondering what all this has to do with our marriage, huh? You see, our strength as a couple was our faith, Karly. We weathered the impatience of the slow accumulation of support to go to Africa. We weathered the horrors of a terminally ill child. We weathered the disappointment of having to give up our dream to be African missionaries and were able to reinvent ourselves into missionaries to the Navajos. We weathered the ups and downs of starting a school and church from scratch. And we weathered the fear and uncertainty of conceiving another child who could have been born with a terminal illness. And through all the difficulties and uncertainties of life we were able to delight in the love and joy and laughter and success that we experienced in abundance."

Edith reached across the table and took Karly's hand. "When things are going well, it is so easy to think life will end happily ever after and that love will conquer all. But the reality of life is that it's *never* predictable and *never* easy. You should go into a marriage with all the positive weaponry you have, and *never, ever* settle for less than you want. Part of being a faithful servant of God is listening to God's still small voice *and then obeying.*

"Is David the right person for you? I don't know. But God does. What do your head and your heart tell you, Karly? Are you settling for less? As wonderful as he seems, is something important missing? Probably, you can answer all of these questions right now if you put your mind to it. But the hard part will be putting all the answers together, realizing what God wants you to do, and acting on it. The wisest choices are rarely the easiest. Stepping out in faith often means doing things that make no sense to your head or your heart, but gives your soul peace." She squeezed Karly's hand. "Have I helped at all, dear?"

Karly nodded. "Yes. Yes you have, Edith. I'm *so glad* I spoke with you."

Walking home, Karly prayed again for God's direction. She asked for wisdom to see the right and the wrong, and then the courage and strength to act on what God made clear to her.

The very next night, when David and she went out to dinner, David asked her to marry him.

And Karly knew what answer she *should* give David. But instead, she asked him for time to think and pray about it.

By the time of the Jamisons' New Years Eve Party, Karly had beaten herself up until she was bruised inside and out. Ten days ago David had proposed to her, and for ten long days she'd kept him waiting for her answer. For the first time since they had been dating she found herself getting unreasonably angry with him. How could this guy be so perfect?

Take all the time you need, Kar. I'm not going anywhere but here, right by your side. How could he be so peaceful and collected? *I'd love to go to the Jamison's party. Ringing in the New Year with the woman I love and the people that are so important to her sounds like the best way to start off a fresh year together.* Why was she being so inconsistent? *You can answer all of these questions right now if you put your mind to it. What the hard part will be is putting all the answers together and realizing what God wants you to do and acting on it.*

David was the most wonderful man she had ever met. *As wonderful as he seems, is there an important part missing that you wish he had but didn't?* YES. She looked back on her life and tried to imagine its course had faith been removed from it. Completely. Not rejected, but simply never having been there at all. It was a bleak picture. The difficult times with her parents darkened almost to blackness, making a childhood that had been unhappy seem unbearable. Her heartache regarding Benjamin magnified to tension and fear at the prospect of the poor decisions and selfish choices she probably would have made regarding him. *You should go into a marriage with all the positive weaponry you have and never, ever settle for less than you want.* If she married David would she be settling for less than she had hoped and dreamed? YES. She wanted marriage and family and children and partnership, and all that she saw with Edith and Sam and Viv and Darin *and not a speck less.* While her head and her heart told her that David was a fine choice, her soul ached with the wrongness of it. *Stepping out in faith often means doing things that make no sense to your head or your heart, but gives your soul peace.*

She sighed deeply. Standing under the red oak tree in the Jamison's back yard just a few hours before midnight on New Year's Eve, she knew that she must speak with David *now, tonight.* It was unfair to keep him waiting, and it was cowardly of her to hide behind the pretext of prayer when she knew the right choice. Karly sighed. She owed David a truthful answer and her answer was NO. She would do it tonight after the party.

Hearing the back door slam, she turned to see Earl striding out of the house and stepping off the porch. Karly sighed at the bad timing of it all. Rarely were her and Earl's brief conversations positive and tonight of all nights she was not in the most positive frame of mind. Why did he always seem angry? If Earl's words didn't communicate it then his body movements sure did. Hands thrust in the pockets of his jacket, his face a fierce mask of impatience and unhappiness, he stood for a moment breathing deeply in the cool night air. "Trying to escape the crush of the party, too?" Karly asked him, giving him an opportunity to adjust to her presence.

He had been unaware of her presence, that was immediately evident, and – *surprise* - he was completely unhappy about it. She watched his already tense body harden into granite. Earl grumbled something under his breath and then pinned her with his dark, annoyed stare. "What's your excuse?"

Theirs was the oddest relationship in the world. They rarely spoke, saw each other only infrequently, and yet seemed to rub each other raw simply if their shadows passed each other. Try as she might, Karly seemed to infuriate him at every turn. It had started with that first day in his home when she had mistakenly allowed Theresa to con her into doing something she shouldn't have. That had made her gun - shy and hesitant around him. Theresa seemed to delight in relaying to Karly all the things Karly did that drove Earl nuts: rearranging furniture (she'd only been trying to help!), giving creative assignments in class that Marion brought home and described *in detail* (that was doing her job!), and spending so much time with Theresa (they were friends!). When Karly sputtered and tried to explain herself, Theresa had only laughed at her. "Hey, Sister, *it's Earl.* You don't need to justify yourself to me. And it's a waste of time and breath to try to explain or understand *him.* I'm telling you all this stuff 'cause I love the fact that Earl's little perfect, organized world is finally getting a wake up call. *You go, Sister.*"

Most annoying of all was an utter rejection of Earl's faith *and* anyone else's. On the brief occasions that they did have contact, he had a mocking quality in the way he spoke to her. And should God or something spiritual come into the conversation, well he did everything but roll his eyes and groan at her apparent idiocy. Theresa's faith, and consequently Marion's, was tenuous at best, and Karly felt she was in a continual uphill battle. When Earl was on the scene, even for brief moments, victory seemed always to belong to him.

Increasingly, Karly found herself feeling just as she did at this very moment of time looking into his angry eyes: apologetic, apprehensive, and unsure of herself. *Enough of this already.* Karly straightened her spine and her shoulders. *You may be a miserable specimen of a man, Earl Nezbegay, but I'll be darned if you'll drag me down or intimidate me anymore. Step back, Jack.*

Standing in the cold darkness of the Jamison's back yard. she heard herself say things to him that she had never dared to even *think*, let alone speak aloud. But there they were, hanging in the air between them: *everything you do offends me, you run away, you have a sarcastic streak that I find particularly offensive, your rejection of God and His call, your own deep seated issues ... Whoa.* When Karly lets loose, *she lets loose.*

How to win friends and influence people, Evil Twin said with stunned amazement.

Earl looked as though his head would explode. He looked like he either wanted to shake her until her head fell off her shoulders or haul off and smack her. She couldn't really blame him. What right did she have to lay bare all of the things she was privy to about his life's heartaches and sorrows? How would she feel were the situation reversed and he was dangling all of her dirty laundry in front of her? She thought of Benjamin and the pain of what she was missing, coupled with the agony of her own poor life choices. Woven in with the difficult decisions she had made was the realization she would *never, ever know until she died* if they had been the right choices or the wrong choices.

Oh God, forgive me for this moment, she prayed suddenly.

The steam that she'd been filled with to put Earl in his place and mark her own territory died a sudden death. The reality was that she prayed for Earl each and every night. Whether she wanted to or not, whether they'd had a run in that day or he'd belittled her yet again, her day was not complete without her mentioning him in prayer before her Lord. Earl was in her head, her heart, and her soul whether Karly wanted him there or not. Remembering Earl in prayer was almost like her job, her mission. She heard Tammy talking to her at the Outer Banks and saying, *It's the worst feeling in the world to give up on your God - given dreams.*

Suddenly, all she wanted to do was comfort him like he was a heartbroken child. The wave of desire to touch him was all - powerful, and she reached up to touch his warm, smooth cheek. Her cool hand warmed almost immediately from the heat of his skin, and she felt the tension and the anger drain out of him instantly. She was unaware of the specific words that she spoke in the dark and the quiet, she just opened up her heart to him and tried to get him to understand ... *things.* She felt inadequate, and lame. Without going into her own personal details that would only muddle the already swirling waters, Karly tried desperately to get him to see that his pain and his guilt were things *he* was holding onto and only *he* could release. It was a precious, private thing that she gave when she admitted that she felt drawn to pray for him nightly.

And standing there in the darkness, proud, handsome, and arrogant, *he mocked her.* Like a beautiful painting a child goes to the trouble to draw for you and inscribe and wrap up ... he crumpled it and threw it in the trash without even glancing at it.

Walk away, Karly, before you say anything more you will regret.

She bit the inside of her mouth to keep herself silent, and still a few choice comments worked their way out.

Walk away, Karly.

Finally, she did.

You step inside my heart
And I am amazed
I love to hear You say
Who I am is quite enough[17]

January, 2002
Huerfano, New Mexico

Eleven: Enlightened Christians Never Lie

If David Shafer couldn't understand the importance of God in Karly's life, he sure as heck couldn't understand her rationale for saying no to his marriage proposal. Their relationship ended bitterly and abruptly, leaving Karly feeling significantly battered and bruised.

Theresa didn't make things any easier. Karly had convinced her to help out in her classroom three times a week with the start of the new year, although Theresa said Karly had only asked for her help because she was cheap labor. The reality was that Theresa had a real gift for communicating with the children. She had the intuition to know who needed her company and support at any given moment. Zipping around the classroom in her motorized wheelchair, some days she seemed to be everywhere at once. Karly always got twice as much accomplished when Theresa was present compared to the days she was not. "Give me a raise then," she'd said with a smirk when Karly had told her. Consequently, their friendship had grown and solidified into a real give and take of advice and emotion. *"Are you nuts?"* Theresa had said when Karly had told her of the break up and reason

---

[17] Beautiful, By Bethany Dillon and Ed Cash, *Bethany Dillon*, 2004

why. "The guy's good looking, his family's rich, he's gainfully employed, he's nice ... Jeeze, is he into quadriplegics? Give him my phone number. I'll marry him in a minute. What are you waiting for anyway? If David Shafer wasn't perfect enough for you then you're in big trouble because I don't think you'll find anyone better."

"I'm not looking for *perfect*," Karly had tried to explain. "I'm not so foolish as to think that *I'm* perfect, and I'm not looking for a man whose perfect either! I want ... certain things that I think are worth waiting for. And I'm stepping out on faith here to believe that God will provide the things that He's encouraged me to make important in my life."

Theresa just shook her head. "Well, I'll encourage you to look around at what else there is to choose from. LouRay Betselie's been looking for a wife for years. Too bad he's not rich because I doubt he's got many more years left in him. I think the one eye would creep me out in bed though." Theresa gave a shiver of revulsion. "And there's always my illustrious brother. I know he's wild about you, but I get the distinct impression that he bugs the heck out of you."

Karly looked at her. "What do you mean he's 'wild about me'? Earl can't stand the sight of me, and when we're together all I ever seem to do is make him absolutely furious – whether I intend to or not."

Theresa gave her a pitying look. "Don't you have a clue about *anything* besides this dusty classroom and these continually annoying kids?" When Karly continued to give her a blank look Theresa sighed. "Look, Earl is ... complicated. No one, including me, has an accurate handle on all the stuff that goes on in that thick skull of his. But one thing I do know, beyond a shadow of a doubt, it that he is absolutely awestruck by you." At Karly's continued disbelief Theresa finally said, "Put it this way. Why do you two clash so powerfully? I think it's because you both care *too much*. But, if I were choosing between Earl and LouRay, I'd pick LouRay. He's a honey. Earl is just a big, controlling pain in my ... butt," she said looking cautiously around to see if any children had slipped in early from recess.

Karly flew to see Darin, Viv, and Benjamin over the Easter holiday. Sam and Edith drove her to the Albuquerque Airport and then picked her up two week's later. Benjamin was now a two-year-old toddler, talking and laughing and interacting with his world. While it was glorious to see him, she was happy to fly home at the end of the two weeks and reassure herself that her life was full and rich and rewarding, even without Ben's presence. Pulling up in front of her trailer, Edith said in stunned awe, "Oh … my … Karly … *You've been busy!"*

The property around her trailer was a mass of spring flowers, a veritable explosion of colors and textures. As she was leaving Karly had noticed an exceptionally large amount of weeds sprouting up from the newly warmed earth, and had intended to get busy once she returned. As the three of them climbed out of the Jamison's car, Karly was stunned at what she saw.

"I had no idea that you worked so hard last fall, Karly, planting all these spring plants!" Edith walked up to the trailer's steps which were framed in the most glorious display of huge purple daisies. "And where did you have time to plant these annuals? Did you do that before you left two weeks ago? My goodness! This must have taken you days and days!" The three of them walked around the trailer, and from every angle there was a glorious profusion of colors and scents. The heavy scent of floral perfume permeated the late afternoon air while the lazy buzz of bumblebees and numerous flashes of butterflies seemed to advertise where the best pollen was located.

When they got back to the car, Karly threw her arms around Sam Jamison. "Oh, Sam! Thanks so much! You shoveled snow whenever it was needed all winter and cleaned the outside of the trailer and repaired the wash shed when I first arrived. *That was more than enough.* But I had no idea you'd planted all of these flowers for me. How did you know I wanted this?"

"Yes," Edith's gaze zeroed in on her husband. Looking at him through narrowed eyes she said, "how *did* you know to do this wonderful thing and where did you ever find the time or the energy?"

Sam glanced at his wife and then at Karly. "I, ah, well, just did it whenever I had a few moments here and there …" he said rather hesitantly.

Karly gave him a kiss on the cheek and another brief hug. "Well, *thank you*. From the bottom of my heart."

"I hope you'll do the same for our garden, Sam. I've been trying to get you to plant a few plants and pull a few weeds for *years."* His wife had her hands firmly planted on her hips and appeared to be working very hard at *not* tapping a toe impatiently.

"Why sure, honey. I'd be happy to do that," Sam said easily.

"Today?"

Sam shook his head. "Well, no not today. I'm a bit tired from driving back and forth to the airport. And tomorrow's Saturday. You know I like to rest on that day so I'm refreshed and at my best for Sunday's sermon. Maybe ..."

"Tomorrow," Edith said with a finality and firmness that made Karly frown. What was going on? "Tomorrow will be just fine, I think. I'm sure you'll get a lot of personal satisfaction of a job well done and *maybe* you can rehearse your sermon in your head while you're working." Edith turned and headed for the passenger side door of the car. "Welcome home, Karly. Come on, *dear*. I think we've got time to go to the nursery in Farmington and pick out just what I want." She got in, shut the door and stared pointedly at Sam through the front windshield.

"Is everything okay, Sam?" Karly said glancing back and forth between the two of them.

Sam sighed. "Yeah, everything is fine."

"Thanks again for the flowers, Sam."

"You're welcome, Karly."

Karly watched the Escort as it drove slowly down the dirt path that led away from her trailer. Edith had her finger pointed at Sam and seemed to be reading him the riot act, making Karly frown again in puzzlement. Maybe she had better get up to their house tomorrow to reciprocate some of the hard word that Sam had put into her garden. He must still be carrying some residual guilt from her initial arrival and the condition of her trailer. Sitting down on the front steps and gently fingering the purple petals she had to smile. The yoga had worked wonders. Sam's back hadn't bothered him in months.   Once the yoga class ended, he'd taken up bicycling and regularly bicycled all over the mission grounds and even back and forth into town.   He'd dropped about fifteen pounds and looked stronger than ever.   Karly had attributed his general new feeling of well being to his snow shoveling this winter at her trailer, too.   She'd definitely have to talk with him privately and tell him they were square after all this time.   Chuckling, she shook her head, stood, and hauled her suitcase into the trailer.

Home.   It felt like home, now.   Furnished in early – American eclectic/bohemian/thrift store/yard sale, it nevertheless had a comfortable welcoming feel about it if she did say so herself.   In the end, she'd replaced the original couch, never able to really believe the idea that the filth could be completely washed or aired out.   The thrift store replacement was big and cushy and had taken her, Sam, and Earl significant negotiation to get it inside.   She discovered the magic of pawnshops in Farmington, and not only had she acquired some really beautiful jewelry at unbelievable prices but had gotten some decorative pieces that reflected her growing love of the southwest and the Navajo culture.

"Hello, Goliath, come give me some sugar," she said to the huge striped tiger cat that was curled up on the corner chair.   The chair was covered with a colorful blanket patterned in the style of an ancient Navajo rug.   The cat studied her from one partially opened eye, apparently trying to decide if he would forgive her for abandoning him for two weeks.   She sat down on the floor near him and began to pet him behind his right ear and under his chin.   Almost immediately, a massive purr began.   "Did you cooperate with everyone while I was away?   Mr. and Mrs. Jamison didn't seem to have any complaints.   Did Marion come and visit you much?"   Goliath had shown up on her doorstep approximately four months ago, right after the New Year when she had been at her lowest after ending things with David.   Full grown and ornery, he'd taken to sleeping on the hood of her car when the engine was warm and under her front porch steps the rest of the time.   When he began leaving her "gifts" of half chewed mice and birds outside the front door, she had decided that feeding him on a regular basis might calm down his killer instinct.   She'd fallen right into his calculating paws. Next thing she knew he was battling to get inside the trailer, settling in like an obnoxious relative. In the end, he had commandeered Karly's favorite chair for himself, took up half the bed each night, and in general, trained Karly to be exactly the type of owner *he* required.

But Goliath was a good listener, never minding the topic, and provided fairly low - maintenance companionship. On school days he'd escort her down to the mission school, waltzing in to take his spot on her classroom windowsill. In the evenings he'd amble back up the hill with her to claim his chair. She'd made naming him into a writing contest that had originally been intended for just her students, but had spread to the entire school. The best essay had come from a child in Naomi's class, a 3rd grader who had cleverly rewritten the story of David and Goliath from the point of view of the rock. The rock, feeling guilty for the demise of the giant it had killed, had requested permission to name the cat in the giant's honor. Karly had been delighted at the skill and cleverness of the writing, Naomi had been put out that one of her students had been enthusiastic regarding some 'ridiculous contest that takes away from the *real* goals of education' and Goliath had received a name - as if he cared. Karly was embarrassed about the number of times she'd thought about him with concern while she visited Viv and Darin's. Goliath most likely had barely spared her a thought.

The following day, Karly worked in the garden with Sam and joined the Jamisons for dinner. Over a casual meal of hamburgers, French fries and a tossed salad, Karly shared stories about her time with Benjamin, Viv and Darin. "I'll get my pictures developed as soon as I finish the roll, and then you'll get to see how cute he is. He's smart, too! Viv says he's doing a whole load of stuff way before the developmental charts say he should." Karly laughed. "They think he might be the youngest member of Mensa."

"Do you realize how fortunate all of you are with this relationship, Karly?" Edith said with a smile. You tell us all these wonderful things and share letters with us. It is so unique and special that Benjamin has you in his life, and at the same time has Viv and Darin as well."

"I know. The Lord has certainly reassured me time and time again that I made a good choice."

"Is it still hard, though?"

Karly thought about it for a moment. She took a deep breath and looked down at the smear of ketchup on her plate. Deep in her heart was an empty spot that she had grown used to, but could never fill or erase. "Yeah. It always will be hard at certain levels. When I was pregnant, I tried never to think of Benjamin as "my baby" or "my son". It made the decision I had to make possible in the end." She looked up at Sam and Edith. "But it didn't stop me from loving him. That's there in my heart, too, and will never stop. I try when I go to visit him to delight in the life he has and the love and care he receives from Viv and Darin. I could *never* have given him what he has now. *Never.* And I wanted the very, very best for him. The fact that I have regular contact and get to see him now and then, and that he will know me, is a wonderful blessing that I never dreamed would be part of the picture."

"Um, changing subject completely, I have something to tell you, Karly," Sam Jamison began.

"What?"

"Well, I, ah, didn't plant those flowers around your trailer," he said rather hesitantly.

Karly stared at him, stunned. "You didn't?"

Sam shook his head. "No, Karly, I didn't."

"Who did, then?"

"Wait, Karly," Edith said pointedly, "Sam's not finished."

Sam flashed her an impatient glance. "Don't get yourself all worked up again, Edith. I'm gonna straighten it all out. Just relax."

Karly frowned. "Straighten what out?"

Sam sighed. "I didn't shovel your driveway, I didn't wash your trailer, and I didn't repair your washer shed."

"You didn't?" Karly said in genuine puzzlement. She looked at Sam's embarrassed face, and then at Edith's stern expression. "Then who did?"

"I don't know for sure, but I could hazard a guess," Sam said after a moment.

"Who?" Karly racked her brain, dismissing people one after another. She even briefly considered David. "I can't for the life of me ..." and then she had a thought and paused.

Edith and Sam looked at her, almost willing her to come to the same conclusion they had. Sam looked slightly smug and Edith looked deadly serious.

"No ..." Karly said shaking her head in denial.

"We vote for Earl," Edith said finally in a rush, as if she couldn't hold it in any longer.

"But, I do *nothing* but infuriate him! And since your New Year's Party, I don't think we've spoken two words to each other. You're telling me that some of those flowers were just planted these past two weeks. That means that he's been doing this all along ..." Karly looked at them, hesitant to reveal the magnitude of what she'd said to Earl that night of their party. In a low voice tinged with embarrassment and regret, she said, "I told him at your New Year's Eve Party that he *offended me,* and that I *pitied him*, and told him that he was *sarcastic and mocking.*"

"Whoa ..." said Sam looking shocked.

"Good for you," said Edith with a subtle smile.

"Edith! Why would you encourage her to say such strong things to Earl?" Sam exploded.

"Has anything else worked with him?" Edith asked her husband and gave him an unblinking stare.

Sam shook his head, defeated. "No, nothing's worked."

"And it's been over almost fifteen years, Sam. *Fifteen years!*" Edith looked at her husband and then to Karly. Almost to her self, she murmured out loud, "I've always wondered, since he so completely rejected his original call, why he stayed *here* of all places. It would have been so much easier to move. But he didn't."

"I always thought he stayed because Theresa wanted to," Sam said finally.

"I always *prayed* that it was because he didn't really reject everything, and was always hoping that someone would make the effort to reach him," Edith said.

"Well," Sam said with a snort, "Karly hammering him over the head with her tough words sure isn't going to do the trick."

"Oh?" Edith crossed her arms and smiled at him smugly, "how many flowers has Earl planted in *your* garden, Samuel Jamison?"

Something told Karly that if she walked up to Earl and questioned him about everything he'd either refuse to answer her or outright lie. Aside from lying in wait like a reconnaissance mission spy, she was at a loss as to how to proceed. Asking Theresa was out, too. Karly didn't trust her friend not to go right to her brother and batter him with questions, insults, and wicked innuendoes.

The answer to her dilemma was waiting on the front steps of school on Monday morning in the form of Marion Goodluck. "You're here early this morning, Marion," Karly said as she unlocked the door.

"Uncle Earl was driving into Farmington to do errands and I hitched a ride." Marion regularly walked the two miles each day to the mission school.

"Smart girl. What's Uncle Earl up to today?" Maybe she could get some information …

"Oh, nothing big. He likes to go to the library when it first opens. He reads the morning paper and checks out magazines he likes."

"Really? Do you know what he likes to read?"

"Oh yeah. He used to get loads of magazines a long time ago delivered to the house, but had to stop when money got tight. He likes mostly Godly kinds of magazines. I think his favorite is Christianity … ah, Today or something like that. He's got stacks of old ones in his shed. Mom told him he should recycle them, that they were a fire hazard, and he told her to mind her own business. That they were "timeless in quality." I remember that because I asked Uncle Earl what that meant and he said it was like me, no matter how old I got I'd always be very valuable.

"He borrows books all the time, too. Mom thinks all he does is woodwork in that shed, but I find him reading a lot, too. He's got a big old sofa over in the corner that he sits in."

"Reading, huh. What else does Uncle Earl like to do?"

"He likes music. But only certain kinds."

"Oh?" Karly had a flash of Snake reciting provocative words to a Foo Fighter song just to stir up trouble and suddenly missing him terribly. Maybe she could get him to come out and spend the summer with her ... "What kind of music?"

Marion looked uncomfortable. "He turns it off whenever I come into the shed and tells me to mind my own business when I ask what he's listening to. I thought it maybe was some music that I shouldn't hear so I ... snuck in one day when he was away to check it out." Marion's uncomfortable expression turned to one of disgust and boredom. "It was *Christian* rock and roll! Can you believe it? It had all kinds of God words and stuff and no cool stuff at *all*."

"Can you remember what were some of the groups he listened to?"

Marion shook her head. "Nah. It was none I'd ever heard of."

"Some Christian rock is really good. Would you do me a favor? Would you sneak into Uncle Earl's shed and write down the names of some of the CDs he already has? Or at least the artists' names? I'd like to know if he's got ones that I don't have."

"Why don't you just ask Uncle Earl himself?"

"Well, uh, I don't want to get you in trouble. If I bring it up, he'll have to figure out where I heard all this from."

"Oh, yeah ..." Marion shrugged her shoulders. "Sure, next time I get a chance I'll do it."

"Thanks Marion."

A gift subscription to 'Christianity Today' would be a nice start to reciprocating Earl's kindness. *Sent anonymously,* of course, Evil Twin said gleefully. *Two can play at this game, Earl Nezbegay.*

Narrow is the road and too high a price to pay
When loneliness is such a sanctuary[18]

June, 2002
Huerfano, New Mexico

Twelve: Fulfilled Christians Have No Reason To Be Sad

Karly had every intention of going home that first summer, regardless of how difficult a visit it would be. She missed Snake, who had refused to come and visit her in Huerfano, she was desperate to see Tammy, who couldn't manage to get away for a full week during the busy summer, and she sincerely wished to show both her parents and those who'd seen her at her lowest that she was happy, peaceful, and content. *At last.*

But God had other plans. Edith Jamison, seemingly ageless and indestructible, fell and broke her hip on the second to the last day of school. In the end her hip was so badly broken that they had no choice but to replace it with an artificial one, and recovery was slow and tedious. It seemed that everything that could go wrong, did. She developed a blood clot and an infection, and just when it looked like things were looking up she came down with a severe case of pneumonia. Sam was beside himself with worry. With Naomi already in possession of plane tickets to go back

---

[18] Famous Last Words, By Haseltine, Odmark, Mason, Lowell, Jars of Clay, 1999, *If I Left The Zoo*

to visit her sister in the east, Karly volunteered to stay behind and pick up the tremendous slack that Edith's incapacitation created. It was the least she could do. She assumed Sunday School coordination and teaching responsibilities at church, organized and ran the summer Vacation Bible School, and even planned all of the activities for the Tent Meeting festivities scheduled just before school opened in September. And that was in addition to inventory and reordering of next year's school supplies, advertising and promoting the school to the local neighborhoods and churches, and handling inquiries and registration for newly enrolling students. Her summer *vacation* turned out to be more work than her school year.

Edith and Sam were eternally grateful and appreciative, but privately Theresa and Karly wondered if their five - year plan to retirement was going to come sooner then they'd wished. Before everyone's eyes the two of them drooped and faded more each day.

"Have you seen Sammy?" Theresa said one day. "He's run ragged. Between driving back and forth to Farmington to see Edith in the rehab center and all the church and ministerial responsibilities he refuses to delegate, he looks like he's about to drop." Karly was cautiously driving the huge, handicapped accessible van that trundled Theresa around regularly enabling her to cause mischief and mayhem. Today, they along with Marion, were traveling to visit Edith and bring her a little bit of humor and good cheer. Theresa glared at her friend. "And *you* look like you're ready to drop as well. When was the last time you sat down and did absolutely nothing? Huh?"

"I can't remember," Karly mumbled. "But there's *no one else* to do things right now, Theresa, and I refuse to let the Jamisons down. They don't deserve to see everything they've worked for crumble at this late date. I'm in for the long haul until God tells me differently. All I can do is pray for healing for Edith, wisdom for the doctors, and strength and stamina for me and Sam." Karly gave Theresa a crooked smile. "Is God going to all this trouble to keep me here because He doesn't want me to go back home to visit my parents? I could have been easily persuaded not to go with a lot less chaos and disaster."

God kept silent, and when the new school year started Karly did all of her work as well as Edith's. Before everyone's eyes Edith went from a vivacious, outspoken powerhouse to an elderly, subdued lady. She tired quickly and was tremendously slow in recovering from the hip replacement. Rehabilitation had been delayed due to the pneumonia, and once therapy resumed, improvements were slow and sporadic. An entire school year slipped by and summer found Edith still moving slowly and painfully with a walker. Karly once again could not even consider traveling home to see her family, and launched into another responsibility packed summer.

Much to everyone's horror, as the new school year started Edith also had a new diagnosis to deal with: a reoccurrence of her colon cancer. Additional surgery was required to remove the tumor, followed by chemotherapy and radiation therapy that made Edith weak and sick. "The cure is as bad as the curse," Edith moaned to Karly on one of her many visits to Edith's bedside.

Two months into the New Year, Karly and Goliath made their way over to the Jamison's house to check on Sam and see what he needed. Edith was once again back in the hospital from complications relating to her radiation. The frequent midweek meals they had all enjoyed as a threesome had all but disappeared. Karly worried if Sam took the time to eat nowadays. She regularly checked to make sure that the basic foods such as milk, eggs, bread, sugar, and coffee were present in the house. Even if Edith was in the hospital, she reasoned, Sam still needed supplies.

She found Sam with his head on the kitchen table, sobbing.

"Oh, Sam," Karly said, pulling up a chair next to him and putting her arm around him. "What can I do?"

"Nothing," his muffled voice came through the cocoon of his arms, "*nothing*." He sat up and mopped his face with a paper napkin. "I just feel so *overwhelmed*. I am sick with worry over Edith, I've got the mission responsibilities, and I'm not sleeping like I should." He couldn't finish the sentence and choked back new sobs. "All I want to do is *be* with her Karly. I don't want to sleep, eat, … or minister right now. I feel absolutely drained."

Karly looked earnestly at Sam. *"Why are you here?* Why aren't you with her?"

Sam's eyes took on a wild sheen. "I've got stuff to do and no one else to do it but me! People depend on me, Karly! I just can't abandon them. I can't ask you to do anything more! And don't tell me you can do anything more than you're already doing. You're so over - burdened already I'm afraid one night you'll decide to run away. I'm here because Sunday's sermon needs to be prepared, the bulletins need to be run off, I've got to make sure the communion supplies are …"

Karly gripped him by the shoulders and shook him. *"Sam. Stop."*

He looked at Karly. "Go wash your face," she said to him firmly. "Take a drink of cold water. Change your shirt. Then get in your car and drive to Edith. What can get done, *will get done.* What can't, will just have to wait. Okay?"

He stared at her and then took a deep, shaky breath. "Okay."

When Sam drove off to Edith, Karly and Goliath made their way back to her trailer. She went inside and got her car keys. As she pulled away from the trailer in a hail of dust and gravel she prayed, *Guide my words, Lord. Guide every single one.*

Earl was, as she had assumed, in his shed. She knew that because she could hear the muted tunes of music drifting on the wind. Marching over to the shed, she didn't bother to knock, just opened the door and stepped in.

Earl looked up from his woodworking bench and turned off the music using a remote control. Sawdust was in his hair and clear plastic protective glasses were perched on the end of his nose. "Just come right on in," he said and went back to work.

"We need to talk."

"Okay," but he made no effort to stop working or even look at her.

Karly didn't waste any time. "You need to take over some of Sam Jamison's ministerial responsibilities."

Earl turned to her with an incredulous look on his face. "*No way.*"

"*Yes way.* You're the most likely candidate. You have the training, know the people, and you even *have the time,* Earl."

Dismissing her, he turned back to his work and said, "There's just one little thing you're forgetting. *I'm done with all that.*" Then he looked up and his dark eyes pinned her where she stood. "Remember how offensive I am to you? You might not recall that talk, but I kind of play it over regularly in my head for its high entertainment value."

Karly advanced on him across the sawdust - covered floor. "Okay, how about this. The Jamisons have been faithful and loving to you and Theresa and Marion for years and years. You *owe* them."

Earl shrugged, seemingly unmoved. "I owe everyone, Karly. Everyone in this whole darn town. Look, just because you feel some big Christian obligation doesn't mean the rest of us do. Take what you can get. Grab all you can. He who takes advantage ends up with the most toys. That's my motto."

Karly was close enough to touch him if she wished. His eyes grew wary and he took off his protective eyewear as she stood there silently, staring at him. "I don't believe you, Earl. Drop the act with me. I *know* you are not the man you pretend to be." He smirked at her like she was a fool, but she forged on. Karly gestured around the shed. "Is this really it for you, Earl? Are you really finished with life? Are you just going to sit here and exist until you die?" She looked into his now carefully blank face. "Are you going to stay mad at yourself forever?" Karly whispered softly, "Haven't you paid whatever dues you think you owe? Theresa doesn't blame you. Marion doesn't blame you. No one blames you but yourself. *Let it go Earl.* Reclaim your life. Aren't you getting tired of all this?"

"What makes you think you can come in here and fix everything, Karly? Why do you even bother?"

She answered him honestly. "Because when I look at you I see what I could have become. Everyone has horrible mistakes in his or her past, Earl. *Even me.* But someone took the time to pull me back from the brink before I went over the edge."

Earl shrugged again. "My life is just fine right now, thank you. Basic. Uncomplicated. No stress."

Karly snorted. "You *have* no life. You simply travel from one destination to the next, marking time. That's not living, that's existing. But I know you're not dead yet. There's some tiny spark deep inside that is still the person you used to be. *I know that* as sure as I'm standing here in front of you. It's a person who cleans trailers and repairs washer sheds and shovels snow each winter and plants glorious flower gardens each spring. I believe that person will help Sam right now because he knows how much is at stake. *Edith is dying, Earl.* Let Sam have as much time with her as he can before there is no time left."

"You know about all that stuff." It wasn't a question, but a statement of fact.

Karly nodded. "Yes, I've known for a long time."

He cocked his head to one side and reached up to touch Karly's ponytail that was draped over her left shoulder. "But you didn't say anything," he murmured. He fingered her hair letting it slowly spill through his fingers, then picked it up to start all over again.

"Two can play at that game." Karly tried not to look smug, but it was difficult.

His face registered dawning realization. "Ahh, the magazine subscription."

She didn't answer, just stared at him.

"And the CDs that appear every now and then that I swear I haven't bought."

Karly tried her best to look blank.

"And that devotional book that just arrived in the mail ..."

She crossed her arms and tried to step back and pull her hair out of his grasp. He gripped her ponytail firmly with a tight fist. When she relaxed he began to play with it again.

"Anything else?" he murmured.

She arched an eyebrow and remained silent.

It was his turn to look smug. "You haven't caught all of mine yet …"

Karly started in surprise. She was so certain that she had … For the first time Earl gave her a small, hesitant smile. "It's a big one, too."

"What …?"

He arched *his* eyebrow at her and remained silent.

"*Why, Earl?* I want to hear you tell me why you've done those kind things."

He looked at his hand still fingering her hair. "Why did you do it for me?"

She gave him an impatient look that communicated that she had noticed he'd not answered her question. "To return the kindnesses. You obviously didn't want to be recognized formally and thanked. Earl, I even thanked Sam Jamison for some of the things you did! So tell me why … "

Earl sighed. "I do lots of stuff because it *needs* to be done. I care for Theresa, I care for Marion, I help people with deliveries and repairs, I wash trailers and repair washer sheds …" He shrugged. "No big deal. That's what I'm good for."

"I'm gonna stand here all night unless you tell me the truth, Earl Nezbegay. *All night.*"

He licked his lips and hesitated as if gathering the right words. "With everyone else I do it because I feel obligated. I do it because I owe them for something they've done for me or Theresa or Marion, whether they've come and spent time visiting or made and delivered a meal, or stopped by and picked up the girls and taken them out for a ride. People watch out for us and it's payback. Like I told you, I'm in this entire town's debt one way or another. So for everyone else it's just as you said, a 'return of kindness'."

He looked her directly in the eye. "But for you it's been different." He sighed, "I did it at first because you were going to be Marion's teacher, and then because you were so kind to Theresa going out of your way to befriend her …"

Earl stopped and let go of her hair and took steps back from her. He made motions of cleaning up his workspace and putting away his tools.

"You ... well ... you're kind of in my head. I ... think about you and it seems that the more I try to avoid you the more you invade my ... space. I hear about you from Theresa and Marion and from the guys down at the mini - mart, and even LouRay Betselie talks about you! I wonder why all of a sudden some beautiful slip of a girl could so completely turn my world upside down. Even spending no time with you and trying never to speak with you, I find I know more about you and think more about you than anyone else." His back was to her as he made the smooth economical motions of hanging tools and winding up power cords. Almost to himself he said, *"How come?"* out loud.

He turned and crossed his arms, leaning back against his now cleared workbench. "But then I did things for you because you were the first person who was honest with me in a long time. You were tough and somewhat brutal, but you were honest. You were so up front with the hard things you said to me that when you said the nice stuff, like I shouldn't feel guilty and about my inability to let it all go, I was able to hear that, too. You've got a pure heart, Karly. There's no hidden agenda. You talk about praying for me and wanting joy and laughter and victory and triumph in my life. That you could look at me and even *attempt to imagine* those things for me is something." No longer able to look at her, he turned and gazed out the small, open window to his right that framed the glorious New Mexico scenery. In a voice no louder than a whisper he said, "You make me think that *maybe, just maybe* I could one day be a better person. I haven't felt that in over a decade."

When she started to say something he reached out a long arm and put his finger to her lips to keep her quiet. "I'll do anything for Sam that you need me to do *except preach.* There's absolutely nothing you can say or do that will make me do that." He took his finger away. "Take it or leave it."

"I'll take it."

"I knew you would."

"What else have you done that I don't know about?"

He gave her another small smile. "If you guess correctly I won't deny it."

"Will you come down to Sam's office and help me start getting things organized? I can't deal with mine and Edith's and now Sam's stuff. I *understand* Edith's responsibilities; I don't even know where to begin with Sam's."

"I'll come down. Just let me make sure Theresa's settled."

"Thanks."

They worked side – by - side that first day and many days thereafter. A temporary preacher from a local Bible college was willing to come out on Sundays to preach, and Earl fell right into all the other tasks: organizing behind the scenes necessities, general maintenance, repair, and upkeep of the mission grounds, transportation and bussing of the students during the school week, and surprisingly doing extensive visiting and comforting of the sick at home or in the hospital. Karly didn't ask how he handled the situations when he most surely had to pray and put on a Godly persona, and he didn't volunteer any information. They both fell into an easy existence, seeing each other far more frequently, and interacting with a cool civility that seemed to work well for everyone involved. Edith surprised everyone by rallying enough that she was able to go home rather than to a rehab facility. Because Earl had relieved Sam of almost all of his duties, the Jamison's were able to cocoon themselves in their house and treasure the precious time they still had. After a few months, Sam even assumed preaching to "keep himself sharp". By the time Karly's third school year ended in June, the shift in power and responsibilities was complete. Like it or not, the Jamison's had found capable and dedicated replacements for themselves in the form of Karly Martin and Earl Nezbegay – *minus the preaching.*

As the year had progressed, Karly had been surprised at how much she enjoyed Earl's company. He had a quick, dry wit that was almost dusty. Half the time, if you weren't paying attention and listening closely you'd miss a quickly worded comment made under his breath. She tried to be helpful without being overbearing, and polite without being sugar sweet. He reciprocated with a dependable presence that immediately made her feel many pounds lighter. Her best times were surprisingly working along side Earl on a list of jobs that was monstrous in proportion. They were a surprisingly good team.

Theresa continued to be her outspoken, irreverent self. "Liking my brother anymore now that the two of you are working side - by - side?"

"*Theresa,*" Karly said in a tolerant, yet somewhat impatient tone (having heard this same line numerous times before). "This is *not* a reality show. We're both working. *Hard.* I appreciate his help in more ways than I can express. But we *are not* romantically interested in each other."

"Is that a mutual agreement or a one sided agreement? Since you're the only one here right now, let's talk about *your side.*"

"There is no *my side.* Will you stop? We always end up in the same discussion every time I come by."

"I'm just trying to be a good friend. You're so stressed about what's going on with the mission that I try to stay off that subject and focus on another one. This one's the most logical."

Karly narrowed her eyes at her friend. "You're a scheming, calculating woman, Theresa Goodluck. Don't you dare hide under the guise of good friend."

For once, Theresa looked absolutely serious. "Listen to me carefully, Karly Martin. *I love you.* You are a wonderful friend. You bring so much light with you, you don't know what life is like in the darkness. Because of you I have watched my daughter blossom, I've watched my world take on a completely different hue, and I've watched my brother become a completely changed man. I call 'em like I see 'em. I'm a selfish son of a ... gun ... and I'd absolutely *love* to have you officially as part of this family so that I know I'm never going to loose you. *I* can't marry you. So why not Earl?"

"What do you mean that Earl is a 'completely changed man'?"

Theresa sighed. "He's come back to life, Karly. He's been ... out of commission shall we say for almost fifteen years now." She saw Karly opening her mouth. "*Hush.* I know that you're going to say you had nothing to do with the change in Earl, but let me finish. He's peaceful.

He's happy. He's free! You may not think that you did any of these things, but you did. God brought you here for more reasons than teaching. You can't argue with me on that one." When Karly shook her head, Theresa said, "Will you agree that you've annoyed him, challenged him, and asked him to help you?"

"Yes, but ..."

"Just answer my questions. Well, I've been doing that for almost *fifteen years*, my friend, and it didn't work. You showed up and accomplished more than anyone else. *Including the Jamisons.* So just own up and shut up, okay?"

Karly stared at her friend.

Theresa looked tremendously smug. "He told me that you pray for him nightly."

Karly nodded. "I do. I pray for you and *all of my students*, too. I can't stand his pain and his sorrow and his guilt. I feel like it's my own sometimes. *I remember* ... I can't imagine carrying it around with me for all this time."

"Well, all I can say is keep up the good work. You don't live with him, but Marion and I do. There is a different man living with us. A *very* different man. I'm not saying that you should throw yourself at him, Karly. I'm just saying that there's more to Earl than meets the eye. Don't equate his silence with indifference. That would be foolish."

Don't equate his silence with indifference. Karly thought about what she already knew about Earl: his dedication to his sister and Marion, his secret kindnesses to her since she'd arrived, the high esteem the Jamison's held him in, and the way the town's people and church family sought him out for everything from handyman work to the newly added bedside visitations. She had a flashback of him standing in the shed playing with her ponytail and giving her that tiny smile of his, and her heart flipped.

Oh no you don't, Evil Twin gasped.

She had built a wall around herself when it came to men. No one knew any better than she how poor her judgment was. Somewhere along the line she'd boxed up and put away that part of her that might be a girlfriend, a wife ... *sigh* ... a mother. Those things were not for her, right?

Right. She needed to keep her nose to the grindstone and follow through on the tasks the Lord had put in front of her. Who needed the complication of a relationship? She surely didn't. One more thing added to her already overloaded life, and she might go off the deep end.

Still, over the next few weeks she couldn't help but notice that Theresa was right. Watching Earl, he *did* seem happier and more peaceful. That big, dark, cloud that used to hover over him was truly gone. Oh, he wasn't skipping through his day tossing daisies over his shoulder. He was the same, quiet, serious person he'd always been, but he just appeared … How had Theresa described it? Oh yeah, *free*. She watched him going about the million and one handyman chores on the mission property, moving in his easy, unhurried stride, long black ponytail swishing back and forth, and had to acknowledge that the difference *was* visible. But her responsibility for it? *No way*.

Get back to work. Never mind Earl Nezbegay. NEVER MIND.

Karly took a week's vacation in July to visit Benjamin. Snake had discouraged her from coming home to visit, telling her he had no plans of being there anymore than he had to. He had managed to finagle a month away at a summer camp affiliated with a church. He again declined to come and spend August in Huerfano, telling her his social life was starting to pick up finally, and he had no interest in being away the entire summer. Whereas last summer had been so busy she had been unable to find time to even take a breath, this summer yawned in front of her open and cavernous. Sure, she had all the responsibilities she had had the last two summers, but having experience under her belt, she was no where as overwhelmed and found that much of the work could now be done almost automatically. The possibility that she might have *free time* was novel to say the least.

In a burst of inspiration she decided to offer 'summer camp' activities for various ages on various days for two weeks in August. All in all it would be good publicity for the school, an excellent outreach to the community and a good bridge between the wide open space of summer and school responsibilities. Having tea with Edith, something she and Goliath did regularly to give Sam a much needed break, they had fun swapping ideas, outlining a budget, and coming up with a structured schedule. Goliath would perch on the edge of Edith's bed, or if she was well enough drape himself across the back of the lounge chair she was sitting in like he was a panther in the wild. Purring loudly enough to cause them sometimes to raise their voices, he regularly rested one massive paw on the top of Edith's sparse white hair. They designed fliers and brochures and even decided to put a little ad in the local newspaper. To their tremendous delight, they soon had a full roster of children for all classes.

"You know what a blessing you are to us, Karly," Edith said one day. "The Lord knew what He was doing when He sent you to us. You've given both Sam and me peace of mind regarding our responsibilities here at the mission, as well as invaluable time for us to relax and spend time with each other. *Thank you.* This is a precious gift from you to us."

The first week of summer camp had been exhausting but fun. Word had spread throughout the community that it was *fun,* and she regularly had spontaneous "additions" each morning at the door. Karly hadn't the heart to turn anyone away, even the group of three hulking seventh graders who had been past students: Ervin, Eddie, and Harley were harmless if a bit mischievous. They'd shown up early in the morning on Friday escorting their younger siblings, and had ended up never leaving. On the whole they were only a minor addition to the chaos, but Karly knew instinctively that she better have some sort of game plan in her pocket should they show up again Monday.

When she arrived home there was someone sitting on the steps of her trailer. That was unusual, for everyone knew they'd have a much better chance of meeting up with her at the mission school, or even at the Jamisons. He wasn't familiar, he wasn't Navajo – his build was too big and his hair was too light underneath his baseball cap. Then he stood up. Karly watched the huge frame unfold and felt as if the world had tilted incorrectly on its axis. *No. It couldn't be. Not here. Not now.* Not when her life was on such a positive, even keel.

Paul Williamson was standing in front of her trailer waiting patiently for her to approach him. *Oh. No. Goaway, goaway, goaway.* He tried hesitancy ("Hey, Kar..."), he tried his abundant charm ("You look as beautiful as I remember you"), and he tried humor ("I was just in the neighborhood and thought I'd stop by and say hello") before she managed to escape him by slamming *and locking* the door in his face.

In one brief moment, the peace and sanctity of her life went up in smoke.

Wanting, needing, guilty and greedy
Unrighteous, unholy, undo me undo me ...[19]

August, 2004
Huerfano, New Mexico

Thirteen: Real Christians Know Rock and Roll Is The Devil's Tool

Earl finished running off the last of Sunday's bulletins, stacking them neatly and banding them with a rubber band. Massaging his aching neck, he glanced at the clock: 11:15 p.m. Jeeze, he'd been going since 5:00 a.m. this morning with the emergency call about Verna Werito being rushed to Farmington General Hospital with chest pains. *Maybe* she'd finally listen to her doctors and cut out eating green chilies for a bedtime snack. Locking up the church office and walking slowly to his truck, Earl couldn't help but chuckle to himself and shake his head. As this was the third time in as many months that he and Verna has prayed together as the sun rose through the emergency room window, Earl was wise enough to know who Verna was going to listen to. And it wasn't going to be any "silly little white boy with a stethoscope" who was going tell her what to eat or not eat.

Nothing could have prepared Earl for this past year. *Nothing.* There had been no smoke on the horizon, no far away rumble in the

---

[19] Undo Me, By Jennifer Knapp, Jennifer Knapp, Kansas, 1997

distance, not even any terrified wildlife seen running for cover. Earl hadn't seen anything coming. But, why should that have surprised him? His life had always been a study in being blindsided. Always by God and His chief messengers of misery and disaster: the women in his life. Earl had *thought* he had had all his defenses in place. With his sister Theresa he had become (almost completely) blessedly numb to her comments, barbs, and innuendoes. Regarding Karly, he had settled on a system that had produced fairly satisfactory results: complete avoidance at all costs. But Earl had foolishly grown complacent. There had been another woman rising up through the ranks that God recognized as worthy of service, but Earl had failed to protect himself sufficiently from. Heck, he hadn't even realized he'd needed to consider safety precautions. But before that day nearly a year ago when Karly had come bursting through the shed door demanding that he shoulder some of Sam's responsibilities, God had laid a solid foundation for Earl's imminent and complete downfall. It had been a brilliant strategy: knock him completely up side the head and then, while he was still reeling in confusion, send Karly in to deliver the death blow kick ...

A year ago, he and Marion had been in his work room. They had an easy and comfortable existence that had developed over the course of many years. After all, whether you were a teenager - or significantly older - sometimes escape from the reality of your life was necessary for your sanity. Normally, Earl didn't mind her company as she wasn't a chatterbox, and when she did speak, usually it was for a good, solid reason. Until that day a year ago when all bets became null and void. When Marion had let loose with a stunning attack that had laid the mighty Earl Nezbegay flat on his back, out for the count.

"Do you believe in God, Uncle Earl?" Marion had been curled up that day, over a year ago, in the corner of the work shed in Earl's battered old sofa. Earl had looked up from the piece of wood he had been busy carving to look at her, but her face had been buried in a copy of *Christianity Today*. "Spirituality For All The Wrong Reasons" the cover said in bold black letters, *Lies and Illusions that Destroy The Church*.

Oh man.

"Sure I believe in God, Marion." *There*, he'd foolishly thought, *that should do it.*

"Mom says you don't."

Oh man, again.

"Yeah, well she's wrong."

Marion had put the magazine down to look at her uncle. "Mom said you used to believe in God but now you don't. She said she's not sure what she believes anymore either. So I'm just asking 'cause I'm trying to decide for myself."

Earl had sighed and walked around his workbench to lean against the edge. Crossing his arms, he stared at his niece and finally – against his better judgment - bit. "Just what are you trying to decide, Marion?"

"If I believe in God, too." Marion's tone implied her uncle should pay more careful attention when she was speaking to him.

"I believe in God, Marion. You should, too."

She seemed highly skeptical. "Do you believe in the Bible?"

Earl had hesitated and rubbed at the tension that was building in the back of his neck. "Yeah," he said slowly and without much conviction, "I believe in the Bible." Even to himself, he had sounded like he was talking about believing in the Tooth Fairy.

Marion squinted her eyes. "*All* of it? It makes sense to me that we should believe all of it. Or none of it. I don't see how it makes sense to do bits and pieces."

Earl remembered wanting to mutter a really foul curse and be very, very *alone*. He'd stared at his niece. She had gazed back at him unblinkingly and the seconds that ticked by in silence seemed to grow heavier and heavier with import. Marion deserved his honesty. The reality was that Marion was smart enough that she would have seen through any attempt at deception anyway. "I used to," he finally ground out rather lamely, and had turned to look out one of the shed's small windows. It had been impossible for him to look her in the eye. Didn't she have someplace to go? Didn't *he* have someplace to go? He glanced at his watch, but had found no escape.

"You *used* to? But you don't anymore?"

Earl had shrugged. "Yeah, something like that." How had he ended up having this conversation anyway?

"You don't believe in the whole thing? Or are there parts you still believe in? If so, what parts do you believe and what parts don't you believe?"

"Give me a break, Marion, will you? What? You want me to go through the book and highlight the sections that I'm okay with or something?" he had said harshly.

Earl got the distinct impression that had his tone not been so impatient and sarcastic Marion might have taken him up on the offer. Instead, she stared at him quietly, his mood effectively putting an end to any discussion that had been brewing.

Oh man ... !

Finally, Earl had walked over to the sofa, sat down, and settled her next to him. They hadn't had time like this in a while, but for both of them there were years of past moments like this. It immediately had felt comfortable and familiar. "Look, Prairie Dog, you're old enough now for me to tell you some things that maybe you've heard and maybe you haven't. But I'm going to tell them to you anyway so you can try to understand where my head is at, okay?"

She had nodded at him solemnly.

Where should he begin, he thought frantically ... desperately? Earl sighed, admitting defeat. There was no place for him to begin but at the beginning. So he had begun to tell his niece the pitiful story of his life ...

"I was a real smart kid growing up, Marion. The teachers always liked me because I was quick and smart and full of confidence. I wasn't so popular with the other kids for the same reasons. They all thought I was a brown - noser, too full of myself, teacher's pet. Really, I was scared and insecure. I had a mother who was ... well, let's just say she was *not* a good mother. I had never had a father to speak of. And I had a burning, all consuming desire to *get away* from home. Anyway I could manage.

"My mother sent me here to this church mission school. Not because she was so all fired up about God, but because she was able to get a free scholarship for me, and in the long run she killed two birds with one stone: she got me an education, and she got rid of me for the entire school year because I lived here in the school dorm."

Earl rubbed his hand along Marion's long, thin back.   Her beautiful, dark eyes had stared at him with an intensity that made him sweat. Talk about pressure. "In reality it could have been a clown school or a school of witchcraft or wizardry.   But it turned out to be a Christian mission school. *So what.*

"I must have been better at some things than even I believed, though," he'd explained absently, lost in the memories. "Looking back on it, I don't ever remember working hard to study *anything.*   The best I remember was thinking, 'Oh, yeah, that makes sense,' when something new or different was presented to me.

"The teachers at the mission school must never have seen anything like me, I guess. They'd get me extra books from the library or their own books and share them with me, and I'd read whatever they gave me from cover to cover. I couldn't seem to get enough." He looked at his niece. "Do you know that pretty much whatever I read I remember exactly?" He pointed to the magazine that now lay on the floor at their feet. "The cover story is by a minister named Eugene Peterson. He's pretty famous for writing a new version of the Bible called *The Message.* One part of the article asks him about aspects of spirituality. Spirituality is often considered by many Christians as something that makes them bigger and better than 'regular' people." Earl spoke from rote, "'It's a kind of specialized form of being a Christian, that you have to have some kind of in. It's elitist. Many people are attracted to it for the wrong reasons. Others are put off by it: *I'm not spiritual. I like to go to football games or parties or pursue my career.* In fact, I try to avoid the word.[20]'" He looked at his niece. "Want me to tell you the whole interview with Reverend Peterson?"

She smiled and shook her head 'no'.

"You know how you can memorize things so easily? How you always win all the Bible memorization contests at church?"

---

[20] "Spirituality for All the Wrong Reasons", Eugene Peterson, *Christianity Today*, 03/04/2005

Marion had nodded her head.

"Well, now you know where you get that from, okay?"

She'd smiled brilliantly and nodded again.

Earl sighed. "Certainly Edith and Sam Jamison hadn't seen anything like me. They hadn't been running the mission for long when my mother managed to finagle me a place there." He shook his head in memory. "Those two adopted me like I was a long lost son or something. I used to hang out with them and do odd jobs when they needed extra help. When most of the kids went home for weekends, nine times out of ten I didn't, and they'd have me up for dinner at their place almost every darn night."

Earl had looked at his niece. "How do you think the other kids treated me, Marion?"

"I'd a hated your guts," she'd said without the slightest bit of hesitation, and in the same direct tone that her mother had used with him that morning when Earl had helped get her dressed.

Earl nodded. "Yup. That about sums it up. They hated me something fierce. I had to decide, was I going to be a teacher's pet or popular and well liked. What do you think I decided? Remember," he said before his niece could answer, "I wanted *out* of this place more than anything in the world."

"You picked teacher's pet."

"Right again, Prairie Dog. I thumbed my nose at those other kids, and they worked real hard to make my life miserable." Earl shrugged. "But it paid off for me in the end. The Jamisons wangled things so I could take some big test for a scholarship for some fancy college. In the end, I got the scholarship and shook the dirt off of this place fast."

Earl chuckled, but the laugh had had little humor in it. "There was one problem, though. I ended up at a *seminary*. That's a school that makes preachers. It was highly ironic that I ended up escaping this town just like I wanted but ended up in a place where I wasn't any more happy or content. In fact, it was almost worse." In a whiny kid voice, Earl said, "*I've worked my tail off for this?!?*"

"What'd ya do, Uncle Earl?"

He had shrugged. "I took the easiest route, Marion. It was no skin off my teeth to read and study and write papers and pass tests. Heck, I didn't have to *believe* anything I was studying, did I? I studied everything objectively, like you'd study say a diagram of an electrical circuit board or the internal organs of a frog. I memorized it, repackaged it, and gave it all back in just the way they wanted it. But did I embrace it? Believe it? Own it?" He shook his head. "Nah, I didn't. In a way, I think I convinced myself that I was above all that somehow. I thought I was smarter and wiser and better than just about everyone else. In the end, I convinced myself that one of the qualities that made me so good was that I didn't fall into the trap of embracing any *one* thing. *I knew them all.*

"I graduated Summa Cum Laude. That means 'with highest honors', and I was offered opportunities to travel and teach and preach and see the world." He fell silent, remembering the way he had been, and shook his head at the ugly memory. "I was an obnoxious son of a gun, Marion."

He had looked at her and smiled, and then pulled her to him and gave her a kiss on her smooth cheek. "While I was doing all this you're mom was home *running wild.* Setting the entire world on fire wherever she landed. She never had good enough grades to get a scholarship – not because she wasn't as smart but just because she didn't give a hoot. Finally, because she was excessively truant and constantly disruptive, she was expelled from the one school Mom had managed to get her enrolled in. She got pregnant and had you the summer she turned seventeen." Earl had shaken his head in disgust. "By then I was already impressing the world with my dazzling intelligence."

Again he was silent for long moments, and this time Marion finally touched his face. "It's okay, Uncle Earl. I know the rest of the story."

Earl shook his head. "No, Prairie Dog. No, you probably don't." He sighed. "But it's time you did. I came home expressly to see you for the first time and to cast some righteous criticism on your mother - my sister - for the low life miserable existence she was choosing to embrace." Earl shook his head again in dismay. "I was so full of myself and my importance and my *wisdom*.

"I came home like some avenging angel, preaching to her about her failures and what she needed to do to 'get herself right'. You know what your Mom said to me, Marion?"

Marion shook her head.

"She looked me right in the eye as she smoked her cigarette and drank her fourth beer while you sat in your car seat neglected and whining and said, 'You know why your eyes are brown, Earl Nezbegay? Because you're full of crap right up to here,' and she held her hand up to the center of her forehead. 'You're so impressed with the sound of your own voice you talk just to make noise. You don't care what you say or who you hurt and you sure as heck don't care what message you deliver in the end. You just want people to understand that you're the best, and if they don't have the sense to appreciate what you have to tell them then they're not worth your time or trouble. Well, I got news for you. I'd rather listen to someone with *less smarts* and *less flowery words* and *less ego*, but who *actually cares about who I am and where I am heading* than you any day of the week.'"

Earl looked at Marion. "Then she calmly informed me that she needed me to drive the both of you to your two month checkup down in Farmington, since she was too drunk to do it herself." Earl shook his head at the memory. "I was *ballistic*. Your mother could always read me like a book, even when she was just a kid, and to have her uneducated, sinful, sorry butt stand there and *condemn me* set me off like fireworks on the fourth of July. I told her I'd drive her to Farmington, but only because I needed to get a haircut and no place in our sorry little town did a decent enough job to suit me. Driving the three of us down that highway, I never said one word to her because I was so enraged. I thought a heck of a lot, though. I was *done*. I was *leaving*. Leaving to never, ever, *ever* come back here. There was not one single thing that could make me stay or make me come back." He sighed and looked at Marion pointedly. "Or so I thought.

"The next thing I knew we were upside down in a ditch on the side of the road. You were in your car seat screaming like a banshee and

Theresa was half in and half out of the passenger side window. I smelled gas, so I hustled you and myself out of the car. I went back and got Theresa and dragged her out."

At that point, Earl had closed his eyes and had put his head back against the sofa, unable to continue. Marion had remained silent, but after a few moments she shifted herself so that she could lean against him and tuck her head under his chin. He had wrapped both of his arms around her. And finally he had said, "The doctors told me that if I hadn't moved her that perhaps her neck injury would have repaired, and she would not be paralyzed. I stayed and cared for you while she spent months in the hospital and rehab. When she finally came home, I stayed and cared for her, too."

He had suddenly felt so tired. "*Now* I think you know the rest of the story."

Still curled against his chest, Marion had asked, "Are you happy, Uncle Earl?"

What a question.

"I mean," she sat up to look intently into his eyes and had continued before he could come up with a politically correct answer for her, "in this whole story you've told me, it sounds like you were never happy in your *whole life*. Like even when you did good on your tests or got to travel like you thought you always wanted. I don't hear you ever saying, 'And then I was happy.' Are you happier *now*, or are you still as unhappy as you *were*?"

Suddenly, her question hadn't been so difficult. Looking into Marion's loving brown eyes he said sincerely, "I'm happier now, Marion. I've got you to keep me company and make me smile and laugh. I've even got a better relationship with your mother, in a bizarre kind of way."

"And you've got your shed with you're woodworking and stuff, and people seem to really like you in town, don't you think?" She had looked so darned intense.

Earl had tenderly touched her shiny crown of black hair. "Yeah, you're right about that, too, Prairie Dog."

Looking tremendously pleased with herself, Marion had given him a dazzling grin. "So we could say you're better off now than before, huh?"

Earl's stomach had rolled. "Now wait a minute! Good grief, Marion! You're mother's a *quadriplegic* for goodness sake! We're *almost* dirt poor, living hand to mouth. We live on your mother's social security, the generosity of others, and the money I bring in from odd jobs. I don't think ..."

In a highly impatient voice, Marion had interrupted him. "*I know my mom is a quadriplegic, Uncle Earl.* You might have a memory of her walking and running, but I sure don't." That shut him up fast. "But I also don't remember someone who smoked or drank or 'set the world on fire wherever she went'. She loves me. *Lots.* I know that as sure as I'm sitting here talking to you. We spend loads of time together laughing and talking and going visiting. From what you just told me, I don't know how things would have been ... otherwise."

Earl looked at this exquisite young woman. *Where did the time go, God?*

"Mrs. Jamison says that we're supposed to be thankful for *all things*, Uncle Earl. Not just the good things, but the bad things as well. She says that people expect God to be the way they want Him to be, but that God is exactly the way *He's* supposed to be. Only He knows what is best. So, when bad things happen, we're supposed to hang on, pray, and trust that God will see us through it all. She says that He loves us and would never give us *less*. Instead, we should always look at the whole picture carefully and see that He always gives us *more*. I look at *my* picture and I see I've got a mother who loves me best of *everything* and *everyone,* and I've got an Uncle who lives with me and loves and cares for me. He takes the time to talk, too. I see I've got the Jamisons who love me and teach me all kinds of good things here at the mission school, and I have lots of friends. I even have Miss Martin, who is the greatest teacher a girl could ever have. I think we've got it pretty good, don't you?"

Earl had been absolutely speechless. He looked at her innocent, intense face and felt all the guilty tension – *almost fifteen years worth* - begin to melt away. Like brain dump, all of a sudden everything he had thought, every hidden agenda he had kept, every meticulously recorded score card he had balanced was wiped absolutely completely and permanently blank. *That was the image she had of her life?* She made it sound like a picnic! She made it sound like she and her mother lived a life of butterflies and rose gardens and long flowing dresses with big pink ribbons. *Hello?* She had sat there as calmly and as seriously as could be, waiting for him to answer her question. His entire perception of the failures and injustices and consequences of his miserable life had faded away like the early morning mist. "So, let me get this straight, Marion. You're telling me that you're very happy with your life …"

Nodding, she had added, "Yup, and so is Mom."

"What do you mean, '*So is mom*'?!"

"*Hello, Uncle Earl,*" she had said in a you're – so - *dumb* tone of voice, "have you been listening to anything I've said? *Of course Mom is happy.* She tells me all the time about how lost and angry and unhappy she was before her accident, and how peaceful and centered and happy she is now. Do you really think I could say I was happy if I knew Mom wasn't?"

He had shaken his head, unable to find any words.

"Sure, she'd like to be able to run around and stuff, but she's said more times than I care to count that 'God only knows where she and I would both be if she hadn't had her accident'. That sounds to me like she maybe isn't exactly *happy* about her accident, but she at least *appreciates* how it's changed her life for the better. Don't you think?"

Besides working to keep his mouth from hanging open in shock, the only thing Earl had been able to do was nod.

"And you just told me only a little bit ago that you're happier now than you've *ever been in your whole life*, right?"

That's not saying much, but it is true … He had been compelled to nod again.

"So, that brings me back to my original question, Uncle Earl. Do you believe in God? 'Cause if you don't, I'd like to know where you think all this good stuff comes from 'cause that's what I've decided I'm going to believe in. I figure anything or anyone that can bring happiness and peace and love and laughter like I've got in my life is worth my believing and trusting in. That makes the most sense, don't you think?"

Out of the mouths of babes ...

The two of them had looked at each other for long moments, and finally, Marion had given him a small smile. "I love you, Uncle Earl," she said and patted his shoulder comfortingly like *he* was the child and she was the adult. "It's okay if I'm putting you on the spot. You can think about all this. That's what Mrs. Jamison always tells me when I'm trying to sort things through in my head. And praying helps a whole lot, too. Mrs. Jamison says she may look like a weak, sick, gray haired old lady, but with the power of prayer behind her she's still moving huge mountains."

A huge mountain named Earl Nezbegay. A lost, bitter, angry, guilt - ridden mountain ...

Marion had sighed, deeply in thought. "Actually, for me, it makes sense that thinking about something and praying about something should probably be the same thing." She had shrugged. "Although I'm sure not everyone feels the same way on that subject." Marion had leaned over and winked at him. "But I guess that's a whole other talk we'll have to have, huh, Uncle Earl?"

That had made him laugh out loud and hug her tightly. "How'd you get so wise and together, Marion Goodluck? It's quite obvious you've got a lot to teach me about the right way of things."

"It's not complicated really," she had said in a tone that implied he shouldn't worry about becoming overwhelmed.

He had thought, *just rub it in why don't you, kid.* "No, you're right, it's not. It's not complicated at all. It's just having enough courage and faith to acknowledge the truth of things. It's just the older, you get the harder that is to do."

Thoughtfully, as though carefully organizing all the ideas that had flowed between them, Marion said, "I also think you can't just pick and choose the pieces you like. I've decided that that's the difference between *faith* and just simply believing in stuff."

"Faith," Earl had murmured to himself and had felt the beginnings of a peace that he hadn't experienced in *forever* bloom in his chest, "being sure of what we hope for and certain of the things that we can't see."

"Yeah, that's it," Marion had said nodding enthusiastically. "That's it in a nutshell."

God had given Earl approximately twenty - four hours before blindsiding him again. Still reeling from Marion's revelations, he had escaped once again to the hoped for peace, quiet and *privacy* of his shed. And if Earl hadn't been expecting the first attack he *for darn sure* had not been expecting the second so quickly after.

That very next day Karly had burst into his shed and had demanded that he assume some of Sam's responsibilities now that Edith was so sick. At first Earl had been stunned speechless that the Lord would work so fast and so furiously. Hadn't he already made one mighty convincing break through just the day before? Then watching Karly rail on him like he was nothing but low - life scum had put his back up more than a bit. It had taken him a while to realize that perhaps, *just perhaps*, this responsibility that Karly was insisting he take on might be an opportunity to continue what he and Marion had only just begun discussing the day before.

In the end, if Karly hadn't been so passionate and serious about the whole thing Earl would have eventually thrown back his head and roared with laughter over God and how He worked. He'd ended up telling Karly things that he'd never even allowed himself to *think* thoroughly through, let alone speak out loud. And finally, aside from the preaching responsibilities, Earl had told her he seriously thought he could handle all of the other day – to - day tasks that Sam usually did. Hence sitting at 5:00 a.m. a year later with Verna Werito with her chili induced indigestion cum false chest pains and working at 11:15 p.m. finishing the church bulletin.

And who in their right mind would have believed that he could feel so good doing it? Felt good in more ways than one. This past year had been a strange journey of self - discovery. Like riding a bicycle, the ministerial responsibilities had come back to him bit by bit with little trouble. But it was all different. So very different. Many of the things he'd said and done before that had felt so superficial and tedious - albeit necessary - now became the most important and spiritually beneficial.

Marion's words stayed with him. Earl realized that he'd spent the majority of his life since he'd come back to Huerfano looking at his life as the glass being half empty. Marion looked at the very same life and viewed the glass as being half full. Why not try viewing life that way? Why not embrace the concept that God was in charge of the good *and* the bad times? Why not believe that God would stay by your side and see you through to the better parts in your life that He promised would come? What good was the life he had embraced with bitterness and anger, self pity and guilt? A life like that was a waste.

Move on, Earl Nezbegay. Move on.

And so he did. Quietly, without any explosions or fanfare, he took steps daily toward healing: mind, body and soul. It felt so good. Like a snowball rolling down hill, each day he felt bigger and better. It was like awakening from a long hibernation and slowly coming back to life.

He dusted off his ministerial skills and took over Sam's visitation role, spending an amazing amount of time with the sick, the elderly, the desperate, the lonely ... Each and every encounter left him different, usually in more ways than one. Often he left a situation feeling overwhelmed with the reality of the hardships of life: illness, poverty, abuse, broken dreams and shattered hearts. But on these visits, he was able to sit and listen, share and talk. The people here *knew him*, they knew of his own personal demons and heartaches and half the time he ended up getting back as much if not more than he gave. With the people he visited, he traded war stories, compared scars, cried a bit, laughed a bit, and tried to come up with a game plan that would get them through to the next day. They bolstered each other's hope, encouraged each other's faith, and championed each other's persistence to continue on.

And it wasn't like last time. The more he ministered to Sam's people, who had always been his friends and neighbors, the more he was humbled with how much he personally didn't know. Oh, he had book learning all right. He could back anyone within a hundred mile radius into a corner with his dazzling quotes and reams of theological knowledge, but when dealing with *people and their lives* it was the humanness and frailty of his own self that made the greatest impact. Not his smarts. The fact that in many instances he'd *been there* and *done that* made the words he imparted - words of comfort, prayer, and spiritual guidance, that much more believable.

Perhaps best of all, he rediscovered his relationship with the Jamisons. In a time of great stress for them, they continued to minister to each other and to those within their close familial sphere. Because Earl assumed so many of Sam's responsibilities, Sam was able to continue to preach. Earl suspected it was good for both Edith and Sam - giving each of them some time apart. No matter how much you loved someone, you couldn't devote yourself 24/7. Individually and together the Jamisons encouraged and championed Earl, but never once asked for more than he was able to give. Like it had been for him as a child, they seemed to almost always know exactly what to say or not to say, and he very much appreciated that.

Who would ever have thought that his greatest trials and failures could turn out to be his greatest ministry? But suddenly, they were. And in embracing them, owning them, *and being able to set them aside and not drown in them*, he found ... freedom. What had Karly said to him at the New Year's Eve Party almost three years ago? *I don't want this part of your life to be your defeat, Earl. I want it to be your victory. That's what I pray for. Triumph. Success. I pray that for you each and every night.*

Which led him to another aspect of his life. Karly Martin. Was she still praying for him? They'd fallen into a carefully maintained relationship, defined by deferential politeness and an eternally willing attitude of helpfulness. Earl suspected that they both were terrified that all of the added responsibilities would push one or both of them over the edge, so they'd better handle each other like highly valuable porcelain dolls. They spent *a lot* of time together planning, trouble shooting, divvying up obligations and fighting impending disasters. In all their time together the predominant conversation was generally no more than: "Would you mind?", "Would it be possible?", "Do you think you could?", "Have you thought about how?", "Thanks so much", "I really appreciate it", "Oh, you're a life saver", "I knew I could count on you", and "No, go ahead, I'll finish up."

In Earl's eyes, Karly grew more beautiful by the day. It was a case of internal beauty shining through more brightly the more he got to see her at work. She was patient, kind, loving, and willing. In every situation and with every person he observed her with, she did her best to be her best. And she treated him like she treated everyone else on the planet it seemed, which drove him absolutely insane. Did she think about him like he did her? Was she as curious about him as he was of her? Did she enjoy those situations where they had to work side - by - side as he did? There was never a glimpse of her thoughts or feelings regarding him while he felt that his feelings were engraved in neon letters on his forehead. As he worked side - by - side with Karly in Huerfano, Earl found his faith *and* fell in love.

At one point, early on as they worked together, Earl sought opportunities to be with Karly, but after a time Earl found reasons to avoid her. He no longer trusted himself to be calm, cool, collected, or to behave like a normal, sane individual. He tried praying about his feelings for Karly. *Hello, God? Isn't this falling in love thing a bit of inappropriate timing?* Wouldn't it be wiser for him to get his head on straight and securely before he added in the complication of love - sick thoughts and dreams? Couldn't he set these feelings for her aside and, perhaps reassess them at a later date? Maybe in another two or three years? But more nights than he cared to admit he ended up behind the mission school parked in his truck at the base of the dirt road leading to her trailer. Sometimes he entertained thoughts of driving up, knocking on her door, spilling his guts, and taking his chances. More often than not, he sat there in the dark underneath the stars - knowing in many instances she was doing the same thing outside her trailer - and prayed. *Keep me on track, God. I can't afford to screw things up a second time. Guide my heart and my head, Lord. I want to please you and do what's right.*

Karly had disappeared for a time every summer since she had first arrived at Huerfano. *Then* Earl had not even taken note; *now* the curiosity factor was immense. These vacations weren't a surprise. In her typical, organized fashion, she made arrangements for everything that needed to be done. Since they now worked together, she spoke at length with Earl about her concerns, and what she planned to do on her return. When he cautiously pressed about where she was going she was vague, while answering all his questions honestly. *Off to see friends. No, she wasn't going to see her family. Flying out of Albuquerque. Five hour flight.* The awkwardness of their relationship rose up and bit him on the butt. They didn't have a serious enough relationship so that he could yell, *Are you going to see a man? Is this someone you care about? Will you miss me when you're away?* Even offering to drive her to the airport was politely refused; Sam had already offered.

He spent a week in hell each time she was gone, worrying about where she was, what she was doing, and who she was with. He got the distinct impression that Edith and Sam knew where she was and what she was doing, but neither volunteered any more information. He wanted to shake someone, but he couldn't figure out who to grab. Earl promised himself that when she got back he'd sit down with her and tell her how he felt. If she rejected him, then she rejected him, but at least he'd be put out of his misery.

And then he could begin a new misery.

Unfortunately, when she arrived back lovely and refreshed, they both fell back into the same old intensely polite pattern of their relationship. The coward that he was refused to risk the relationship they had for the possibility of it becoming less. He caught himself slipping into dangerous old patterns with her that he had managed to file away. Out of his mouth came sarcasm and biting dry wit that more often than not made her stop, stare and then finally purse her lips to keep from mouthing back. Like a child that craved negative attention rather than no attention, Earl decided that having her give him a piece of her mind was almost as appealing as her giving him a piece of her heart.

He continued to sit at the edge of her road two, three, okay, maybe sometimes five nights a week. Nobody knew. He wasn't hurting anyone. He was loosing some much needed sleep. So what was the harm, right? Pulling into the driveway one Saturday night in August he was stunned to see another car parked, exactly where he usually parked and leaning against it was another man. Oh, this was just too much. What, did she have a whole collection of idiots like him pining away for her and baying at the moon? So many that they were doubling up in spots? Anger, hot and red, surged through his veins.

Rolling down the truck's window, he ground out in unfriendly tones to the huge guy leaning against the side of his rental car, "You're on private property."

The guy, who had to be at least six foot four or five, looked directly at Earl and said, "Look's like you are too."

"True. But only one of us has a right to be here."

"Look, I'm not looking for a fight. I'm minding my own business. Why don't you do the same, okay?"

They stared at each other for a few intense moments and then Earl shrugged. "Sure, no problem." He killed the engine, turned and slouched down in the seat, tipped his hat down over his eyes, and stuck his booted feet out the passenger side window.

"What are you doing?" came the question a few moments later.

"Minding my own business," said Earl from underneath his hat. "Right here along with you."

He could hear a muffled curse, and underneath his hat he smiled. Some of his tension eased when the car engine roared to life and gravel spit out from spinning tires. Long after the guy had left, Earl sat under the stars thinking about Karly.

And trying to pray.

Amazing grace I feel you coming up slowly now
Like the sun is risin'; heat on my face
Oh love that keeps on shinin'
Don't let the shadow come[21]

August, 2004

Huerfano, New Mexico

Fourteen: Learned Christians Know God Has No Sense of Humor

Karly could hear Paul's rich baritone loudly and clearly over the congregation Sunday morning. He was in a back row, to the far right of the meeting room.

Amazing Grace! How sweet the sound.
That saved a wretch like me!
I once was lost, but now am found.
Was blind, but now I see ...[22]

Who ever said that God didn't have a sense of humor? A wave of fury swept over her at Paul's intrusion into her world. He did not belong here. He had no right to be here.

No right? The occasionally reformed evil twin AKA the Utmost of Christian Consciences challenged her.

She sighed in frustration, arguing with herself. Absolutely. He has no right to be here. He had his chance and he BLEW IT. Tough luck. End of story. Stay the heck out of my life.

---

[21] Amazing Grace, Jars of Clay, Who We Are Instead, 2003

[22] "Amazing Grace", Words by John Newton, Olney Hymns, London, W. Oliver, 1779

So, he isn't entitled to a second chance? Evil Twin said, voice dripping with derision. *Let me get this right. He's the only human being on the face of the earth who is exempt from being forgiven. No turning the other cheek? No forgiving seventy times seven? Who gave you the right to rewrite the Bible?*

She didn't care how it sounded. Yeah, that was right, she told herself, he's the only human being on the face of the earth who is exempt from being forgiven. Given the circumstances, it didn't seem unreasonable at all.

Karly had managed to avoid Paul all day Saturday. She had gotten up at the crack of dawn and drove to Farmington to do needed errands, had spent part of the day with Theresa and Marion, and then had stayed as late as politely possible at the Jamisons. As Sam had resumed his preaching responsibilities (the only area that Earl still refused to consider) and needed some uninterrupted preparation time, keeping Edith company on Saturday and cooking dinner in the kitchen for the three of them (Goliath didn't count) was something she often did.

During the summer, church school consisted of one group of children ages three through five and another group for children ages kindergarten through third grade. Karly enjoyed teaching the little ones for a change, while Shoshanna Werito usually taught the older group. Consequently, encountering Paul in the adult Bible class was not something she needed to worry about. Filing out after church, however, was a different story.

She could hear Paul conversing with Sam, giving his name, and saying that he was "visiting someone in the area". In such a small church community it would have been unthinkable for him to have escaped notice. "Karly! Come here! I'd like to introduce you to someone!" Sam called to her enthusiastically while she was making every effort to appear invisible as she picked up used bulletins and put pencils back where they belonged. Straightening, she met Paul's eyes across the sanctuary. It was impossible to avoid him.

"Karly, this is Paul Williamson. He's from back east, like you. He's here visiting a friend and decided to grace us with his presence." Sam turned to Paul. "Who did you say you were visiting? I know just about everyone around these parts. I could point you in the right direction."

"If you don't mind," Paul said politely, "it's sort of a surprise. If I have any trouble though, I'll be sure to look you up for assistance."

Not everyone likes surprises, Evil Twin said with venom.

"Sure, sure, you do that. My wife, Edith and I live right up the hill behind the mission school in the ranch house," Sam pointed in the correct direction even though you couldn't see the house. "She's not here. Been real sick, I'm sorry to say." Karly watched him visibly war with himself regarding concern for Edith and continuing to do his pastoral duties. "How long will you be in the area?"

"Not much more than a few days."

"Oh, that's too bad. Our annual Tent Meeting is at the end of this week. Good food, fellowship and fun. If there's any chance you can stay through the weekend, it's something you don't want to miss."

"Thanks, I'll consider that. Could you point me to a decent restaurant in the area? I've been eating fast food, and my body's starting to feel the drain. Should I drive all the way to Farmington?"

Oh no, Evil Twin moaned. As Sam opened his mouth Karly burst out, "There's a halfway decent diner about two thirds of the way between here and Farmington. You wouldn't have to go all the way into town. It's no more than a twenty minute drive."

Paul allowed his attention to focus completely on her. "Oh. Okay. Thanks."

"No, no! Won't hear of it! Simply won't hear of it! Since my wife's been sick, everyone's been so kind and generous. I've got a huge casserole cooking in the oven right now back at the house." He smiled a self - depreciating smile at Paul. "It's the closest I come to cooking – reheating!"

"No, no, I couldn't impose," Paul said quite sincerely.

"Edith's probably not up to it either, Sam," Karly said hoping to reinforce the wisdom of Paul's not attending.

"Don't be silly. She felt pretty good this morning. We actually thought – for about five minutes mind you – of trying to get her down here for the service. In the end we knew that would ruin her for the day so we passed. But she'd love to see a new face besides mine and Karly's." He winked at Karly. "No offense."

"Karly's going to eat with you?"

Sam chuckled. "Oh sure. We try to feed her and take the best possible care of her, because without her this mission school and church would have collapsed this past few years. She's been a Godsend, she has." He looked at Karly. "I invited Earl, too."

Oh great, Evil Twin said, *just when it didn't seem to be able to get any worse.*

"And he said he'd come?" Karly burst out incredulously, feeling as if she was in a Candid Camera prank.

Sam laughed and shrugged his shoulders. "Go figure, huh? How many times have I invited him over for a meal? Probably *hundreds*. And today of all days he said yes. I'll have to mark this day down on the calendar."

Oh, you do that, Sam. You do that.

So Karly trudged up the hill in Paul and Sam's wake. She listened to Paul ask interested questions about the mission school and the church. The delicious aroma of baked ziti and garlic bread greeted them the moment they stepped in the front door. "Give me a moment," Sam said to Paul and Karly, "to check on my girl. Karly, fetch Paul and yourself some iced tea from the fridge."

As Sam walked down the hall to their bedroom, Karly walked away from Paul as fast as she could to get the drinks. She *felt* him follow her, even though his steps were silent. She got out glasses and took ice from the trays in the freezer. Pouring two glasses, she turned and handed Paul one without a word.

"Thanks," he said and gave her a hesitant smile. She walked away to stand in the living room and looked out the large bay window. It was a glorious view, a picture postcard scene of the mission school and chapel and the surrounding beautiful countryside. On the far horizon, if you knew where to look, was the white top of her trailer.

"I see you're not any more pleased to see me today than you were on Friday," he said from behind her.

Karly felt completely disinclined to answer him. *You wanted this, boyo,* Evil Twin hissed.

"It's not my purpose to come and disrupt the life you've established here, Karly." She turned briefly to look over her shoulder and glare her disbelief at him. "Obviously you will find this hard to believe, but I've simply come here to apologize and try to set the record straight."

What?!

She whirled around to face him, ready to let fly anything and everything that was going to spew out of her mouth. He took a small step back and seemed to flinch as if getting ready to take whatever she threw at him. Karly felt the screams begin to boil up, opened her mouth and ..."

"Have I missed anything yet?" came a voice from the front doorway. Sticking his head in, Earl gave Karly his typically shuttered look, and then his gaze settled on Paul. He stepped into the house, automatically wiping his feet on the small rug. "Hey," he said in a cautious tone walking forward, "welcome to Huerfano. My name's Earl Nezbegay."

Earl made eye contact with Karly, waiting for her to make introductions, but she couldn't do it. Who cares if she looked rude? *It was just Paul and Earl.* She turned her back to both of them to look stone - faced out the window again.

"Paul. Paul Williamson. Ah, it's nice to meet you, Earl. I'm worried that I'm intruding on dinner here, but Reverend Jamison pretty much insisted."

"Don't have to try to explain to me. I've been avoiding eating dinner here for close to fifteen years. Still can't figure out how I manage to be standing here today."

"Gee, fifteen years," Paul said. "Is there something I should know about the cooking in this house?"

Karly heard Earl chuckle. "No, more likely you should learn that the couple in this house *never give up* on anything they set their mind to. They may have been trying to get me to stop by and have dinner with them for more than fifteen years, but it was never a question of *if* it was going to happen, simply *when*."

"Ahh," Paul said, and Karly knew by the tone and the inflection that he was smiling, "so it simply says a great deal about your strength of will versus mine."

"You've got that right. But don't take it too hard, you had no idea what you were dealing with. Did he Karly?" Earl said trying to bring her back into the conversation.

Not turning around Karly said with venom, "No. Mr. Williamson had no idea what he was dealing with when he came to Huerfano." The attention of both men - Earl's shocked expression and Paul's pained one - was drawn from her by the sounds in the hallway.

Karly looked to see Sam helping Edith down the hallway toward them. Even on this 'good day' she had a fragile, ethereal quality about her that gripped Karly's gut before she sprang to life and moved purposely past Paul and Earl to greet her friend. "Edith," Karly whispered when she got to her side, "you're not up to having all of us here for dinner. Let me make excuses so you can have a quiet afternoon."

"I've had a quiet morning. I could use a little action to keep me awake, Karly. This company is just what I need. Introduce me, please." She smiled up at Paul.

"Edith Jamison, this is Paul Williamson. He's visiting the area."

Paul stepped forward, bending his huge frame over to respectfully take Edith's frail hand in his. "It's a pleasure to meet you, Mrs. Jamison. I really enjoyed Reverend Jamison's sermon this morning. I'm worried that unexpected guests are too much for you, though."

"Oh, you're a charmer, aren't you? Have a seat and tell me about yourself, young man. When I've had enough of all this company I'll tell you to go, won't I Earl?"

"Yes, Ma'am, that you will," Earl said with an easy smile.

They had all settled down into the chairs and couches in the living room, when a yowling of astronomical proportions began outside the front door. "Karly, go let that beast of a cat of yours in, will you?"

Smiling, Karly went over to the front door to open it for Goliath. "Who invited you?" she asked, but reached down to scratch him behind his ears just the same. Goliath had everyone trained in the Jamison's house to give him the treats that Edith kept under the kitchen sink. The first order of any visit was to travel over to the sink and sit and wait for someone to serve him. The most optimal situation was for only one person at a time to be aware of his presence, therefore insuring numerous treats over the course of one visit. If you were too slow, then the yowling would begin, followed by a paw scratching the cabinet door. "You are so spoiled," Karly said giving him a treat and listening to the purring begin. She got out a serving tray and put three more glasses with ice and the pitcher of iced tea on it. Carrying it into the living room, she poured drinks for Sam, Edith, and Earl.

The conversation, which Karly remained completely out of, flowed smoothly. Through Sam, Edith, and Earl's innocent questioning she learned about Paul's family (all of whom were well), his job (truck lineman for the local power company), and bits about his personal life (owned his own home, was single, still loved to play all kinds of sports). But what was most startling was his firm profession of faith when Sam asked him about his religious upbringing and personal beliefs. "It's been a long time in coming," Paul said quietly to all of them, but looking directly at Sam and Edith, "but I've finally come to the realization that the only life to lead is one rooted in Jesus Christ. Some years ago I rededicated my life to the Lord, and I've worked diligently to remain on that path." He gave a self - depreciating laugh, "I slip up all the time but it only makes me more determined. Lately," Paul glanced at Karly who was giving him a shocked stare, and then back to the Jamisons, "I've worked hard at trying to come to terms with *most* of the glaringly foolish choices I've made over the course of my life. I know I can't go back and change the mistakes I've made in the past, but I'd like to have the courage to fix or settle up with the things I can. I've made peace with my family, I've … met a truly wonderful young woman who the Lord has seen fit to bless me with and … I feel that maybe, *just maybe*, I might become a fruitful, productive, solid man after God's own heart. I still have a few major hurdles I need to get over before

I can begin to look completely forward, but each day is better. That's what we should pray and aim for, right? That each day is better than the one before?"

"It's a nice goal," Earl said.

"It's an excellent goal that I wish more people subscribed to," Edith said with conviction.

The oven timer sounded and Karly went to get everything set. When Sam got up to help she waved him back and told him to entertain his guests. Earl followed her into the kitchen though. "I don't need any help," she grumbled as she pulled the large tray of baked pasta out of the oven and peeled back the lid to check it.

"Aren't you just the friendliest person today?" Earl said, leaning against the counter with his arms crossed, studying her. "If I didn't know better I'd think you and I had a personality switch last night through some magical incantation under the full moon. Either that, or Paul Williamson is no stranger to you, and you're trying to put on a good front."

"I'm not in the mood, Earl. Go be your unbelievably cheerful and entertaining self somewhere else where it's appreciated."

Karly opened the cutlery drawer to take out a serving spoon and stir the pasta mixture. Earl grabbed her hand and leaned into her line of vision when she refused to look up at him. "What gives, Little Miss Cheerful and Light? Having trouble putting the past behind you and forgiving and forgetting? Seems to me over the past few years I've had this little bird in my ear preaching love and forgiveness of oneself and others and about *letting go*." Karly tried to pull her hand free, but Earl held on tightly. "Paul says he's here to surprise someone and see them. I'll bet anything that that person *is you*. Could it be that you haven't done as much forgiving and forgetting as you thought, but instead have embraced *running and hiding* and got them all confused?"

The kitchen closed in on her and she felt unable to breathe. It seemed as if there was no oxygen, and her lungs were paralyzed. Karly looked up at Earl to tell him to leave her alone, but instead felt tears choke her throat and begin to slide down her face.

"Oh. Damn," he said as he released her hand. Earl reached for the oven mitts, picked up the tray of pasta, and shoved it back in the oven. Reaching up to shut off the oven, he shouted over his shoulder, "Pasta looks good, but I forgot to do something. I'll be back in a minute. Karly's going to keep me company." Before anyone could respond, they were out the door and driving down the highway in his truck.

They didn't drive far, just to the first shaded area on the side of the road. Huerfano Mountain rose up blocking the sun and creating a quiet shady nook tucked alongside the road. "You can sit there until you get calmed down and then we'll go back, or we can talk. No pressure though. I just wanted to get you out of that house so if you were going to have a crisis, you could do it in private."

"It wouldn't be private. You're here."

"My lips are sealed."

Karly sighed, sniffling and wishing for a tissue. Earl handed her a neat, white men's handkerchief. "My momma always told me preacher men were never to be trusted and to always make sure I had a clean handkerchief in my pocket. She was one wise woman."

"Why are you being so kind, Earl?"

He had the audacity to look offended. "What's that supposed to mean?"

"Earl, you've never gone out of your way to be overtly kind or comforting to me. You've been helpful, reliable, yes, but always distant."

He shrugged. "You've never needed it before. You're always together, in control, and in command. But when you looked at me with those big, sad, blue eyes in the kitchen, I just … melted." He gave her a small smile. "You must be feeling better; you're already giving me a hard time." Then he sighed and massaged the back of his neck. "I have to be honest with you and tell you that I knew Paul had an interest in you. I caught him snooping around your driveway last night and gave him a hard time. That's why I accepted when Sam invited me to Sunday supper. I figured at least I'd keep an eye on you. Paul and I exchanged glances in church a few times."

Karly wasn't surprised that Paul was near her place but she was stunned that Earl was. "What were you doing in my driveway?" Her driveway was behind the mission school. Only a purposeful visitor would come upon it.

Earl waved an impatient hand at her question and looked supremely satisfied. "So you *do* know him. He refused to answer any questions I threw at him last night, so I wasn't completely sure. He finally just drove off when I parked my truck right next to his and made it clear I wasn't leaving."

"You looked so calm and collected when you walked into the Jamisons."

"Well, last night we were just having the who – can – shoot – it - farther pissing contest guys get into when they're trying to make a point. Plus, it wasn't like we could come out swinging in the Jamison's living room."

"Paul is the father of my son, Earl," Karly blurted out. "He abandoned me on the day of our wedding. I haven't seen him or spoken to him in almost five and a half years."

Earl looked like he was trying to shove a brick into his ear. "Your ... *son* ... ?"

She nodded. "His name is Benjamin. I gave him up for adoption almost four and a half years ago."

Like lights turning on in a dark house, Earl suddenly seemed to understand. "The thing in your past that is out of sight but not out of mind or heart or soul ..."

Karly nodded and felt the tears begin again. Looking out the window, clutching Earl's handkerchief, she said in a whisper, "You're right. I didn't forgive and forget. I just ran and hid."

Earl slid across the seat as best he could and did the only thing that made complete sense to him: pulled her into his arms. "Aww, I've got a big, big mouth. I said things that I've got no right saying. You never ran or hid. You took care of everything you needed to, made sure that baby of yours was safely taken care of, and then you went on with your life. And you're doing a bang up job, if I do say so myself. Look! You're doing your own job, Edith's job, and who'd you finally manage to explode out from under the rock where he's been hiding for the past fifteen years? *Me.* Good God, Karly. You're a veritable miracle worker!"

She shook her head in disbelief and tried to get out of his embrace.

"Don't," he said quietly into her hair, "let me do this. It's because of what you've been pushing me to do this past year that I'm even capable of attempting this." He held her tenderly, her back pulled against his chest and both his arms wrapped around her. She felt him rest his chin on top of her head. "Tell me about your boy."

She sighed. "He's not *my* boy. He belongs to a wonderful couple, Viv and Darin. It's an open adoption, so we communicate regularly and I even see him. He's smart and sweet with big blue eyes and sandy brown hair. His favorite food is dill pickles. I was there just last month for a week."

So that's where she was. "Do you have pictures?" He felt her nod in his arms. "Will you show them to me?" She was still for a moment and then she nodded a little more slowly this time. "Paul has to know about the boy," he finally said.

"Oh, he does. He had to sign release papers when the adoption was finalized. From what I understand he never even contacted the agency or even asked one question. The papers just all showed up signed, sealed, notarized, and dated. He was so efficient that the agency didn't even need to fly out to see him. *He couldn't wait to be rid of me or the baby.*"

Earl's arms tightened around her. "Or maybe, his life was already so far out of control that it was the only sane thing he could do." Earl reached up and fingered her hair. *God he loved the feel of it.* "Why's he here? Do you know?"

Karly shook her head. "Well, based on what he told the Jamisons, he's not interested in starting up things again with me. Seems like his life is perfectly fine right now as it is." She sounded bitter even to herself.

"Do you wish he was coming back for you?"

"*No!*" she exploded.

"Why?" he persisted, needing to hear what she had to say a little more desperately than he needed air right then.

The words poured out of her. "Because I don't love him. Because I don't think I ever really truly loved him. Because my life is *right* now; *on track*. I feel peaceful and happy. I don't think of him or miss him." Earl felt her relax against him just a little bit and whisper almost to herself, "There are times when I am even happy he did what he did and backed out of the marriage. We would never have made it ..."

Earl's breath tickled her ear as he spoke. "So you've got your head on straight regarding you and the relationship you had with him. Do you believe what he says about the changes he's made in his life?"

Karly shrugged. "He was always very vocal about how little he thought of God and religion when we were together. I can't imagine him saying anything of the sort without really believing it himself."

"I felt that he was sincere, too."

Karly twisted around in Earl's arms to look at him. "You did?"

He nodded his head and his hair slipped off his shoulder between them. It was in a neat, tight braid today that ran all the way down his back. "Um - humm. I did."

Karly reached up to touch his hair. Like a thick, glossy rope, it filled the palm of her hand. "Why do you always touch my hair?" she asked.

It was the first time Karly recalled him rolling his eyes. "We're sitting here in the close confines of my truck and you're in my arms," Earl said patiently to her. "You're also in a highly emotional state, and I'm thinking it might be better to continue this conversation at another time, because ..."

Kiss him, Evil Twin said all of a sudden. *Trust me on this one.*

"Does your sister give you as hard a time about me as she gives me about you?"

He hesitated for a moment, and she was certain he glanced once at her mouth. "Yeah, I'd say she's relentless."

"I'm not a very good judge of character where men are concerned. I've kind of decided that I should just avoid that area in my life."

"Oh yeah?" He tucked a stray strand of her hair behind her ear. "That's about the dumbest thing I've ever heard you say."

"Now you sound exactly like your sister."

"And that's the scariest thing I've ever heard you say."

She laughed. "But I have been thinking about you."

Earl swallowed. "And?"

"Well, if I was the only one who thought you were something special then I'd have my doubts. But there are a lot of people who think very highly of you. Theresa, Marion, the Jamisons, people in town, people at church … Seems like you've got a regular fan club around here. Seems like lots of people think you're pretty special."

"Now that's the *smartest* thing I've ever heard you say," and he gave her one of his sweet smiles.

She pulled his head down by drawing on his braid and kissed him. And wonders of wonders he kissed her back like a man who had been starving for something all his life and finally, *at last,* had found it. His one hand held fast to the back of her head where he had been stroking her and trying to calm her, and the other hand worked its way up to grasp her face and hold her right where he wanted her.

Earl finally broke the kiss and leaned his forehead against hers. "Karly, I …" she felt him tense, "I was going to say I was sorry for that, but damn if I am! I've been wanting to kiss you like that for almost as long as I've known you. And I touch your hair because from the first moment in your trailer on the very first day I've wondered about the texture of it! And once I did touch it in the shed that day, I could not believe it was as glorious as I had dreamed." He groaned in the back of his throat. "It only made me wild to want to touch it again."

He sat up and held her face in both of his hands. "Look. We have to talk, okay? Not fight. Not lecture. Not discuss church issues or stopped up toilets or leaky roofs. I'll do my best to keep the sarcasm and provocative humor at bay. You and I have to talk about …" Earl looked at Karly in an anguished way, "can I say 'us'? Can I say we have to talk about us?" He untangled his arms, turned away from her and put his hands on the steering wheel before she could respond. "I have no right ..."

Karly slid across the seat. On her knees, she put her arms around his shoulders. Then, cupping his face, she leaned in and kissed his smooth, warm cheek and inhaled his scent that was reminiscent of soap and woodchips. "Don't go annoying me now, Earl Nezbegay. I'd be honored to talk about 'us', okay? We'll make it our first official ... *date.*" Sitting back on her heels she turned his face to hers, making him look her in the eye. "*Okay?*" She smoothed the worry line from his forehead with her hands. "Don't go away on me now, Earl. Hang around for a while and see if it's worth all the time and trouble."

He reached over to run a rough calloused thumb across her mouth in disbelief that she was sitting there and he was touching her. "You are the most beautiful woman I have ever seen *in my life,*" he murmured, and his eyes traveled over her facial features as if feasting on them. "My brain shuts down when you look at me and my mouth trips all over itself. I become a bumbling idiot."

She beamed a blinding smile at him. "And I get feisty and defensive, bossy and overbearing. It sounds like a match made in heaven," and she leaned in to kiss him again, unable to wait a moment longer.

They went back to the Jamisons for dinner. In the driveway before they went in, Earl looked at her and said, "I think you should talk with him. By your own words you've admitted his apparent sincerity, and there seems to be no confusion about what you need or want from him."

"I want *nothing* from him," Karly said through gritted teeth.

"Exactly," he said, nodding. "If you're going to continue to claim that your life is the Lord's and that He is in charge then you have to acknowledge that He played a part in bringing Paul here to your doorstep." When she didn't argue with his logic, he quietly said, "I'll sit with you when you talk with him if you want."

She seemed to be processing what he had said to her, slowly and methodically. Finally she turned to him with a stunned expression, "You're talking *God* talk to me, Earl Nezbegay. *Good* God talk."

Earl gave her one of his quiet, slow smiles and, unable to help himself, reached out and touched her hair one more time. Running his rough finger down the smooth plane of her cheek he said, "Yes, Karly Martin. I'm talking good God talk. I told you that you make me want to be a better man. Well, here he is ..."

If you could show me the story of love
I would write it again and again
And then you could be the woman you need
If you would just let me be the man that I am[23]

August, 2004
Huerfano, New Mexico

Fifteen: Realistic Christians Know That Some Sins Just Can't Be Forgiven

By 3:00 p.m. on Monday afternoon Karly was exhausted but content with her day. Sixteen children, ranging in ages from ten to fifteen, had shown up that morning and they'd had a wonderful day of crafts, games, Bible stories, and free time. The casual schedule gave the day a different feeling than the structured day of normal school. She was particularly complimented that two of the children specifically asked her to tell a *longer* Bible story than the one she'd told today. She'd used felt figures and had told the story of Deborah the judge, prophet, poet, and Mother of Israel. It was a particular favorite of hers and she'd really gotten into it, talking about the struggles of the Israelites and the oppression of the Canaanites from the city of Hazor. She riffled through her mental file of stories and thought that she would tell the story of a strong, positive male Biblical figure tomorrow. Maybe Joseph?

"You seem lost in thought," came Paul Williamson's voice. He looked hesitant and uncertain, unsure of the reception he was going to

---

[23] "Climb On", by Shawn Colvin, John Leventhal, Caedmon's Call, *40 Acres*, 1998

receive. She stood staring at him probably, she realized, with the same identical expression for the same identical reason.

"I'm trying to decide which Bible story to tell tomorrow. Today's was a big hit and I've been asked to do a repeat performance."

He fell into step with her as she walked up the hill toward her trailer, asking questions about the day and her work. His questions were tentative and careful, as if he was afraid to push the one button that would eject him right out of this tenuous space into the stratosphere of fury and resentment that pressed in on every side.

Outside her trailer, he stood with his baseball cap and sunglasses on and hands in his pocket. He didn't ask. She sure as heck didn't want to offer. *If you're going to continue to maintain that your life is the Lord's and that He is in charge of it all, then you have to acknowledge that He played a part in bringing Paul here to your doorstep.*

Shut up, Earl.

"Would you like to come in and have a drink? It's not much but it's my home."

He nodded. "I've traveled a couple of thousand miles just for an offer like this."

Paul wandered around the tiny space, made significantly smaller by his enormous six foot five frame that was literally a few scant inches from the ceiling. Karly had forgotten how huge he was. He took off his baseball cap and sunglasses and carefully set them on the small table in the kitchen. He studied the Navajo artifacts she'd accumulated, and touched the woven macramé wall hanging that Shoshanna had made for her. Whether he realized it or not, he was headed to the photograph she kept on display of Benjamin near her bed. Karly walked into the living room space carrying two glasses of iced tea, sat on Goliath's chair, and waited.

Karly knew exactly the moment he saw the picture because he froze, literally suspended in time. Paul simply stood there for long, long moments not moving, just staring and staring. Then she heard him sniff and she realized he was crying.

For a moment she had a strong urge to walk over to him and try to comfort him. But she couldn't do it. That was no longer her place, and she felt that as certainly as it was no longer her place to call herself Benjamin's mother. Instead, she said a quick prayer, *Guide my words. Give him peace.* And then, quite suddenly, one more thought came into her head. *Thank you for this opportunity, Lord. And thank you for Viv and Darin.*

"You can have the picture, Paul. I can have reprints made."

He turned to her and made no effort to disguise his distress or his tears. "Really? You mean that?"

Suddenly her throat was choked closed, and she was unable to speak. Karly nodded. He bent over to reverently pick up the photograph while she sat with her legs curled under her, watching and waiting. Finally Paul turned around and, carrying the photo, made his way over to the couch and sat down.

What exactly do you say? Where do you start? Both of them sat for the longest time in a silence that was profound, yet not uncomfortable, like suspended animation. Then a yowling of astronomical proportions began. Paul looked at her with an incredulous expression. "What in heaven's name is that?"

Karly gave him a rueful smile. "My cat. Goliath." She got up and opened the trailer door. Goliath entered with all the pride and confidence of a king and went directly to the cabinet under the sink. Karly took the time to give him his treat and then came back to sit. She gave Paul another smile. "Watch."

Having finished his treats, Goliath came sauntering into the room licking his chops. He stopped and looked up at Karly with a look of pure affront. Patient for a few moments, but incensed that she was in his chair, he finally tipped back his head and meowed in annoyance.

"I was here first," she said to him. "Get over it." To Paul she said, "He may think he's king and this is his palace, but I still rule this roost."

"Oh yeah, it shows," Paul said with real humor.

Goliath jumped into Karly's lap and gave her a direct stare which she returned unblinkingly. Finally he made his way to the back of the chair and stretched out like he was a panther on a high jungle limb. The roar of his purr began and finally, as he settled his enormous head on the back of his chair, he plopped one of his big paws on top of her head and began to knead.

"What a performance," Paul said.

Karly laughed. "You're telling me. You should try living with him on a day to day basis." Goliath's large paw contracted and bunched a clump of her blonde hair. She shrugged and smiled, reaching back to stroke the cat's fur. The purrs, amazingly, got louder.

Paul cleared his throat. "I, I'm going to be honest and tell you I don't really know why I'm here, Karly. I was serious when I told everyone yesterday at the Jamisons that I'd made a profession of faith and had been working very hard to get my life on the right track. Things are *finally* falling into place it seems, but I just *could not* go on with my life without settling things with you. I ... need to be accountable for the mistakes I've made and the responsibilities I failed in and the ... massive hurts I know I caused you ..."

Paul looked down at his hands and the picture he held there. "I'm trying really hard to do what I feel the Lord wants me to do. I know He wanted me to come here and see you, but now that I'm here ... well," he shook his head in frustration, "now I don't know what I'm supposed to do. The words "I'm sorry" seem so completely inadequate and trite." He met Karly's gaze. "I'm dating a woman now. I've told her about you and how I ... messed up ... so badly with you. She knows about the baby," he swallowed, "Benjamin," he looked down at the picture again. "She said I was looking for closure. She said that I owed you the opportunity for closure, too. But she told me that in the end I might feel even worse after seeing you than I did before."

Still looking at the picture, he swallowed and said in a voice choked with emotion. "I'm so sorry, Karly. I'm sorry for all the hurt I caused you and for being a coward. I'd like to say had I known about the baby on the day of the wedding I would have been more noble and stepped back up to the plate and seen my responsibilities through." He laughed so bitterly that she felt a wave of pity for him. "But the way I was back then makes me sincerely doubt I would have made such an honorable choice. Hell, I probably would have run faster."

Karly couldn't help saying, "The agency said you never even called to inquire about me or the baby. You just sent all the papers, signed and sealed. It was what we'd prayed for - that you wouldn't fight the adoption, but I, I felt abandoned a second time." Oh man, she had never intended to rip open the old feelings or tell him private thoughts and hurts. Things were *over and done*. Past history. *Ancient* history.

Paul looked at her. "I was going to fight you. I couldn't believe that you would hate me so very much that you would throw our baby away. I was royally pissed when I first found out."

Karly gasped and opened her mouth to speak, but Paul held up his hands and his voice was anguished. "Wait, let me finish. *Please.*" She shut her mouth and gripped her hands, which she held tightly in her lap.

"Then I looked at my life and the person I was and the future I was headed for and I knew that I had absolutely *nothing* positive to offer anyone, especially a baby." He looked into Karly's tear - filled eyes. "And I remembered the person you were and I knew that no matter how much you might hate me you would *never* hurt any child, let alone your own. So I had to face the fact that you were always more together and mature and focused and *good* than I ever was, and that this choice of adoption must have been what you felt was the best and wisest thing for the child. And suddenly, I wanted to do something wise and good and noble *for once.* So I signed the papers and sent them back. I tried to do the right thing." Paul looked at her tear - streaked face, and slowly his eyes filled with tears, too, making wet tracks down his cheeks. *"Did I?"*

Earl's voice in the truck yesterday afternoon came back to her. *Or maybe, his life was already so far out of control that it was the only sane thing he knew he could do.*

Karly stood up, and from the small bookcase near the front door took out two photo albums. She walked over to Paul. The top of her head was messed and knotted from Goliath's attention. She held out the photo albums. "Here," she said holding them out to him. "You need to look at these." She looked at him pointedly. "Take the time to read *everything.* I'm giving you permission. It will take you a while. There's iced tea in the fridge and cold cuts and bread there, too." She looked at her watch. "I'll be back in about ... two hours."

Paul took the photo albums from her. "You don't have to go ..."

Karly almost rolled her eyes. "Oh, yeah I do. You're going to need time alone. Don't let Goliath con you into anything." And she left him alone with her cat and all that she had left of their baby.

The first album was a story book of sorts, with photographs and narrated short paragraphs. It introduced Paul to a couple named Viv and Darin, telling how they met, where they lived, what they loved, how they spent their time, and what hobbies and talents they had. It painted a wonderful picture of a couple in love who had a full and vital life rooted in God and His unfailing love and grace. A life so full and so vital that they wanted to share it with someone other than just themselves. Carefully pressed in the back of the album were email print outs. Pages and pages of them. Paul realized that they began during Karly's pregnancy and then continued right up until Karly came here to Huerfano. They were communications that painted lovely snippets of a life with a beloved baby, then an active toddler. In addition, they championed and encouraged Karly, commiserating over disappointments and offering insights and suggestions for future path choices. After the email pages there were letters that Karly had received while in Huerfano, delighting over her successes and accomplishments. Every missive offered prayerful support and bore sincere love and concern for Karly.

The second album held just photos, each picture carefully dated with notations of the child's age.

Benjamin in the hospital delivery room.

Benjamin being held by Karly sitting in a hospital bed.

Benjamin with a beaming couple dressed in hospital gowns.

Benjamin in a car seat with ridiculous sunglasses on his baby face.

Benjamin in a Winnie The Pooh outfit with a hood that gave him little cloth bear ears.

Benjamin with spaghetti sauce covering every inch of his head.

Benjamin sitting on a linoleum floor with an entire box of Cheerios spilled all around him, grinning a mischievous toothy baby smile.

Benjamin standing on fat baby legs by a coffee table.

Benjamin in a bathing suit, wearing Tigger sandals and a Tigger baseball cap covered in chocolate ice cream.

Benjamin and Karly sitting on a porch swing staring at the camera with identical blue eyes and identical smiles.

Paul set the albums down on the coffee table, put his face in his hands and sobbed. He cried for opportunities that would never be, for sins that were forgiven, and for consequences that would never be forgotten.

Oh dear Lord ...

What? What was he going to pray for? That brought him up short. He stood and walked over to the kitchen sink, blew his nose on a paper towel, and splashed cold water on his hot face. He looked around at Karly's tiny, cramped trailer and realized he liked it. It was homey and cozy and *her.* It was a sanctuary that you could come home to after a long day, like escaping into a peaceful cocoon.

Paul thought about Karly. She seemed happy. That's the impression he'd gotten anyway, until he'd put in his appearance. She certainly was well thought of by the Jamisons. Jeeze, they acted like she practically walked on water. He'd watched her laughing and responding to the kids after the summer school class today. Teasing and joking and exhibiting such spontaneous joy.

He thought about Earl. Paul was no fool. Something was going on between the two of them. Earl seemed like a stand up guy, in spite of the macho tough guy act the other night. Paul had to admit that had the situation been reversed, he would have behaved similarly.

The truth of the matter was, given the circumstances that Karly had been put in after he'd abandoned her, she had done the absolute best for the child, and in the end for herself as well.

Paul remembered Karly's parents in flashes of encounters while he and Karly had been a couple, and his own visit with them before he'd come down to Huerfano. There was not one, single, positive or happy experience when they had been part of the picture. Karly, in choosing such wonderful parents for the baby, had inadvertently found a strong, spiritual, support system for herself as well. Jeeze, from the letters, it was obvious that they were the ones who had first hooked her up with the people here in Huerfano. This was not a relationship that smacked of 'thanks for the baby, birth mother, now have a nice life'. This was *family*. An odd, one - of - a - kind family most certainly, but a loving family nonetheless, rooted in faith and God's perfect plan.

Standing at the kitchen sink, looking out the window at the desert that was Karly's backyard, Paul suddenly knew what to pray. *Oh dear Lord, thank you. Thank you for Your faithfulness, goodness, care, guidance …*

Karly didn't exactly regret giving him the photo albums, but as she walked away from her trailer she felt naked. No one had seen the complete set of memorabilia ever. Tammy had seen the book about Viv and Darin. Mrs. Jamison and Theresa had heard snippets of the letters that described funny things that Benjamin had said or done. But no one had seen the whole collection. Not only did it paint a pretty vivid picture of Viv, Darin, and Benjamin, it painted a pretty clear picture of Karly as well. Paul couldn't help but see how lost and desperate she was in those early months, and she wasn't particularly sure she wanted him to know that part of herself. She shrugged fatalistically. Oh well.

Thinking about Paul's reason for signing the papers made her feel … *good*. She felt somewhat vindicated. Even from a distance, even without any direct communication, even with their relationship absolutely severed, he had been able to figure out amidst the shock, the reasons behind her decision to give Benjamin up for adoption. To this day she doubted that anyone truly could comprehend how a woman could give away her child. Certainly her parents still didn't fully understand and she knew they never would, despite endless attempts to explain. There was a dark stigma attached to the term "birth mother" that brought with it implications of failure, desperation, promiscuity, and callous disregard. For Karly, giving Benjamin up remained the single most difficult, brave, mature decision she had ever made. The love she had for that little boy had made the options that she had had to offer him miserable, dark, and … hopeless. It was not a legacy she wanted to give to any child, most especially her own. But trying to get others to understand that was pretty much impossible.

But Paul had figured it out. Paul had gotten it. Paul had understood it so clearly and so completely and had trusted her so totally that he, too, had signed the papers giving away his child. It was a powerful testimony to the person he obviously believed her to be. With Paul, she hadn't had to say one word in explanation or defense today. He'd just gotten it. *Thank you, God.* Didn't the fact that he had been able to figure everything out on his own validate and vindicate her choices? She thought so. Her step suddenly felt lighter, her heart unexpectedly felt freer, and her future all of a sudden seemed brighter. *Did I say thank you, God?*

Walking back to the mission school, Karly figured that she'd use these two hours to get her classroom set and in order for tomorrow. Maybe when she told the Bible story, she'd let the kids act it out instead of just sitting and listening. Make them active instead of passive. Give them each parts and a funny prop, and use them like gigantic puppets while she told the story. Yeah. That sounded like fun. She stopped and looked off into the distance, but wasn't really seeing, she was so lost in thought.

"I'd like to think you're staring at me in awe and wonder, but something tells me I'm afraid you haven't noticed that I'm even standing here." Earl stood in front of her in his standard uniform: battered jeans, battered cowboy hat, battered boots, and a dusty white pocket tee shirt.

"Will your ego be destroyed if I admit your fears are correct?" She smiled walking slowly toward him as he leaned against his truck.

"Nah. I've got an ego the size of Huerfano Mountain. No pint size white woman is going to cause it any damage."

"I'm glad to hear that."

Karly got close enough to him that he could reach out and take her hand, and he did. "I came to claim my date."

"Oh?" She smiled at him but didn't say anything else.

"Yeah. Would you go to dinner with me tonight?"

"I'm not sure what state I'll be in by tonight. I've got Paul Williamson up in my trailer looking at all my things about ... Benjamin." She glanced at her watch. "I told him I'd be back in two hours, and then I'm sure we'll talk some more."

Earl looked at her for a moment and then gently pulled her into the circle of his arms. "Is this okay?" he said against the top of her head. She nodded. "Are you okay?"

"Surprisingly, yes," she said against his chest. She sighed and wrapped her arms around his waist. "You were right."

"How's that?"

She shrugged against him. "About the reason he signed the adoption papers and how it's absolutely God's design that he's here to see me. It's the first time in more than five years that thoughts of him don't generate fury."

"Oh? What emotion do thoughts of him generate now?"

Karly tipped her head back and looked at him. "Jealous?" She grinned at him.

"Nooo ... that's not the emotion that's on my mind right now, I can assure you."

"What emotion is on your mind?" She looked intensely curious.

"I asked my question first," he said, and his big hand reached up and pushed her head back against his chest and tucked it under his chin.

She sighed. "I feel pity for him. I know what he's going through right now. I still can't look at all the stuff about Benjamin and his adoption without it tearing me up. I can't imagine what it must be like to see it all at once for the first time."

Earl's deep voice rumbled through his chest against her ear. "It's good of you to share it with him. You didn't have to do that. I know that, and I know he realizes it as well." He stroked her pony tail and smoothed his hand down her back. "Don't worry about dinner tonight. I'll just take a rain check." He couldn't keep the disappointment out of his voice though.

"I didn't say I didn't want company. I just didn't know if I'd be up to much as far as heavy duty talks and scintillating conversation. That's all."

Hope filled his voice. "How 'bout I stop by about 7:30 and bring dinner with me? Would that work for you?"

She straightened up, pulling out of his embrace, and his hands settled on her hips. "That'd be perfect."

"Wanna know what emotion I was feeling?"

She nodded.

"It's directly related to this." His hands came up from her waist to cup her face, and he pulled her forward for a kiss. Karly felt his hands tangling in her hair and could feel his heart pounding against her palms as she touched his chest.

Earl broke the kiss by dropping his hands to her waist and making her take a few steps back from him. He readjusted his hat and gave her a sideways grin. She gave him a little stunned look and her mouth formed a perfect O of surprise. "See you about 7:30," then he swung himself into his truck and roared off.

She had trouble concentrating on school things and two hours later when she let herself back into the trailer, she had no clear memory of what she'd actually accomplished.

When Karly quietly entered the trailer she found Paul leaning against her kitchen sink. Head bowed, face still puffy from crying, he was obviously praying silently. He looked up at her leaning against the door and gave her a tired smile. "You were right. I needed to be alone." He straightened up and walked towards her. She stiffened at his approach. Paul reached out and took both of her hands in his. "*Thank you.* That was *very private, personal stuff* that you never had to share with anyone, let alone me. You have … given me … something else to carry in my head besides memories of my stupidity and volumes of my guilt. I now have pictures of …" he took a deep shuddering breath, "a beautiful little boy who has everything going for him to help him become a tremendous man." Paul squeezed her hand so tightly she almost flinched. "I came here," he sighed, "*I thought* for things I thought I owed and needed to give you. But I feel like I've done nothing but disrupt your life and cause you needless stress and trouble. *I'm* the one who's gotten a truckload of satisfaction and peace. What can I do for you?"

Let go of my hands. You're breaking my fingers, Evil Twin gasped. Karly laughed softly and wiggled her fingers to get him to loosen his grip. She smiled. "I'm not sure I can explain this correctly, but I'll try. You may think that you've not done anything in coming here, but without realizing it you've given me the single most valuable thing you possibly could have. Something so valuable that I never could have asked you for it because I didn't believe it was possible."

Paul looked absolutely stunned. "What did I do?" If it hadn't been such a serious discussion, his expression would have almost been comical.

Karly felt tears gather behind her eyes, pool, and finally spill. She took a deep, shuddering breath and said, "You believed in me, Paul. You believed that I only wanted what was best for Benjamin. I didn't even have to try to explain or convince you. You did it all on your own, based on what you knew of me and about me. Even with everything you must have been struggling with and going through you didn't doubt me, my motives, or my faith. That's a huge gift. *Thank you.*"

He couldn't answer because of the emotions that choked his throat.

Come fallen ones, Dance in the healing stream
He has faithfully kept you, Brought you out of captivity
Rejoice with all your hearts[24]

Late August, 2004
Huerfano, New Mexico

Sixteen: Erudite Christians Always Have the Right Thing To Say

Karly shrugged. "So I gave him Viv and Darin's email address and he said thanks again, and I guess we cried a little bit more, and then … he left."

Earl was sitting on the couch in her trailer watching closely as she related how things had gone with Paul Williamson. Earl wanted to grab her, pull her onto his lap, and hold her, but he just sat politely, listening and sipping his iced tea. "Are you okay?" he finally asked. "Was it better or worse that he came here?"

She got up and walked to the door of the trailer in answer to the tremendous howling that had begun. "I told you, you were right. Paul's visit filled in spots that I didn't even know needed … filling. I feel," she sighed and squatted down to pat Goliath and then followed him obediently to the sink cupboard to give him his treats, "I feel *free*. Vindicated. Peaceful." She smiled a smile that made his toes curl inside of his boots. "I can hardly believe I'm saying this but I'm much better off for Paul

---

[24] "Exodus", By Bethany Dillon and Ed Cash, *Bethany Dillon*, 2004

Williamson's visit." While Goliath munched on his treats, she padded back to the big chair covered in a Navajo blanket and settled herself, curling her legs underneath her. "I owe you sincere thanks. You gave good, solid, wise advice." She grinned. "Hey! Maybe you should consider a career in advice? Like," she tilted her head to the right and tapped her lips in thought, "psychologist or school counselor or," she sat up with a twinkle in her eye as if she'd discovered the perfect idea, "talk show host!"

Earl settled back on her couch and let the wonder of being alone in her company seep into his muscles. He felt that he had been running, walking, and crawling his whole life to get *right here*. Her monster cat jumped up on the couch, yowled once, and then settled into his lap. "Hey Goliath. How's it hanging, old man?" As Earl scratched behind the cat's ears a rumble of contentment filled the room.

Karly stared at him intently, no longer flirty and teasing. "You brought me Goliath, didn't you? That's the other thing you gave me that I hadn't figured out." At Earl's silence she narrowed her eyes. "You said you wouldn't deny it if I guessed right."

Looking at the gigantic pile of fur draped across his lap Earl said, "Guess our secret's out, huh, cat?" He looked at Karly and shrugged. "Some old Navajo woman who I helped out regularly got too elderly to live on her own and had to go into a nursing home in Farmington. The only thing she cared about was her darn cat, and was refusing to move because she couldn't take him along with her. I promised her that I'd find the cat a good home. I dumped him by your trailer, and each morning and each evening for about a week I showed up and fed him from the old lady's stash of cat food. I just left it under your front steps." He gave her a sly smile. "I knew that he'd reel you in mighty quick, and sure enough he did." Earl scratched Goliath's ear and Karly watched the cat contentedly knead his paws into his denim-clad leg. "The rest is history. And the old lady enjoyed the stories about her cat and you - the contest to pick a name with the kids, how he follows you around and hangs out in your classroom, how he's got everyone 'proper trained'." He sighed and closed his eyes briefly. "She went home to be with the Lord just a few months ago."

"You're a good man, Earl Nezbegay."

"It's nice you see me that way."

Karly gave him a pointed look. "Name someone who doesn't."

He closed he eyes and rested his head on the back of her couch, avoiding the question and her eyes. "I haven't been in this trailer since that first day," he said slowly. "You've done nice things with it. It's a home now."

"I thought I had upset you or something that first day. You left so abruptly, without even saying goodbye."

"Oh, you upset me all right," he said without moving, lost in the memory.

"What did I do?"

Still with his eyes closed, he sighed. "You smiled at me and I lost my heart."

At her absolute silence he finally lifted his head and looked at her across her small living room. She was staring at him with wide, serious eyes. "Don't worry," he said, in what he hoped was a light, teasing tone. "It wasn't love at first sight or anything like that." He dropped his head back wondering if the heat he felt filling his face was visible against his dark skin. "Just at first smile."

He heard her get up and then felt the shift of the couch as she sat down next to him. Concentrating, he was certain he could feel a warmth on his left side from her nearness. Taking a deep breath, he could smell the soap and shampoo she was partial to. He didn't move.

"When you told me that we needed to talk I didn't think you meant you needed to tell me that you loved me."

Earl couldn't look at her. God only knew what he'd say or do if he looked into her eyes and didn't see what he so desperately wanted to see. Karly was waiting for him to say something. Oh Jeeze. He shrugged again, trying to lighten the serious mood with his gifted abilities at comedy. "Just trying to be different and unique. Heaven forbid I be typical or predictable."

He felt her reach for the hair he'd braided that morning. Just this past week he'd thought about cutting it; it hadn't been cut for almost fifteen years. He'd never gotten to the haircut the night of the accident so many, many years ago, and something had kept him from ever following through on it. Yeah, maybe he'd get it cut …

"I've never had anyone love me, you know."

He gave a short laugh, knowing she was kidding him.

She continued. "Paul said it, but he said it in response to my own declaration of love, and to get me in bed with him. My mother's surely never said it. I guess my dad has, but he says it in a whisper, making sure no one else hears it. Somehow that diminishes it," she spoke barely above a whisper, "when someone tells you they love you but they have a hidden agenda or are not willing to let anyone else know." She was silent for a few moments. "The kid's I've taught sometimes say, "I love you, Miss Martin," and Viv and Darin have Benjamin tell me he loves me." Earl couldn't help himself, and he opened his left eye to peer at her. She wasn't even looking at him as she played with his braid, but was staring, unseeingly, out the small window behind the couch. Her brow wrinkled in thought. "No, I'm certain that no one has ever truly loved me *just because*."

He picked his head up to stare at her and she released his braid as she stared out the window. She *was* serious. She *wasn't* kidding.

I love you, Uncle Earl.

I love you, you annoying, demanding, pain - in - my - ass brother.

Karly had really never believed that someone loved her purely and simply just because? Heck, even he, in his most miserable times, knew that he was loved. Didn't feel he deserved it, mind you, but he had had it just the same.

He sat up and looked at her. He reached and touched her face under her chin, turning her to look at him. "I love you, Karly Martin. I've loved you from your first smile. It's a love that has grown and continues to grow with each and every day. It's a love that's made me examine my head and my heart and, having found the state of them so pathetically lacking, work long and hard to remedy that situation. It's a love that's made me understand what's important and what's not, what's worth fighting for and what's worth letting go." He reached up to cup her cheek and his thumb brushed the tear that was making a slow track down her face. "I told you that you made me a better man. What did you think I meant?"

She pulled away from his hand, shook her head, and looked down at her lap. Her shoulders shook and he saw more tears splash down onto her legs. "Aww, Girl. Getting told someone loves you isn't supposed to make you miserable. Didn't anyone ever *at least* tell you that?" He pushed Goliath down and pulled her across the couch and into his lap. She sobbed against Earl's chest, soaking his shirt and he rocked her like she was a small child, crooning nonsense words against the top of her sweet - smelling hair.

He finally started to sing to her, clutching her to him. It was a new song he'd been listening to while he worked in the shed, the words so powerful the first time he'd heard them that they'd made him stop still. It was another one of those mysterious CDs that continued to appear in his collection that he had no memory of purchasing. *"Would I believe you when you say, Your hand will guide my every way? Will I receive the words You say, every moment of every day? Well, I will walk by faith, even when I cannot see it. Well, because this broken road, prepares Your will for me. Help me to win my endless fears, You've been so faithful for all my years. With the one breath You make me, Your grace covers all I do. Well, I'm broken, but I still see Your face. Well, You've spoken, pouring Your words of grace. Well, hallelujah, halleleu, I will walk by faith ...*[25]"

She quieted after a time, drawing shuddery breaths. "Some first date, huh?" Earl managed to say finally in the silence. Even Goliath had stopped purring and was busy giving himself an extensive bath in the chair with the Navajo blanket.

Karly gave a hiccupping laugh and he relaxed a bit. "They're good tears, you know," she finally mumbled.

"Oh, man, don't tell me that. I don't think I could handle *bad* tears."

She sat up in his lap and sniffed loudly. Leaning over he fished out his handkerchief. "It's clean."

After wiping her face and blowing her nose, she finally made eye contact with him. "I'm a mess."

---

[25] "Walk By Faith", Jeremy Camp,

"Actually, you're kind of cute with a red nose. I have to be honest and tell you that I don't think there's anything you could do where you wouldn't still be the most beautiful woman I've ever laid eyes on."

She put her hand against his warm, smooth cheek. "Where do we go from here, Earl?"

"Well," he said reaching up to tug on her pony tail, "off the top of my head I think we should work on you loving me as much as I love you. I think that's the best plan, don't you?"

Nodding, Karly leaned over and gave him a slow, lingering kiss. "And certainly the most fun."

Late Saturday evening in the midst of the Tent Meeting weekend, Edith Jamison fell into a coma and was rushed to the Farmington Hospital. Told that his wife would probably not survive the weekend, Sam Jamison shut down all outside stimuli other than his wife and her care. Karly and Earl, having rushed to the hospital as soon as they heard, stood at the foot of Edith's bed at a loss as to what to say or do.

"Tell us what we can do, Sam," she said gently. When he didn't answer, Karly walked over and gently put a hand on his shoulder. "Sam? What do you need for us to do?"

Turning, Sam looked at both of them and then focused on Earl. "You'll have to preach the sermons tomorrow at the Tent Meeting, Earl. It will be impossible to get anyone else on such short notice. Can you do that?"

Karly looked at Earl and held her breath. Earl took a deep breath and closed his eyes briefly. "Yeah. I'll do it Sam. Don't worry about a thing, okay?" But Sam had already turned back to his wife forgetting about anything but her.

"Are you okay?" Earl had been absolutely silent on the drive home from the hospital. Karly pressed on in the face of his continued silence. "In the best of circumstances it would be impossible to come up with a sermon on such short notice. Why don't we just do a hymn - sing or invite people to give their impromptu testimonies or something like that?" She finally reached over and touched his arm as it gripped the steering wheel. "Hello? Earl? Have you heard anything I've said?"

"Huh? Oh, sorry, I'm just thinking about my sermon tomorrow, that's all." He gave her a wink and a smile. "Guess how much sleep this man's gonna get tonight."

"You're okay with this?"

He shrugged. "It's obvious that it's been on its way. I've done fine with all the other ministerial responsibilities. I *used* to preach a pretty good sermon. Certainly my head and my heart and my soul have repaired themselves enough to be able to handle my preaching. I've come to realize that I'm a stubborn, sedentary individual, and God regularly works best by blasting my sorry butt into action. It doesn't seem to have made me change my tune very much, but I've found that I'm less and less surprised when the explosions occur." He reached across the dark truck cab to put a warm hand on the back of her neck. "And one of the explosions in the form of a beautiful, blonde - haired, blue - eyed woman isn't half that bad in retrospect."

"In retrospect?"

He shrugged while his hand sought and found hers. "You've got to admit you were pretty brutal with me during our first few encounters. I was practically in flames after at least one or two of them. It's tough to be smiling and thankful about something when you're covered in smoke, soot, and ashes."

"Hmpff," was all she could manage while he chuckled and then fell silent once again.

The next day dawned a gorgeous, late summer morning and the sunshine was uninterrupted in a cloudless blue sky. "Everyone here knows the story of Noah and The Ark, right?" Earl started his sermon standing on the scrub grass behind the battered wood pulpit underneath the huge tent awning. "He's the poor guy to whom God said, "Hey, Noah. Go build a big huge boat over on the plain. Get your family to help you. Here's the plans and the lists of materials you are to use. Don't listen to the criticisms that the townspeople are going to levy at you because every single one of them is wicked. They are so evil that I plan to destroy them all. Every single one of them. Only you and your family are worth saving in this entire world."

Earl walked around the pulpit, leaned his elbow against it and crossed his legs. He was wearing a dark suit, a white shirt, and a carefully knotted dark blue tie. Karly had never seen him in anything but jeans. He looked unbelievably handsome in her unbiased opinion. "I imagine those neighbors and townspeople of Noah had plenty to say. He probably even became a bizarre tourist attraction. Can you just hear it all? Excuse me, Noah? Don't you think it's a problem that you're not next to any *water?* Hey Noah, sure hope your God is mighty powerful. Everyone knows that a boat that big won't float! Noah! How are you managing to support your family doing such a lengthy project? Don't expect us to give you any handouts. Oh, Noah? Let me know when this big flood is coming. I'm going to need to get my laundry in and gather my sheep into the corral."

Earl sighed. "The Bible doesn't say anything about *one single person* other than family helping build that ark that must have taken years and years to complete." Earl shook his head. "It must have been some lonely existence, don't you think? How many of you would have liked being given that job?"

Karly looked around at the attentive audience. Some smiled and chuckled. Others shook their heads.

"But, the picture of the type of man that Noah was *before* God gave him this assignment is detailed in the Bible. Genesis, chapter six verses nine and ten say," Earl picked up his Bible and to Karly's surprise put on a pair of wire - rimmed glasses, "'This is the history of Noah and his family. Noah was a righteous man, the only blameless man living on earth at the time. He consistently followed God's will and enjoyed a close relationship with him." Earl looked up at his audience, and his glasses flashed with the reflection of the bright sunlight. "Wow. Some description, huh? I'll tell you something. Based on this description, *it let's me off the hook for building any arks in the near future."* A significant part of the audience roared with laughter.

"I like what Genesis, chapter six verse twenty - five says, 'So Noah did everything exactly as God had commanded him.' How many of you wouldn't just *love* an employee or a child just like that? Huh?"

Earl put his Bible down, took off his glasses and set them down, unbuttoned the jacket of his suit, and thrust his hands in his pockets. "You know the rest of the story. Everything that God had predicted came true: the animals were collected, the rains came, the flood rose, and only Noah and his family survived …

"When I found out that I was going to be preaching this morning, I struggled with what to speak about. We've already prayed for Edith and for Sam this morning, so everyone knows the difficult circumstances that have me wearing a suit and tie and doing something I haven't done in almost fifteen years. I got thinking about Noah and his ark. And you know what I asked myself? Could Noah have done everything God told him to do without Mrs. Noah? Take a minute and think about the type of woman Mrs. Noah would have had to be for Noah to have accomplished all that he did. Do you think that she was selfish? Or argumentative? Spoiled and lazy? How about ungodly?"

Earl took one hand out of his pocket and scratched the side of his cheek. "You know, the more I thought on it, the more I was convinced that Mrs. Noah must have been one amazing woman. I realized that when God called Noah for this heroic, once - in - a - lifetime adventure, that Noah and Mrs. Noah must have been one amazing *couple* who set the mold when it came to amazing couples."

He walked back around to the pulpit and rested both hands on the side of the podium. "But, I realized that perhaps *one* of my thoughts wasn't completely correct. You see, I think over the course of history, God raises up great men *and women* to do seemingly insurmountable tasks, just like Noah and Mrs. Noah. Those two may have been the *first* amazing couple but I don't believe they were the *only*.

"Edith and Sam Jamison came to this place over thirty five years ago and built another ark. It's an ark that doesn't save animals, it saves people - Navajo people: children,   mothers,   fathers,   aunts,   uncles, grandmothers, grandfathers." He walked over and put his hand on his sister Theresa's shoulder. "People who have been dealt such great hardships in their lives that they must learn to persevere and conquer." He walked over to LouRay Betselie, who wasn't sitting, but leaning off to the side against one of the tent posts. "People who have been dealt injustices and faced unfair prejudices that have made many give up on the belief that life could have anything good to offer." He and Earl exchanged glances and Earl gave him a nod of respect.

Earl wandered over to a woman Karly knew whose twin sons had been killed in a drunk driving accident just three years ago. "People who know sorrows so deep and so painful that living seems too difficult at times." He squeezed her shoulder, and she gave him a tremulous smile as he walked away.

He wandered back to the front of the audience, and the people were so silent she could here his boots crunching in the scrub grass and gravel. "It's an ark that draws people to it and gives our lives joy and laughter." He made eye contact with Karly, and she felt a warm flush from the top of her head to the tip of her toes. His gaze didn't leave her face as he continued, "They come from all parts of the country and bring talents and insights, challenges and encouragement. They infuse us with boundless love and endless courage."

He walked over and patted Naomi French, the other mission school teacher, who smiled for perhaps the first time ever that Karly could recall. "They teach us." Earl wandered over to Shoshanna Werito and put his hand on her shoulder. "They exhibit uncommon bravery and mythical patience by being dorm parents and Sunday school teachers." Everyone laughed. Sitting next to Shoshanna was her mother, Verna. "They devote hundreds of volunteer hours to remind us of the richness of our culture and the pride of our Navajo heritage." Walking through the audience, he stopped by numerous people and simply said things like, "They always are willing to help when asked," and "They cook delicious meals for homes where only inexperienced bachelors rule the kitchen," and "They have a hammer and screwdriver and aren't afraid to use them," and "They pray unceasingly for us," and "They always have a glass of iced tea and a listening ear." He rested his hand on little Roderick Yazzie's head, who said "Uh, Oh," in a loud voice and made everyone laugh out loud again. "It's an ark that saves young and old alike, and will have far - reaching benefits that only God can truly know. By the time he had finished walking through the audience everyone not only felt honored, but experienced a feeling of empowerment and pride.

Wandering back up front, he stood to the right of the pulpit with his hands clasped behind his back. "It's an ark that draws the best out of those of us who were already here, offering us a life of eternal love and grace and happiness.

"Today, Sam Jamison sits beside the bed of his beloved wife, Edith, as she spends her last remaining days with us here on earth. For those of us who will be left behind it is a sad time, for we will miss her love and laughter, encouragement and prayers. I will personally miss her wise advice and unwavering belief that I *would someday* make wise choices. For some of us, it is a time of worry and fear, a time when we pray for miracles and make heartfelt requests. But it is important to remember that we sit here in the shade of the Jamison's Ark. They've built it, just as Noah and Mrs. Noah did, with their own blood, sweat, and tears according to God's design and instructions. We are fortunate people to benefit from the Jamison's dedication and the Lord's love and grace. We are Huerfano Mission School and Church, and we are proud to be a part of this amazing journey." Karly heard murmurs of agreement ripple throughout the crowd.

"May God bless us with many more years. May we remember where all of this goodness and mercy and love and hope comes from: Our Lord and Savior, Jesus Christ. Let's close in prayer."

It took a long time for everyone to finish shaking Earl's hand. Theresa, sitting next to Karly, mumbled, "I don't care what anyone says, I'm *not* going to head up his fan club," making Karly laugh out loud and drawing Earl's brief attention before he went back to shaking hands.

"Uncle Earl did really good, didn't he, Mom?" Marion said in a voice tinged with awe. "I think he's almost as good as Sam."

"Well don't go telling him that, okay Marion? You don't know what it's like living with him when he's got a swelled head. It's ... heck ... on earth."

"Did he always preach like that?" Karly asked Theresa.

Theresa gave her a solemn look. "I'll never admit it to his face, but he's *absolutely gifted*. He didn't become the obnoxious son of a gun he became way back when because he was lucky or in the right place at the right time. It was because every time he opened his mouth practically pure poetry would come out. This was *nothing*. You should see him on a big pulpit in a fancy church when he's had time to really prepare. You've never seen anything like it. He is absolutely *dazzling* when he preaches."

"I had no idea," Karly said and looked back at the subject in question as he bent over to speak with a stooped Navajo woman.

After Marion and Theresa had been dropped off and settled at home, Earl drove Karly home. "You're awfully quiet," he finally said to her, "Gonna tell me any of those thoughts I can practically hear roaring around in your head?"

"You did an amazing job preaching this morning."

He glanced at her and then looked back at the road. "I can do better. It was just so last minute."

"I don't think I've ever seen an audience so captivated and enthralled by what a minister was saying. You truly have a gift."

He shrugged. "I enjoy doing it, too. I'd forgotten that until I got up there. It's a huge adrenaline rush and half of the stuff I say is often inspired in the moment. That's why I never bother with notes. They sort of slow me down and cramp my style." They stopped outside her trailer and sat surrounded by the sounds of the desert night.

"You are destined for great things, Earl."

He gave her a funny look in the twilight of the truck cab. "I *used* to think I was destined for great things, and look where it got me. Right where you found me when you showed up: miserable, bitter, and alienated from God. If there's one thing the last fifteen years have hammered home to me - right through my thick stubborn skull - it is that *this* is where I belong: here in Huerfano, caring for Theresa and Marion, and ministering to these people that have always been a part of me. That's about as great as I want and as great as I plan to be."

"Are you sure?"

He gave her the most tender of smiles. "There's only one thing I'm more sure of. Loving you."

Karly felt her heart expand and a warm rush consume her from head to toe. She saw her time here in Huerfano flash before her eyes: the breath - taking scenery, the sincerity of the Jamisons as they told their story, the smiles of the children she taught, the laughter and teasing of the many Navajo faces that had welcomed her and made her feel like she belonged, the expression on Theresa's face when she was going to say something irreverent and teasing, the look on Paul's face as he stared at Benjamin's picture. And then there was Earl: Earl closed and dark, Earl angry and bitter, Earl resigned and silent, Earl with a slow smile and a sharp, teasing comment ready on his lips, Earl caring and soothing while she cried and told him of Benjamin and Paul, Earl blushing on her couch as he admitted he'd loved her at first smile, and Earl standing today preaching and looking right at her when he said, "boundless love and endless courage." Right now she had never felt so peaceful, so right, so content, and so blessedly happy. *Thank you for my life, God.* "I love you, Earl."

He let out a whoop of astronomical proportions and dove across the front seat of the truck to pull her into a crushing embrace. "Well, Girl, it's about time!"

Have you ever been haunted the way I've been by you?
And have you ever felt the measure of the days
That I've spent waiting pining for you?[26]

Labor Day Weekend, September, 2004
Huerfano, New Mexico

Seventeen: Only Well Behaved Christians Go To Heaven

Edith Jamison went home to be with her Lord in the very early hours of Monday morning while her husband of forty - three years sat by her side telling her he loved her and would see her again soon.   Sam Jamison, handyman, bus driver, minister, friend, father, son, brother, uncle, and simple man knew that the best and brightest part of his life had been when he'd worn the label 'husband'.   Driving home from the hospital, after making all the tedious arrangements and endless decisions, he drove his battered Ford Escort not towards home but towards Huerfano Mountain.   The drive was steep and the car seemed to object now and then, but he made it to the end of the road and into the small parking area.   Slowly walking the remaining distance, he found himself facing a glorious early morning sunrise in a world of which Edith was no longer a part.

For long moments grief engulfed him, sucking him down into a pit of despair that seemed bottomless.   He and Edith had always said they

---

[26] "Edge of Water", Jars of Clay

wanted to go together. All their lives they'd joked about it and said that they'd filed their exit papers with the same departure date from this world to the next. When Edith had battled colon cancer that first time so many years ago, he'd faced the reality of their mortality and the realization that perhaps God was not going to honor their simultaneous departure request. But Edith had rallied, and the false sense of security that they would live - not forever but a lengthy indeterminate number of years - had crept back into his hopes and dreams.

This last year had been hell watching Edith deal with the pain and discomfort, the complications and the disappointments. Sitting beside her, feeling well and healthy and pain free, had gnawed him with guilt and frustration. But this year had also been an immeasurable blessing. *They'd had this past year.* Without the business and chaos of the school and the million and one other responsibilities, they had had time to sit and talk and hold hands and reminisce and … renew their love for one another. He'd always been the softy, and she'd always been the rock. He'd always been the scatterbrained mess, and she'd always been the organized go - getter. She'd always been the one to do the worrying, and he'd always been the one to say "you know, we'll be looked after, we always are." She'd always been the one to plan for disasters, and he'd always been the one to plan for picnics.

One of the last coherent things she'd said to him, besides telling him she loved him, was, "You're my best friend, you know."

His greatest fear had been being left without Edith. Standing on top of Huerfano Mountain, this sorrow threatened to engulf him completely, and if that didn't succeed, the fear of being separated and on his own for the rest of his life waited patiently for its turn at him. He felt the tears build like a tidal wave and howls of anguish fill his lungs …

I earnestly expect and hope that I will in no way be ashamed, but will have sufficient courage so that now, as always, Christ will be exalted in my life. For me, to live is Christ and to die is gain.[27] Sam sighed. That had been Edith's favorite Bible verse. He remembered it like it was yesterday, coming upon her

---

[27] Philippians 1:20-21, New American Standard

sitting on a bench at the Bible college they'd both attended. "I've got to memorize this one, Sam. It's going to be the theme for my life." She'd been young and eager and ready to take on the world. Her faith had sustained her through Rudy's sickness and death, her cancer, his bouts with anger, indecision, and frustration, and a full measure of disappointment and failure. But she'd never lost her spark. If her faith had wavered she'd never let him see it.

She'd been his rock, and now she was gone. *Oh, dear Lord, I can't do this ...* A sob escaped his chest.

What is faith? It is the confident assurance that what we hope for is going to happen. It is the evidence of things we cannot yet see.[28] That had been his theme.

Faith had been the cornerstone, the bedrock, and the foundation of their marriage. Sam took a deep shuddering breath. His faith wasn't going to waver now.

I go to prepare a place for you. If it were not so I would not have told you.[29]

He could do this. He would do this. "Give me strength and peace and courage, Lord, to face these days ahead of me without Edith by my side." Edith had always loved it up here on the top of Huerfano. Said that it was a special, spiritual place for her. After Rudy had died, she'd trudged up here almost every night for months. Maybe he'd do that, too. Start some new habits. Doing something like this would make him feel close to Edith and give him time to pray.

"Help me get through these next couple of days, Lord. I just want to crawl under my bed and stay there for the next few years or so. Help me to continue to be a good example and a man after Your Heart. Guide my words and actions.

"And Thank You For My Life With Edith, Lord. Your goodness to me knows no bounds."

Even from death, Edith's organization and planning was evident. Despite Sam's refusal to discuss it, she'd apparently planned her own funeral. She'd chosen the hymns, selected the scripture readings, and had even chosen who was to speak. The fact that she'd not asked these people

---

[28] Hebrews 11:1, New Living Translation
[29] John 14:2, King James Version

to do this somewhat difficult chore or given them the opportunity to accept or decline had not caused Edith to hesitate or reconsider for, you see, she'd also provided them with scripts for what she wanted them to say. On the evening of the day of Edith's death, Theresa Goodluck – chauffeured around in her trusty handicapped equipped van - visited a number of individuals in the community and delivered the letters she had been entrusted with.

And, in the end, no one, least of all her husband, was surprised.

Earl was provided a letter that detailed how she wanted her funeral conducted: closed casket, no wake, and an evening service at the chapel. For the service, he was to make sure to leave a bit of time for the few people she'd asked to speak (he shouldn't worry, she had letters that were to be delivered detailing what she expected from them). She'd asked Marilu Curley to play a selection of her favorite hymns (Marilu to receive her own large manila envelope with all the songs and music carefully enclosed, as well as a personal note detailing the hours and hours of blessing Edith had received from her God - given musical talent). Edith wanted Stephanie Edsitty and her husband Edgar to sing two solos (manila envelope and personal note also to be delivered as requested), and she wanted Earl to say a few words. In Earl's personal note, she stressed the phrase *few words,* and having written the note before he had preached, wrote a strong paragraph reminding him of his God - given gifts and talents and *responsibility* (another word that was stressed). Earl smiled and shook his head. *Ahh, Edith, I'm going to miss you.* She had finished her note to him in her spidery script, with a paragraph telling of her love for him, of her belief that God had sent him to be the son to take the place in her heart after Rudy had died, and of her delight and pride in him. He spent long moments after he'd finished taking deep breaths and wiping his wet face with his handkerchief thinking about Edith. *Thank you, God, for Edith Jamison.*

On Wednesday evening everyone gathered in the chapel at 7:00 p.m. for the memorial service for Edith Jamison. She'd misjudged herself (humility being one of her many qualities), and the chapel was overflowing with people. In the end, all the doors and windows were thrown open and people ended up sitting outside on the few fold up chairs that hadn't been used inside, on the bumpers of their pick - up trucks, and on any other place they could park themselves. *What a testimony to your ministry, Edith,* Earl thought as he carefully wove his way through the clusters of people outside, and then inside.

His sister was zipping around in her wheelchair directing and passing out memorial bulletins (typed by Edith and apparently run off by Karly). Theresa greeted him as he strode up the aisle. "You go find Sam and get him to sit with you. He needs your moral support. I'll let you know when you're up."

"Hey, who's in charge here?" he said, but there was a twinkle in his eye.

"My note said I am, you wanna see it?" Although her tone was tough, he could see that she was on the edge of tears. She hated to cry because she wasn't able to manage blowing her nose on her own.

"You okay?" he said to her as he touched her cheek.

"Stay away from me and don't start being nice or ministerial or anything. Remember, I see you regularly in your underwear, and it's not a pretty sight." She zipped away from him before he could give her a suitable comeback.

Earl made his way to Karly and squatted in front of her. "How's everything?"

Her eyes were red and puffy from crying, but she managed a small smile for him. "Thank God Edith told Theresa she was in charge. If she'd asked me, nothing would have ever happened." Two tears made slow paths down her cheeks, and he noticed a paper clutched tightly in her hand. "I can't read this letter she's given me, Earl, *I can't.*"

He reached up and wiped away the tears that were quickly replaced by new ones, leaned forward, and in front of everyone gave her a light kiss. "You say a prayer about it, I'll say a prayer about it, and then we both know that if you still don't think you can do it, Edith's got someone in the wings with a letter that says, "If Karly's too upset to read my note, go over to wherever she's sitting and tell her to pull herself together and do her job."

That made her laugh and hiccup at the same time. "I suppose you're right."

He leaned forward and whispered, "Tell me," into her ear.

"I love you, Earl Nezbegay," she whispered in his ear.

He stood and smiled at her. "That's all I need to keep me going. I'm going to find Sam." He touched her hair and was gone.

Sam was standing outside one of the fire exit doors that had been propped open for a breeze. Tim Jamison, who had flown in from California just yesterday with his family, stood beside his father at a loss for words and awash with grief. Out of deference to both of them, the crowd that was waiting to collect at the door was milling off to the side. Earl wandered up to stand next to Sam, and at his continued silence, finally said, "Hey Sam. It looks like we're ready to go. You two want to come in and take a seat?"

"No," Sam responded without even glancing in Earl's direction.

"Okay." Earl loosened his tie and leaned back against the door with his hands in his pockets. Long moments passed.

"You going to stand there all day?" Sam finally asked him.

"Yup."

"Jeeze, Earl, can't you leave a guy to be miserable in peace?" Sam growled. Tim cast a glance at his father, a glance at Earl, and then went back to silently staring at the desert horizon.

"Yeah, I could, but I won't." After a few beats, Earl said to Sam, "You know what I was just remembering?"

Sam sighed impatiently. "No."

"I was remembering that night you came to the hospital after the accident and I had just found out that Theresa was paralyzed from the neck down, and that it was probably my fault that she'd never walk again." Sam was silent, his profile seemingly carved out of marble. Tim turned to look at Earl as he spoke. "Do you remember what you said to me that night, Sam?" Sam made no response. "You told me, 'Earl, sometimes life just sucks.'" Earl chuckled and shook his head at the memory. "It was the last thing I thought you were going to say, and being the big, impressive minister that I was back then, I, for the life of me, couldn't imagine where you were headed with that statement. But if you'd said anything else to me I would have just tuned you out, knowing you were just handing me the standard lines from 'Helping Those With Grief 101'. Instead you went on and on about how life sucks. You talked about Rudy's death and Edith's cancer, and a pile of other horrible things that had happened to people in the area. Then you asked me a question. Do you remember what you asked me?" By now, Sam had turned around and was looking at Earl, too, silently waiting for him to continue. "You asked me if I thought God felt sadness."

Now it was Earl's turn to look away into the parking lot at the people milling around. "You said that life here on this earth was not perfect and was never going to be perfect. We were all going to face sorrow and grief and hardship all of our lives, and anyone who believed they could have a life without those things was plain crazy. Then you said, 'I think God's sorrowing right along with us, don't you, Earl? I think he's grieving right along with you over what's happening here tonight. But I have every confidence that He's still in charge, and that eventually you'll make it through to the other side of all this. Theresa, too. And little Marion as well.'"

Sam snorted. "Had no idea it'd take you more than a decade and a half to come around though, for pity's sake."

Earl smiled and shrugged his shoulders. "Yeah, well, some people's skulls are thicker than others."

"I suppose."

"I don't think God's too sad about today, Sam." When Sam looked at him in surprise, Earl continued. "I think He's conscious of your grief right now, and understands the depths of your mourning, but I think He's real glad to have Edith home with Him. I think He's telling her right now, 'Well done My good and faithful servant'. I think He's feeling tremendous satisfaction for the brilliant job that's been well done. What do you think, my friend?"

"I think you're going to be one heck of a preacher man, Earl Nezbegay, now that God's got your head screwed on straight."

"I'll take that as a compliment, Sam."

"You do that."

The service went off without a hitch. Tears were shed, but voices were raised in song and praise, and laughter was heard a number of times when people gave tribute and reminisced. Karly choked her way through her note and managed to bring just about everyone to tears. Earl said his *few words* and made them laugh when he said he was worried because, although Edith had said a 'few words', she hadn't given him an actual acceptable word count and he would have to live the rest of his life wondering if she was pleased with him or not.

Just when Theresa was ready to dismiss everyone, (Shoshanna had a note asking her to give the closing prayer), Marion Goodluck stood up. "I've got a note I'm supposed to read, Mamma," she said to Theresa. "My note says you'll be surprised, because it's not mentioned in your letter and it wasn't one of the letters that you were instructed to deliver. I'm to tell you that Mrs. Jamison gave me my note about six months ago and told me to put it in a safe place, and that after she died I was to open it up and read it. There's personal stuff for me, but there's also something I'm supposed to read out loud to everyone."

She was fifteen, but she exhibited a poise and beauty that some adults would never achieve in their whole lives.

"Do you want to come up front to the podium, honey, or stand where you are?" Theresa asked.

"I guess I'll come up front." She made her way forward and stood by the same battered podium that Earl had used during the Tent Meeting just last Sunday. She looked out over the crowd and then down at the paper clutched in her hand. "My name is Marion Goodluck," she began to read, "and I'm the daughter of Theresa Goodluck and the niece of Reverend Earl Nezbegay.

"I stand before you," she read, "as a representation of all that brought Edith and Sam Jamison here to Huerfano. I represent the future. I represent opportunity. I represent promise and hope, excitement and life. The Jamisons didn't come here to Huerfano to build a megachurch or to save thousands or to become famous. They came here because of me. Just one. *Only one.*

"Being a success in God's terms has nothing to do with volume or size. It has everything to do with accomplishing the purpose and plan God has for your life. It means that you look around at what you have and what you can do and what you're interested in, and then fashion it all up into a ministry that is pleasing to the Lord. That's what Edith and Sam Jamison did.

"That's what you all need to do. You need to look inside yourselves, confess those things that aren't right with God, commit your future steps to doing what is pleasing to the Lord, *and then get walking."*

Looking out at the assembled group of people she said, "I am Marion Goodluck. I am fifteen years old. I told Mrs. Jamison that I asked the Lord to come into my heart and to guide me where He wants me to go. I think I want to be a teacher, but maybe a missionary, too. I'm not so sure."

Marion searched for Sam. "Mrs. Jamison told me that she fell in love with you at church youth group when she was just a teenager, Sam." She looked down at her paper and began to read again. "The two of us were always better together than separate, Sam. You halved all my sorrows and doubled all my joys. You are the greatest gift the Lord ever gave me and you are my best friend." Marion looked up at Sam again, his face a silent wash of tears. "I pray that I'll be blessed with the same type of best friend at some point in my life, Sam."

Marion looked down at her piece of paper and smiled. "I'm supposed to remind you to do the laundry once a week, don't forget to take your vitamins, and you're to stay away from those extra hot chili peppers you love so much because you know what terrible indigestion they give you."

She looked up and took a deep breath and her lip trembled just a bit. "And that she loves you with all her heart, right through and into eternity. She's waiting for you, but remember she's learned to be very patient so take your time."

There wasn't a dry eye in the house.

The new school year began. Karly found it hard to believe that she had been here four years. In some ways it seemed like she had been here forever, while in others it seemed she had only just arrived. She was consumed with the responsibilities of the mission: teaching, coordinating, trouble - shooting, and mentoring. Earl continued with all of his responsibilities at the mission and, whether he had spoken directly with Sam or not, began to preach as well. Numerous people checked in on Sam on a regular basis, and on the surface he seemed to be coping well with Edith's death, but privately all who knew him well noticed the subtle changes. He was quiet, withdrawn, and distracted.

As a group, Earl, Theresa, and Karly approached him and suggested that he visit his son Tim and his wife and grandchildren in California. Earl pointed out the need to get away for a bit, Karly pointed out the benefit of being surrounded by family, but it was Theresa who put it all in perspective. "What would Edith tell you to do, Sam? She'd tell you to stop dragging everyone down with your sorry old face and make the most of the time God's given you. There is nothing here at the mission that you *have* to do. Karly and Earl can either handle it themselves or they have a whole passel of people willing to do anything they ask. You've lost years and years of opportunity being able to spend time with Tim and his family because you had no one to relieve you here. The Lord's given you this chance. *Now take it.* Stay as long as you want and come back when you feel like it."

Sam looked at the three of them with a resigned expression. "Okay."

"I'll take you to the airport," Earl said. "Just let me know the day and time."

Three weeks later, the mission school received a postcard from San Diego. On the front it said, "Having Fun, Glad You're Not Here!" On the back Sam had written just three words: *You were right.*

The bench was there one evening as though it had been there forever. Intricately carved, it was a masterpiece of time, effort, and talent. Standing outside enjoying the beautiful autumn evening bright with moonlight Karly looked down at the bench in stunned awe. She ran her hands over the smooth, cool wood tracing the patterns of dark and light that she could see in the moonlight. It was placed under a large New Mexico privet tree that had become Karly's favorite spot to pray. In the spring the tree bloomed with tiny yellow flowers, in the summer it bore berries that attracted numerous birds to keep her company with their chatter and song, and in the fall, as it was now, it was alive with bright yellow leaves just getting ready for its winter sleep. She could make out carvings of vines and leaves across the back rest, along with elaborate patterns that trailed off into areas too dark for her to see clearly. Sitting down on it, she thought she detected animal faces, and bent over to see if she could discern exactly what they were.

"That's a black - tailed prairie dog," came Earl's voice from the shadows. "Marion has the same kind of expression on her face when she's studying something intently, trying to figure it out." Stepping out into the moonlight, Karly gave him a welcoming smile.

"Do you make it your habit to hide in the shadows and frighten your parishioners on a regular basis, Reverend Nezbegay?"

"Nah," he said as he joined her by the bench, "just a select one. I thought I could drop the bench off and disappear, but you caught me as I was escaping." He squatted down beside her so that he could point out more of the carvings but took the time to lean into her, inhale her scent and kiss her neck a bit. He finally pointed to another face barely discernable in the twilight. "This is a kit fox, which is what Theresa reminds me of." He chuckled briefly. "They have exceptionally keen senses of hearing, sight, and smell." He traced the ears carved carefully into the wood. "They're not particularly noisy or vocal, but they bark and growl when they're alarmed or upset. Sounds like Theresa, doesn't it?" Earl gave her a small smile.

"Who else is on here? Tell me."

He shrugged in a self - depreciating way. "Edith and Sam are here," he pointed to another spot and Karly slid over, hoping to be able to see better.

"I want to get a flashlight."

"No," he chuckled, "trust me, it looks a darn sight better in the dark. These two coyotes are the Jamisons. Coyotes get a bad rap a lot of the time, but they have many positive qualities. Did you know they mate for life?"

Karly shook her head.

"Yeah, they mate for life, both parents are active in the raising of the young, and they are amazingly adaptable and resilient no matter where they choose to make their home. Coyotes are found all over North America."

"Where am I?"

Earl was quiet for a bit. Karly reached out and touched his cheek, and he turned his face into her palm and kissed it. He sighed, settled himself down on the ground near her, and finally rested his head against her knee. His hair was caught back in a loose ponytail, and Karly felt it's silky softness against her hand as it rested on the bench. "You're the chickadee. It's carved on the back. You can't see it unless you walk around."

"Why am I a chickadee? Cause I'm tiny and flighty?" she teased.

"Chickadees are tiny, but they're uncommonly brave for such a small bird. They've been seen defending their nests against birds and animals significantly larger than themselves. But they're tough, too, Karly. They've been known to survive the harshest of winters up in northern Minnesota – I'm talking 60 below! - and the fiercest of droughts down in Mexico. They're fantastically adaptable, get along well with numerous other species of birds, and have shown examples of cooperative feeding and mutual defense when attacked. I've read up on most of the birds and wildlife in this area and the most fascinating thing about chickadees is that scientist have discovered that they continually allow selective brain neurons to die as new ones are produced to replace them. It gives them the ability to adapt and flourish as their environment changes, and to be constantly positive and forward - thinking." Earl's warm hand wrapped around her jean - clad calf and Karly felt its warmth seep through. "That's you, Karly: brave, tough, adaptable, constantly positive, and forward - thinking." He paused, then said in a rush, "Being with you, all those qualities are kind of infectious, too."

Karly leaned over and embraced Earl as he leaned against her. "I love you, Earl."

"I suppose you're going to ask me if I'm an animal on here."

"Eventually."

He sighed and then shrugged. "I'm the badger: mean - tempered, solitary, and traditionally the cause of bad luck. There's a saying, 'Should one hear a badger call, And then an owl cry, Make thy peace with God, good soul, for thou shalt shortly die.'" He picked his head up to look at her. "I know I don't fit that description so much lately, but I've been working on this bench for ages and it was one of the first things I carved."

"Thank you for this."

"I was working on it the day you stormed into the shed and told me I had to take over Sam's ministerial responsibilities. It's because of you that it didn't get finished sooner. You've kept me too busy." He winked at her. "I wouldn't have it any other way."

Earl seemed to want to say something, and then thought better of it. "What?" she prompted.

"Do you have that flashlight handy after all?" he finally said.

"Yeah …"

"Why don't you go get it?"

Filled with curiosity, she headed off to her trailer and was back moments later, the flashlight clutched in her hand.

"You were supposed to find the bench on your own, but I couldn't bring myself to walk away when you came out." He looked at her, and even in the moonlight she could see his tension. "There's other stuff on the bench."

Switching on the light, she directed the beam towards the bench while he sat quietly besides her, watching. Suddenly she looked up at him. "Psalm 34:8," she said and then looked frustrated. "Earl! I'm not good like you. I don't have all this scripture memorized."

He gave her a wicked grin. "Oh, too bad then."

"Earl …"

Chuckling, he said, "*Taste and see that the LORD is good. Oh, the joys of those who trust in him!*[30] He's brought me great joy in bringing you here, Karly." Earl nodded to the bench. "Keep looking."

He scooted out of her way as she climbed over him in search of more hidden things. Karly grinned at him, "Ecclesiastes 4:9!" she said breathlessly.

"Come on, you *have* to know *that* one." When she shook her head he said, "*Two are better than one; because they have a good reward for their labor.*[31] We make a good team here at the mission school, Karly. It's been pure enjoyment each morning getting up, facing the day, knowing that at some point over the course of it you and I would be together to plan, troubleshoot, and provide encouragement." At her look he smiled and nodded, "Yeah, keep looking."

On the armrest she found Genesis 2:18. "I know it has to do with Adam and Eve, but that's it," she said in a frustrated tone.

"*GOD said, "It's not good for the Man to be alone; I'll make him a helper, a companion."*[32] I've been alone my whole life, Karly. Even in a crowd I'm alone." She stood there looking at him in the night, illuminated by the flashlight that she held casually in her hand. "First you made the solitary life obvious to me, then you made my choice to be so seem empty and lacking, and then finally you made the void unbearable, craving only you and your brightness." Sitting casually in the dirt and scrub grass, he gestured to the bench. "There's more."

"Oh, Earl …" her voice was tremulous with tears.

"Don't fall apart on me now, Girl. Come on! I've been working on this for years. The least you can do is look."

On the back, near the exquisite carving of a chickadee, she found Song of Solomon 8:6. Karly looked at him. "Song of Solomon is the book of love, Earl. I can only imagine what this one says." She came around,

---

[30] New Living Translation
[31] King James Version
[32] The Message

and before she could sit by him in the dirt he stood and sat on the bench. When she sat next to him, he enfolded her in his arms.

Whispering against her ear he said, "'*Hang my locket around your neck, wear my ring on your finger. Love is invincible facing danger and death. Passion laughs at the terrors of hell. The fire of love stops at nothing, it sweeps everything before it.*'[33] I love you, Karly Martin. Will you wear my ring on your finger? Will you marry me?" He held open his hand and in it was a ring, flashing in the moonlight. The band was intricately carved and was topped with an ornate, carved flower that was inlaid with pieces of mother of pearl and turquoise.

"There's one more verse, but something tells me that you're finished searching," Earl said to her as she snuffled against his tee shirt. "It's Psalm 73:25 and the verse says, '*You're all I want in heaven! You're all I want on earth!*'[34] I knew my life was sorely lacking before you, but I had no idea how enormous the void was until you came into my life. Nothing would make me happier, nothing would make me feel ready to conquer whatever the world's got to throw at me than having you by my side. Of course," he said as he kissed the top of your head, "you're stuck with Marion and Theresa. I feel inclined to warn you about that before you give me a final decision. Marion's in the midst of puberty – heaven help us all, and Theresa found three gray hairs today and you would have thought the world had stopped rotating with the fuss and bother she created about it. *I'm* not sure I can handle the two of them, let alone subject you to them constantly. So if you want some time to mull all this over …"

"You know, when we first met you were much less talkative than you are now. Will you be quiet and give a girl a chance to get a word in edgewise?" He stared at her in silence, but his eyes still spoke volumes. "I love you, Earl Nezbegay. I'm a better person for knowing you and have only just begun to appreciate the joy of being loved by you. Yes, I'll marry you – right this minute in fact."

"Yeah? You don't want the big, fancy wedding with the dress and the flowers?"

"Well …"

---

[33] The Message
[34] The Message

He laughed and shook his head in mock defeat. "I thought so."

"No, we can talk. Actually, I was thinking more that there were some special *people* I wanted present, rather than special trappings. I'd love Viv and Darin and Benjamin to come, and," she sighed, "I'm guessing my parents would want to be here." Karly's voice held no enthusiasm for that prospect. "I'd want Snake and my friend, Tammy, too." She looked at Earl. "Is that okay?"

"I've waited my whole life for you, Karly, I can wait a few more months." He reached over to slip the ring on her finger. "I designed it myself. I've got a friend down in Ship Rock who makes beautiful, handmade jewelry and we spent quite a bit of time designing and planning this ring. He said he'd make us complimentary wedding rings, too."

Karly threw her arms around him. "Can I be there when you tell Theresa and Marion? I know you won't be able to keep this secret, and I want to see their faces when they hear." She pulled back and looked at Earl. "Unless they already know …"

Earl rolled his eyes. "Theresa suspects something because I've been so closed mouthed around her and trying to not make much eye contact. Just you wait. The woman is positively creepy how she can read minds." He looked at her, and touched her face. She closed her eyes and leaned into his palm, and he couldn't resist. He leaned over and his kiss was long and sweet. "We need to talk about our future, and what changes we'll need to make so that both of our lives can come together happily and without too much confusion and trouble. But it's only," he looked at his watch, laughed and rolled his eyes, "twelve - thirty in the morning. Maybe Theresa's still up. Shall we go see?"

I lift my eyes and thank You for, This life you've granted me
I pray that every day I live, Your heart will be pleased[35]

Nine Years In The Future
Huerfano, New Mexico

Epilogue

"DAAAAAD!!! Mom says she needs you *right now!!!!*"

"I'm up to my elbows in engine grease, Jacob, can it wait a few moments?" Earl looked to his right to see a dirty pair of Batman sneakers standing in the gravel and sunshine next to the truck.

"She said to tell you to *drop everything.* That doesn't sound like you can wait, does it, Dad?"

Earl scooted out from underneath the pickup and looked frantically around for a rag. "She okay?"

Jacob, his five - year old face intent with concern, shook his head. "I don't think so. She's holding on to her stomach and mumbling a lot under her breath and breathing *real funny.*"

Oh man. Earl, unable to find a rag, began to wipe his hands on his tee shirt while at the same time running pell - mell toward the house.

Karly was sitting on the couch, clutching her enormous stomach, and doing her 'who – who – who - hee' focused breathing. "I'm sorry, Earl," she gasped, "the labor's just come on all of a sudden."

---

[35] "All I Ever Wanted", Margaret Becker

Earl knelt down beside her, tenderly touching her arm and then sliding down to grasp one of her hands. "Oh, man, Girly! We're four weeks early!"

"They told us twins are always early. I guess we should have listened." She gave him a weak smile and went back to breathing.

Earl felt a huge wave of panic. "The truck ..." he said frantically, "I'm in the middle of draining the oil pan ... !"

His wife nodded. "Know that," she panted, "Called Marion. On the way." As she spoke, the insistent honk of a car horn and the crunch of gravel as a car tore up their driveway could be heard.

Earl turned to his son. "Where's Lydia?"

"She went with Uncle Snake and Auntie Tee into town a bit ago. I wanted to go, but she said I couldn't." Jacob still looked annoyed at being excluded. Whenever Jacob's big sister Lydia, Uncle Snake, and Auntie Tee were together exciting things were guaranteed to happen. No one in their right mind *ever* missed an opportunity to be part of their adventures. That is unless a bossy seven – year - old big sister could come up with a good excuse. "She said I didn't finish my chores so I had to stay."

"Hmmm," Earl said, reaching up to push a dark lock of hair out of his son's enormous brown eyes, "well, look at it this way: you're the first one to know that the babies are on their way."

Jacob's eyes got wide, looking first at his mother and then to his father. *"Today?"*

Earl smiled and nodded. "Yup. Today." As Karly began to do her breathing again he glanced at his wife. *"Now."*

Marion exploded through the door. "I'm here! Let's go! Car's running!"

"Jacob, run and get your Mom's suitcase in the bedroom, okay?" He and Marion grasped Karly's arms on either side and pulled her to standing. "Easy does it, Girly. Let's get you to the car."

Less than two hours later Earl sat by Karly's bedside, brushing sweat damp tendrils of hair from her face. "That was way too close, Mrs. Nezbegay," he said and kissed her tenderly by her temple. "Next time ..."

"Don't you 'next time' me, Earl! This is *it!!*" But she gave him a tender smile and sighed contentedly as he wiped her forehead with a damp cloth. She glanced over at the nurses who were caring for their new son and daughter. "Everything okay?"

Earl looked over to where all the action was happening. "That's what they told me. I was told to be patient, wait just a few minutes, and they'd bring the babies over shortly. Even though they're early, they seem to be pretty sturdy and breathing on their own. One nurse said she thought they were both over five pounds. That's what we were praying for, huh?"

Karly closed her eyes, smiled, and nodded. "Yup. Just what we prayed for."

"Are we still fighting about the names?"

Karly opened one eye to peer at him. "I don't know, are we?"

Earl sighed in mock frustration. "When was the last time I won an argument? *Isn't it my turn?*"

"Edith hated her first name. She told me that on more than one occasion. Sam's said that every time we've talked to him on the phone. She'd be furious if we named our daughter Edith and you know it," Karly said.

"I gave in when we had Lydia."

"So follow one wise choice with another." Karly sighed. "And you forget, you got your way with Jacob."

Earl snorted. "*That doesn't count!* You didn't have any name you felt strongly about! That's the only reason I got my way with Jacob!"

With her eyes closed she grinned, and reminded Earl of the Cheshire cat in Alice in Wonderland. "You knew you were doomed when you married me and brought me home to live with Theresa and Marion. I told you back then not to set any precedents that you weren't willing to follow through on. You've spoiled me rotten from the start and I expect it to continue right to the end."

Earl's heart swelled with love. "I suppose Esther's a good name," he said tenderly, touching her smiling mouth with a gentle finger. "But I'm not budging on Matthew. Are you going to fight me on that one?"

"No," Karly said in a sleepy voice. "I'm not going to fight you ..."

The nurse brought over two tiny bundles and put them both into Earl's arms. One was wrapped in a pink hospital blankets and one was wrapped in blue. "Hey, Esther. Hey Matthew. I'm your Poppa," he said in a crooning, singsong voice. Both of the little round faces stared back at him with eyes that weren't quite brown but were already too dark to be called blue. None of their four children were going to have anymore than a dash of Karly's fair skin and hair. Theresa described it best when she said that all of Earl and Karly's kids had skin that looked like the most delicious kind of chocolate milk. "Hey, sleepy Momma, look what I've got here," he said quietly to Karly.

When he had settled the both of them into Karly's arms and kissed his wife, Earl stood. He couldn't resist and reached out to touch the top of his wife's head as she bent down to kiss the babies. He never seemed to tire of touching her. "*We know that all things work together for good to them that love God, to them who are the called according to his purpose*[36]," he murmured under his breath.

"You quoting scripture to me, Earl Nezbegay?!" Karly looked up at him with a wry smile.

"No," he said smiling back at her, "I'm just reminding myself of a proven truth that's all."

"Oh yeah? What's that?" Karly fought against an enormous yawn and failed miserably.

"I was just saying that all things work together for good to them that love God. I look at you lying here with our two new babies, and I think about who's waiting for us down the hall, and I think about our life and all the things we have to make us happy and content, and I'm just getting sentimental I guess, about how far we've come." He looked a little sheepish and shrugged. "That's all."

"All things work together for good to them that love God. Hmmm," Karly said, bending down to brush her lips against Esther's downy head. "That's a pretty good recipe for life, wouldn't you say?"

---

[36] Romans 8:28, King James Version

"It's worked spectacularly for me, that's for sure," Earl said with a huge grin. "I've got a gorgeous wife, four beautiful children, a loving family, a job I love, and an eternal future. What more could I ask for?"

Karly looked at him then, a look full of love and happiness and hope, and her eyes filled with tears. "I can't think of a thing I need or want," she whispered to him, and he bent over closely not to miss a word. "Every prayer has been answered. Even things I didn't know *to ask for* have been given to me. I look at you, looking at me with that *expression,* and there are many times I can't believe all of this is real."

"Oh, *I'm real* all right, Mrs. Nezbegay, don't you ever doubt that!" Earl gave her a long, lingering kiss. "Keep an eye on those babies for me. I'm going to go get Marion and Jacob. Maybe Lydia, Snake, and Theresa have shown up by now."

"Mmmm," Karly said, and gave him a tired smile. "You do that, Daddy."

Walking down the hospital corridor to the waiting room, Earl felt a huge rush of peace and contentment. *Thank you, God, for my life.*

Every prayer was answered in the most perfect way. The mission school was thriving thanks to a steady flow of dedicated and caring people. Sam had reinvented himself as a doting grandfather and part - time preacher when needed. Earl felt appreciated, fulfilled, and content in both his professional and his personal life. Standing, unobserved in the doorway of the hospital waiting room looking at his family, the feelings of love and happiness grew by leaps and bounds. Marion had her dark head bent down looking intently at something Lydia was showing her in a book cradled in her lap. Jacob sat on Theresa's lap, snuggled against his aunt in her wheelchair watching the television that was bolted to the ceiling tuned to some crazy cartoon show. And Uncle Snake was lounging indolently in one of the hospital chairs doing his favorite thing: watching Aunt Marion.

One visit. It had taken only one visit - the occasion of their wedding - to convince Karly's brother Michael, still known by almost one and all as 'Snake', that life in Huerfano had a truckload more to offer then any other place else he'd like to consider hanging his hat. A truckload to offer by the name of one Marion Goodluck. Perhaps it hadn't been love a first sight, but the hook had been set that day, and each summer, each winter vacation, each spring break had found Snake at their door eking out every last minute before he had to return east. Once college was finished (journalism), he'd shown up on their doorstep with all his worldly possessions and a smart aleck remark about the state of the living room couch where he planned to sleep.

Marion, her mother's daughter in all ways except a wheel chair, had strung him along through thick and thin: college (teaching), mission trips (Spain, Canada, and Mexico), and life in general. Earl wasn't sure, but he figured Snake probably qualified as one of the top ten most frustrated men this side of the Mississippi. Through Karly, Earl knew that the poor guy had proposed to Marion not once but *four times,* and in each and every instance she'd told him 'no' with a precise (and highly rational) reason why not. Why he hung around (now with his own apartment in Farmington and a job at the local newspaper) was a testament to true love that even Earl doubted he could top.

"Hey everybody," Earl said as he stepped into the room, "I'm a daddy again, times two!"

"I knew first!" Jacob crowed and made a flying leap at his father who caught him with practiced ease.

"Yes sirree, you knew first," Earl said to his son, kissing him and then setting him down.

"You two still fighting over the names or have you finally caved?" Theresa said.

"I caved. *Esther* weighed in at five pounds, two ounces and *Matthew* weighed in at five pounds even. The babies are doing fine, but will have to stay here for a few days. Karly's tired but great, too. Wanna come have a peek?"

There was a mad scramble for the door that left Earl and Snake standing in the empty waiting room. "How ya doing, brother – in - law?" Earl said clapping him on the back.

Snake rolled his eyes. "I've just spent the afternoon with your daughter and your sister. How do you think I am?"

Earl chuckled. "I'd say that if you were a drinking man, you'd be packing a case in the trunk of your car on a regular basis."

Snake gave him a pointed stare. "That's not something I've tried …" Both men laughed and made their way down the hall.

"You want to call your parents or shall I?" Earl asked.

Snake shrugged. "You can have the honors. Every time I call, I catch it from my mother because I haven't managed to get Marion to marry me. Who ever would have thought that *my mother* would not only *approve* of someone other than herself but the very same woman *I'm* trying to get to marry me?" He shuddered. "It creeps me out at times. Makes me think, *have I missed something? Am I loosing my mind? Could I really be agreeing with my mother over a choice of anything, let alone a woman?*" He shrugged. "Then I take one look at Marion and my head turns to mush again."

Earl laughed. "She loves you, you know. Marion has only ever had eyes for you. She's just got an agenda before she's going to settle down."

Snake looked at Earl like he was nuts. "You think I would hang around if I didn't know that?"

The object of their conversation came up and looped her arms around Snake's neck. Marion gave him a kiss on his cheek, carefully wiped off a smudge of lipstick, and then said, "Hey! What's all this serious talk I see? Come see your new niece and nephew, Uncle Snake."

"When are you going to put this man out of his misery, Marion? A guy can only take so much, you know," Earl said half in jest and half seriously.

Marion studied Snake's profile. "Are you miserable, Baby?" she crooned to him and gave him another kiss and a hug.

Snake gave Earl a calculated look, waggled his eyebrows, and winked. "I'm so miserable, I don't think I can stand myself much longer, Mar."

Marion reached up a tanned hand to lay against his cheek. "Awww, why didn't you say so? We better go get married. *And quick.*"

Snake immediately lost his teasing demeanor. "Don't joke with me about that, Mar," he said in all seriousness. "You know I told you I can't play around with that topic."

"I guess we better talk serious then, hadn't we?" Marion said solemnly in a low voice.

Earl watched Marion and Snake stare at each other communicating without words and decided they'd reached a level of conversation that didn't need him in the audience. As he walked away, he heard Snake say earnestly, "I told you I would only ask you one more time, Mar. You tell me 'no' for the fifth time and I'm outta here."

"I'm not gonna tell you no for the fifth time, Michael James Martin."

"You're not?"

"No, Love, I'm not …"

Dear Karly,

Mom and Dad said to tell you congratulations on the twins! I'm loosing count of how many half brothers and sisters I have! They say that if you can handle the chaos, we will be down for Thanksgiving again for the whole long weekend.

Mom wants to know if Lydia wants to come and spend Easter break with us like she did last summer. I told Mom that she's okay for a girl but I'd rather have Jacob come instead. Mom says that maybe both of them could come visit and to ask you what you think. What do you think about that, Karly?

Will Uncle Snake be there when we come down in November? Don't tell Mom, but when he took me out hiking we saw a rattlesnake. He said next time I come out he'll try to catch one and cook it. All the kids at school would go nuts if I came back with a rattlesnake tail.

I made the baseball traveling team. I'm one of two pitchers. The other guy, Johnny, is better than me really, but at least I get to pitch every once in a while.

Paul came out and visited me for a long weekend a while ago. We went to a Twins game and he took me skating at the local hockey rink. He says he thinks I'm going to be as big as him when I'm fully grown up. Mom and Dad said I could go out again this summer and visit his whole family. I had such a good time last summer. We even went and saw a Yankee's game! He's got something like fifteen nieces and nephews, plus his three kids. Cool, huh?

We had to do a report on our family heritage in school last month. I had pictures of you and Paul and me and Mom and Dad. My teacher, Ms. Palombo, said that when she read my report she cried.

Mom always says that we are a _unique_ family because of me being adopted and still knowing you and all. I think you made really good choices, Karly. I think that our family isn't so unique. It's just got lots of love, right? But just in case, thanks for making good choices. I can't wait to see you at Thanksgiving. Send pictures as soon as you can, okay?

Love,

Benjamin

About The Author

Susan McGeown is a wife, mother, daughter, sister, friend, aunt, uncle (don't ask), teacher, author ... but, most importantly, a "woman after God's own heart." Living in Bridgewater, New Jersey, with her husband of over fifteen years and their three children, writing stories is just about the best way she can imagine spending her free time. Each of Sue's stories champions those emotions nearest and dearest to her: faith, joy, hope and love.

Philippians 1:20-21

For I fully expect and hope that I will never be ashamed, but that I will continue to be bold for Christ, as I have been in the past. And I trust that my life will bring honor to Christ, whether I live or die. For to me, living means living for Christ, and dying is even better.

www.ingramcontent.com/pod-product-compliance
Lightning Source LLC
Chambersburg PA
CBHW020611260626
47157CB00003B/956